Publisher
MIKE RICHARDSON

Collection Editor
SUZANNE TAYLOR

Collection Designers
KRISTEN BURDA/JULIE E. GASSAWAY

This book collects issues one through six of the Dark Horse comic-book series
Usagi Yojimbo™ Volume Three and stories from issues 13, 15, and 16
of the Mirage comic-book series *Usagi Yojimbo™ Volume Two.*

Published by
Dark Horse Comics, Inc.
10956 SE Main Street
Milwaukie, OR 97222

First edition: August 1998
ISBN: 1-56971-297-2

Limited hardcover edition: August 1998
ISBN: 1-56971-298-0

3 5 7 9 10 8 6 4 2
Printed in Canada

USAGI YOJIMBO™

THE BRINK *of* LIFE
—— AND DEATH ——

*Created, Written,
and Illustrated by*
STAN SAKAI

Introduction by
KURT BUSIEK

DARK HORSE COMICS®

Usagi Yojimbo

Discoveries

I HAVE TO ADMIT TO A CERTAIN THRILL, sitting down to write this introduction. This is *Usagi Yojimbo*, after all. There'll be a *Usagi Yojimbo* trade paperback out there that I had something to do with. I like the thought of that, and that's why I said, "Sure, you bet!" the moment I was asked to do this.

But that leaves me with a problem. Now I've got to write the piece, and there's not a lot I can tell you, whether you're new to *Usagi*, or a longtime reader like me.

I can't, for instance, tell you much about Stan Sakai. I could tell you about the time we went up in a hot-air balloon together — Stan had come up to my neck of the woods for a comics convention, and one of the things the convention organizer (the ever-affable Richard Finn) likes to do is show the guests a fun time in return for signing autographs and such at the con. On this particular day, we got up at the crack of dawn and watched as the folks from the ballooning company laid out the brightly colored balloon, fired up the burners, and filled it with hot air until it was straining to be aloft. And then a bunch of us piled in and took to the sky.

It was spectacular — being above the familiar countryside turned it strange and exotic: the early-morning mists, the sensation of absolute stillness as the world rolled on beneath us, the sudden awareness of speed as we descended to just above the treetops. If you're a comics creator and Richard Finn ever invites you to a show, by all means say yes; you'll get to do this yourself, or go river rafting, or skiing, or some other such similar delight. But Stan? He was the quiet guy at the back. I can't say I got to know him, memorable though the trip was.

Other than that, I've talked to Stan on the phone a time or two, and seen him at conventions signing books and doing rabbit-head sketches for healthy lines of *Usagi* devotees. He's a nice guy — pleasant, friendly, modest, and amazingly talented — but I don't really know him well enough to share any incisive insights about him.

And I can't exactly rattle on about 16th-century Japan, setting the stage for the adventures you're going to be reading. For one thing, Stan's already taken care of it, with the elegant and informative four-page prologue to the first Dark Horse issue of *Usagi*, which was done to bring new readers up to speed, and which I expect runs either at the beginning of this collection or at the start of the two-part "Noodles" story it originally introduced. And for another, I don't really know that much about the subject. Basically, all I know about feudal Japan, I learned from James Clavell novels and *Usagi Yojimbo* — and probably some Wolverine comics, but I have my doubts about their dependability as historical resources.

It's funny. I'm a big proponent of doing comics for specific audiences, catching readers' attention with the content rather than trying to tempt customers into buying stuff they're not interested in — if you want to attract mystery buffs, do mystery comics, don't do superhero comics with mystery elements and expect that'll be enough. If you want to attract romance buffs, do romance comics, and so forth. And I firmly believe this — but I'm the antithesis of the argument, since feudal Japan and samurai adventures aren't a big interest of mine. It's not like I go out of my way to avoid such material — but I don't seek it out either.

And yet, the setting and culture of *Usagi Yojimbo* are immensely important to the series. Story after story features introductions to and explanations of aspects of feudal Japanese culture and legend, and this volume is no exception — from the seaweed farmers of "Kaiso" to the authentic (if corrupt) village justice system and soba merchant of "Noodles" to the repercussions of Western intrusion into Japan in "Bats, the Cat, and the Rabbit" and more.

And I've got to say, I love it all.

That brings me to the third thing I can't tell you that much about, which is the comics themselves.

I can tell you my reaction to them, which is flat-out awe. I referred to some of Stan's work as "elegant" a few paragraphs back, and that's an understatement. In an industry overwhelmed by in-your-face spectacle, Stan is a master of restraint, setting the stage slowly and deliberately and letting the story amble forward at an unhurried pace, which seems peculiarly appropriate for the adventures of a samurai traveling on foot. But it also results in comics far more exciting than the gaudiest of the in-your-face stuff, since the restraint provides a context against which the violence and danger that permeate these stories come as a shock, an ugly interruption of life.

I could point out examples: look at the first page of "Lightning Strikes Twice," at the panels Stan has chosen — birds over the woods, the high aerial shot of the road, and the slow zoom-in that introduces us to ordinary, everyday people going about their business — only to break that carefully constructed mood in a single panel, as the people turn out to be anything but ordinary, and Inazuma reacts to their imminent attack. And then we turn the page and the scene explodes in action, the peace and beauty shattered. How much less effective would that have been if Stan had opened with the action, without first giving us time to relax into the setting? (Of course, Stan does open stories with action, but they're worth a careful look, too, as in the way "Noodles" intercuts between the anger and emotion of the chase and Usagi's slow, relaxed walk, building to a gag rather than an explosion.)

And I could point to the way Stan frames his panels — no dramatic angles for the sake of it, no wild layouts to "jazz up" the page — just clear, straightforward storytelling that lets the beauty of the drawing come through, focuses on content and mood, and always, always, tells the story rather than distracts from it.

I could explain why it is that the setting and culture fascinate me so much here, how Stan is such a good storyteller, such a good explainer, that the history and mythology lessons we get along the way don't feel like lectures but discoveries — as you'll see in the many pages of "Kaiso" that are devoted to showing the reader (and Usagi) what seaweed farming entails, and how it shapes the lives of those who make their living at it.

But that's the thing, isn't it? You're going to see it in "Kaiso." You're going to read that first page of "Lightning Strikes Twice," and the opening sequence of "Noodles." You have the book. If you're a longtime *Usagi* reader like me, you know this stuff already. If you're a newcomer, you're about to find out. And either way, you don't need me telling you about it ahead of time. There's stuff I'd love to talk about — the heartbreak in these stories, the moments of poetic justice, the treachery and resourcefulness — but I don't want to spoil it for you. You'll read it in the stories, as you should.

So what is there for me to tell you? These are the stories from the final two issues of Mirage Publishing's run of *Usagi Yojimbo* and the first six issues of Dark Horse Comics' run (plus a stray backup story from an earlier Mirage issue). You're gonna love 'em. That's all you need to know.

But humor me — if you see me at a convention and you've got this book, pretend like I accomplished something in this intro, okay? I've wanted to be a part of this series for years, and I'd hate to think I was *completely* irrelevant . . .

KURT BUSIEK, MARCH 1998

CONTENTS

To Todd Bustillo and Glenn Masuda
and the other members of the
Usagi Dojo website with much thanks.
(WWW.USAGIYOJIMBO.COM)

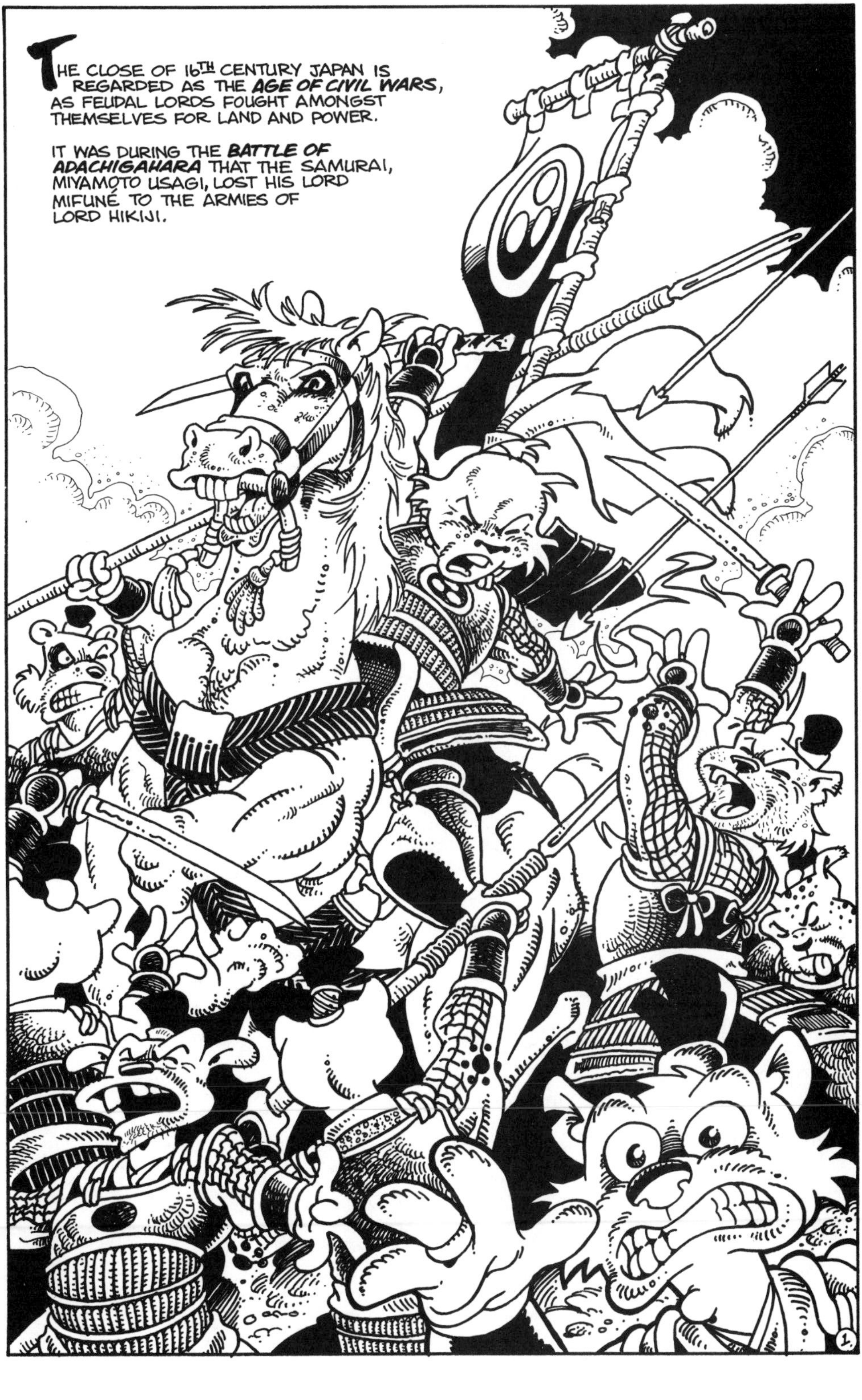
THE CLOSE OF 16TH CENTURY JAPAN IS REGARDED AS THE AGE OF CIVIL WARS, AS FEUDAL LORDS FOUGHT AMONGST THEMSELVES FOR LAND AND POWER.
IT WAS DURING THE BATTLE OF ADACHIGAHARA THAT THE SAMURAI, MIYAMOTO USAGI, LOST HIS LORD MIFUNÉ TO THE ARMIES OF LORD HIKIJI.
1.

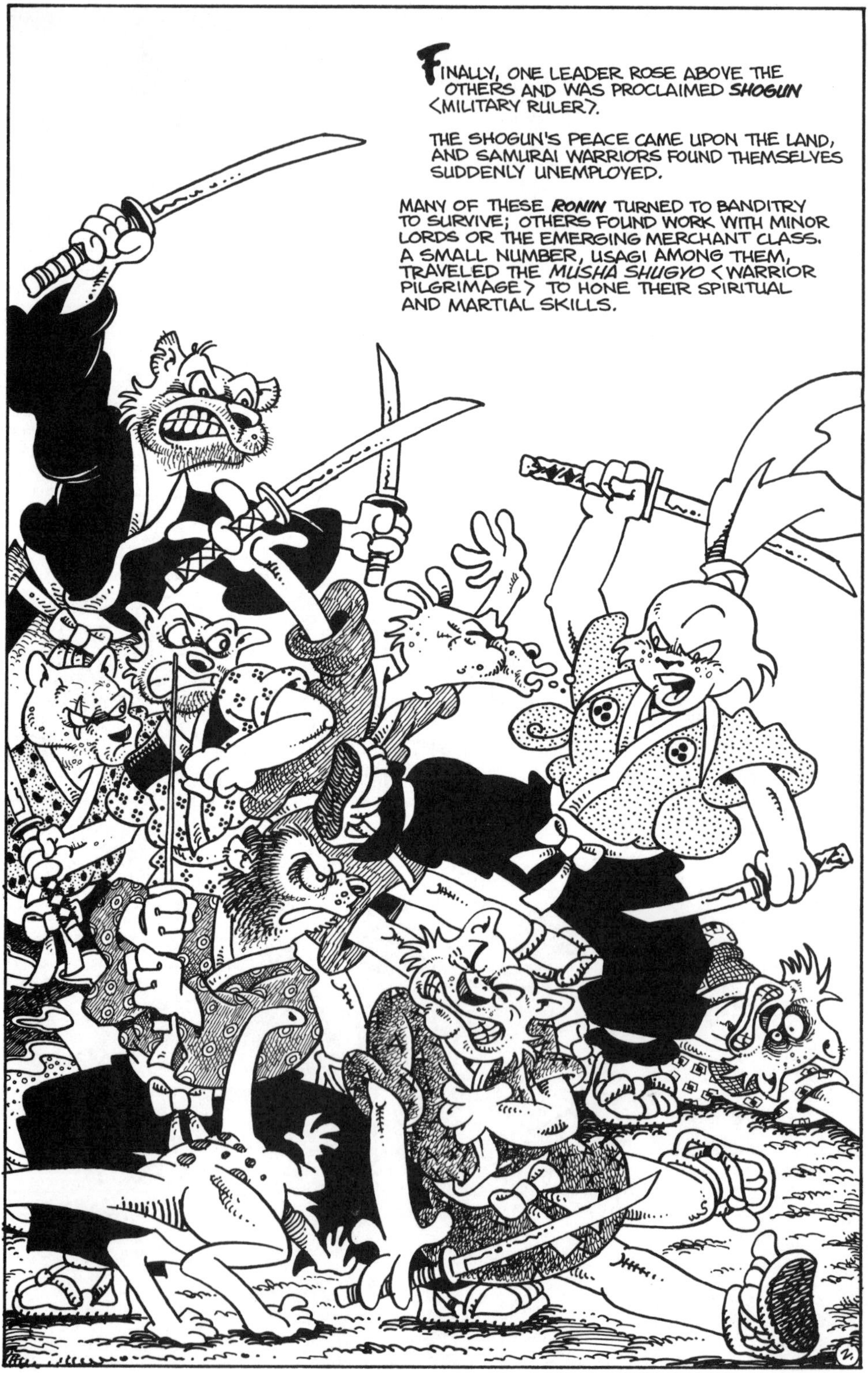
FINALLY, ONE LEADER ROSE ABOVE THE OTHERS AND WAS PROCLAIMED **SHOGUN** <MILITARY RULER>.
THE SHOGUN'S PEACE CAME UPON THE LAND, AND SAMURAI WARRIORS FOUND THEMSELVES SUDDENLY UNEMPLOYED.
MANY OF THESE ***RONIN*** TURNED TO BANDITRY TO SURVIVE; OTHERS FOUND WORK WITH MINOR LORDS OR THE EMERGING MERCHANT CLASS. A SMALL NUMBER, USAGI AMONG THEM, TRAVELED THE *MUSHA SHUGYO* <WARRIOR PILGRIMAGE> TO HONE THEIR SPIRITUAL AND MARTIAL SKILLS.
2.

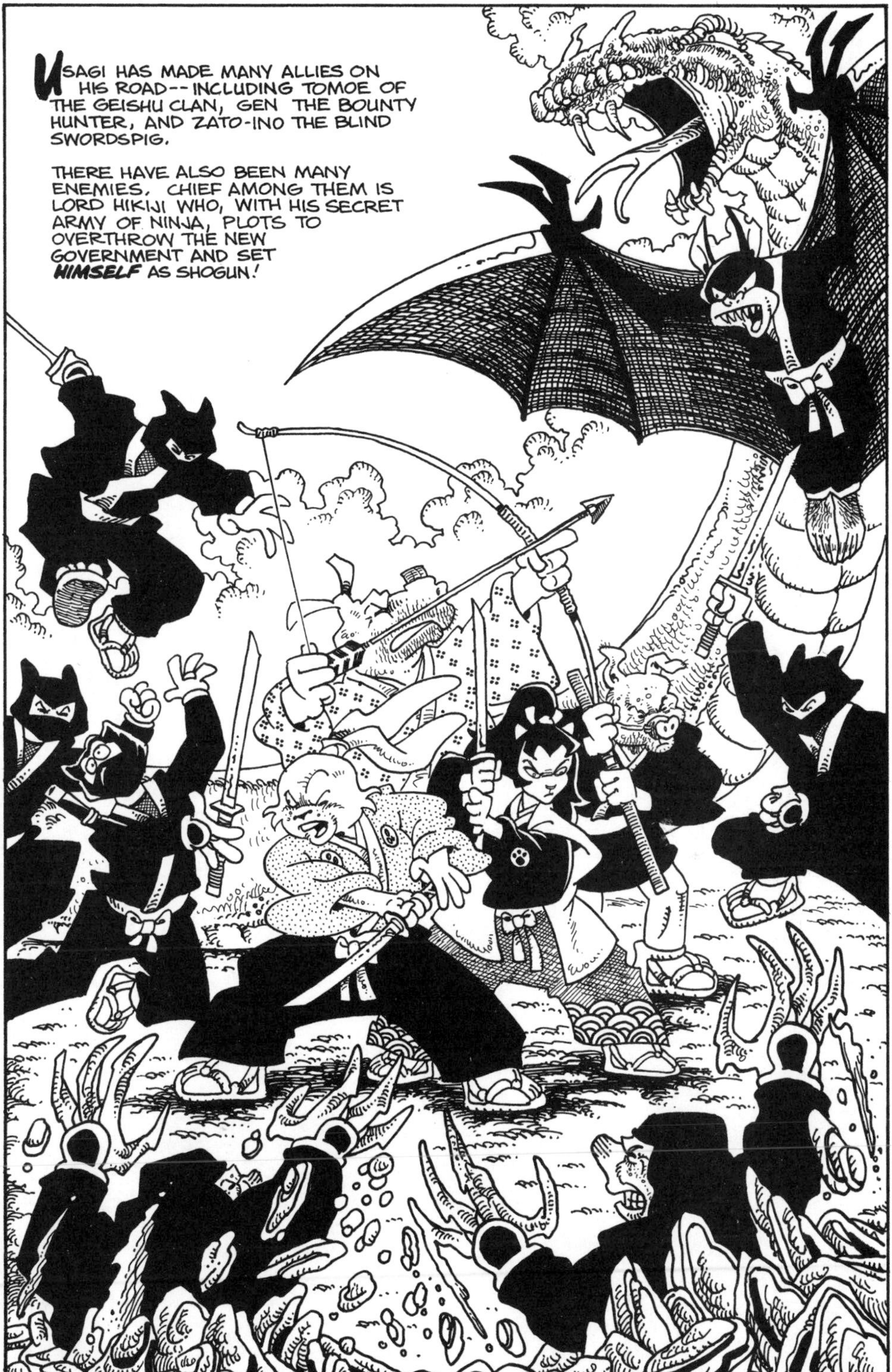
USAGI HAS MADE MANY ALLIES ON HIS ROAD-- INCLUDING TOMOE OF THE GEISHU CLAN, GEN THE BOUNTY HUNTER, AND ZATO-INO THE BLIND SWORDSPIG.
THERE HAVE ALSO BEEN MANY ENEMIES. CHIEF AMONG THEM IS LORD HIKIJI WHO, WITH HIS SECRET ARMY OF NINJA, PLOTS TO OVERTHROW THE NEW GOVERNMENT AND SET *HIMSELF* AS SHOGUN!

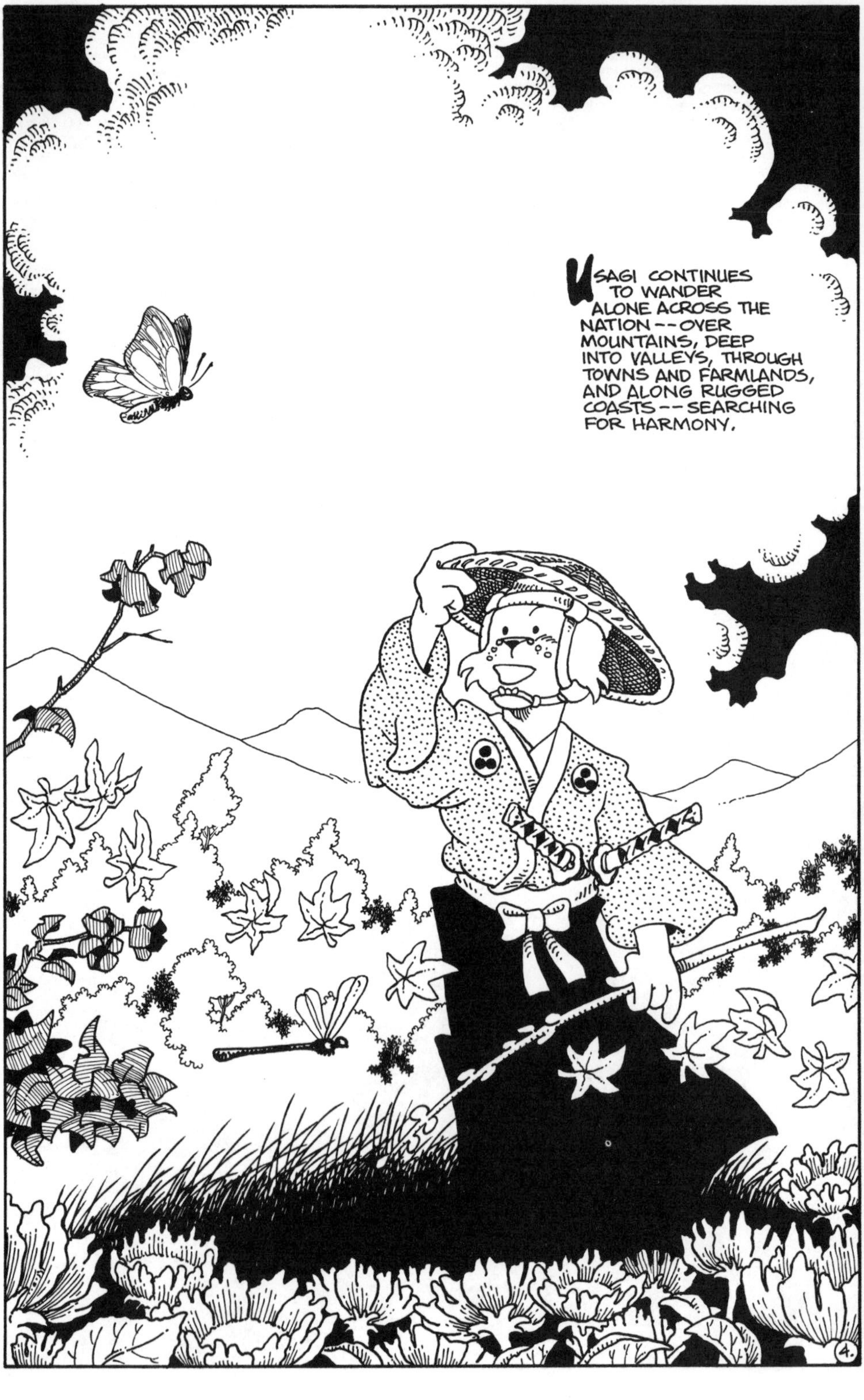
USAGI CONTINUES TO WANDER ALONE ACROSS THE NATION -- OVER MOUNTAINS, DEEP INTO VALLEYS, THROUGH TOWNS AND FARMLANDS, AND ALONG RUGGED COASTS -- SEARCHING FOR HARMONY.
4.

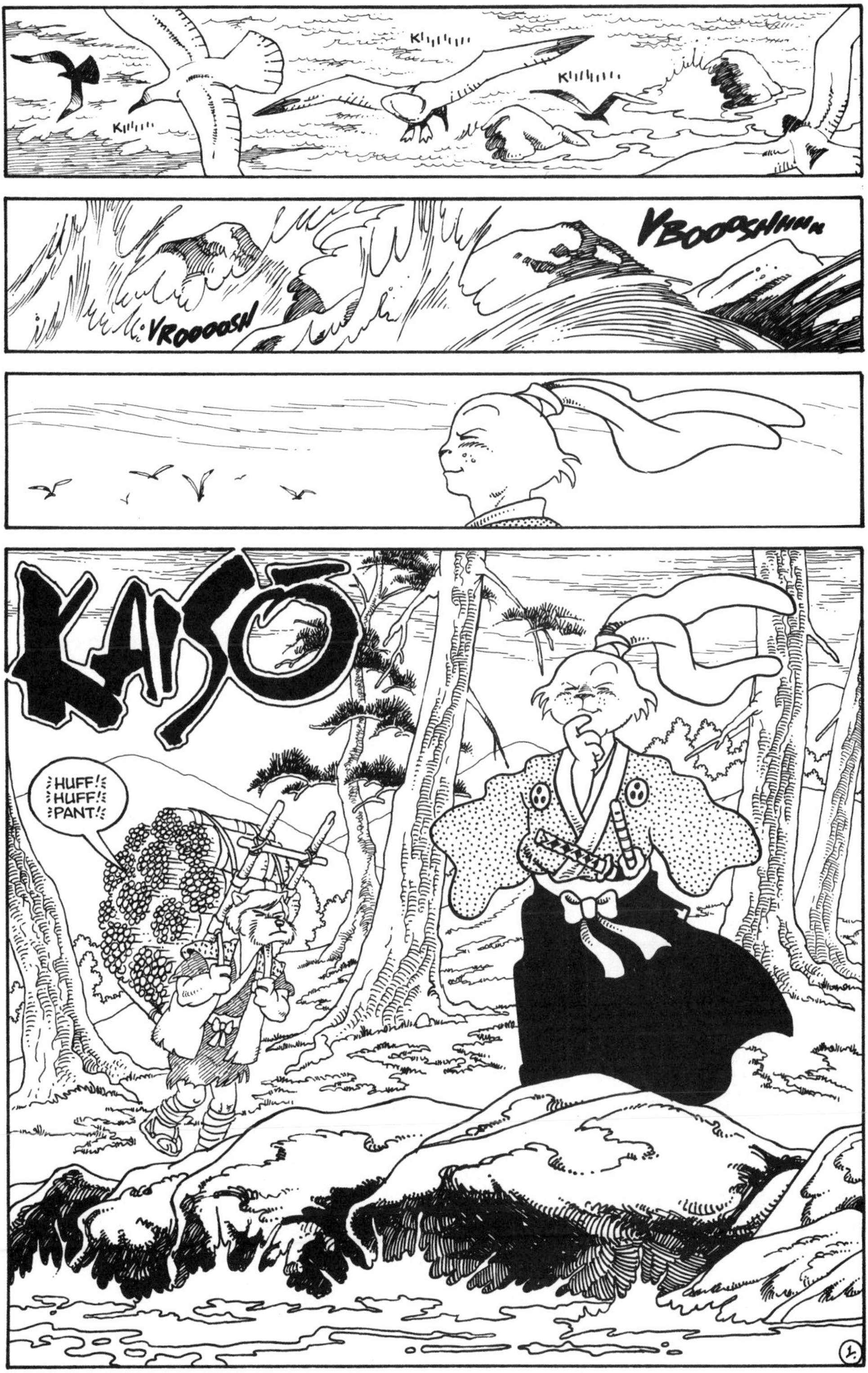
KIIIIII
KIIIIII
KIIIIII
VROOOOSH
VBOOOSHHHH
KASŌ
HUFF! HUFF! PANT!
1

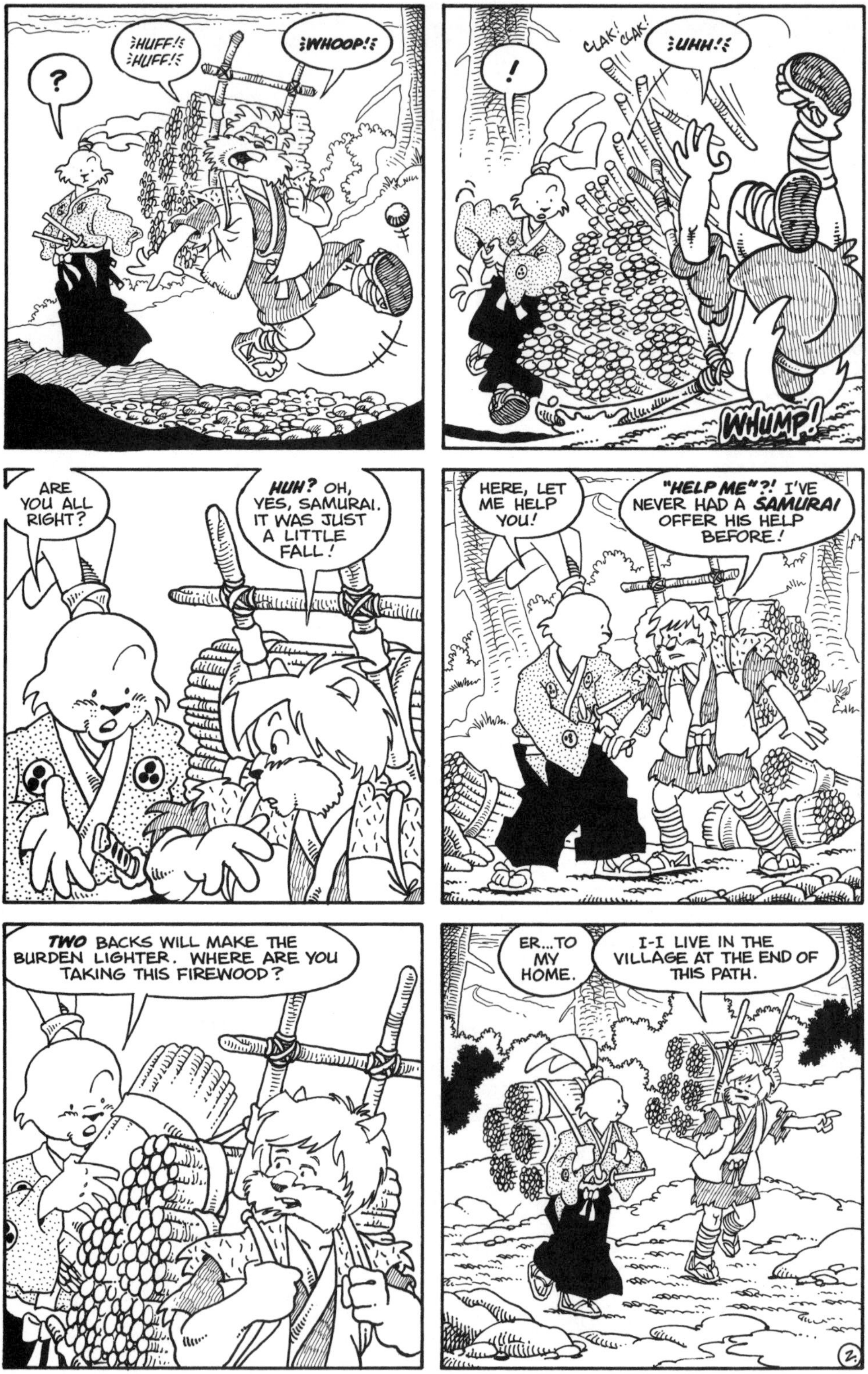
?
HUFF! HUFF!
WHOOP!
CLAK! CLAK!
!
UHH!
WHUMP!
ARE YOU ALL RIGHT?
HUH? OH, YES, SAMURAI. IT WAS JUST A LITTLE FALL!
HERE, LET ME HELP YOU!
"HELP ME"?! I'VE NEVER HAD A SAMURAI OFFER HIS HELP BEFORE!
TWO BACKS WILL MAKE THE BURDEN LIGHTER. WHERE ARE YOU TAKING THIS FIREWOOD?
ER...TO MY HOME.
I-I LIVE IN THE VILLAGE AT THE END OF THIS PATH.
2.

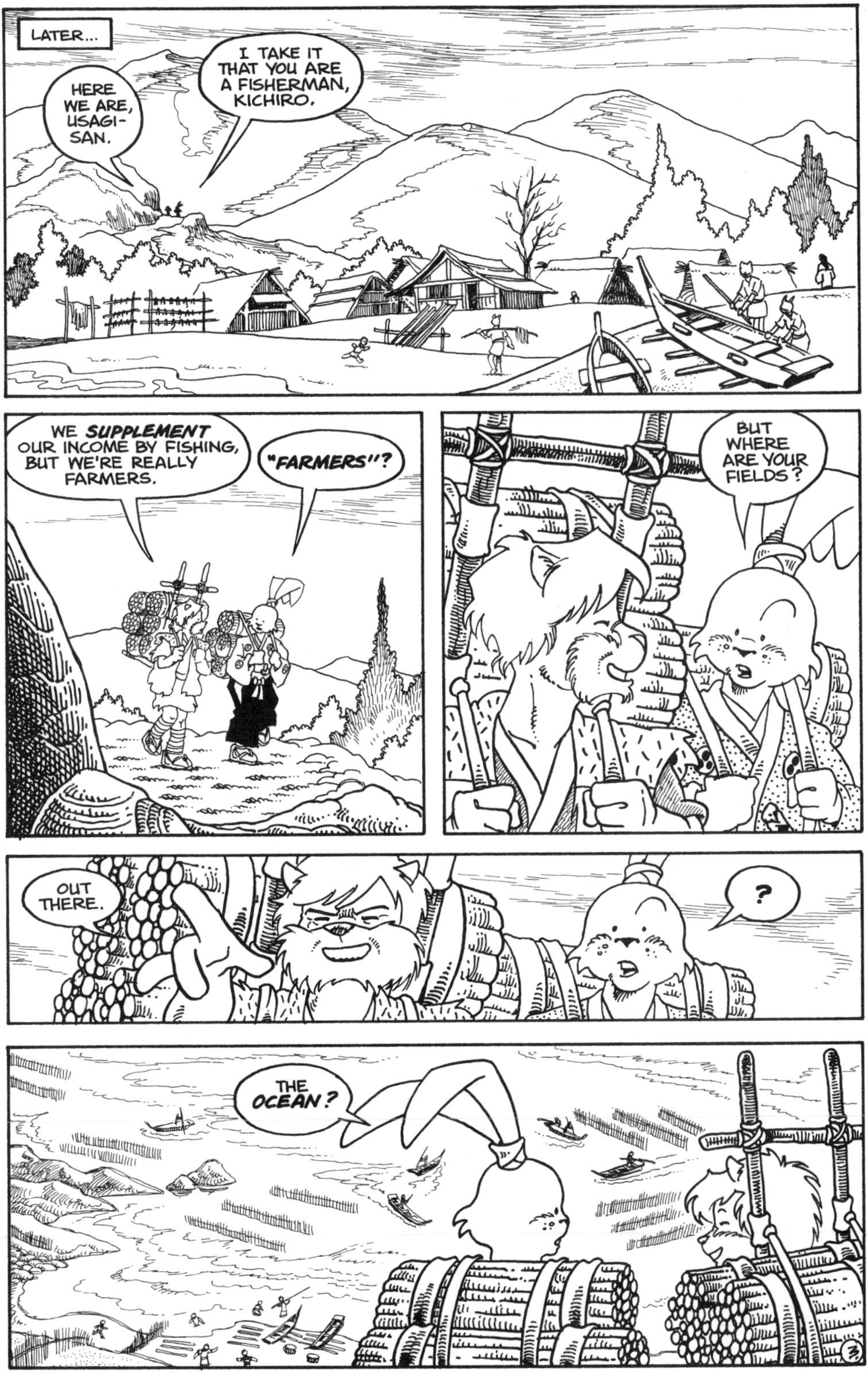
LATER...
HERE WE ARE, USAGI-SAN.
I TAKE IT THAT YOU ARE A FISHERMAN, KICHIRO.
WE *SUPPLEMENT* OUR INCOME BY FISHING, BUT WE'RE REALLY FARMERS.
"FARMERS"?
BUT WHERE ARE YOUR FIELDS?
OUT THERE.
?
THE *OCEAN*?

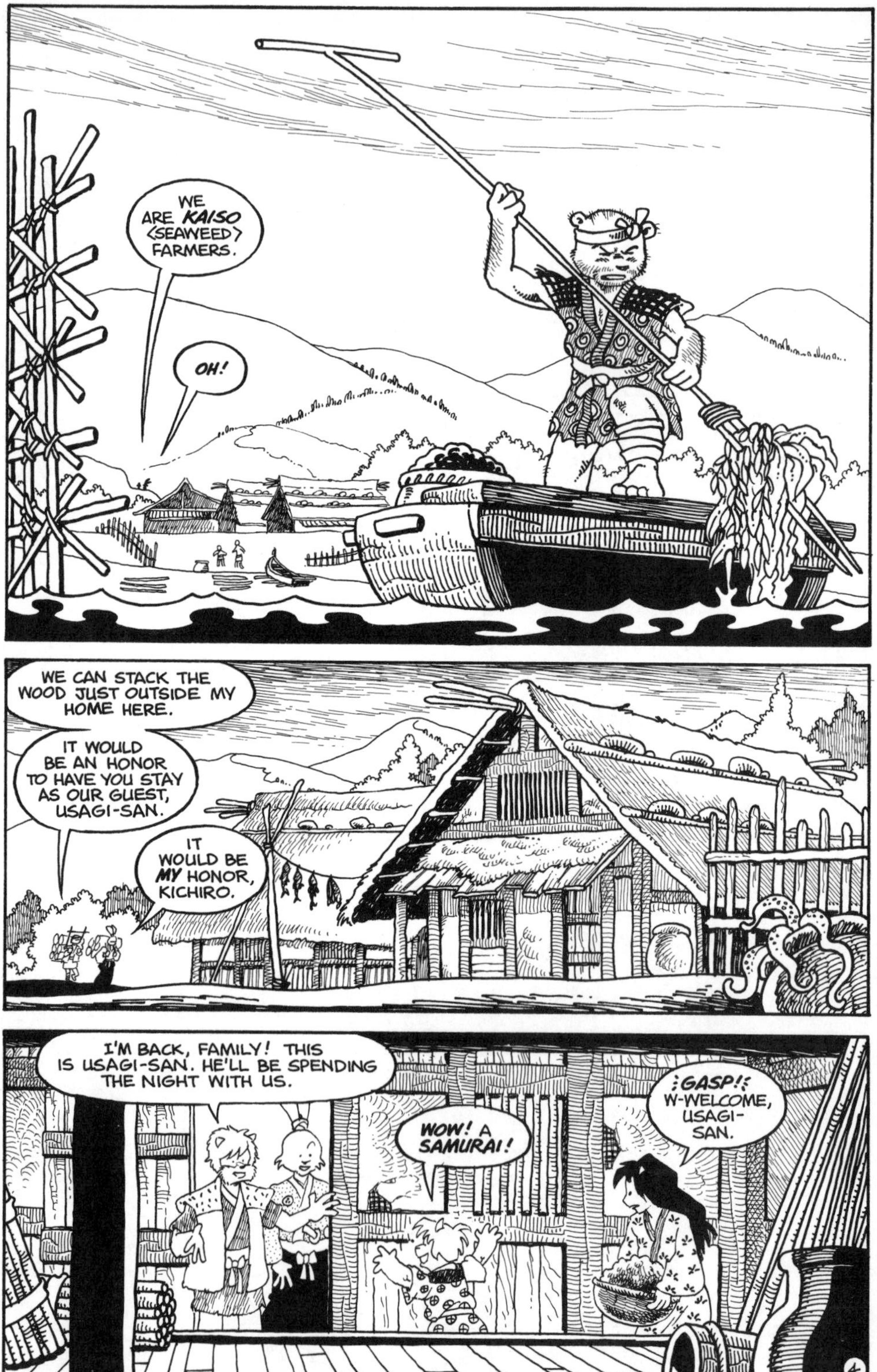
WE ARE KAISO <SEAWEED> FARMERS.
OH!
WE CAN STACK THE WOOD JUST OUTSIDE MY HOME HERE.
IT WOULD BE AN HONOR TO HAVE YOU STAY AS OUR GUEST, USAGI-SAN.
IT WOULD BE MY HONOR, KICHIRO.
I'M BACK, FAMILY! THIS IS USAGI-SAN. HE'LL BE SPENDING THE NIGHT WITH US.
WOW! A SAMURAI!
:GASP!: W-WELCOME, USAGI-SAN.
4.

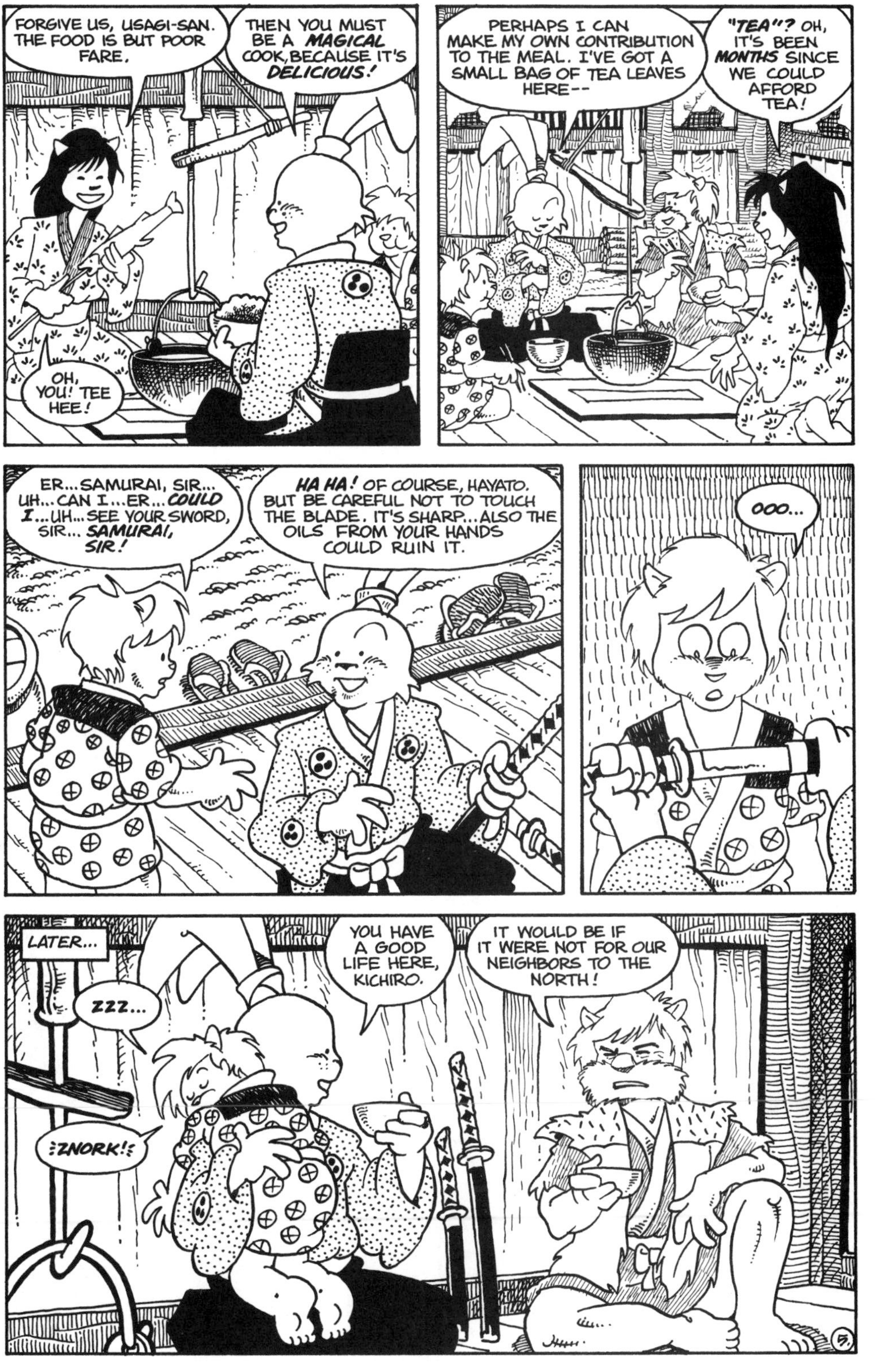
FORGIVE US, USAGI-SAN. THE FOOD IS BUT POOR FARE.
THEN YOU MUST BE A MAGICAL COOK, BECAUSE IT'S DELICIOUS!
OH, YOU! TEE HEE!
PERHAPS I CAN MAKE MY OWN CONTRIBUTION TO THE MEAL. I'VE GOT A SMALL BAG OF TEA LEAVES HERE--
"TEA"? OH, IT'S BEEN MONTHS SINCE WE COULD AFFORD TEA!
ER...SAMURAI, SIR... UH...CAN I...ER...COULD I...UH...SEE YOUR SWORD, SIR... SAMURAI, SIR!
HA HA! OF COURSE, HAYATO. BUT BE CAREFUL NOT TO TOUCH THE BLADE. IT'S SHARP...ALSO THE OILS FROM YOUR HANDS COULD RUIN IT.
OOO...
LATER...
ZZZ...
ZNORK!
YOU HAVE A GOOD LIFE HERE, KICHIRO.
IT WOULD BE IF IT WERE NOT FOR OUR NEIGHBORS TO THE NORTH!

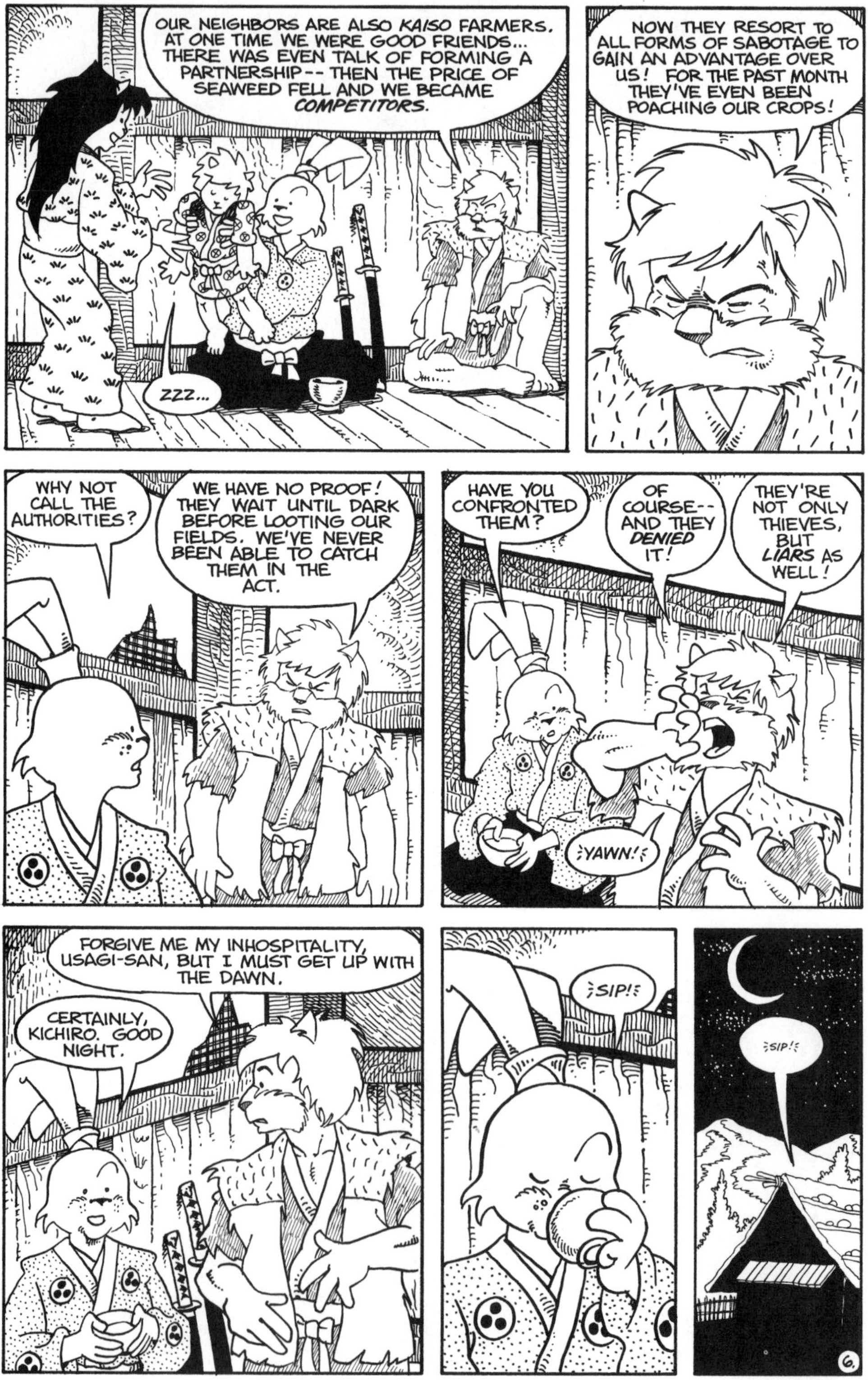

OUR NEIGHBORS ARE ALSO *KAISO* FARMERS. AT ONE TIME WE WERE GOOD FRIENDS... THERE WAS EVEN TALK OF FORMING A PARTNERSHIP-- THEN THE PRICE OF SEAWEED FELL AND WE BECAME *COMPETITORS*.
ZZZ...
NOW THEY RESORT TO ALL FORMS OF SABOTAGE TO GAIN AN ADVANTAGE OVER US! FOR THE PAST MONTH THEY'VE EVEN BEEN POACHING OUR CROPS!
WHY NOT CALL THE AUTHORITIES?
WE HAVE NO PROOF! THEY WAIT UNTIL DARK BEFORE LOOTING OUR FIELDS. WE'VE NEVER BEEN ABLE TO CATCH THEM IN THE ACT.
HAVE YOU CONFRONTED THEM?
OF COURSE-- AND THEY *DENIED* IT!
THEY'RE NOT ONLY THIEVES, BUT *LIARS* AS WELL!
YAWN!
FORGIVE ME MY INHOSPITALITY, USAGI-SAN, BUT I MUST GET UP WITH THE DAWN.
CERTAINLY, KICHIRO. GOOD NIGHT.
SIP!
SIP!
6.

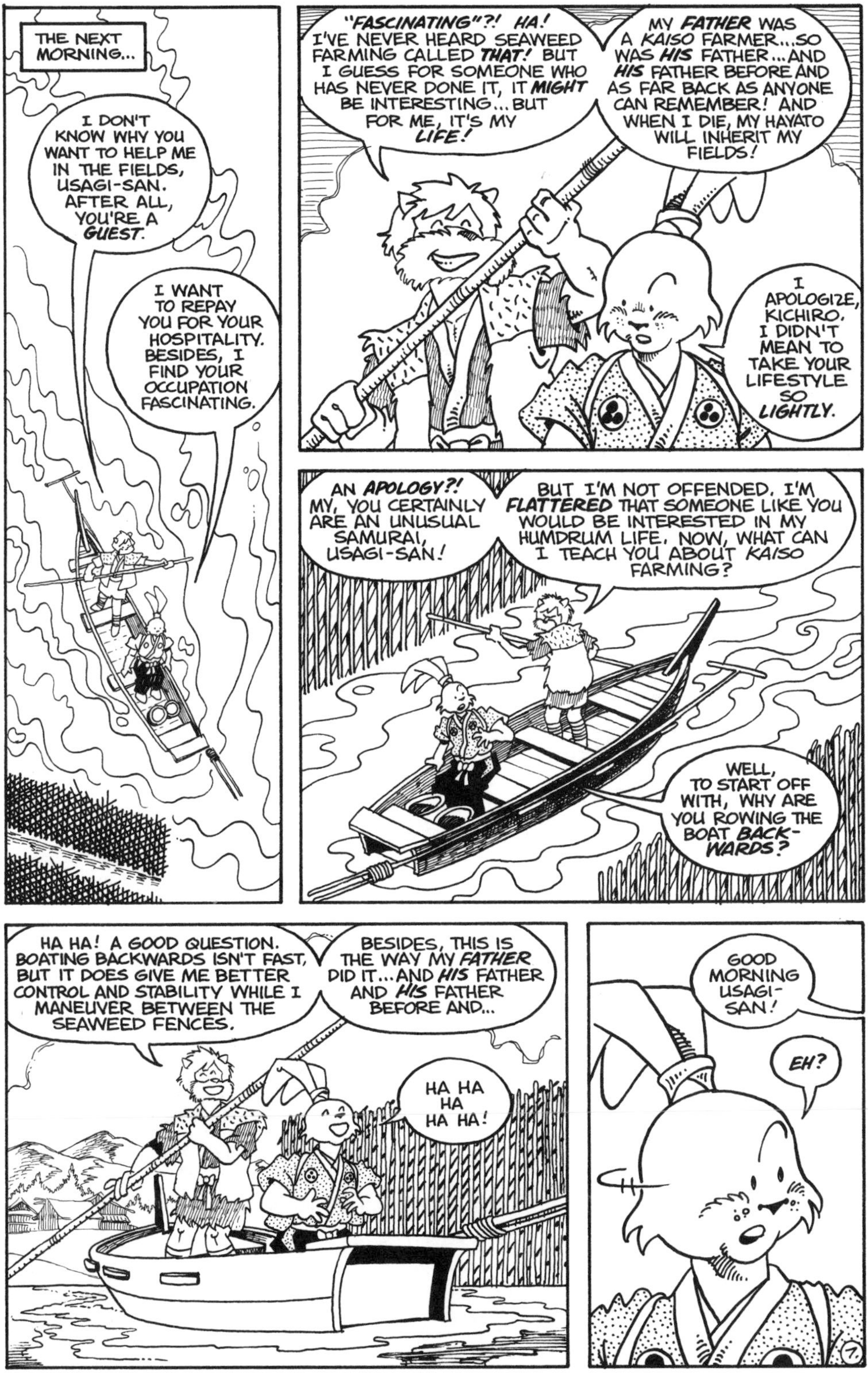
THE NEXT MORNING...
I DON'T KNOW WHY YOU WANT TO HELP ME IN THE FIELDS, USAGI-SAN. AFTER ALL, YOU'RE A *GUEST*.
I WANT TO REPAY YOU FOR YOUR HOSPITALITY. BESIDES, I FIND YOUR OCCUPATION FASCINATING.
"FASCINATING"?! HA! I'VE NEVER HEARD SEAWEED FARMING CALLED *THAT!* BUT I GUESS FOR SOMEONE WHO HAS NEVER DONE IT, IT *MIGHT* BE INTERESTING... BUT FOR ME, IT'S MY *LIFE!*
MY *FATHER* WAS A *KAISO* FARMER... SO WAS *HIS* FATHER... AND *HIS* FATHER BEFORE AND AS FAR BACK AS ANYONE CAN REMEMBER! AND WHEN I DIE, MY HAYATO WILL INHERIT MY FIELDS!
I APOLOGIZE, KICHIRO. I DIDN'T MEAN TO TAKE YOUR LIFESTYLE SO *LIGHTLY*.
AN *APOLOGY?!* MY, YOU CERTAINLY ARE AN UNUSUAL SAMURAI, USAGI-SAN!
BUT I'M NOT OFFENDED. I'M *FLATTERED* THAT SOMEONE LIKE YOU WOULD BE INTERESTED IN MY HUMDRUM LIFE. NOW, WHAT CAN I TEACH YOU ABOUT *KAISO* FARMING?
WELL, TO START OFF WITH, WHY ARE YOU ROWING THE BOAT *BACK-WARDS?*
HA HA! A GOOD QUESTION. BOATING BACKWARDS ISN'T FAST, BUT IT DOES GIVE ME BETTER CONTROL AND STABILITY WHILE I MANEUVER BETWEEN THE SEAWEED FENCES.
BESIDES, THIS IS THE WAY MY *FATHER* DID IT... AND *HIS* FATHER AND *HIS* FATHER BEFORE AND...
HA HA HA HA HA!
GOOD MORNING USAGI-SAN!
EH?
7.

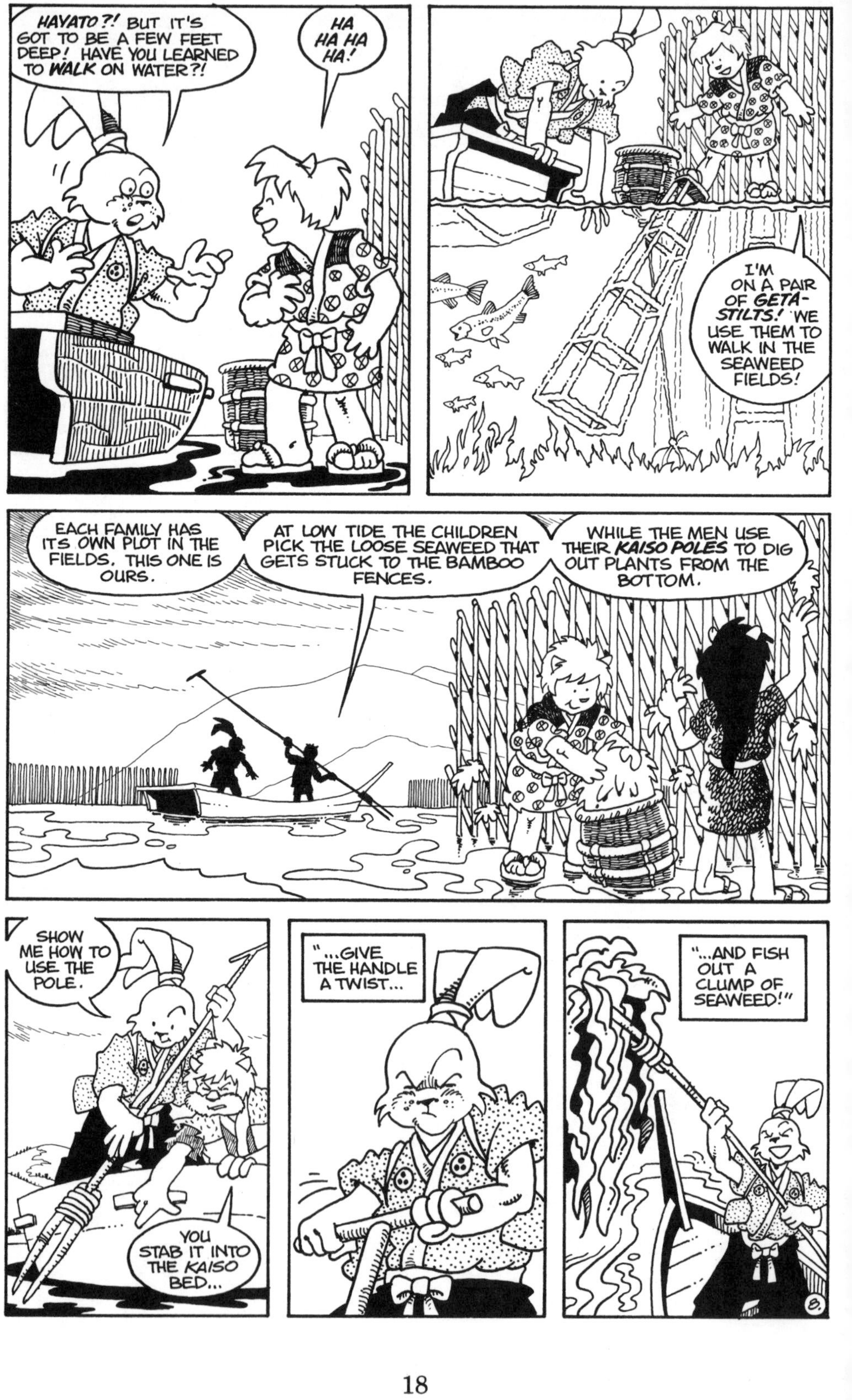

HAYATO?! BUT IT'S GOT TO BE A FEW FEET DEEP! HAVE YOU LEARNED TO WALK ON WATER?!
HA HA HA HA!
I'M ON A PAIR OF GETA-STILTS! WE USE THEM TO WALK IN THE SEAWEED FIELDS!
EACH FAMILY HAS ITS OWN PLOT IN THE FIELDS. THIS ONE IS OURS.
AT LOW TIDE THE CHILDREN PICK THE LOOSE SEAWEED THAT GETS STUCK TO THE BAMBOO FENCES.
WHILE THE MEN USE THEIR KAISO POLES TO DIG OUT PLANTS FROM THE BOTTOM.
SHOW ME HOW TO USE THE POLE.
YOU STAB IT INTO THE KAISO BED...
"...GIVE THE HANDLE A TWIST...
"...AND FISH OUT A CLUMP OF SEAWEED!"
8.

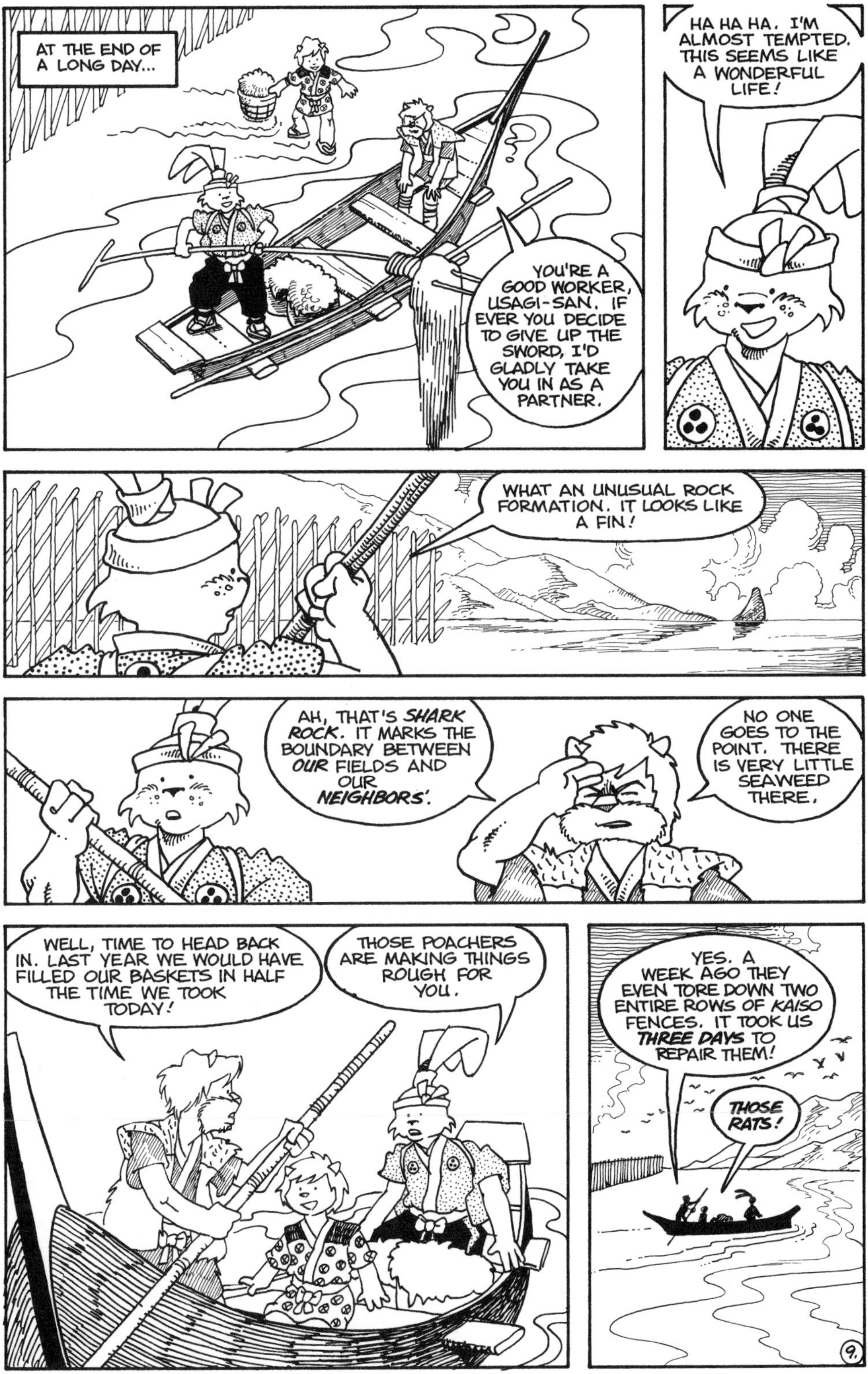
AT THE END OF A LONG DAY...
YOU'RE A GOOD WORKER, USAGI-SAN. IF EVER YOU DECIDE TO GIVE UP THE SWORD, I'D GLADLY TAKE YOU IN AS A PARTNER.
HA HA HA. I'M ALMOST TEMPTED. THIS SEEMS LIKE A WONDERFUL LIFE!
WHAT AN UNUSUAL ROCK FORMATION. IT LOOKS LIKE A FIN!
AH, THAT'S SHARK ROCK. IT MARKS THE BOUNDARY BETWEEN OUR FIELDS AND OUR NEIGHBORS'.
NO ONE GOES TO THE POINT. THERE IS VERY LITTLE SEAWEED THERE.
WELL, TIME TO HEAD BACK IN. LAST YEAR WE WOULD HAVE FILLED OUR BASKETS IN HALF THE TIME WE TOOK TODAY!
THOSE POACHERS ARE MAKING THINGS ROUGH FOR YOU.
YES. A WEEK AGO THEY EVEN TORE DOWN TWO ENTIRE ROWS OF KAISO FENCES. IT TOOK US THREE DAYS TO REPAIR THEM!
THOSE RATS!
9.

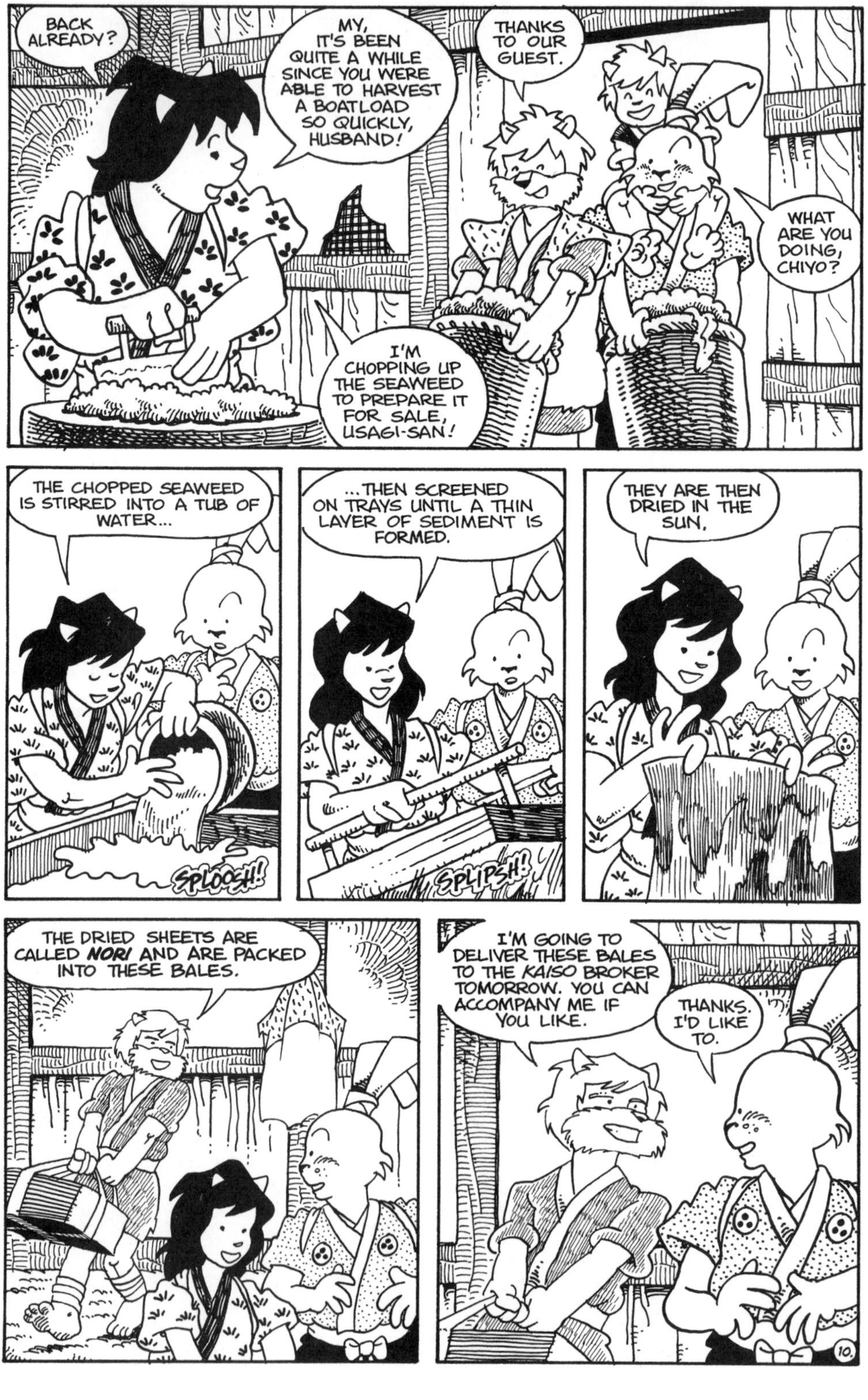
BACK ALREADY?
MY, IT'S BEEN QUITE A WHILE SINCE YOU WERE ABLE TO HARVEST A BOATLOAD SO QUICKLY, HUSBAND!
THANKS TO OUR GUEST.
WHAT ARE YOU DOING, CHIYO?
I'M CHOPPING UP THE SEAWEED TO PREPARE IT FOR SALE, USAGI-SAN!
THE CHOPPED SEAWEED IS STIRRED INTO A TUB OF WATER...
SPLOOSH!
...THEN SCREENED ON TRAYS UNTIL A THIN LAYER OF SEDIMENT IS FORMED.
SPLIPSH!
THEY ARE THEN DRIED IN THE SUN.
THE DRIED SHEETS ARE CALLED *NORI* AND ARE PACKED INTO THESE BALES.
I'M GOING TO DELIVER THESE BALES TO THE *KAISO* BROKER TOMORROW. YOU CAN ACCOMPANY ME IF YOU LIKE.
THANKS. I'D LIKE TO.
10.

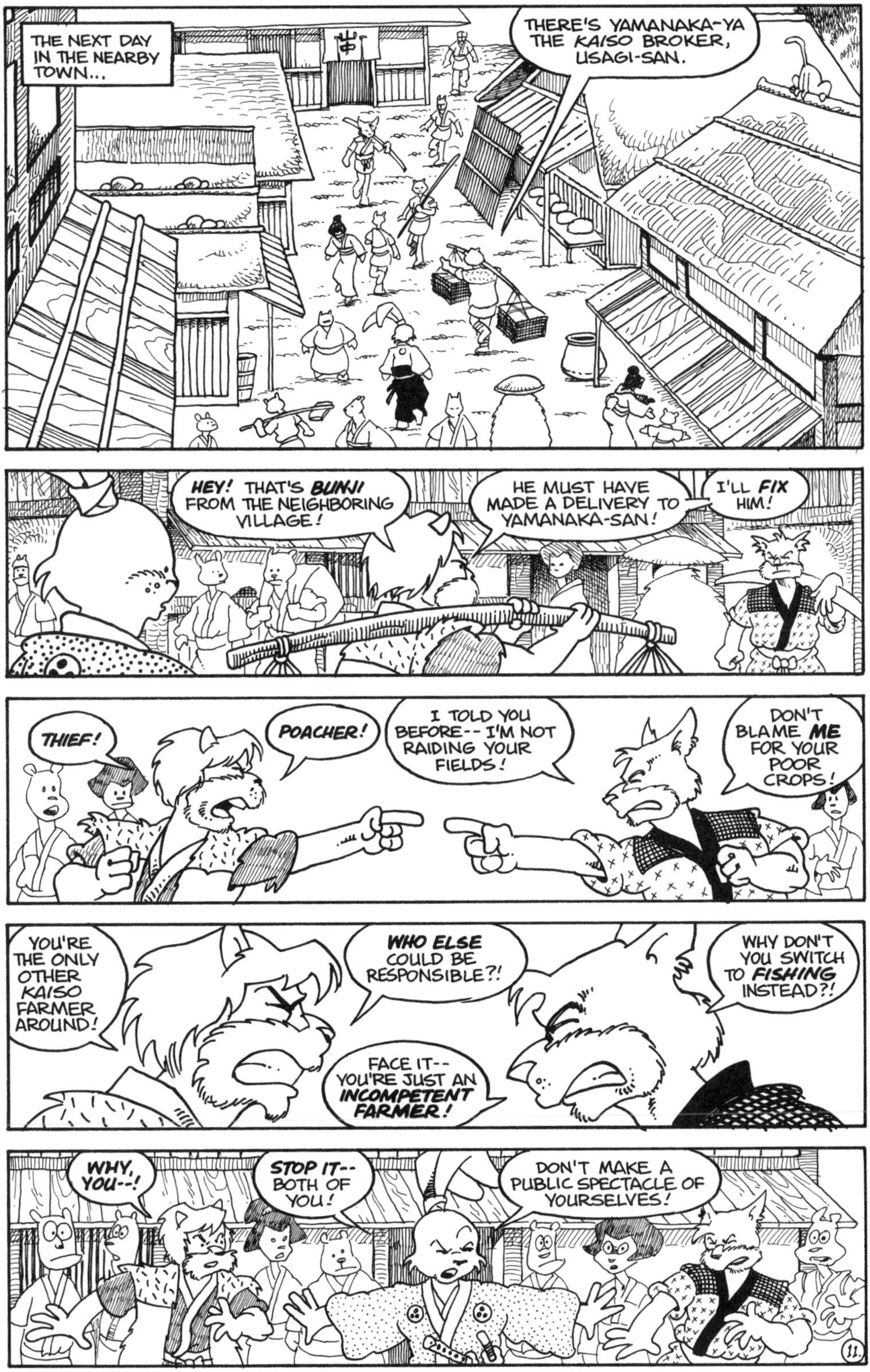
THE NEXT DAY IN THE NEARBY TOWN...
THERE'S YAMANAKA-YA THE KAISO BROKER, USAGI-SAN.
HEY! THAT'S BUNJI FROM THE NEIGHBORING VILLAGE!
HE MUST HAVE MADE A DELIVERY TO YAMANAKA-SAN!
I'LL FIX HIM!
THIEF!
POACHER!
I TOLD YOU BEFORE-- I'M NOT RAIDING YOUR FIELDS!
DON'T BLAME ME FOR YOUR POOR CROPS!
YOU'RE THE ONLY OTHER KAISO FARMER AROUND!
WHO ELSE COULD BE RESPONSIBLE?!
WHY DON'T YOU SWITCH TO FISHING INSTEAD?!
FACE IT-- YOU'RE JUST AN INCOMPETENT FARMER!
WHY, YOU--!
STOP IT-- BOTH OF YOU!
DON'T MAKE A PUBLIC SPECTACLE OF YOURSELVES!
11.

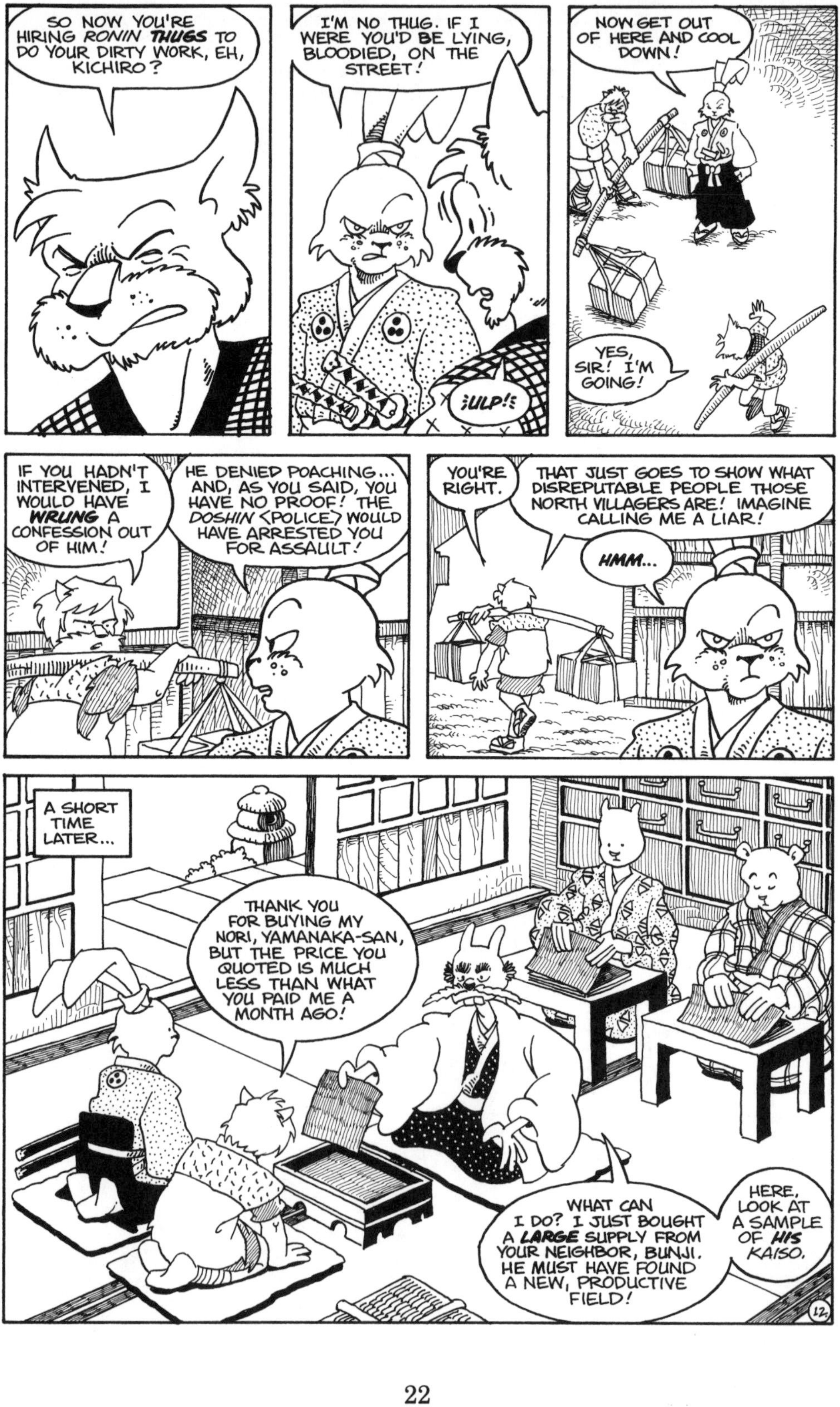
SO NOW YOU'RE HIRING *RONIN* **THUGS** TO DO YOUR DIRTY WORK, EH, KICHIRO?
I'M NO THUG. IF I WERE YOU'D BE LYING, BLOODIED, ON THE STREET!
¡ULP!¡
NOW GET OUT OF HERE AND COOL DOWN!
YES, SIR! I'M GOING!
IF YOU HADN'T INTERVENED, I WOULD HAVE **WRUNG** A CONFESSION OUT OF HIM!
HE DENIED POACHING... AND, AS YOU SAID, YOU HAVE NO PROOF! THE *DOSHIN* <POLICE> WOULD HAVE ARRESTED YOU FOR ASSAULT!
YOU'RE RIGHT.
THAT JUST GOES TO SHOW WHAT DISREPUTABLE PEOPLE THOSE NORTH VILLAGERS ARE! IMAGINE CALLING ME A LIAR!
HMM...
A SHORT TIME LATER...
THANK YOU FOR BUYING MY NORI, YAMANAKA-SAN, BUT THE PRICE YOU QUOTED IS MUCH LESS THAN WHAT YOU PAID ME A MONTH AGO!
WHAT CAN I DO? I JUST BOUGHT A **LARGE** SUPPLY FROM YOUR NEIGHBOR, BUNJI. HE MUST HAVE FOUND A NEW, PRODUCTIVE FIELD!
HERE, LOOK AT A SAMPLE OF **HIS** *KAISO.*
12

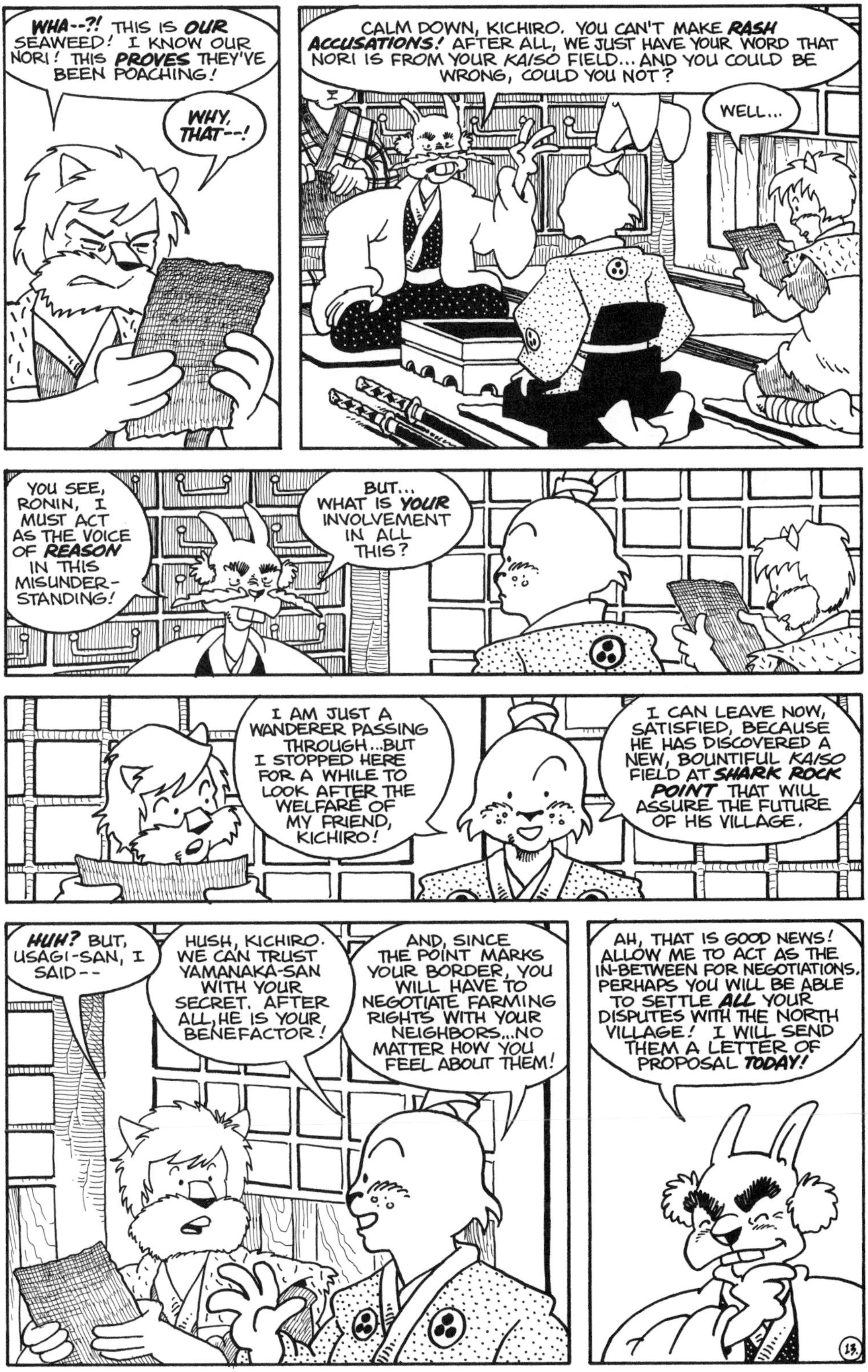
WHA--?! THIS IS OUR SEAWEED! I KNOW OUR NORI! THIS PROVES THEY'VE BEEN POACHING!
WHY, THAT--!
CALM DOWN, KICHIRO. YOU CAN'T MAKE RASH ACCUSATIONS! AFTER ALL, WE JUST HAVE YOUR WORD THAT NORI IS FROM YOUR KAISO FIELD... AND YOU COULD BE WRONG, COULD YOU NOT?
WELL...
YOU SEE, RONIN, I MUST ACT AS THE VOICE OF REASON IN THIS MISUNDER-STANDING!
BUT... WHAT IS YOUR INVOLVEMENT IN ALL THIS?
I AM JUST A WANDERER PASSING THROUGH...BUT I STOPPED HERE FOR A WHILE TO LOOK AFTER THE WELFARE OF MY FRIEND, KICHIRO!
I CAN LEAVE NOW, SATISFIED, BECAUSE HE HAS DISCOVERED A NEW, BOUNTIFUL KAISO FIELD AT SHARK ROCK POINT THAT WILL ASSURE THE FUTURE OF HIS VILLAGE.
HUH? BUT, USAGI-SAN, I SAID--
HUSH, KICHIRO. WE CAN TRUST YAMANAKA-SAN WITH YOUR SECRET. AFTER ALL, HE IS YOUR BENEFACTOR!
AND, SINCE THE POINT MARKS YOUR BORDER, YOU WILL HAVE TO NEGOTIATE FARMING RIGHTS WITH YOUR NEIGHBORS...NO MATTER HOW YOU FEEL ABOUT THEM!
AH, THAT IS GOOD NEWS! ALLOW ME TO ACT AS THE IN-BETWEEN FOR NEGOTIATIONS. PERHAPS YOU WILL BE ABLE TO SETTLE ALL YOUR DISPUTES WITH THE NORTH VILLAGE! I WILL SEND THEM A LETTER OF PROPOSAL TODAY!
13.

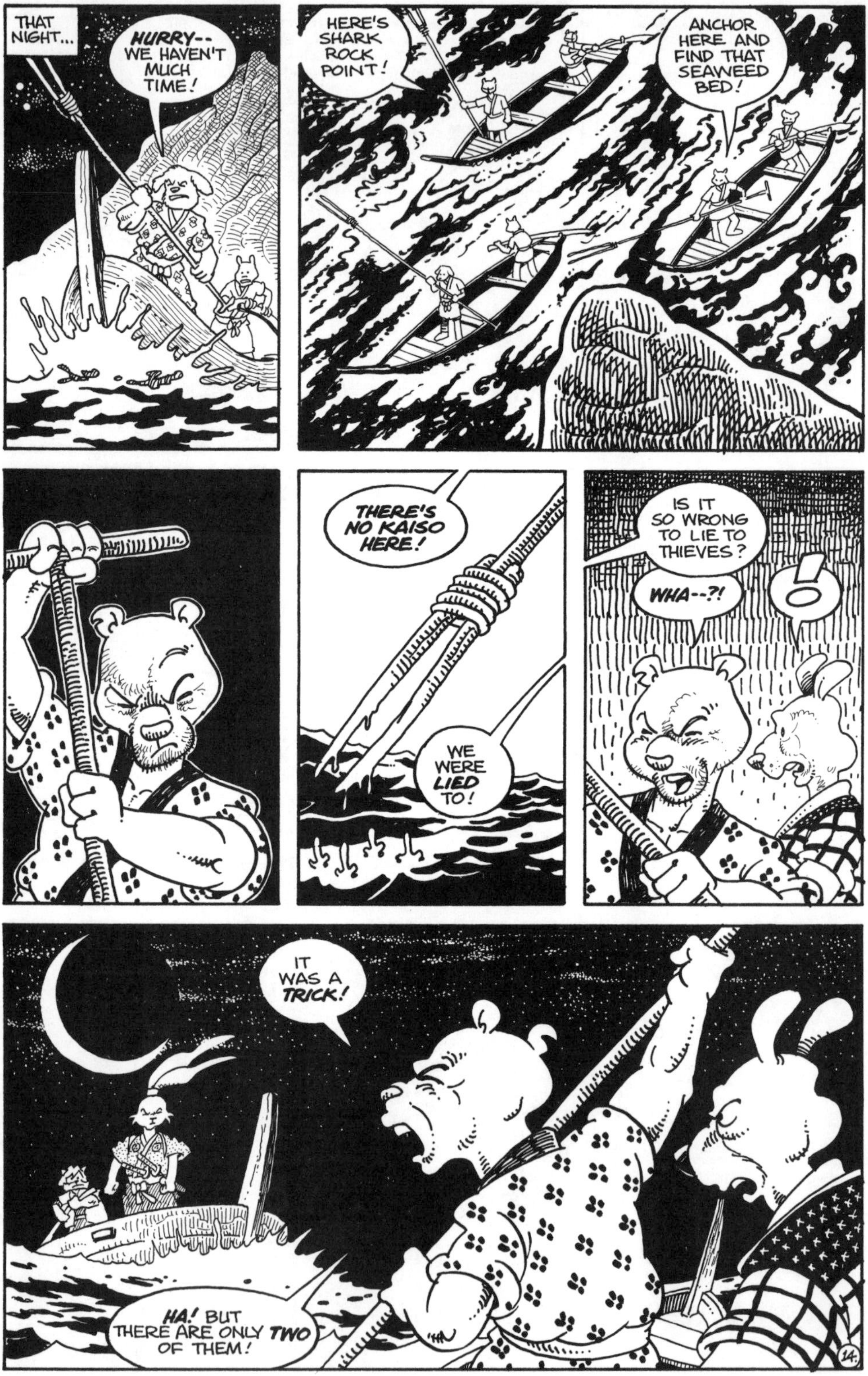
THAT NIGHT...
HURRY-- WE HAVEN'T MUCH TIME!
HERE'S SHARK ROCK POINT!
ANCHOR HERE AND FIND THAT SEAWEED BED!
THERE'S NO KAISO HERE!
WE WERE LIED TO!
IS IT SO WRONG TO LIE TO THIEVES?
WHA--?!
!
IT WAS A TRICK!
HA! BUT THERE ARE ONLY TWO OF THEM!
14.

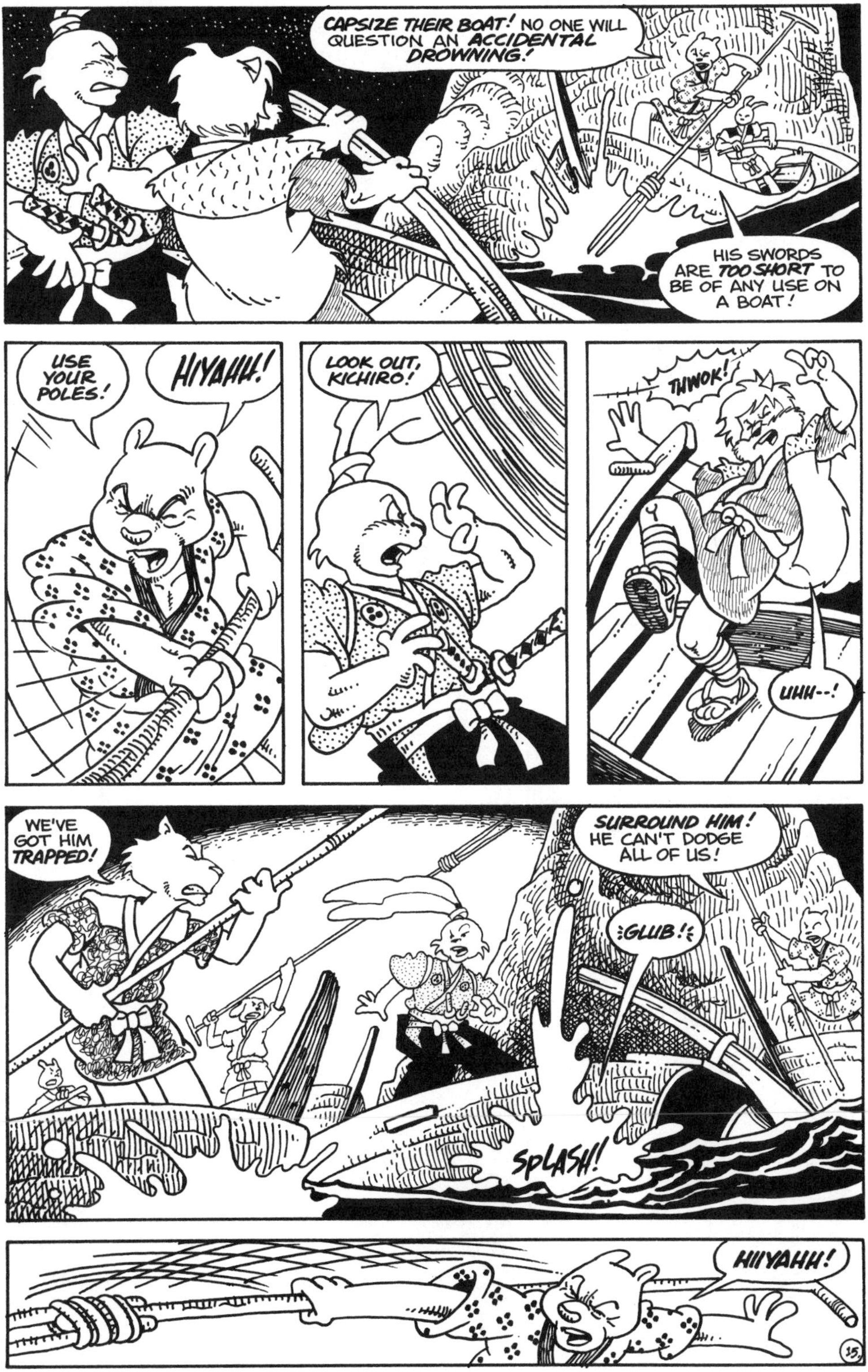
CAPSIZE THEIR BOAT! NO ONE WILL QUESTION AN ACCIDENTAL DROWNING!
HIS SWORDS ARE TOO SHORT TO BE OF ANY USE ON A BOAT!
USE YOUR POLES!
HIYAHH!
LOOK OUT, KICHIRO!
THWOK!
UHH--!
WE'VE GOT HIM TRAPPED!
SURROUND HIM! HE CAN'T DODGE ALL OF US!
GLUB!
SPLASH!
HIIYAHH!
15

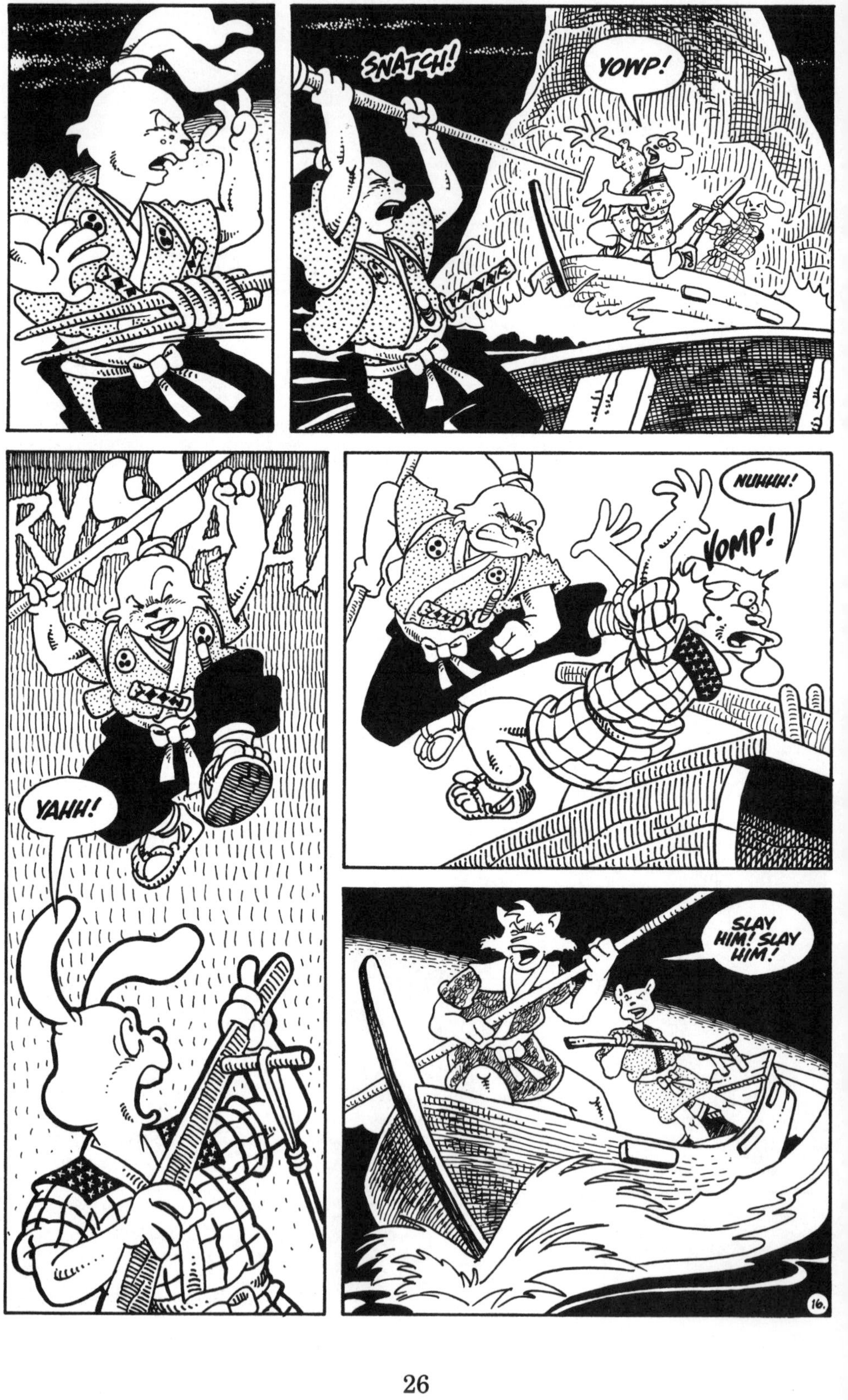

SNATCH!
YOWP!
YAHH!
NUHHH!
VOMP!
SLAY HIM! SLAY HIM!
16.

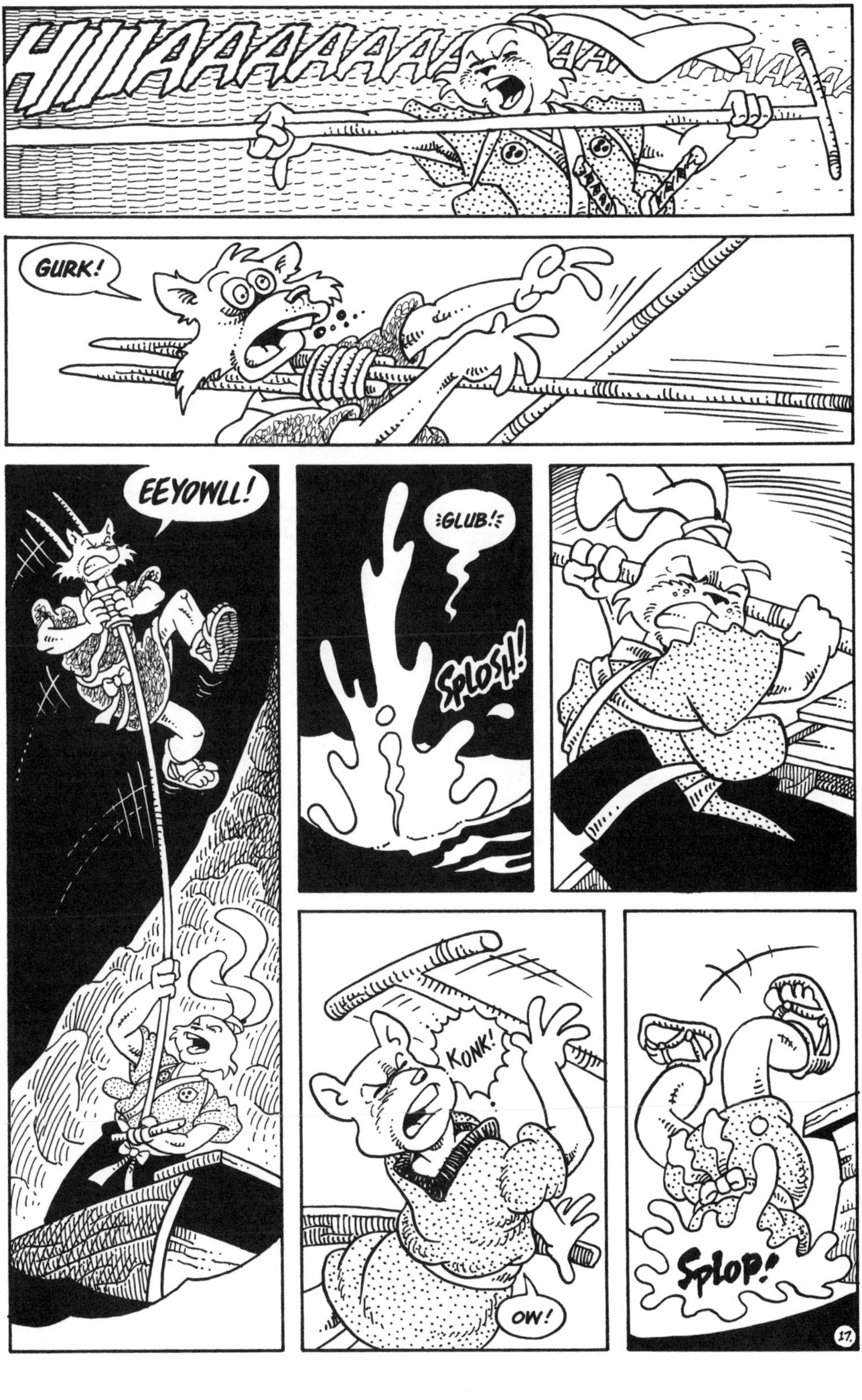
HIIAAAAAAAAAAAAAAAA
GURK!
EEYOWLL!
GLUB!
SPLOSH!
KONK!
OW!
Splop!
17.

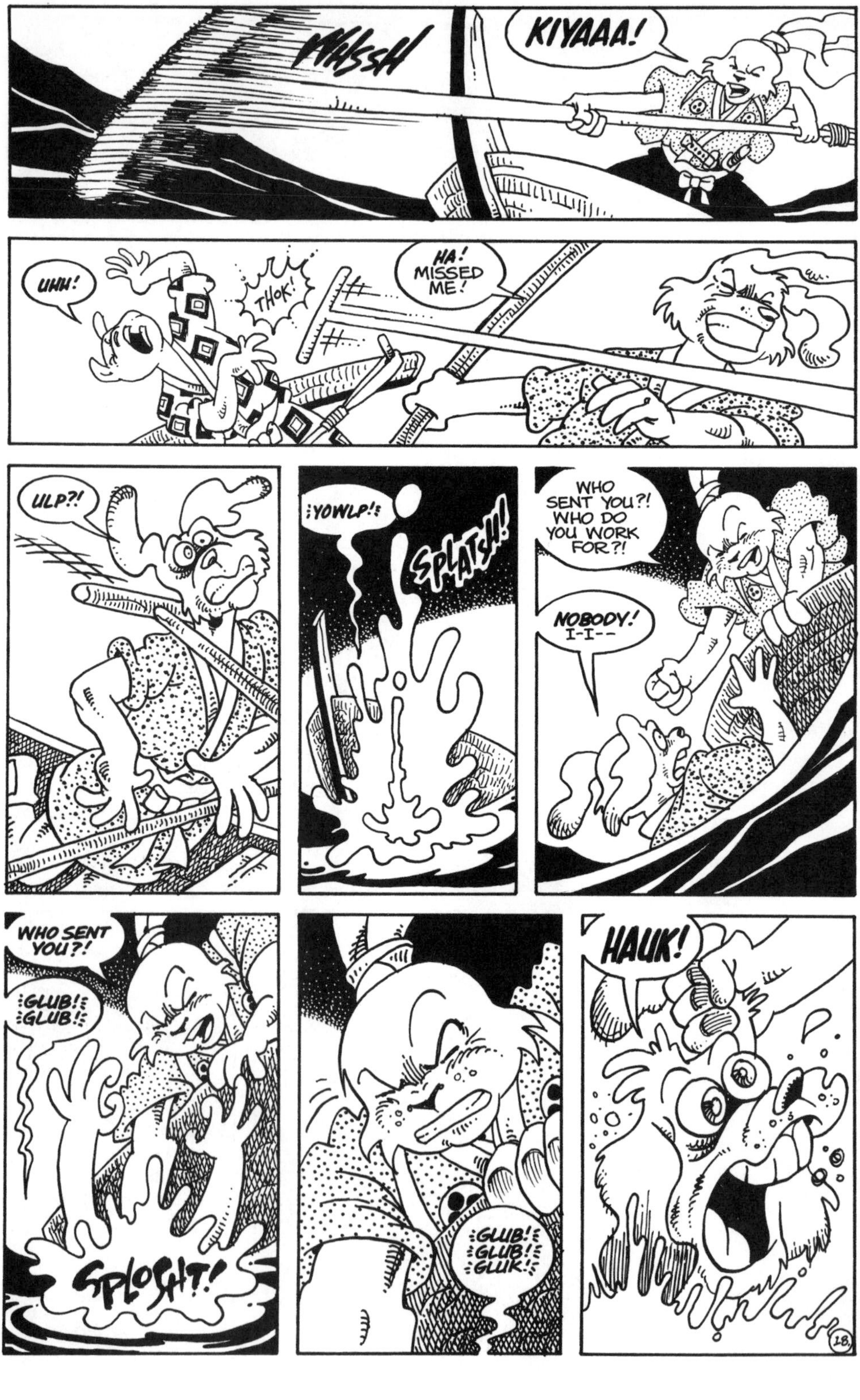

WHSSH
KIYAAA!
UHH!
THOK!
HA! MISSED ME!
ULP?!
YOWLP!
SPLATSH!
WHO SENT YOU?! WHO DO YOU WORK FOR?!
NOBODY! I-I--
WHO SENT YOU?!
GLUB! GLUB!
SPLOSHT!
GLUB! GLUB! GLUK!
HAUK!

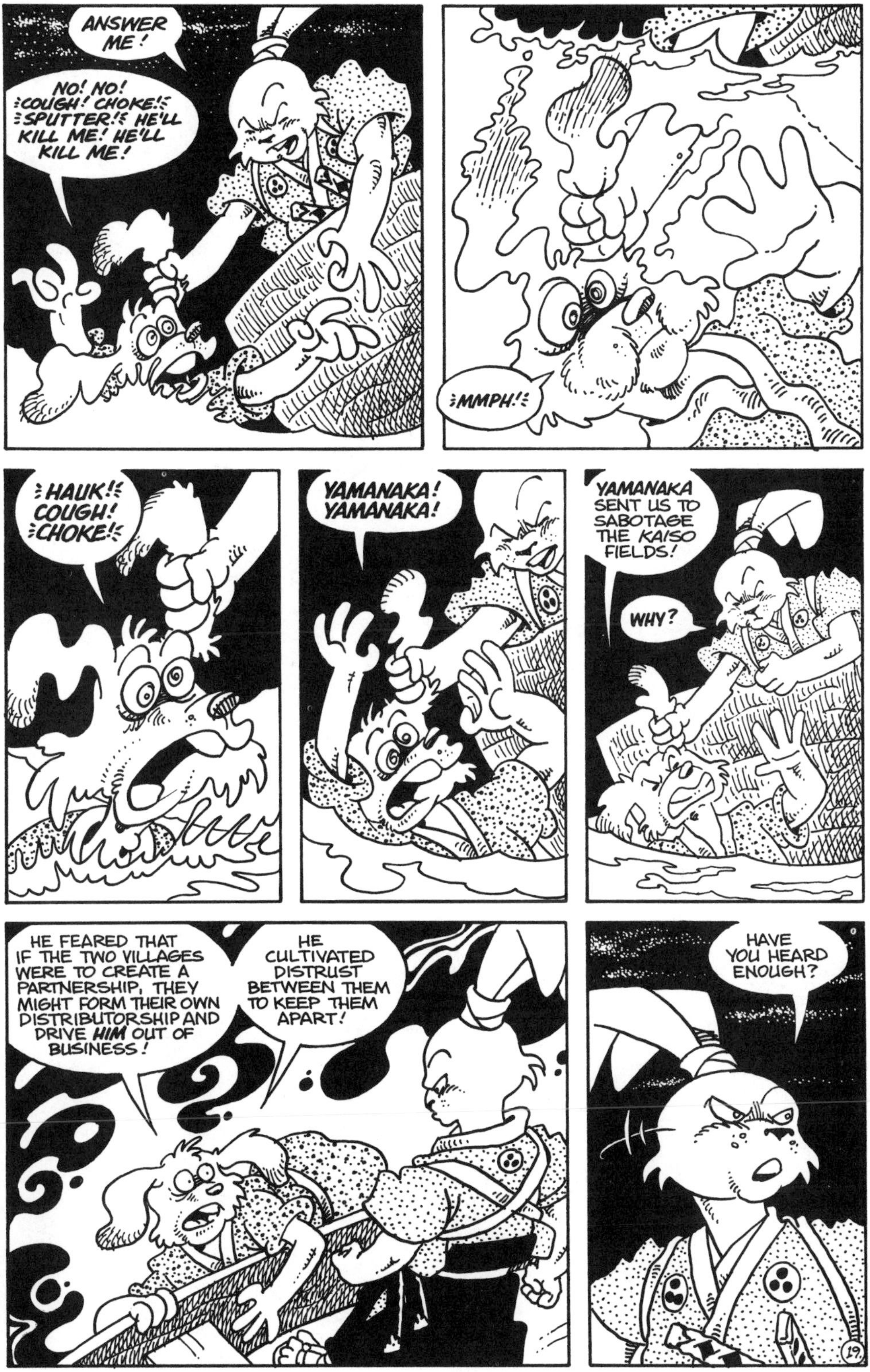

ANSWER ME!
NO! NO! COUGH! CHOKE! SPUTTER! HE'LL KILL ME! HE'LL KILL ME!
MMPH!
HAUK! COUGH! CHOKE!
YAMANAKA! YAMANAKA!
YAMANAKA SENT US TO SABOTAGE THE KAISO FIELDS!
WHY?
HE FEARED THAT IF THE TWO VILLAGES WERE TO CREATE A PARTNERSHIP, THEY MIGHT FORM THEIR OWN DISTRIBUTORSHIP AND DRIVE HIM OUT OF BUSINESS!
HE CULTIVATED DISTRUST BETWEEN THEM TO KEEP THEM APART!
HAVE YOU HEARD ENOUGH?
19

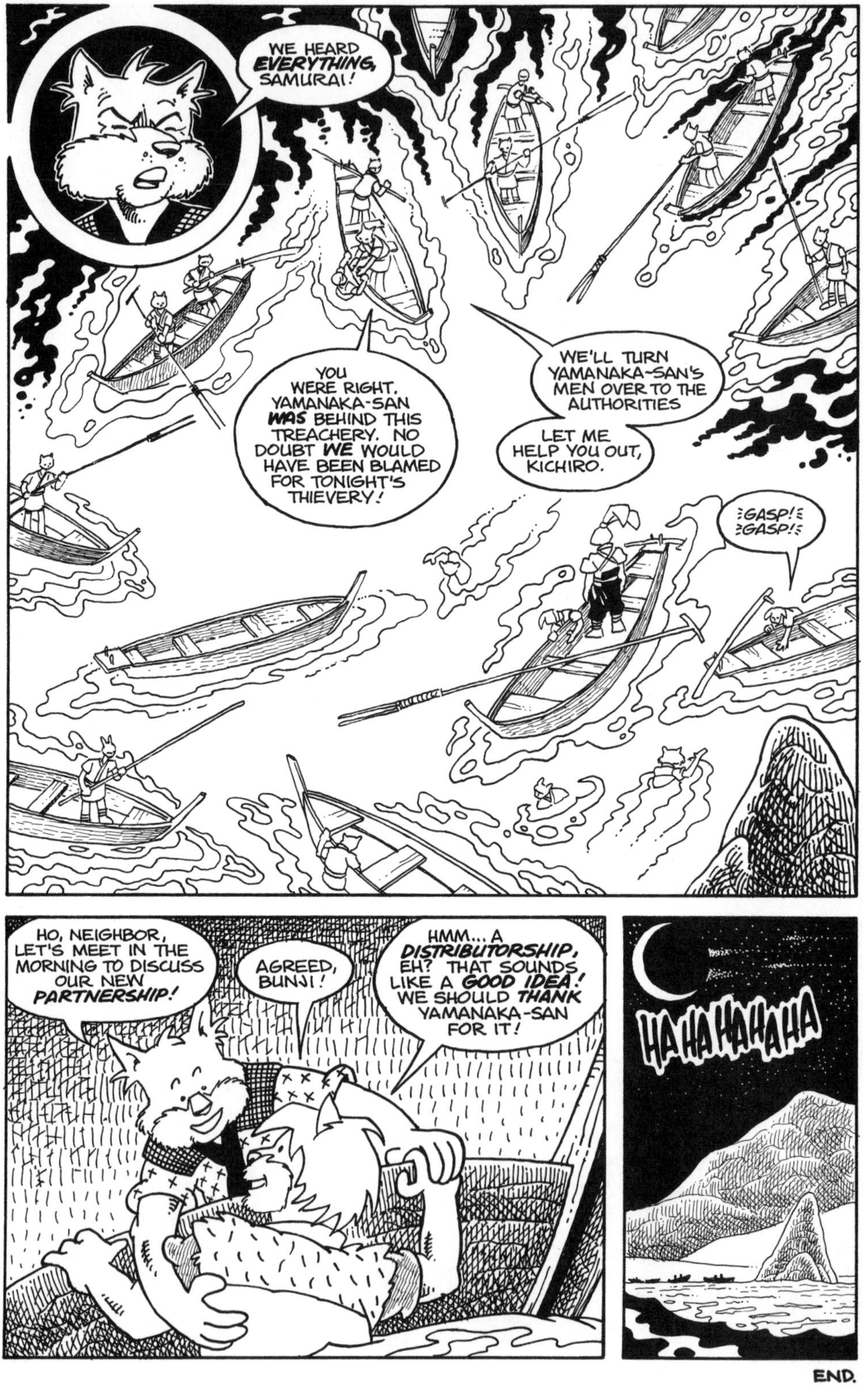
WE HEARD EVERYTHING, SAMURAI!
YOU WERE RIGHT. YAMANAKA-SAN WAS BEHIND THIS TREACHERY. NO DOUBT WE WOULD HAVE BEEN BLAMED FOR TONIGHT'S THIEVERY!
WE'LL TURN YAMANAKA-SAN'S MEN OVER TO THE AUTHORITIES
LET ME HELP YOU OUT, KICHIRO.
GASP! GASP!
HO, NEIGHBOR, LET'S MEET IN THE MORNING TO DISCUSS OUR NEW PARTNERSHIP!
AGREED, BUNJI!
HMM... A DISTRIBUTORSHIP, EH? THAT SOUNDS LIKE A GOOD IDEA! WE SHOULD THANK YAMANAKA-SAN FOR IT!
HA HA HA HA HA HA
END.

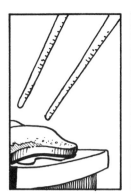

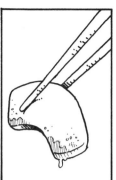

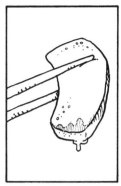

MUNCH!
MUNCH!
MUNCH!

.....

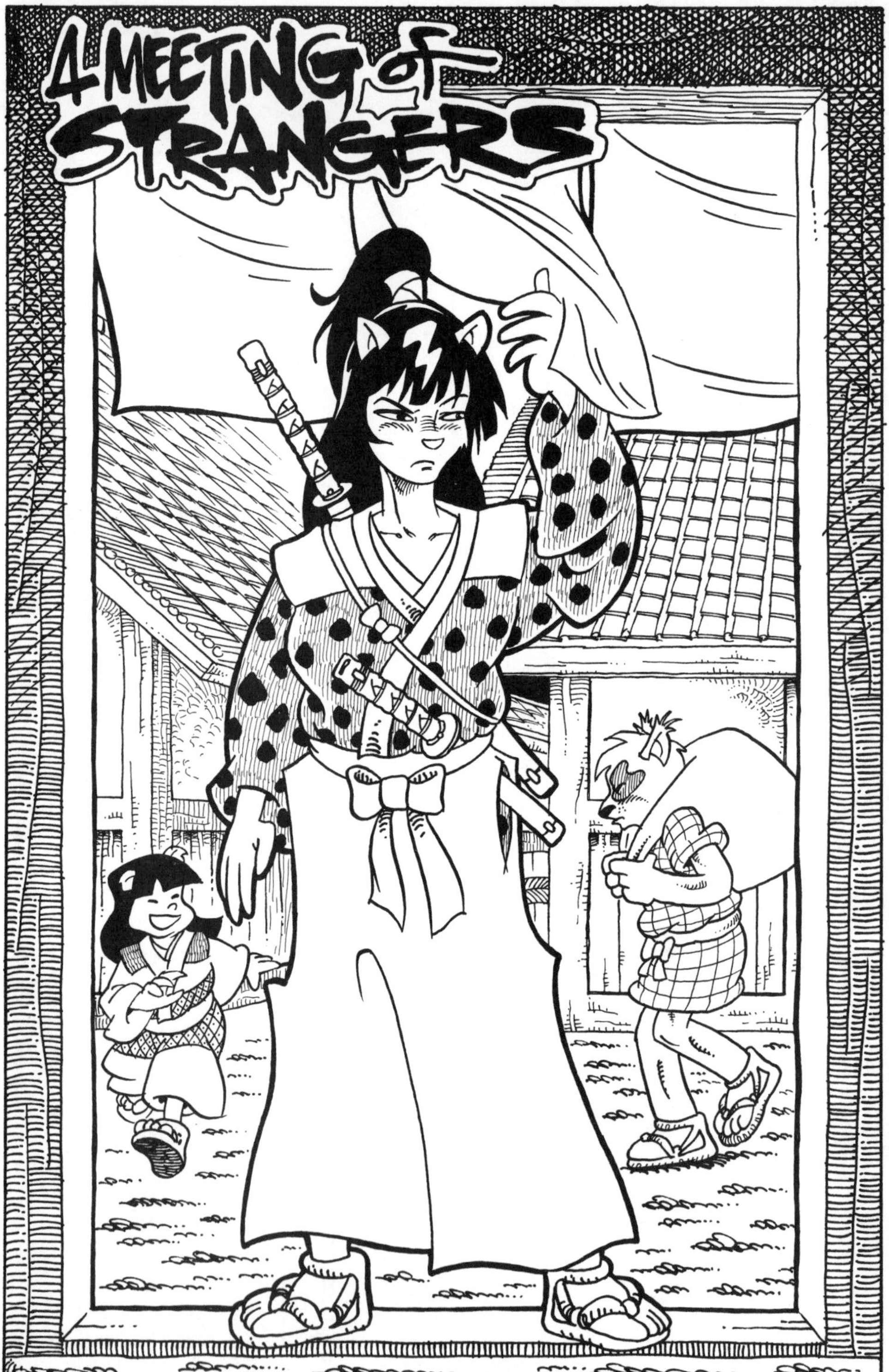

4 MEETING of STRANGERS

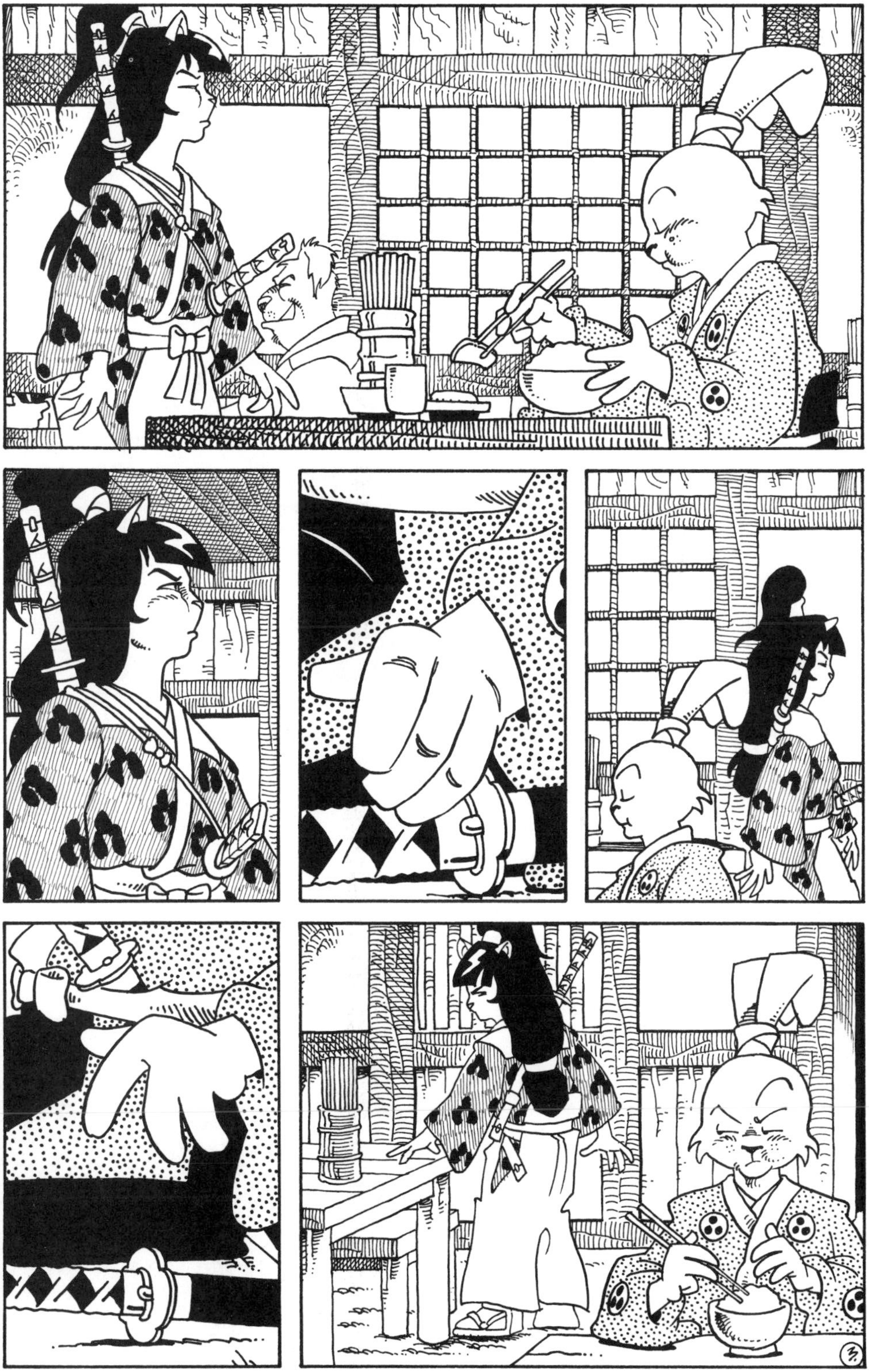

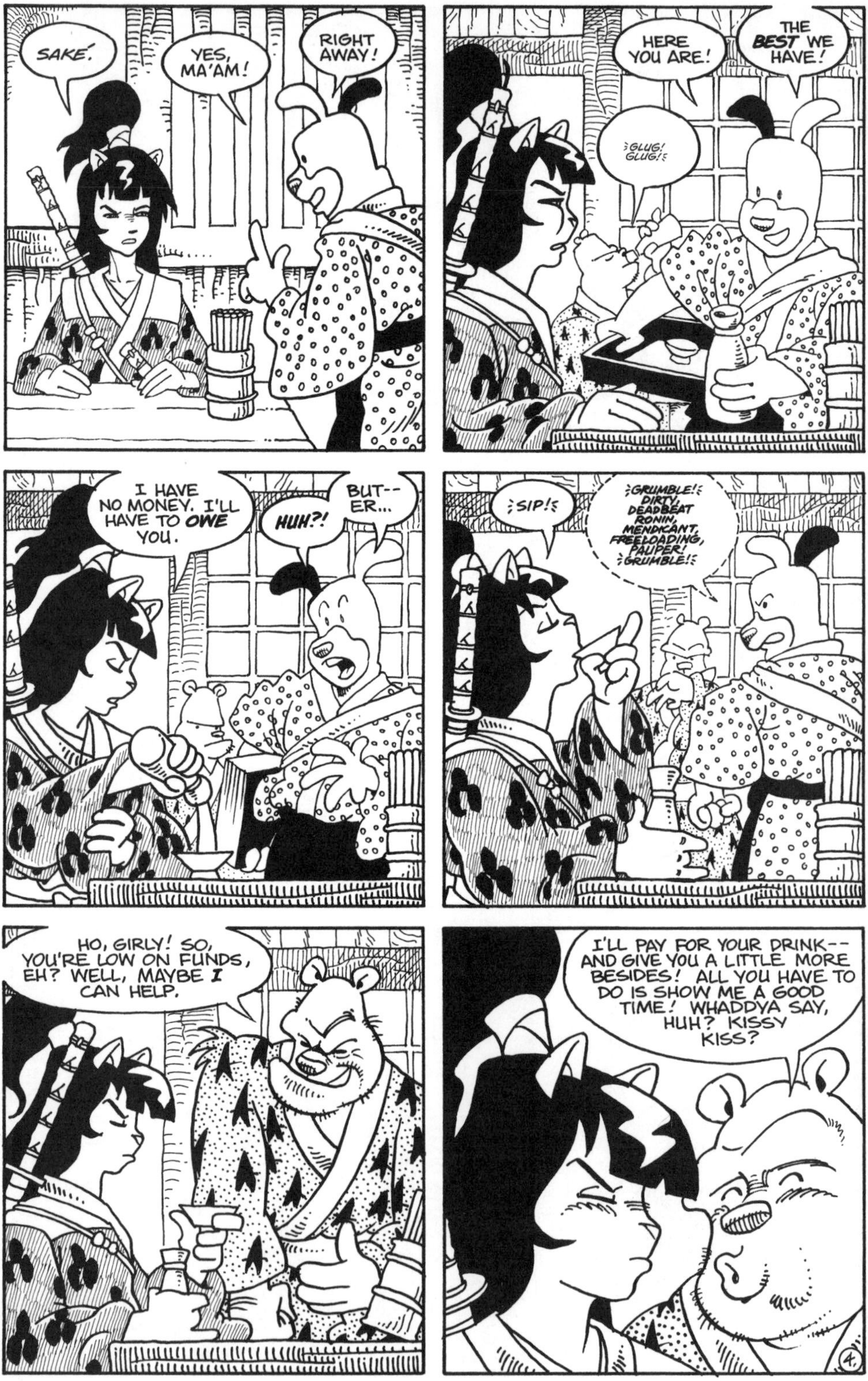
SAKE!
YES, MA'AM!
RIGHT AWAY!
HERE YOU ARE!
THE BEST WE HAVE!
GLUG! GLUG!
I HAVE NO MONEY. I'LL HAVE TO OWE YOU.
HUH?!
BUT-- ER...
SIP!
GRUMBLE! DIRTY, DEADBEAT RONIN, MENDICANT, FREELOADING, PAUPER! GRUMBLE!
HO, GIRLY! SO, YOU'RE LOW ON FUNDS, EH? WELL, MAYBE I CAN HELP.
I'LL PAY FOR YOUR DRINK-- AND GIVE YOU A LITTLE MORE BESIDES! ALL YOU HAVE TO DO IS SHOW ME A GOOD TIME! WHADDYA SAY, HUH? KISSY KISS?
4.

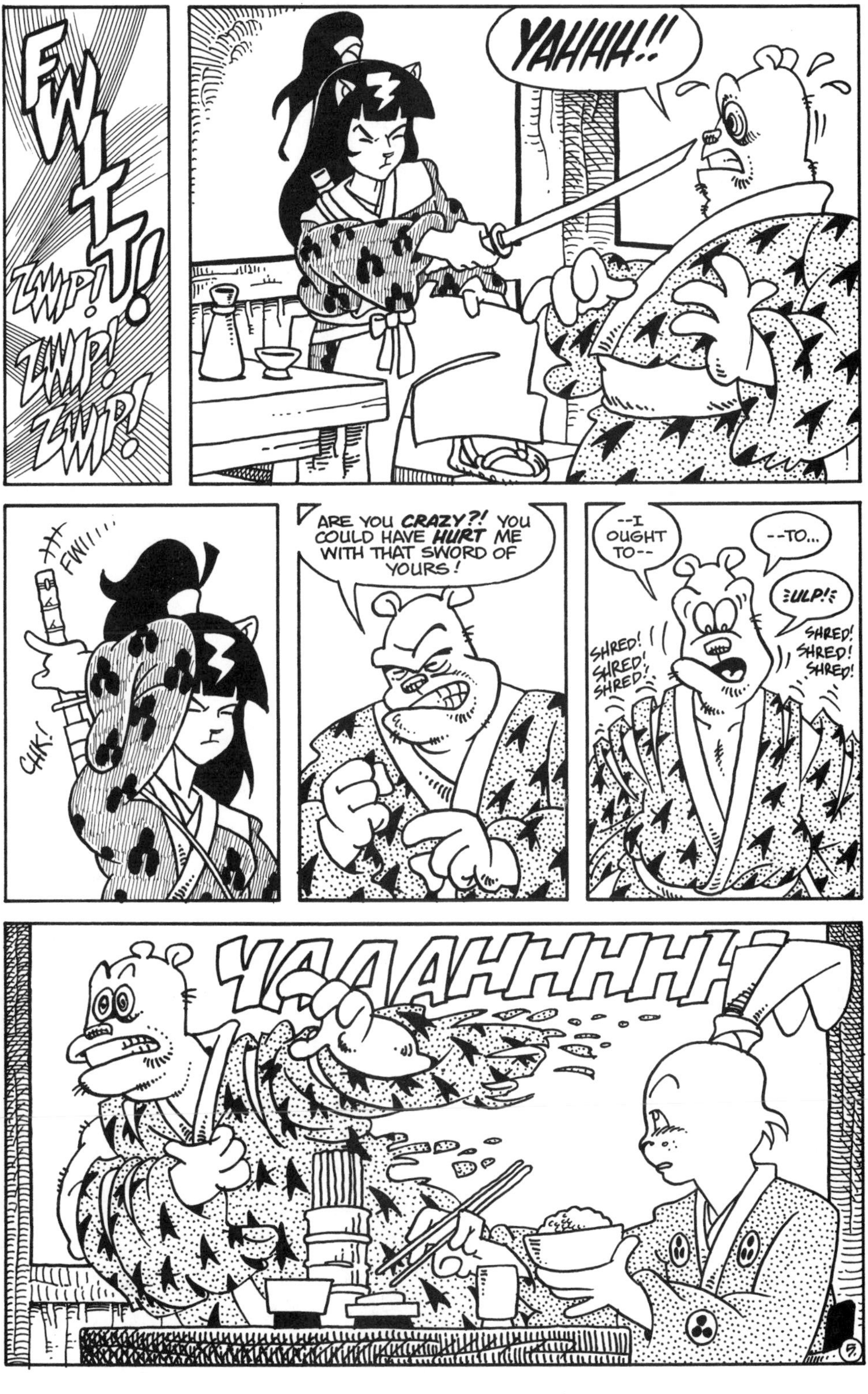
FWITT!
ZWIP!
ZWIP!
ZWIP!
YAHHH!!
FWIII
CHK!
ARE YOU CRAZY?! YOU COULD HAVE HURT ME WITH THAT SWORD OF YOURS!
--I OUGHT TO--
--TO...
ULP!
SHRED! SHRED! SHRED!
SHRED! SHRED! SHRED!
YAAAHHHHH!

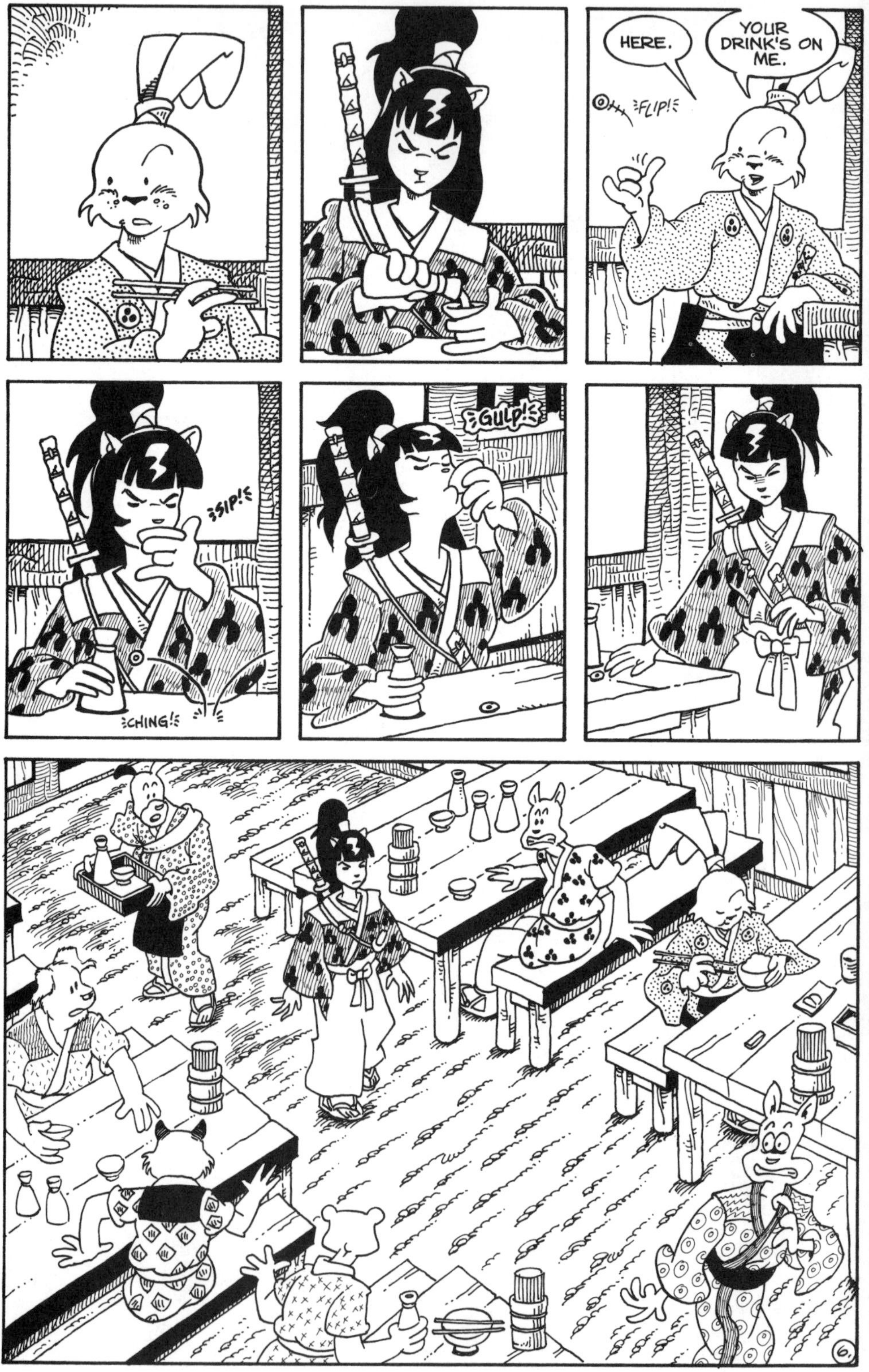
HERE.
YOUR DRINK'S ON ME.
FLIP!
SIP!
CHING!
GULP!
6.

RONIN.

EH?

THANKS.

I OWE YOU ONE.

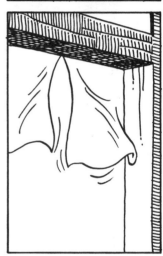

THREE MINUTES EARLIER...

HURRY! HURRY!

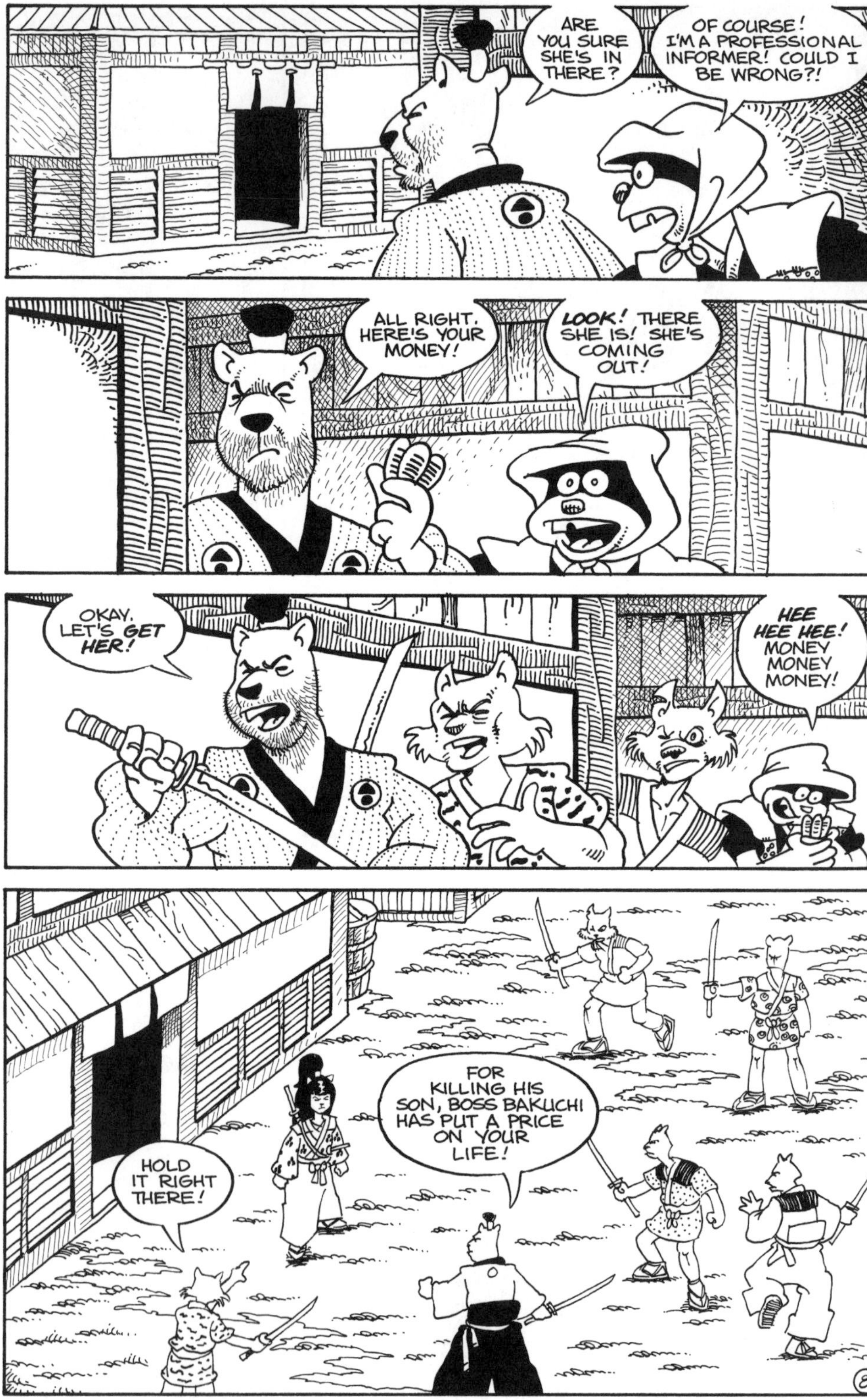
ARE YOU SURE SHE'S IN THERE?
OF COURSE! I'M A PROFESSIONAL INFORMER! COULD I BE WRONG?!
ALL RIGHT. HERE'S YOUR MONEY!
LOOK! THERE SHE IS! SHE'S COMING OUT!
OKAY. LET'S GET HER!
HEE HEE HEE! MONEY MONEY MONEY!
HOLD IT RIGHT THERE!
FOR KILLING HIS SON, BOSS BAKUCHI HAS PUT A PRICE ON YOUR LIFE!
8

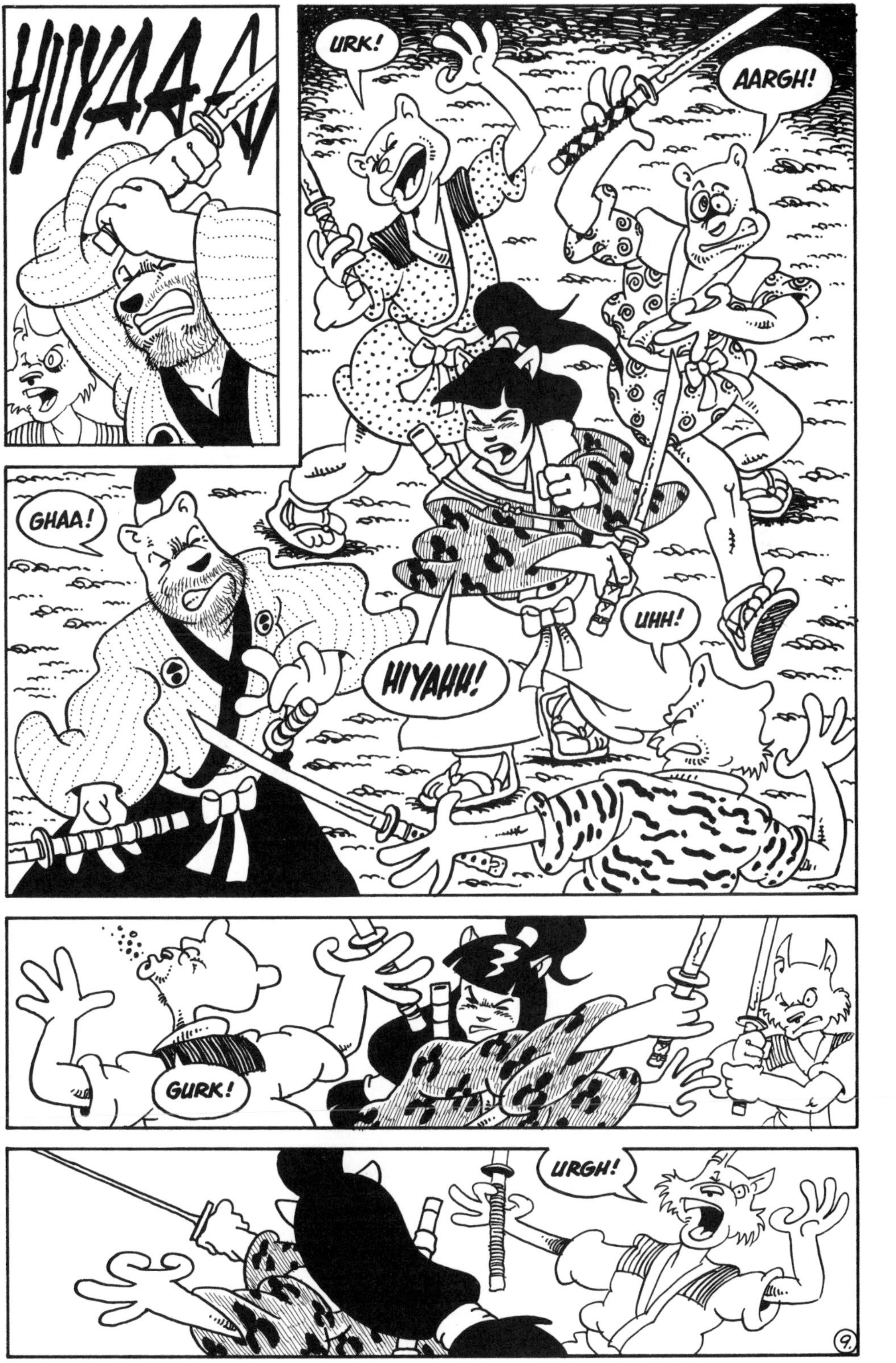
HIIYAA A
URK!
AARGH!
GHAA!
HIYAHH!
UHH!
GURK!
URGH!
9.

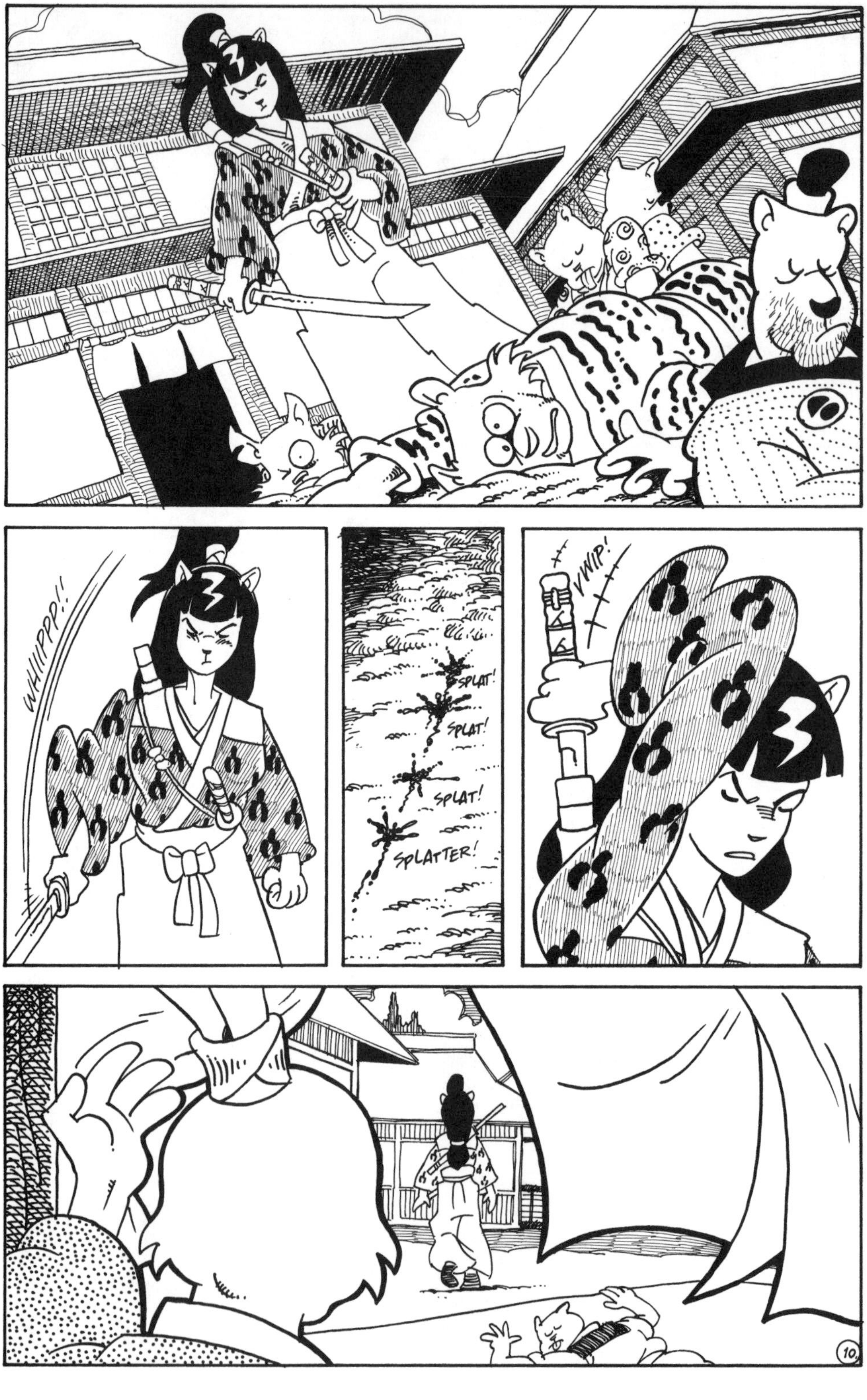
WHIIPPP!!
SPLAT!
SPLAT!
SPLAT!
SPLATTER!
VWIP!
10

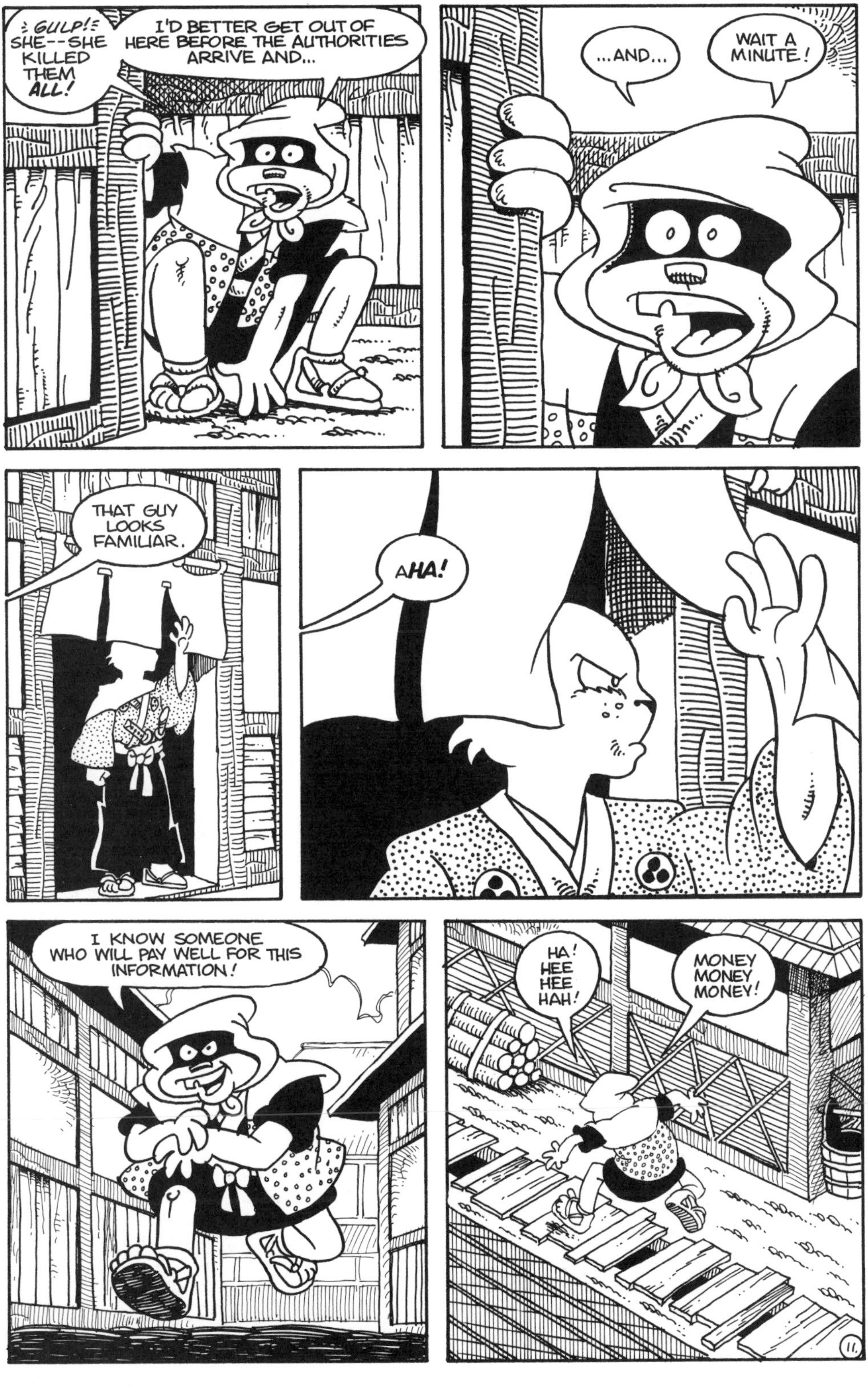
GULP! SHE--SHE KILLED THEM ALL!
I'D BETTER GET OUT OF HERE BEFORE THE AUTHORITIES ARRIVE AND...
...AND...
WAIT A MINUTE!
THAT GUY LOOKS FAMILIAR.
AHA!
I KNOW SOMEONE WHO WILL PAY WELL FOR THIS INFORMATION!
HA! HEE HEE HAH!
MONEY MONEY MONEY!
11.

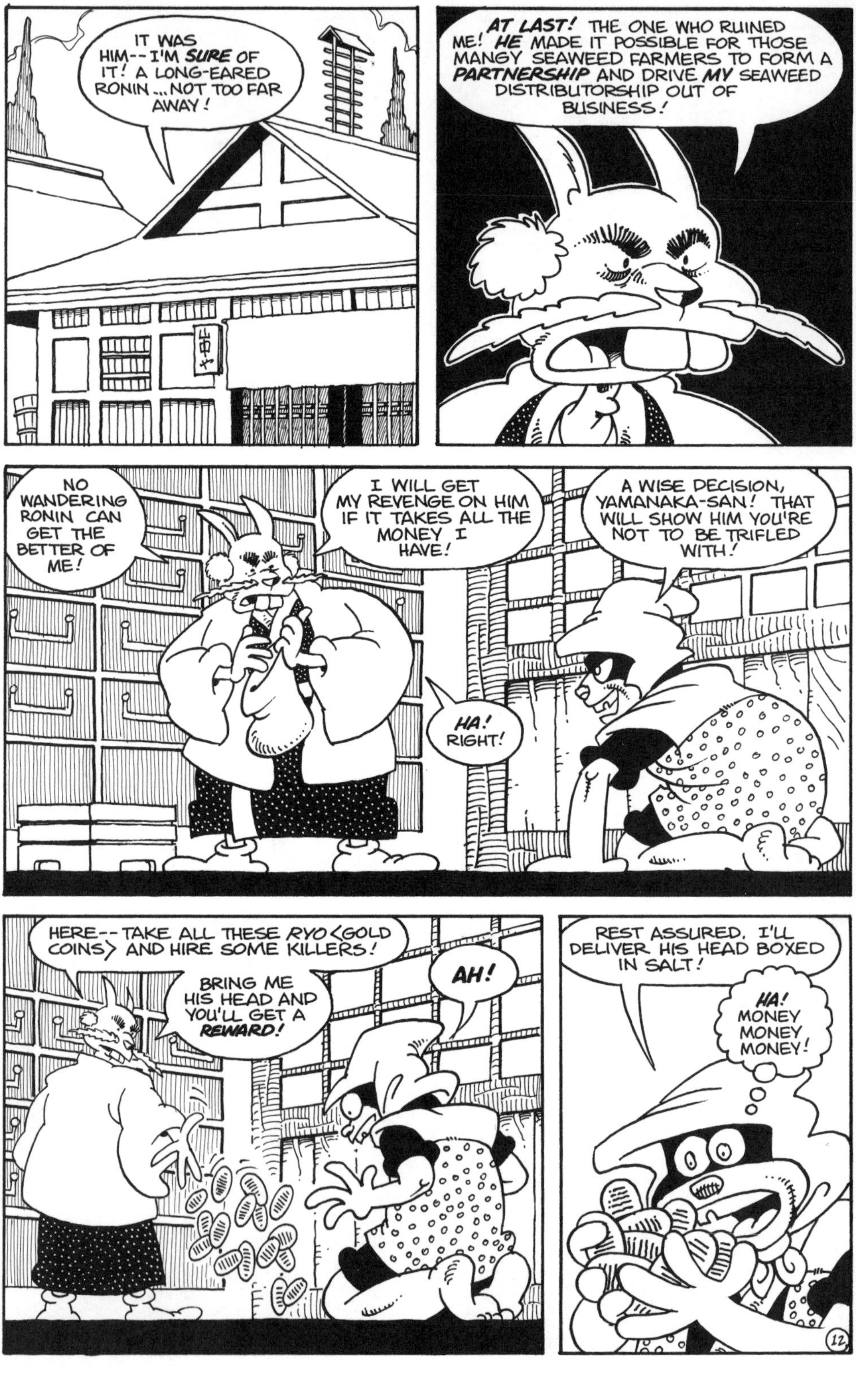
IT WAS HIM-- I'M SURE OF IT! A LONG-EARED RONIN ... NOT TOO FAR AWAY!
AT LAST! THE ONE WHO RUINED ME! HE MADE IT POSSIBLE FOR THOSE MANGY SEAWEED FARMERS TO FORM A PARTNERSHIP AND DRIVE MY SEAWEED DISTRIBUTORSHIP OUT OF BUSINESS!
NO WANDERING RONIN CAN GET THE BETTER OF ME!
I WILL GET MY REVENGE ON HIM IF IT TAKES ALL THE MONEY I HAVE!
A WISE DECISION, YAMANAKA-SAN! THAT WILL SHOW HIM YOU'RE NOT TO BE TRIFLED WITH!
HA! RIGHT!
HERE-- TAKE ALL THESE RYO <GOLD COINS> AND HIRE SOME KILLERS!
BRING ME HIS HEAD AND YOU'LL GET A REWARD!
AH!
REST ASSURED. I'LL DELIVER HIS HEAD BOXED IN SALT!
HA! MONEY MONEY MONEY!
12

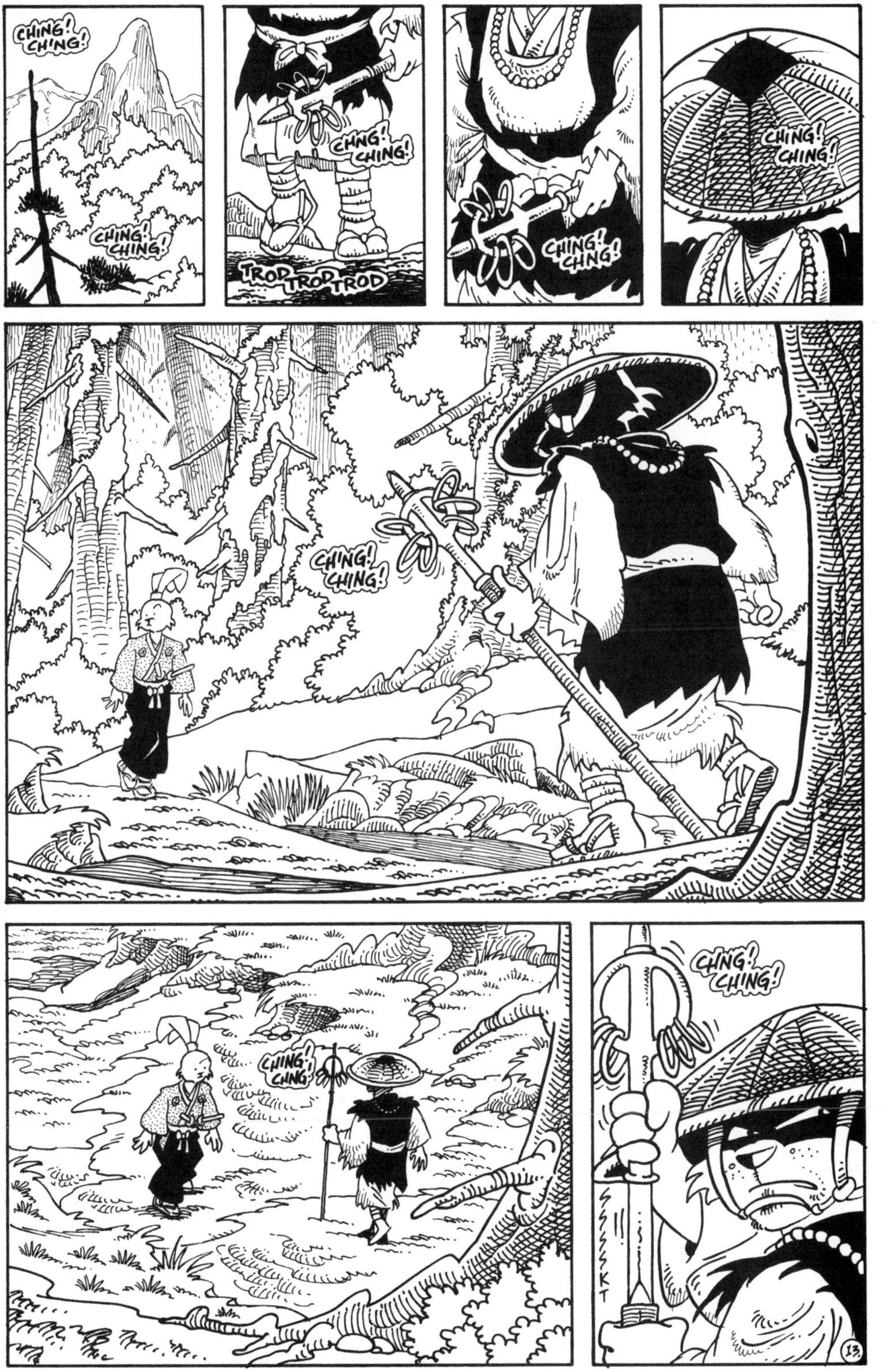
CHING! CHING!
CHING! CHING!
CHNG! CHING!
TROD TROD TROD
CHING! CHNG!
CHING! CHING!
CHING! CHING!
CHING! CHNG!
CHNG! CHING!
SSSSKT
13

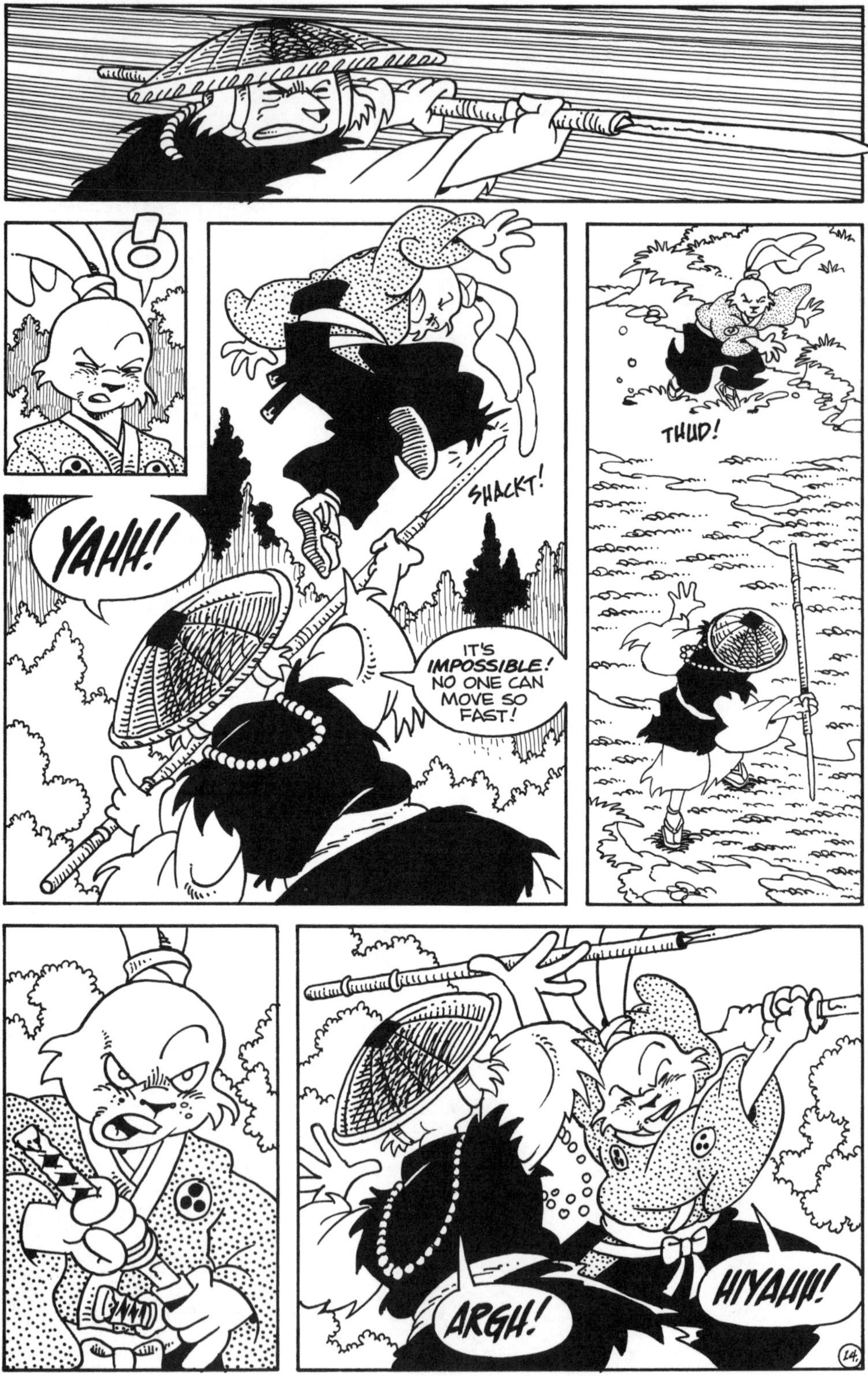
!
YAHH!
SHACKT!
IT'S IMPOSSIBLE! NO ONE CAN MOVE SO FAST!
THUD!
ARGH!
HIYAHH!
14.

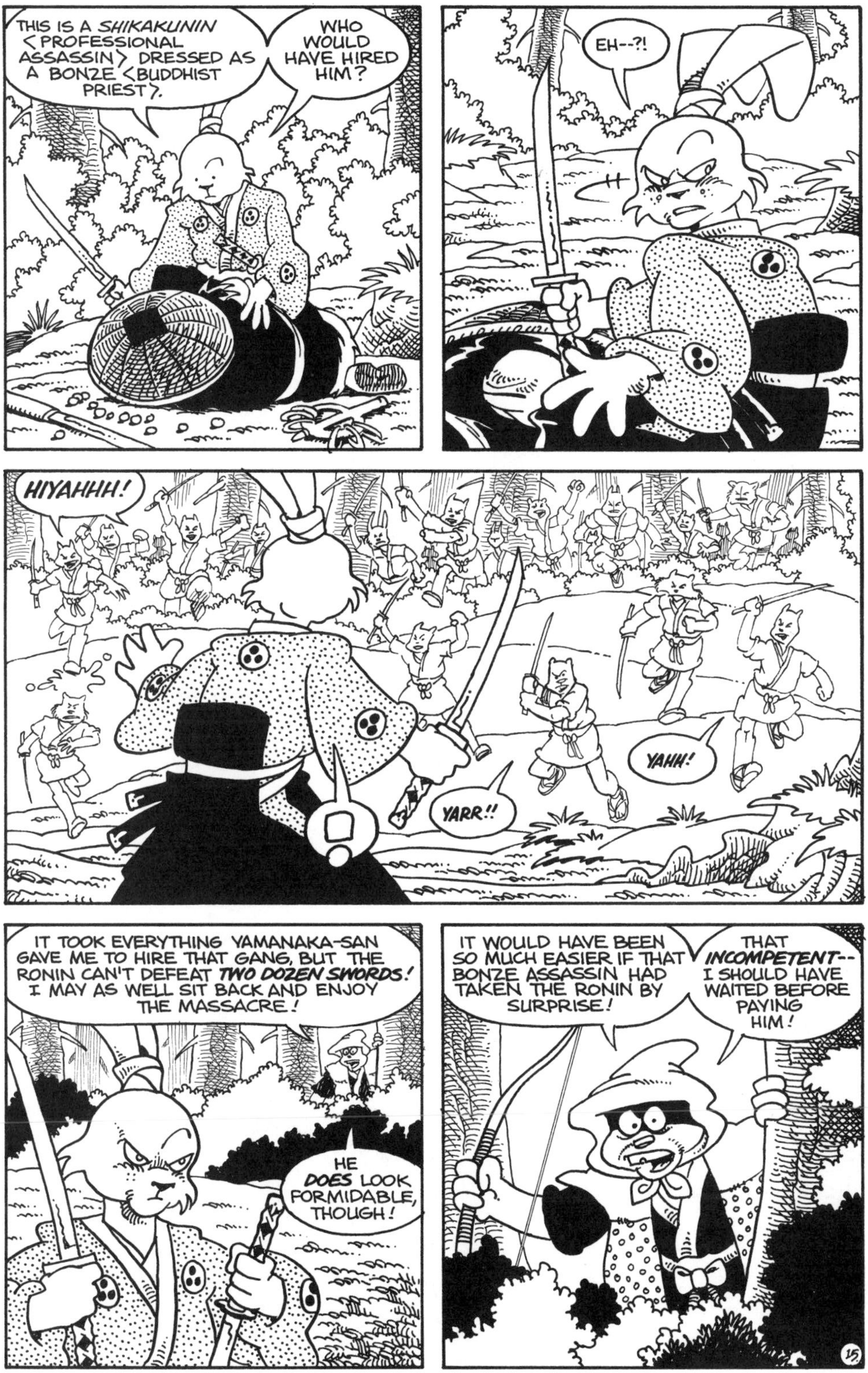

THIS IS A SHIKAKUNIN <PROFESSIONAL ASSASSIN> DRESSED AS A BONZE <BUDDHIST PRIEST>.
WHO WOULD HAVE HIRED HIM?
EH--?!
HIYAHHH!
YAHH!
YARR!!
IT TOOK EVERYTHING YAMANAKA-SAN GAVE ME TO HIRE THAT GANG, BUT THE RONIN CAN'T DEFEAT TWO DOZEN SWORDS! I MAY AS WELL SIT BACK AND ENJOY THE MASSACRE!
HE DOES LOOK FORMIDABLE, THOUGH!
IT WOULD HAVE BEEN SO MUCH EASIER IF THAT BONZE ASSASSIN HAD TAKEN THE RONIN BY SURPRISE!
THAT INCOMPETENT-- I SHOULD HAVE WAITED BEFORE PAYING HIM!
15

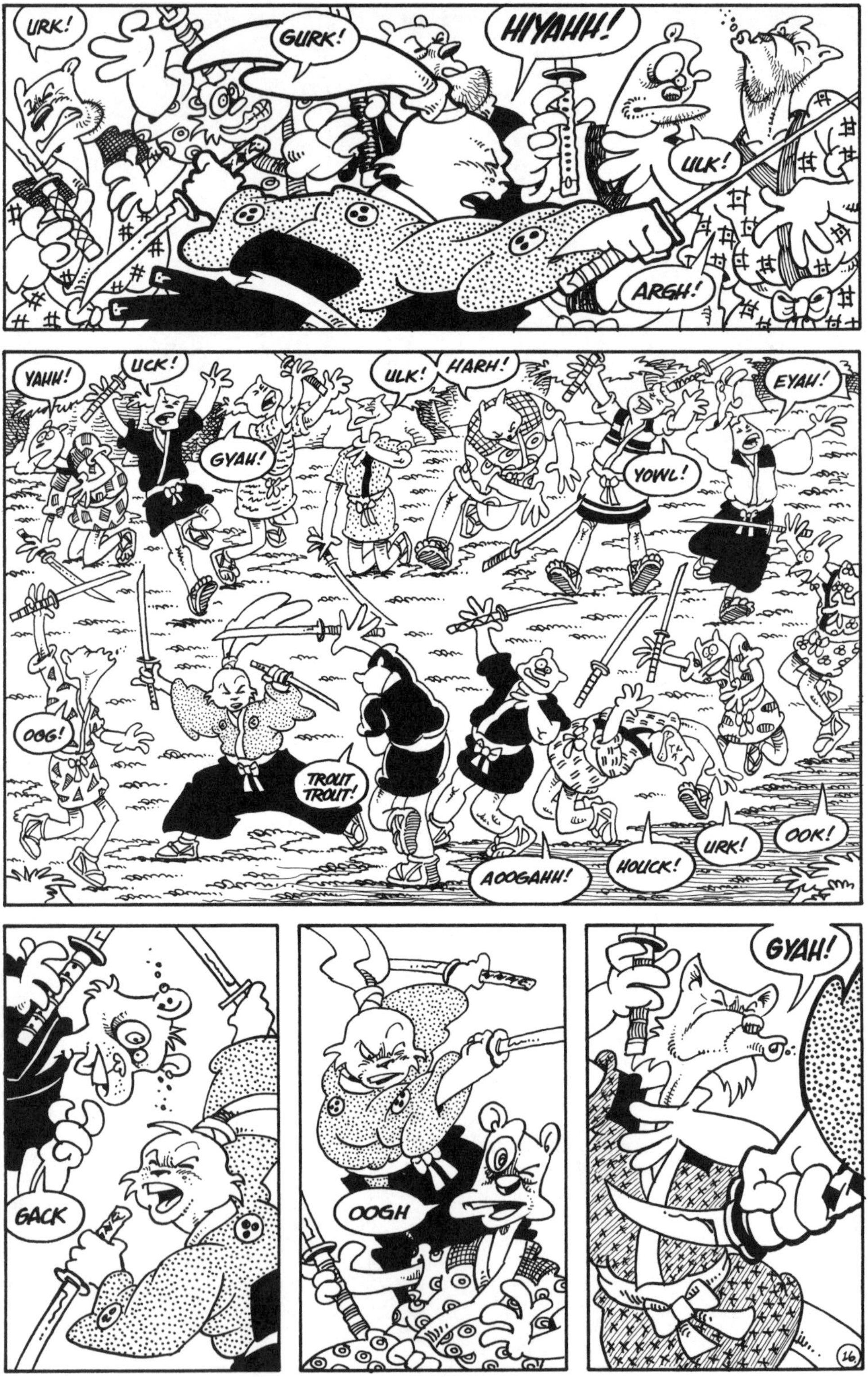
URK!
GURK!
HIYAHH!
ULK!
ARGH!
YAHH!
UCK!
GYAH!
ULK!
HARH!
YOWL!
EYAH!
OOG!
TROUT TROUT!
AOOGAHH!
HOUCK!
URK!
OOK!
GACK
OOGH
GYAH!
16

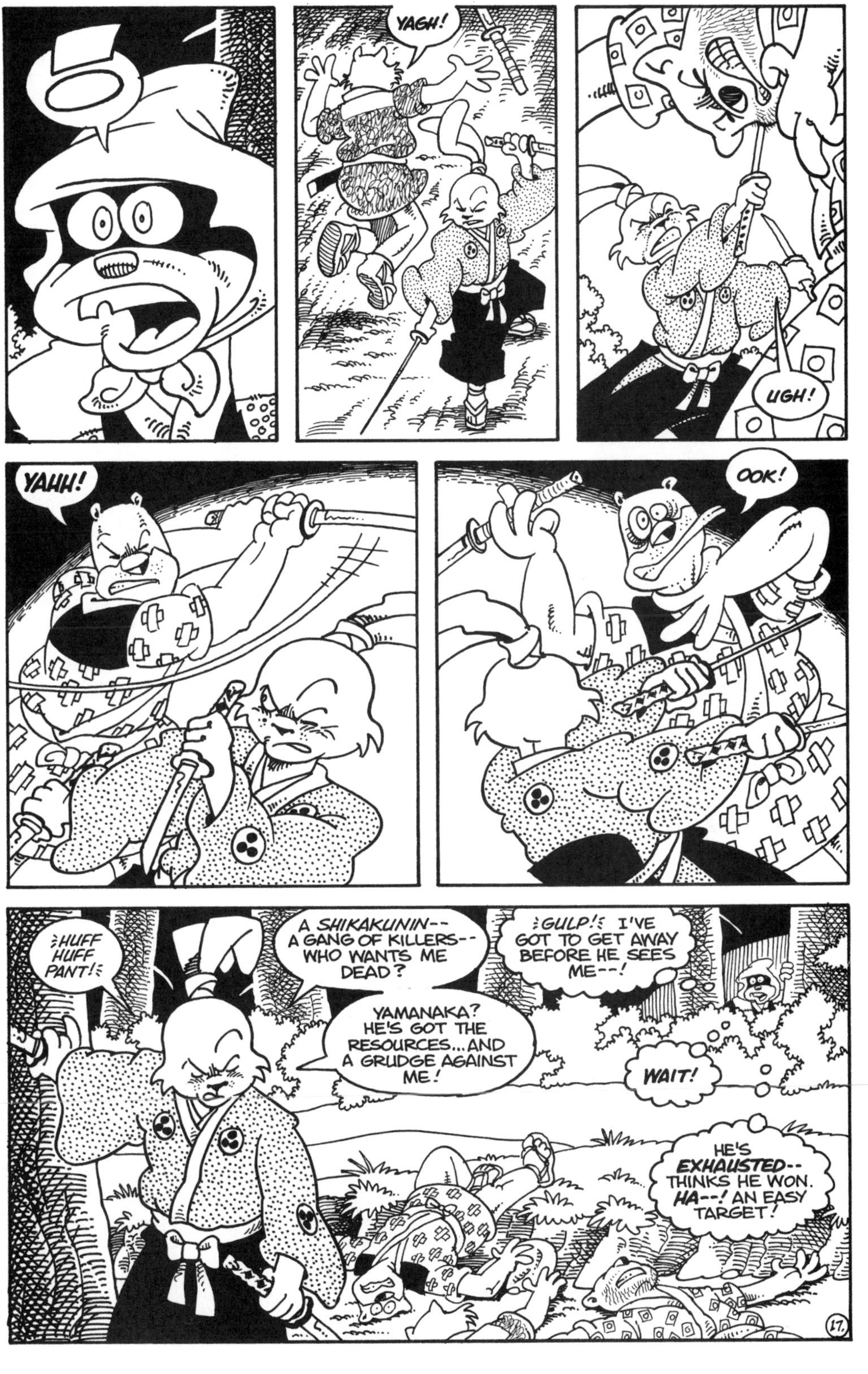
YAGH!
UGH!
YAHH!
OOK!
HUFF HUFF PANT!
A *SHIKAKUNIN*-- A GANG OF KILLERS-- WHO WANTS ME DEAD?
YAMANAKA? HE'S GOT THE RESOURCES...AND A GRUDGE AGAINST ME!
GULP! I'VE GOT TO GET AWAY BEFORE HE SEES ME--!
WAIT!
HE'S ***EXHAUSTED***-- THINKS HE WON. ***HA***--! AN EASY TARGET!
17.

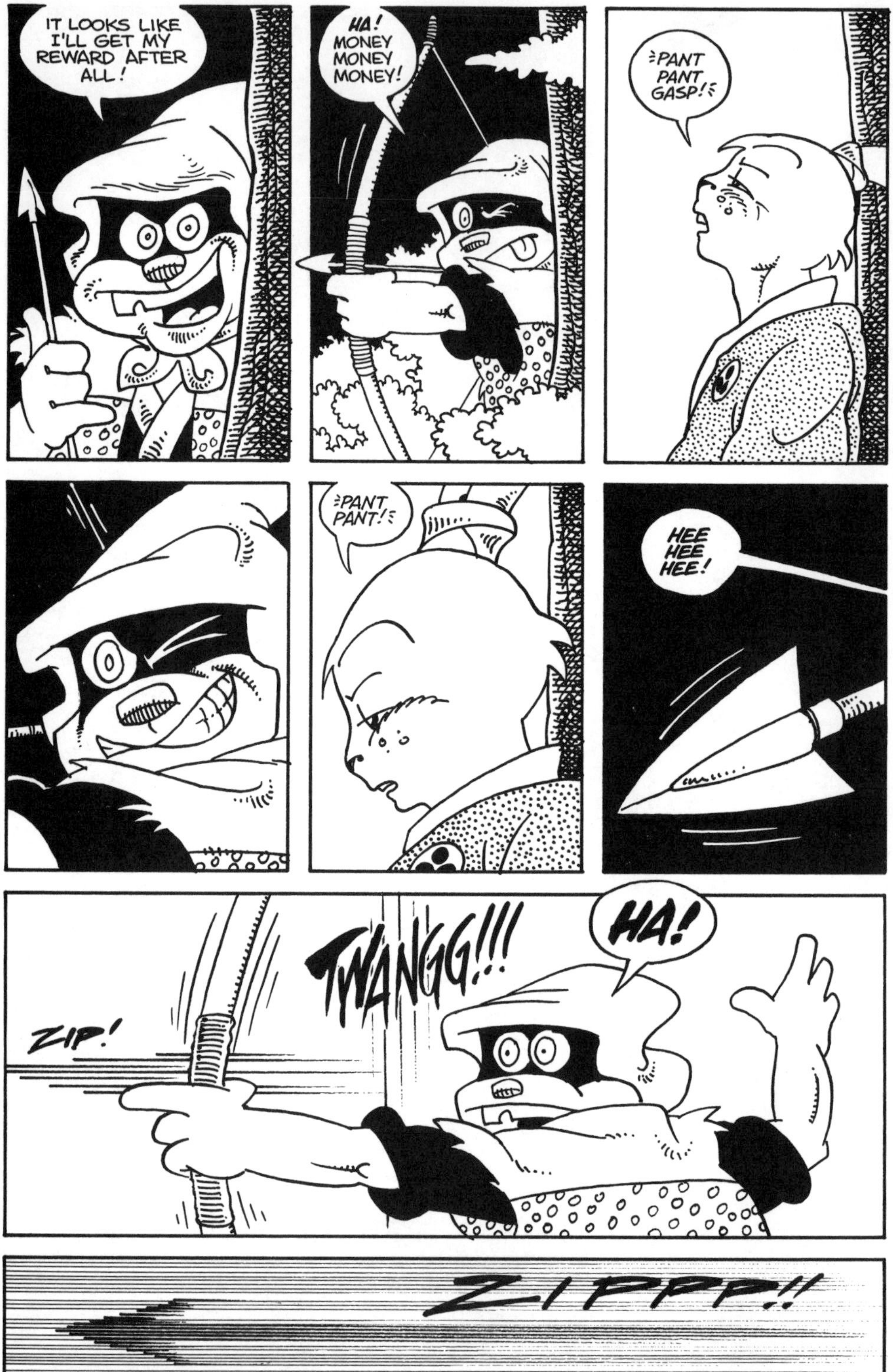
IT LOOKS LIKE I'LL GET MY REWARD AFTER ALL!
HA! MONEY MONEY MONEY!
PANT PANT GASP!
PANT PANT!
HEE HEE HEE!
TWANGG!!!
HA!
ZIP!
ZIPPP!!
18

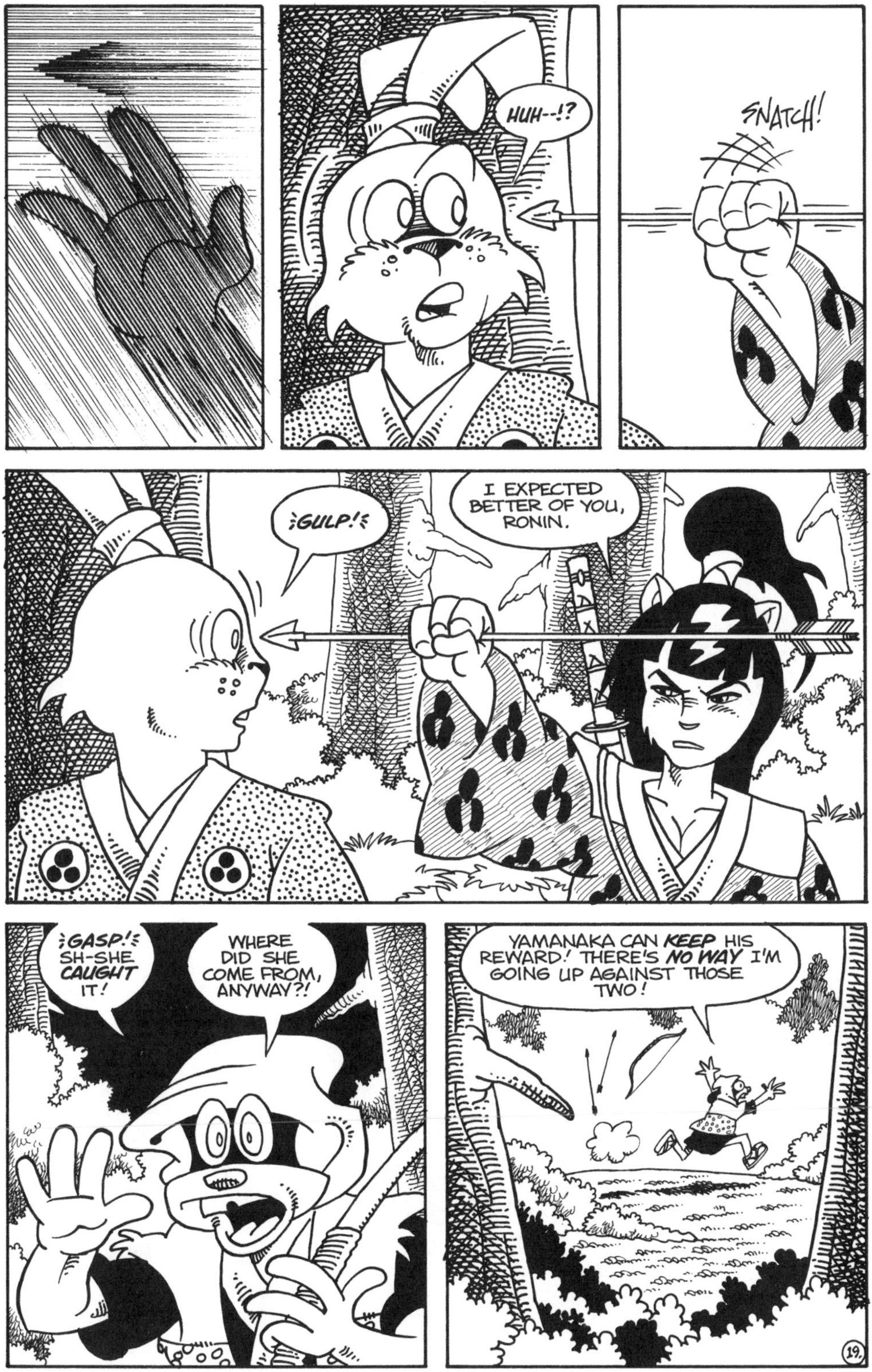
HUH--!?
SNATCH!
GULP!
I EXPECTED BETTER OF YOU, RONIN.
GASP! SH-SHE CAUGHT IT!
WHERE DID SHE COME FROM, ANYWAY?!
YAMANAKA CAN KEEP HIS REWARD! THERE'S NO WAY I'M GOING UP AGAINST THOSE TWO!
19.

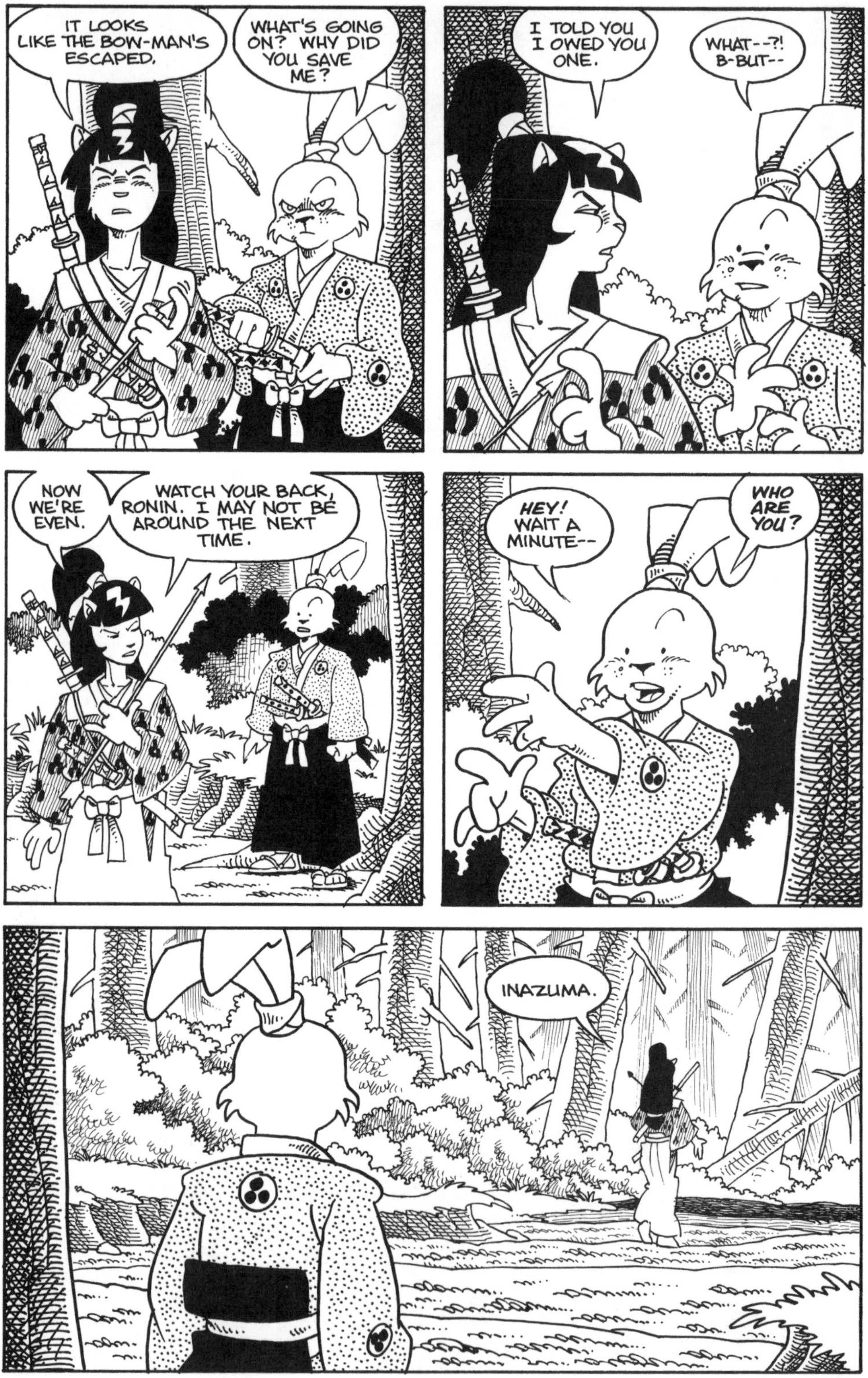
IT LOOKS LIKE THE BOW-MAN'S ESCAPED.
WHAT'S GOING ON? WHY DID YOU SAVE ME?
I TOLD YOU I OWED YOU ONE.
WHAT--?! B-BUT--
NOW WE'RE EVEN.
WATCH YOUR BACK, RONIN. I MAY NOT BE AROUND THE NEXT TIME.
HEY! WAIT A MINUTE--
WHO ARE YOU?
INAZUMA.

END.

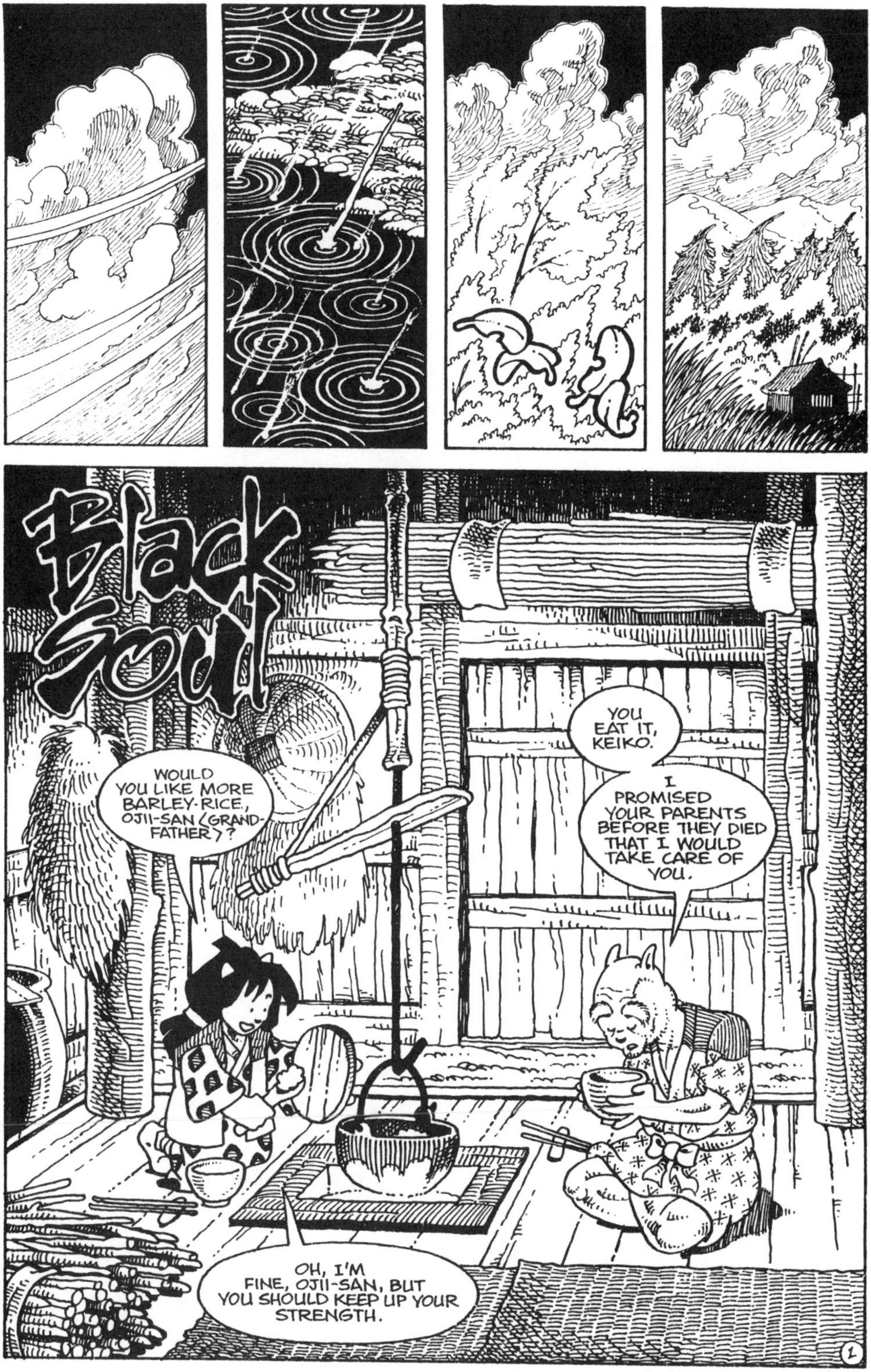
Black Soul
WOULD YOU LIKE MORE BARLEY-RICE, OJII-SAN <GRAND-FATHER>?
OH, I'M FINE, OJII-SAN, BUT YOU SHOULD KEEP UP YOUR STRENGTH.
YOU EAT IT, KEIKO.
I PROMISED YOUR PARENTS BEFORE THEY DIED THAT I WOULD TAKE CARE OF YOU.

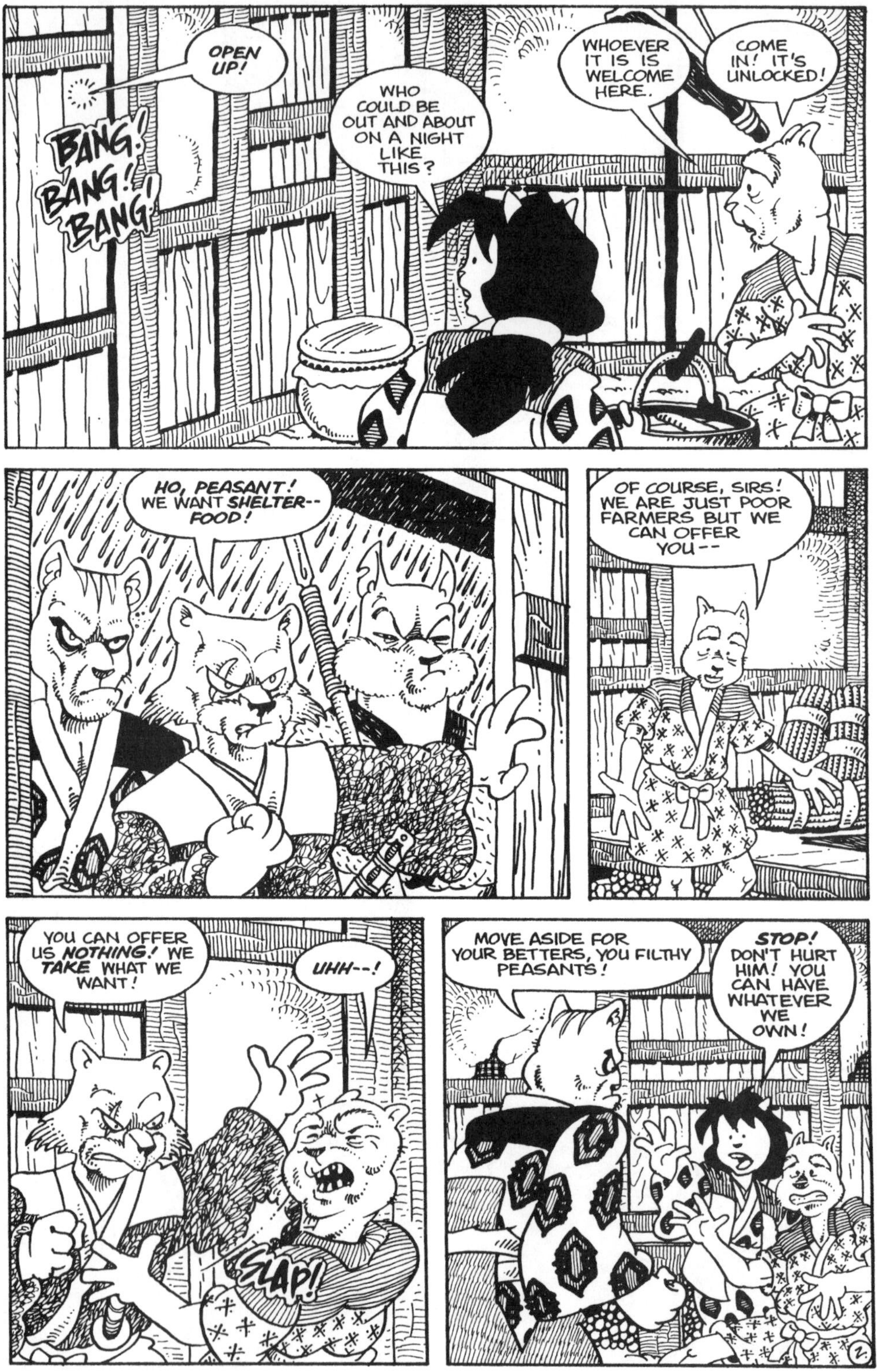

OPEN UP!
BANG! BANG! BANG!
WHO COULD BE OUT AND ABOUT ON A NIGHT LIKE THIS?
WHOEVER IT IS IS WELCOME HERE.
COME IN! IT'S UNLOCKED!
HO, PEASANT! WE WANT SHELTER-- FOOD!
OF COURSE, SIRS! WE ARE JUST POOR FARMERS BUT WE CAN OFFER YOU--
YOU CAN OFFER US NOTHING! WE TAKE WHAT WE WANT!
UHH--!
SLAP!
MOVE ASIDE FOR YOUR BETTERS, YOU FILTHY PEASANTS!
STOP! DON'T HURT HIM! YOU CAN HAVE WHATEVER WE OWN!
2.

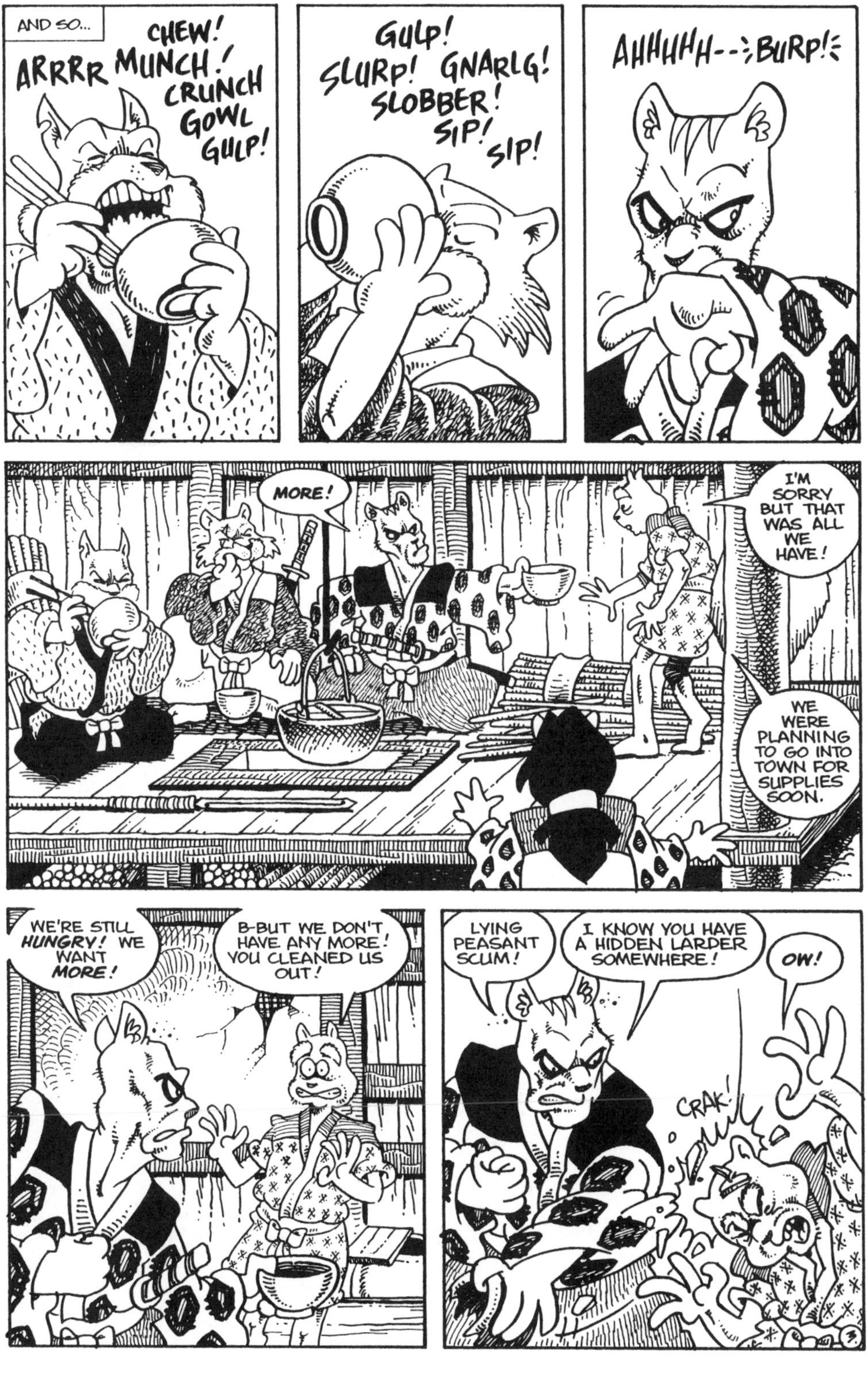
AND SO...
ARRRR MUNCH! CHEW! CRUNCH GOWL GULP!
GULP! SLURP! GNARLG! SLOBBER! SIP! SIP!
AHHHHH--BURP!
MORE!
I'M SORRY BUT THAT WAS ALL WE HAVE!
WE WERE PLANNING TO GO INTO TOWN FOR SUPPLIES SOON.
WE'RE STILL HUNGRY! WE WANT MORE!
B-BUT WE DON'T HAVE ANY MORE! YOU CLEANED US OUT!
LYING PEASANT SCUM!
I KNOW YOU HAVE A HIDDEN LARDER SOMEWHERE!
OW!
CRAK!

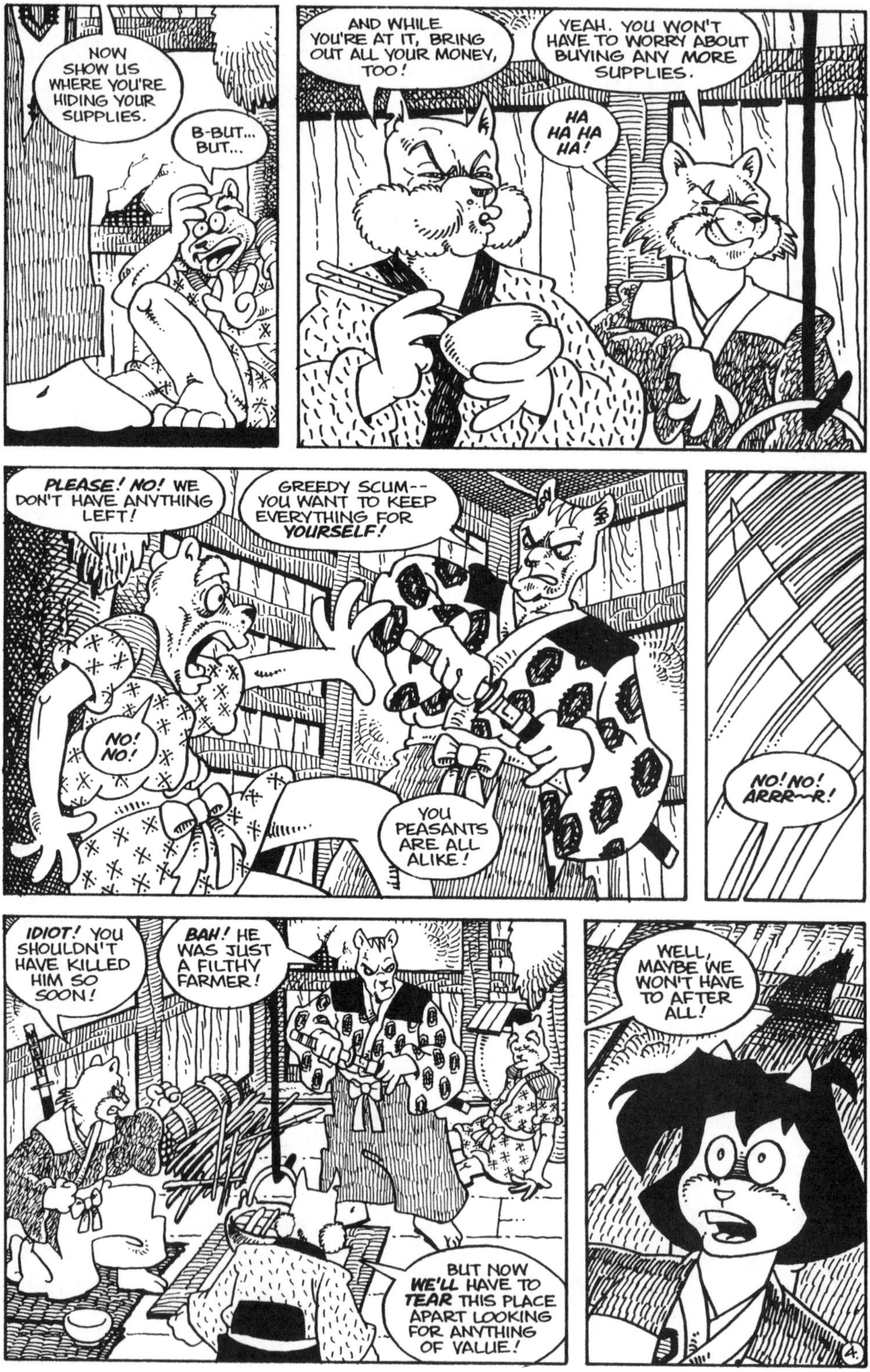
NOW SHOW US WHERE YOU'RE HIDING YOUR SUPPLIES.
B-BUT... BUT...
AND WHILE YOU'RE AT IT, BRING OUT ALL YOUR MONEY, TOO!
YEAH. YOU WON'T HAVE TO WORRY ABOUT BUYING ANY MORE SUPPLIES.
HA HA HA HA!
PLEASE! NO! WE DON'T HAVE ANYTHING LEFT!
GREEDY SCUM-- YOU WANT TO KEEP EVERYTHING FOR YOURSELF!
NO! NO!
YOU PEASANTS ARE ALL ALIKE!
NO! NO! ARRR~R!
IDIOT! YOU SHOULDN'T HAVE KILLED HIM SO SOON!
BAH! HE WAS JUST A FILTHY FARMER!
BUT NOW WE'LL HAVE TO TEAR THIS PLACE APART LOOKING FOR ANYTHING OF VALUE!
WELL, MAYBE WE WON'T HAVE TO AFTER ALL!
4.

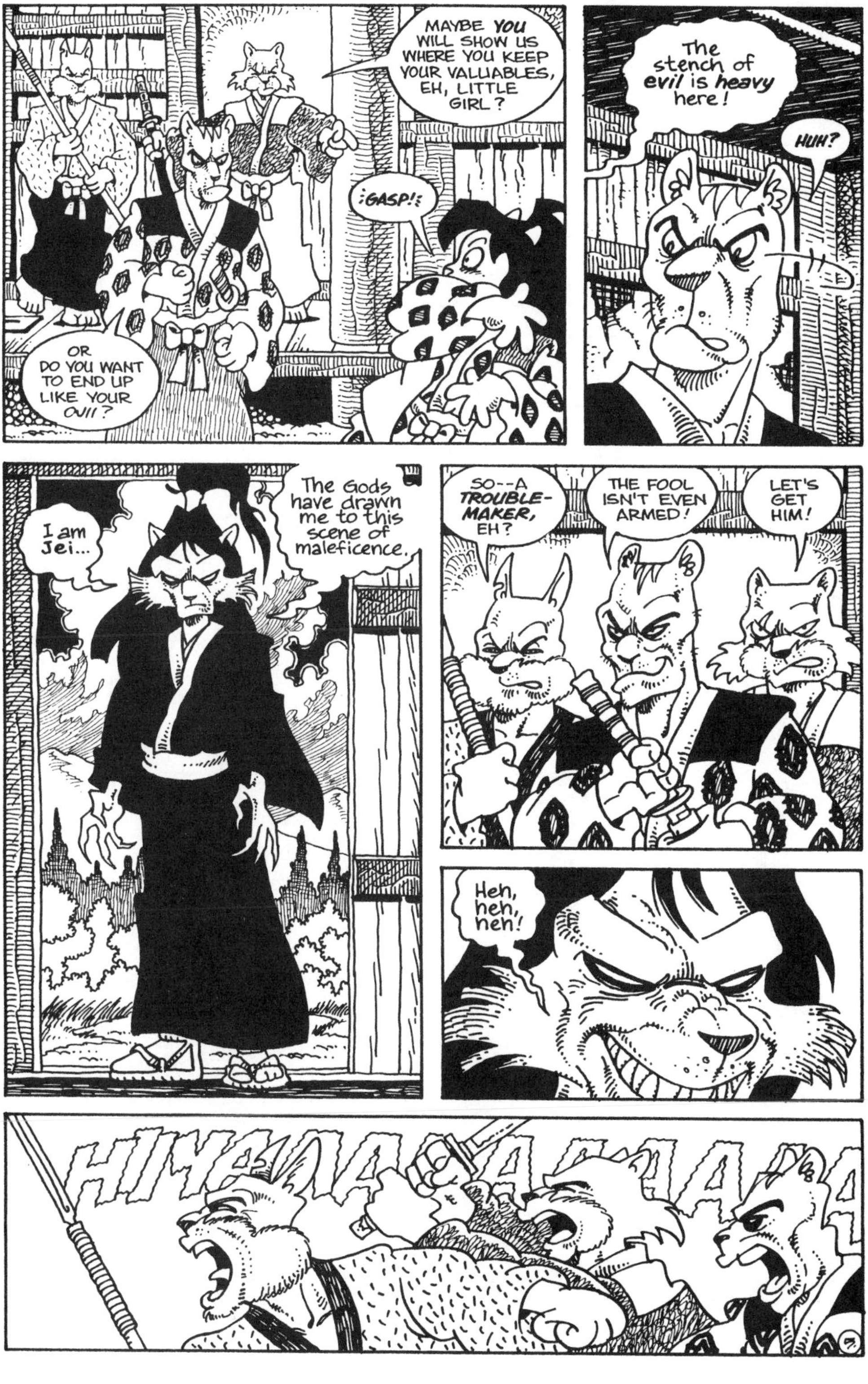
MAYBE YOU WILL SHOW US WHERE YOU KEEP YOUR VALUABLES, EH, LITTLE GIRL?
OR DO YOU WANT TO END UP LIKE YOUR OJII?
GASP!
The stench of evil is heavy here!
HUH?
I am Jei...
The Gods have drawn me to this scene of maleficence.
SO--A TROUBLE-MAKER, EH?
THE FOOL ISN'T EVEN ARMED!
LET'S GET HIM!
Heh, heh, heh!
HIYAAAAAAAA

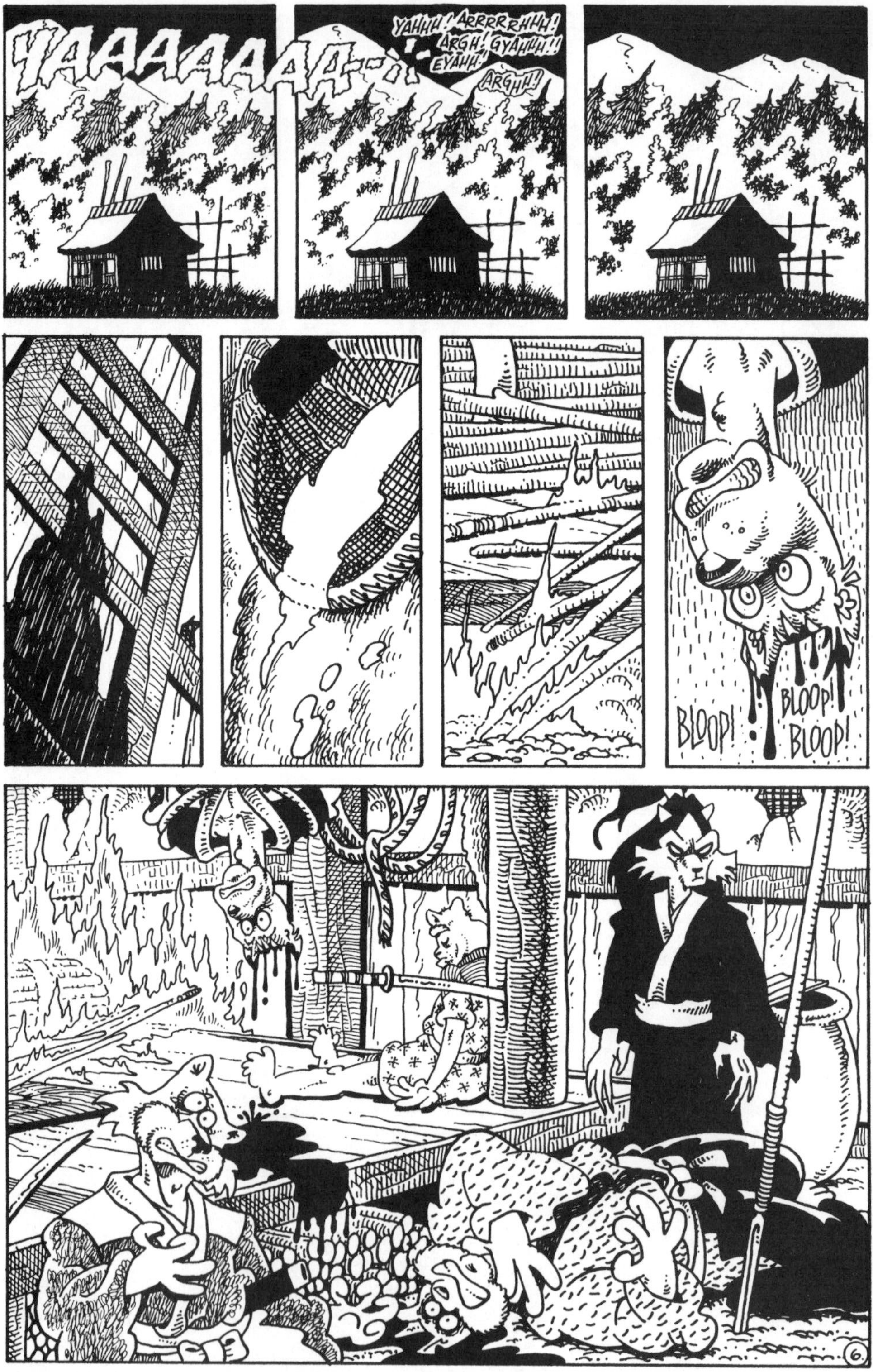

YAAAAAAA-!!
YAHHH! ARRRRRHHH!
ARGH! GYAHHH!!
EYAHH!
ARGHH!
BLOOP!
BLOOP!
BLOOP!
6.

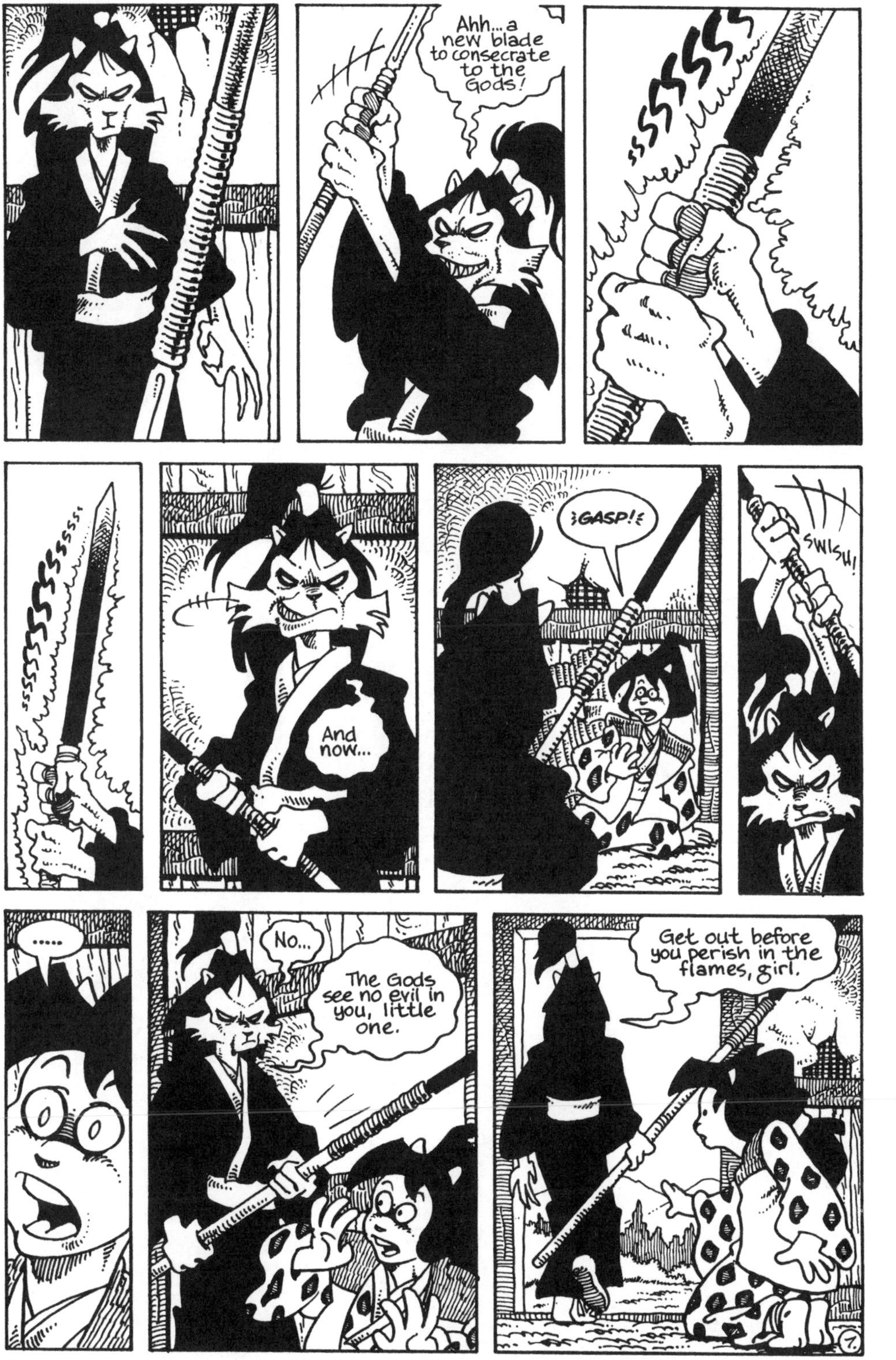
Ahh... a new blade to consecrate to the Gods!
sssSSSSSS
sssSSSSSSSssss
And now...
¡GASP!¡
SWISH!
.....
No...
The Gods see no evil in you, little one.
Get out before you perish in the flames, girl.
7.

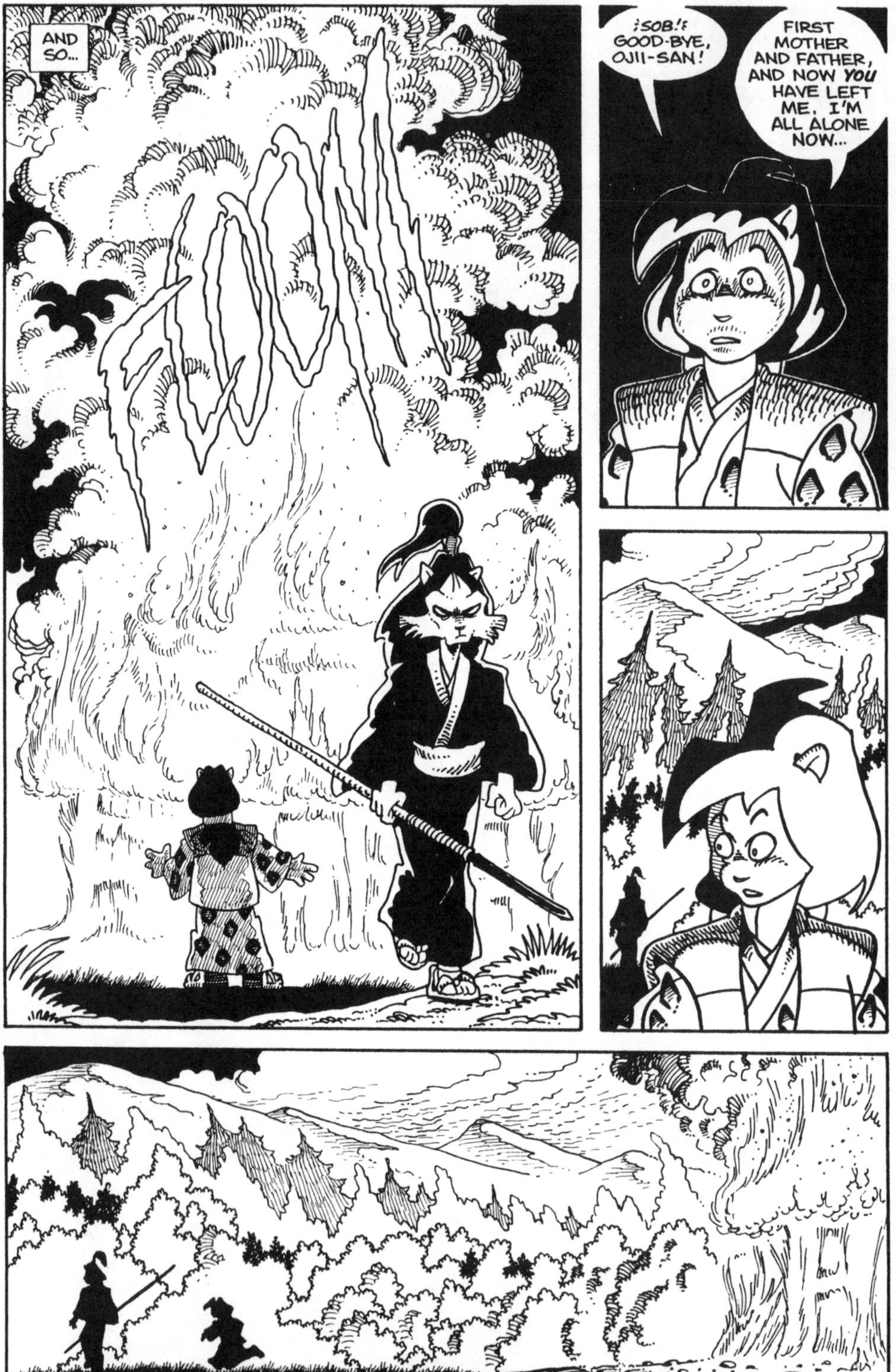
AND SO...
FOOOM
¡SOB!¡ GOOD-BYE, OJII-SAN!
FIRST MOTHER AND FATHER, AND NOW YOU HAVE LEFT ME. I'M ALL ALONE NOW...
END.

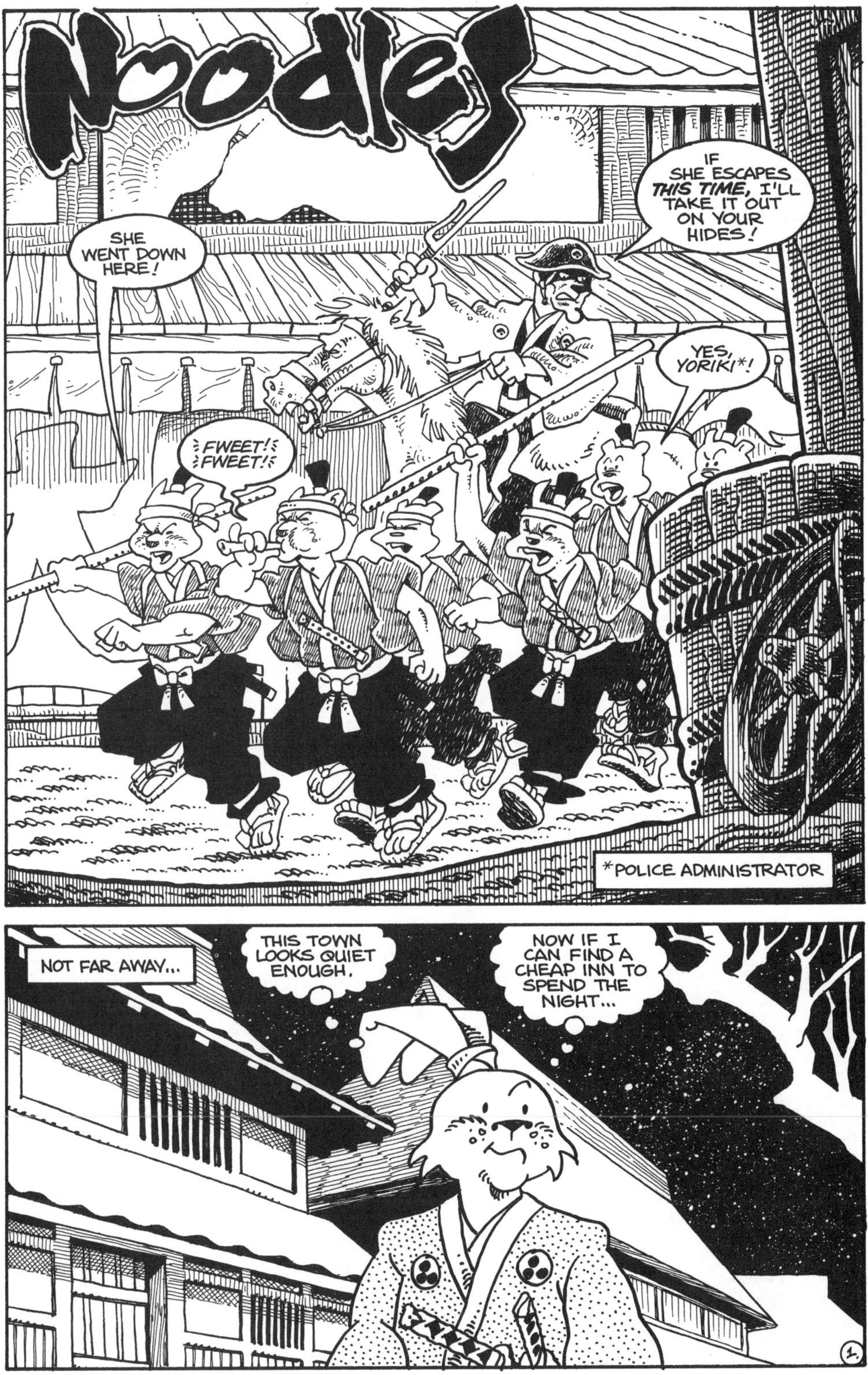
Noodles
SHE WENT DOWN HERE!
IF SHE ESCAPES THIS TIME, I'LL TAKE IT OUT ON YOUR HIDES!
YES, YORIKI*!
FWEET! FWEET!
*POLICE ADMINISTRATOR
NOT FAR AWAY...
THIS TOWN LOOKS QUIET ENOUGH.
NOW IF I CAN FIND A CHEAP INN TO SPEND THE NIGHT...
1.

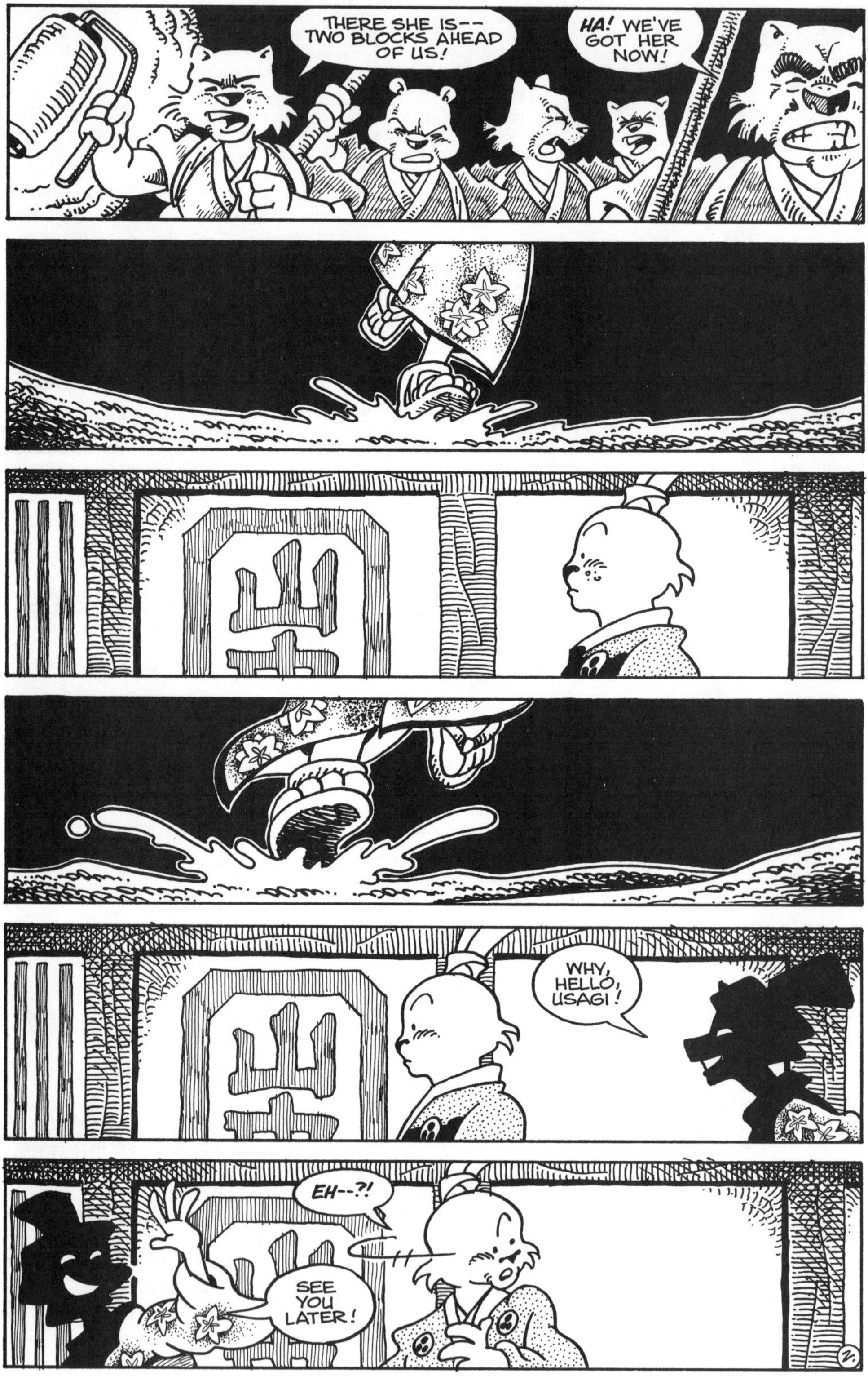
THERE SHE IS-- TWO BLOCKS AHEAD OF US!
HA! WE'VE GOT HER NOW!
WHY, HELLO, USAGI!
EH--?!
SEE YOU LATER!

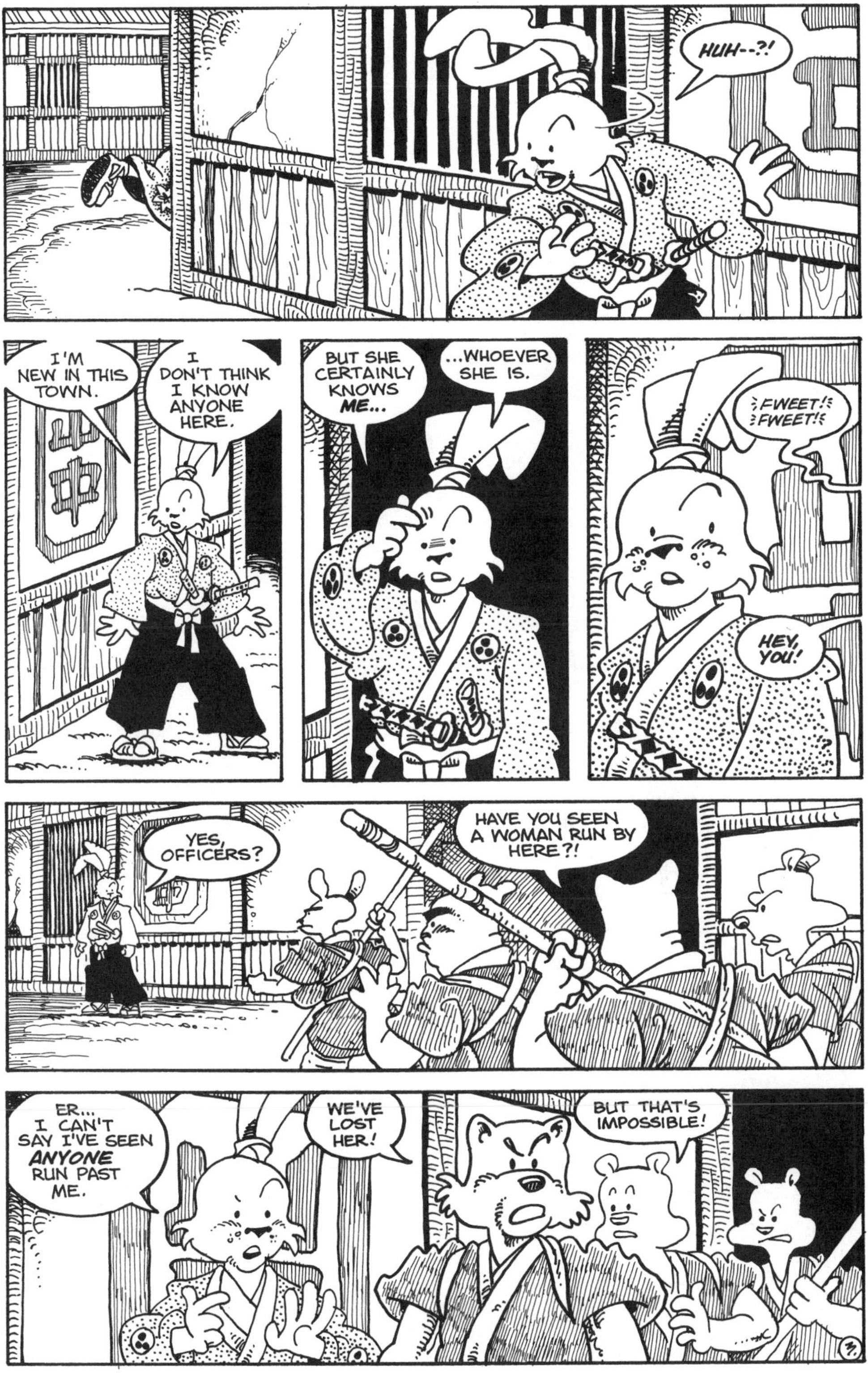
HUH--?!
I'M NEW IN THIS TOWN.
I DON'T THINK I KNOW ANYONE HERE.
BUT SHE CERTAINLY KNOWS *ME*...
...WHOEVER SHE IS.
FWEET! FWEET!
HEY, YOU!
YES, OFFICERS?
HAVE YOU SEEN A WOMAN RUN BY HERE?!
ER... I CAN'T SAY I'VE SEEN *ANYONE* RUN PAST ME.
WE'VE LOST HER!
BUT THAT'S IMPOSSIBLE!

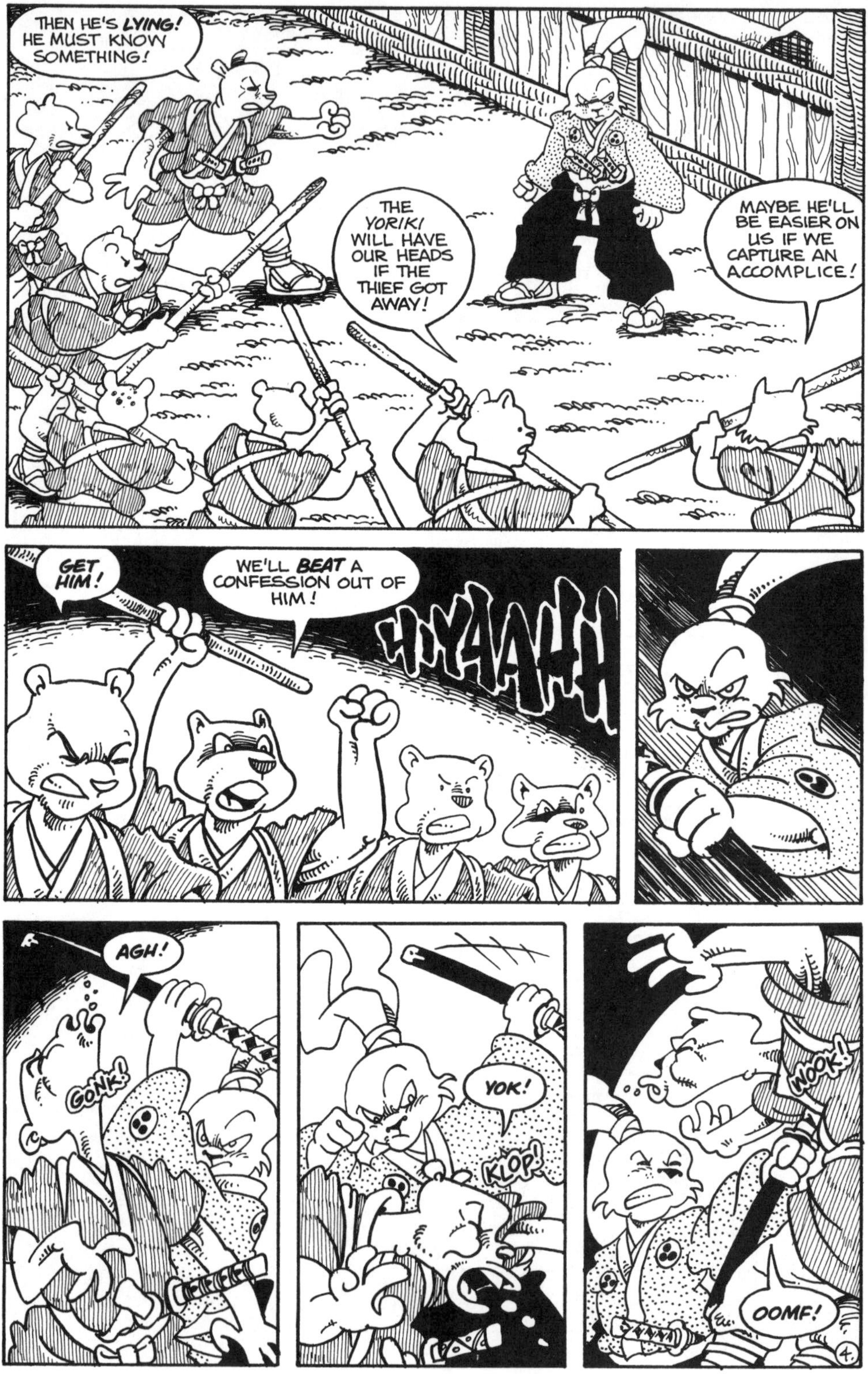
THEN HE'S LYING! HE MUST KNOW SOMETHING!
THE YORIKI WILL HAVE OUR HEADS IF THE THIEF GOT AWAY!
MAYBE HE'LL BE EASIER ON US IF WE CAPTURE AN ACCOMPLICE!
GET HIM!
WE'LL BEAT A CONFESSION OUT OF HIM!
HIYAAHH
AGH!
GONK!
YOK!
KLOP!
WOOK!
OOMF!
4.

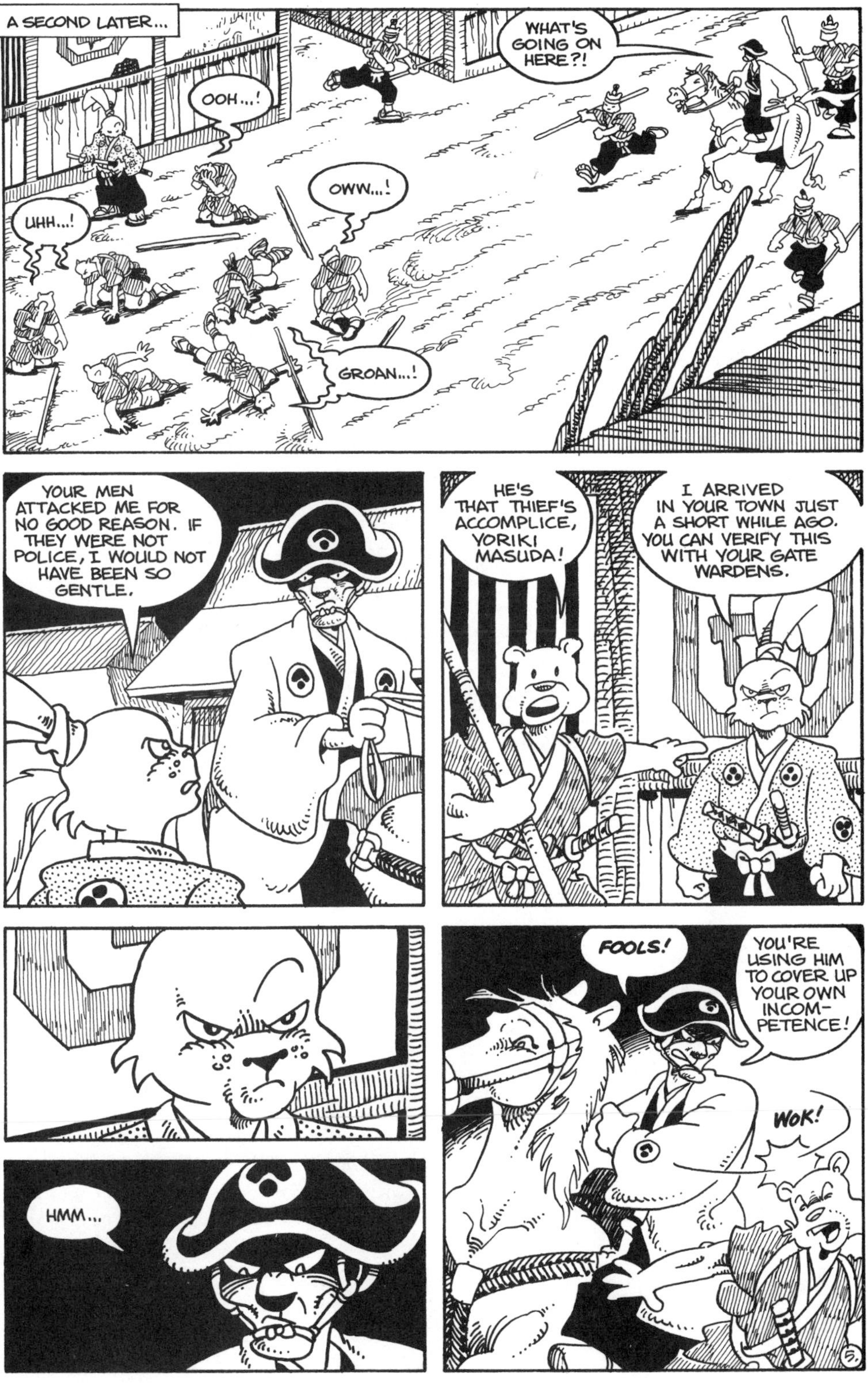
A SECOND LATER...
WHAT'S GOING ON HERE?!
OOH...!
OWW...!
UHH...!
GROAN...!
YOUR MEN ATTACKED ME FOR NO GOOD REASON. IF THEY WERE NOT POLICE, I WOULD NOT HAVE BEEN SO GENTLE.
HE'S THAT THIEF'S ACCOMPLICE, YORIKI MASUDA!
I ARRIVED IN YOUR TOWN JUST A SHORT WHILE AGO. YOU CAN VERIFY THIS WITH YOUR GATE WARDENS.
HMM...
FOOLS!
YOU'RE USING HIM TO COVER UP YOUR OWN INCOMPETENCE!
WOK!

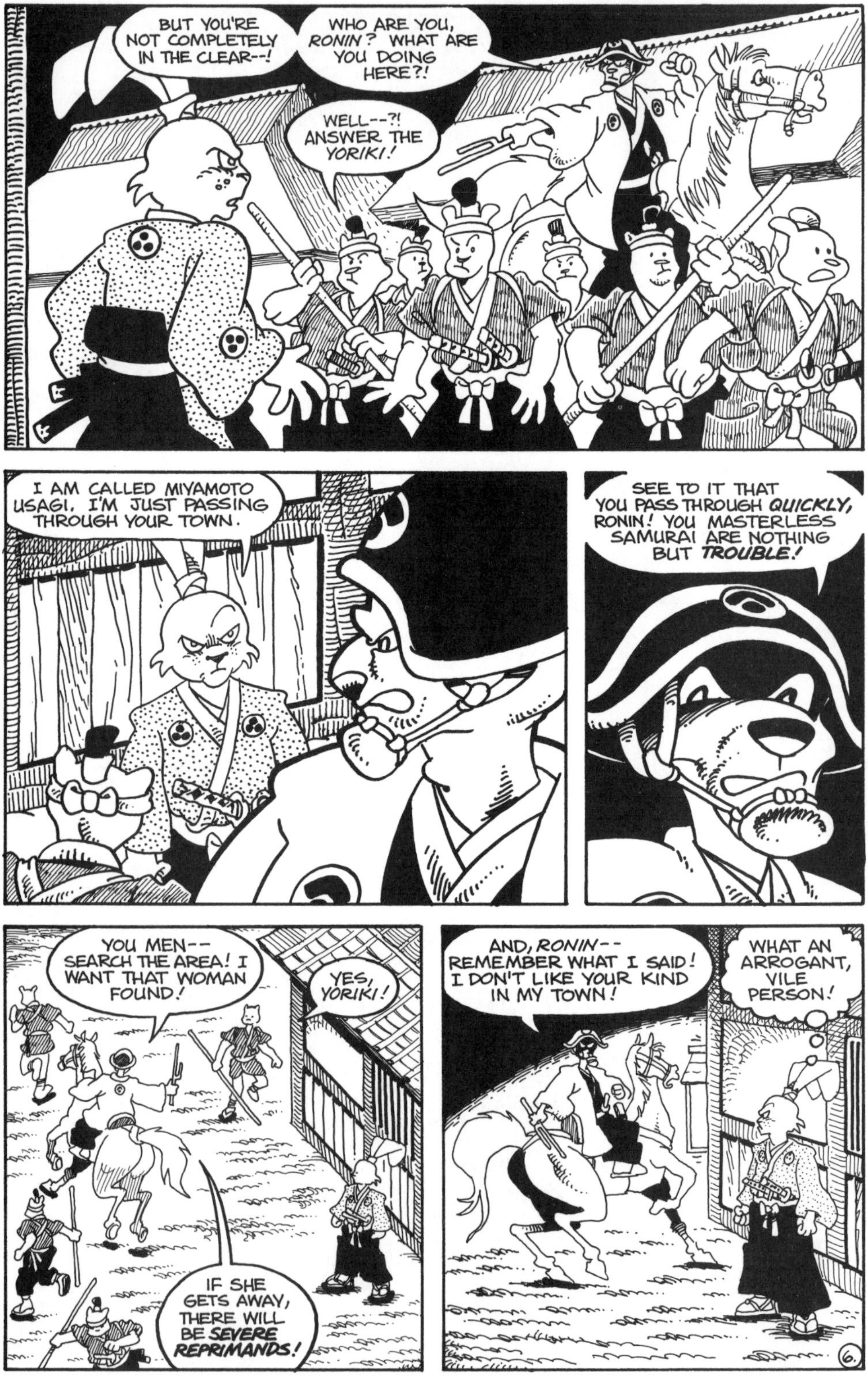

BUT YOU'RE NOT COMPLETELY IN THE CLEAR--!
WHO ARE YOU, RONIN? WHAT ARE YOU DOING HERE?!
WELL--?! ANSWER THE YORIKI!
I AM CALLED MIYAMOTO USAGI. I'M JUST PASSING THROUGH YOUR TOWN.
SEE TO IT THAT YOU PASS THROUGH QUICKLY, RONIN! YOU MASTERLESS SAMURAI ARE NOTHING BUT TROUBLE!
YOU MEN-- SEARCH THE AREA! I WANT THAT WOMAN FOUND!
YES, YORIKI!
IF SHE GETS AWAY, THERE WILL BE SEVERE REPRIMANDS!
AND, RONIN-- REMEMBER WHAT I SAID! I DON'T LIKE YOUR KIND IN MY TOWN!
WHAT AN ARROGANT, VILE PERSON!
6.

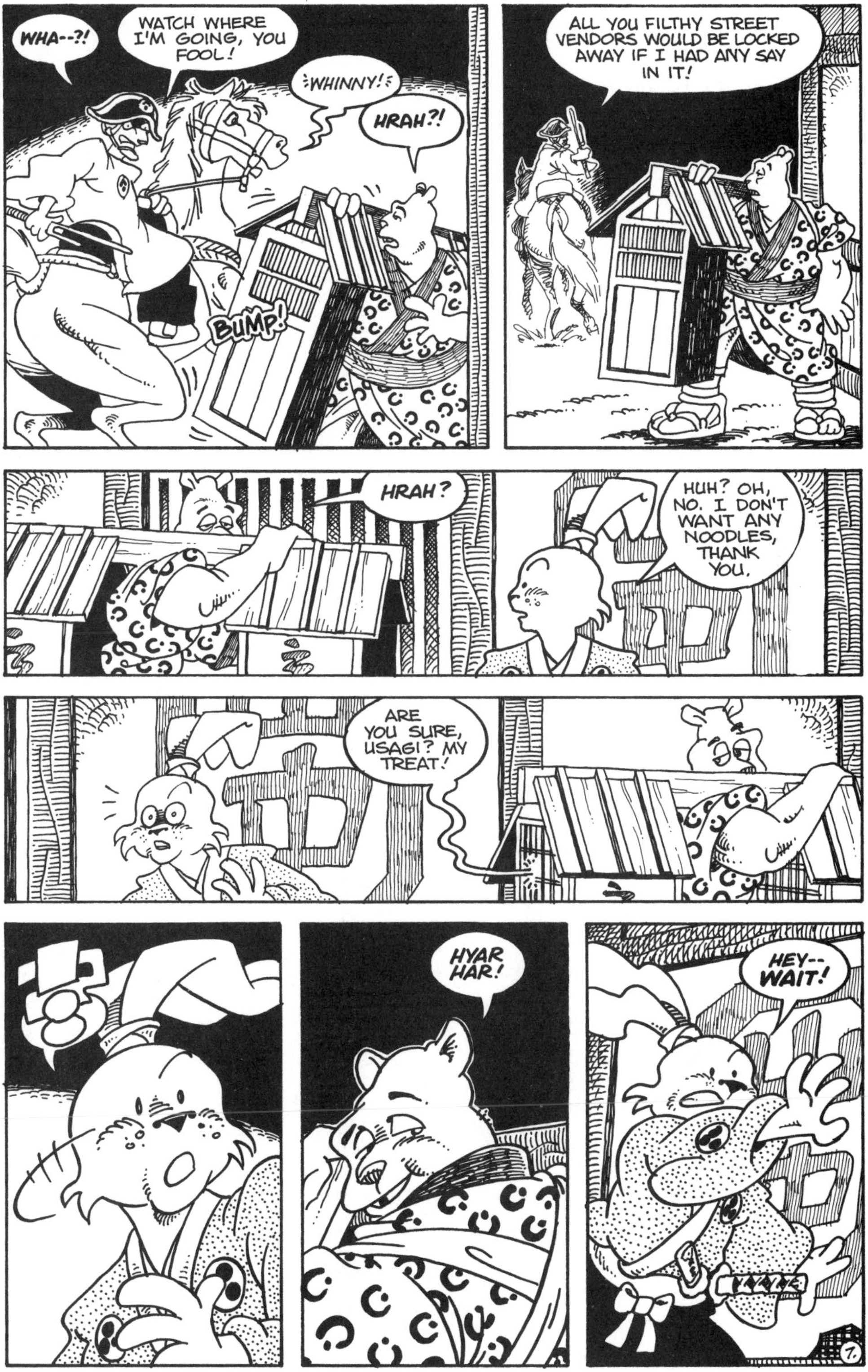
WHA--?!
WATCH WHERE I'M GOING, YOU FOOL!
WHINNY!
HRAH?!
BUMP!
ALL YOU FILTHY STREET VENDORS WOULD BE LOCKED AWAY IF I HAD ANY SAY IN IT!
HRAH?
HUH? OH, NO. I DON'T WANT ANY NOODLES, THANK YOU.
ARE YOU SURE, USAGI? MY TREAT!
HYAR HAR!
HEY-- WAIT!
7.

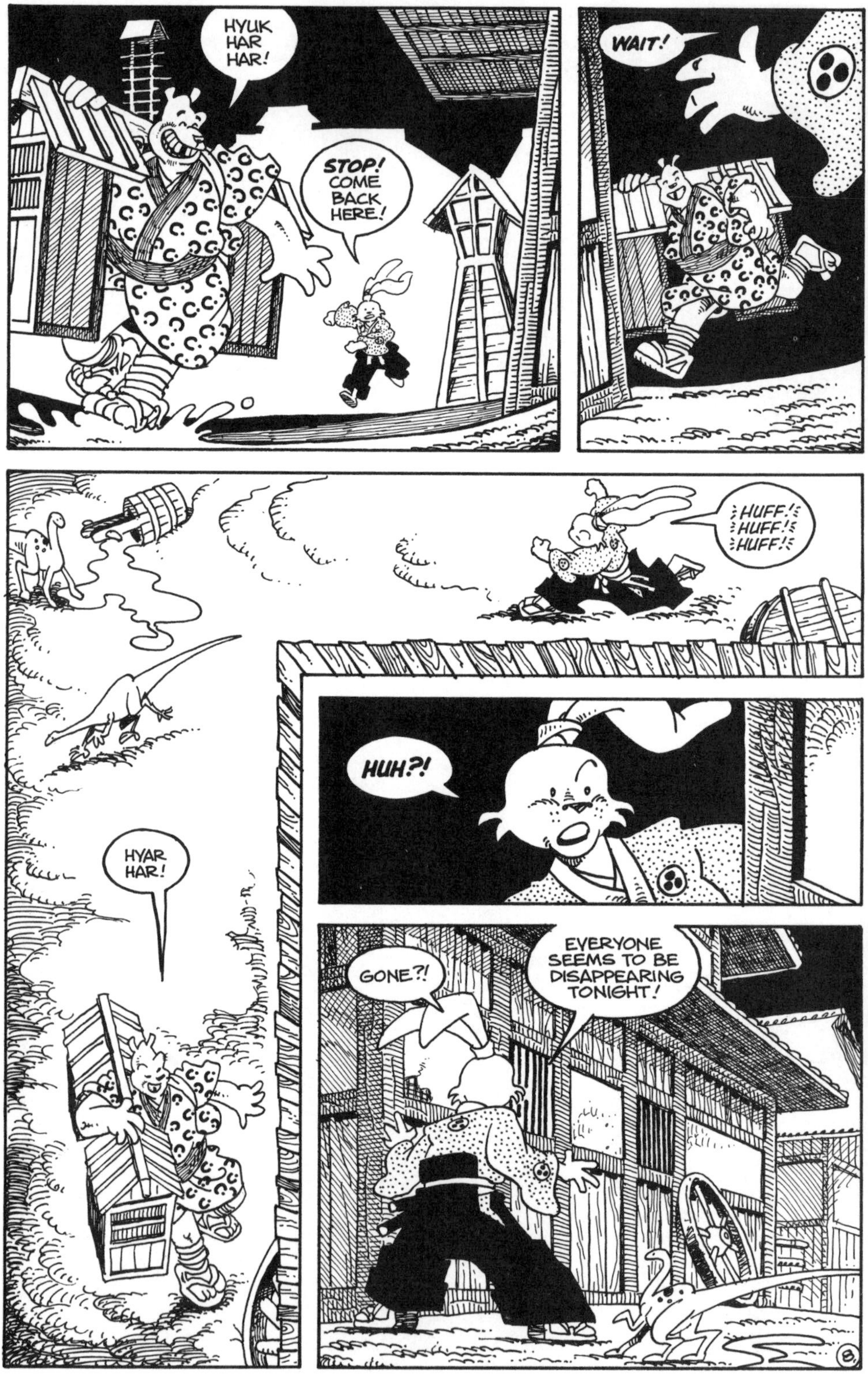
HYUK HAR HAR!
STOP! COME BACK HERE!
WAIT!
HUFF! HUFF! HUFF!
HYAR HAR!
HUH?!
GONE?!
EVERYONE SEEMS TO BE DISAPPEARING TONIGHT!
8

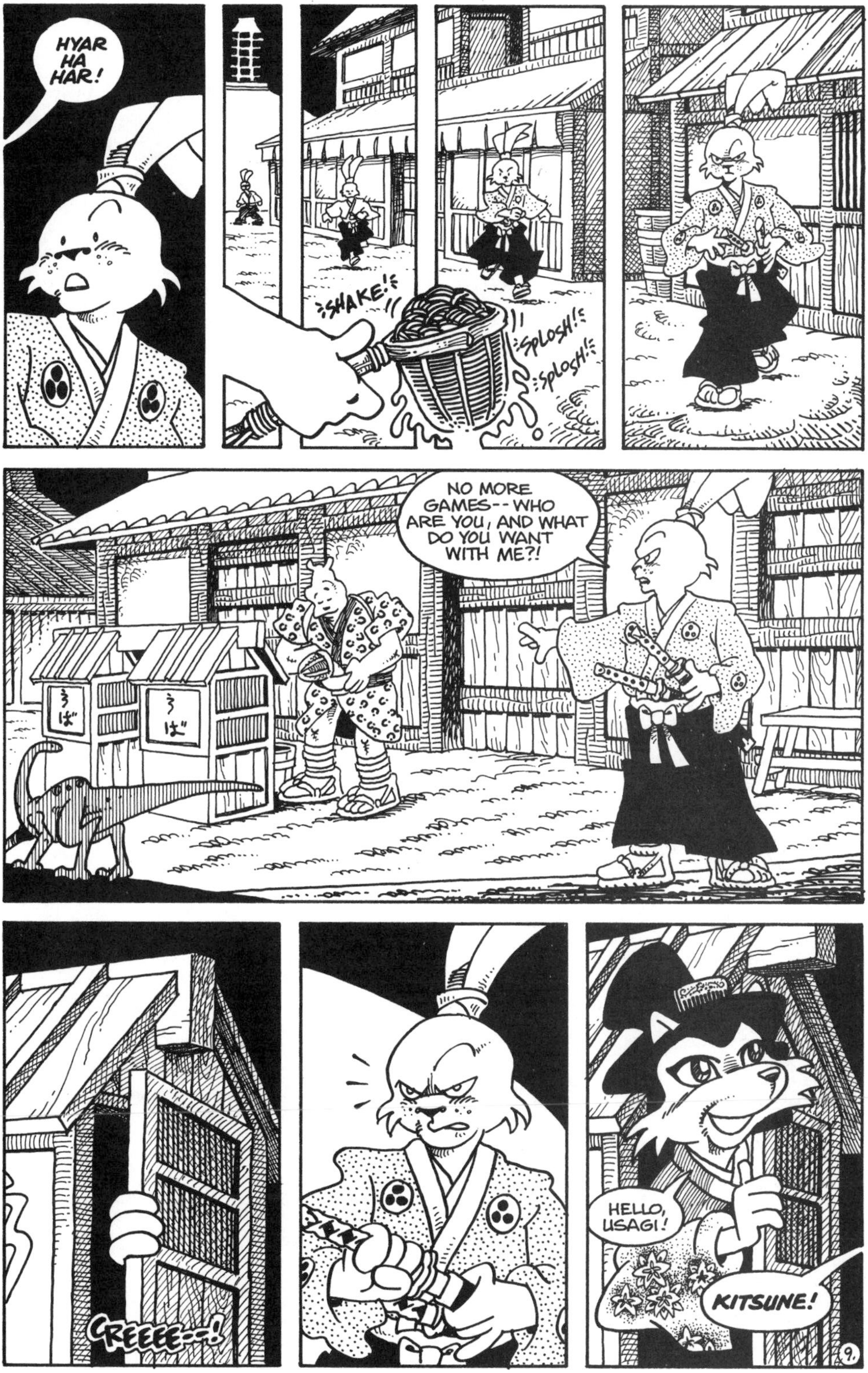
HYAR HA HAR!
SHAKE!
SPLOSH!
SPLOSH!
NO MORE GAMES-- WHO ARE YOU, AND WHAT DO YOU WANT WITH ME?!
うば
うば
CREEEE--!
HELLO, USAGI!
KITSUNE!
9.

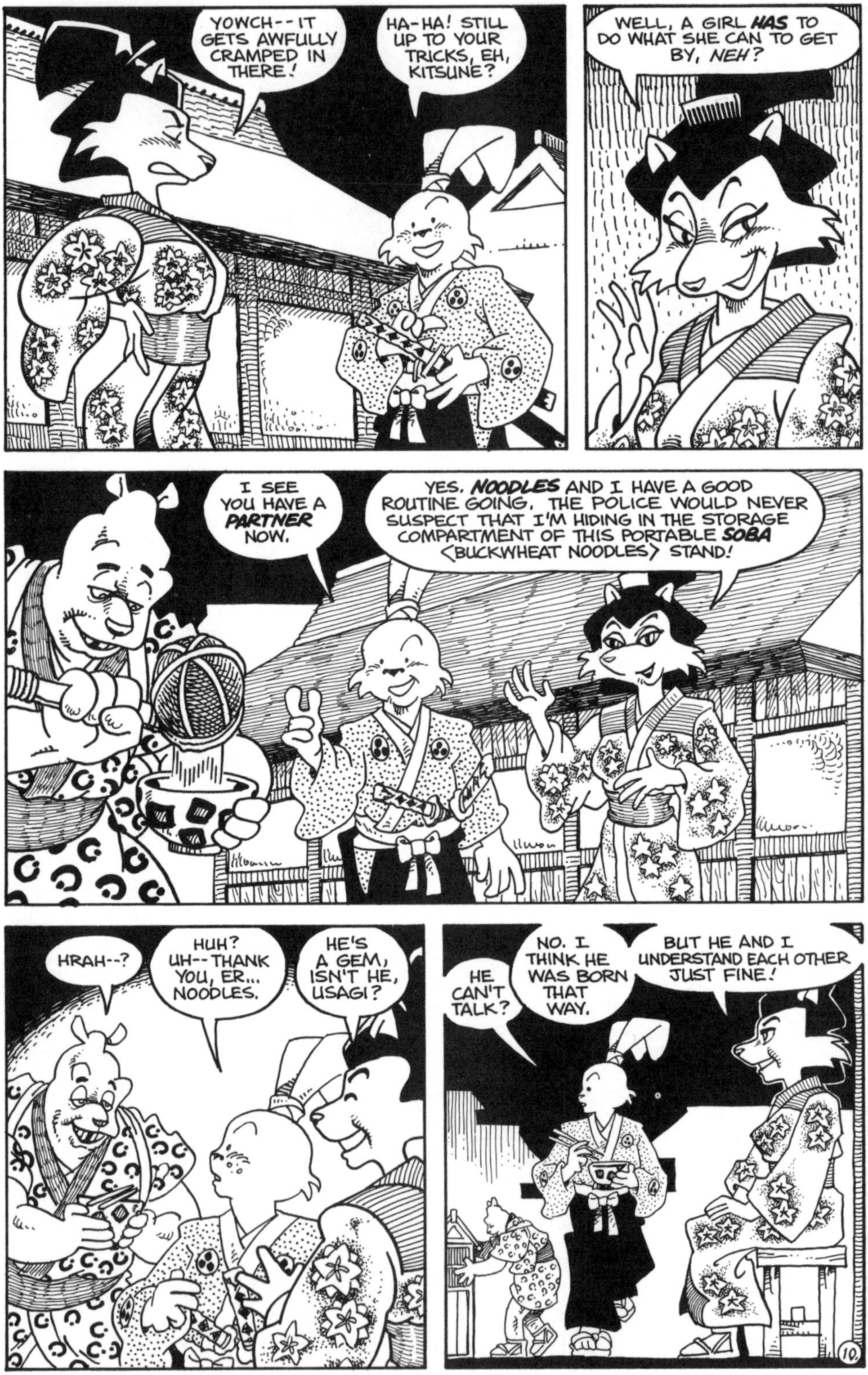
YOWCH--IT GETS AWFULLY CRAMPED IN THERE!
HA-HA! STILL UP TO YOUR TRICKS, EH, KITSUNE?
WELL, A GIRL **HAS** TO DO WHAT SHE CAN TO GET BY, *NEH*?
I SEE YOU HAVE A ***PARTNER*** NOW.
YES. ***NOODLES*** AND I HAVE A GOOD ROUTINE GOING. THE POLICE WOULD NEVER SUSPECT THAT I'M HIDING IN THE STORAGE COMPARTMENT OF THIS PORTABLE ***SOBA*** <BUCKWHEAT NOODLES> STAND!
HRAH--?
HUH? UH--THANK YOU, ER... NOODLES.
HE'S A GEM, ISN'T HE, USAGI?
HE CAN'T TALK?
NO. I THINK HE WAS BORN THAT WAY.
BUT HE AND I UNDERSTAND EACH OTHER JUST FINE!
10

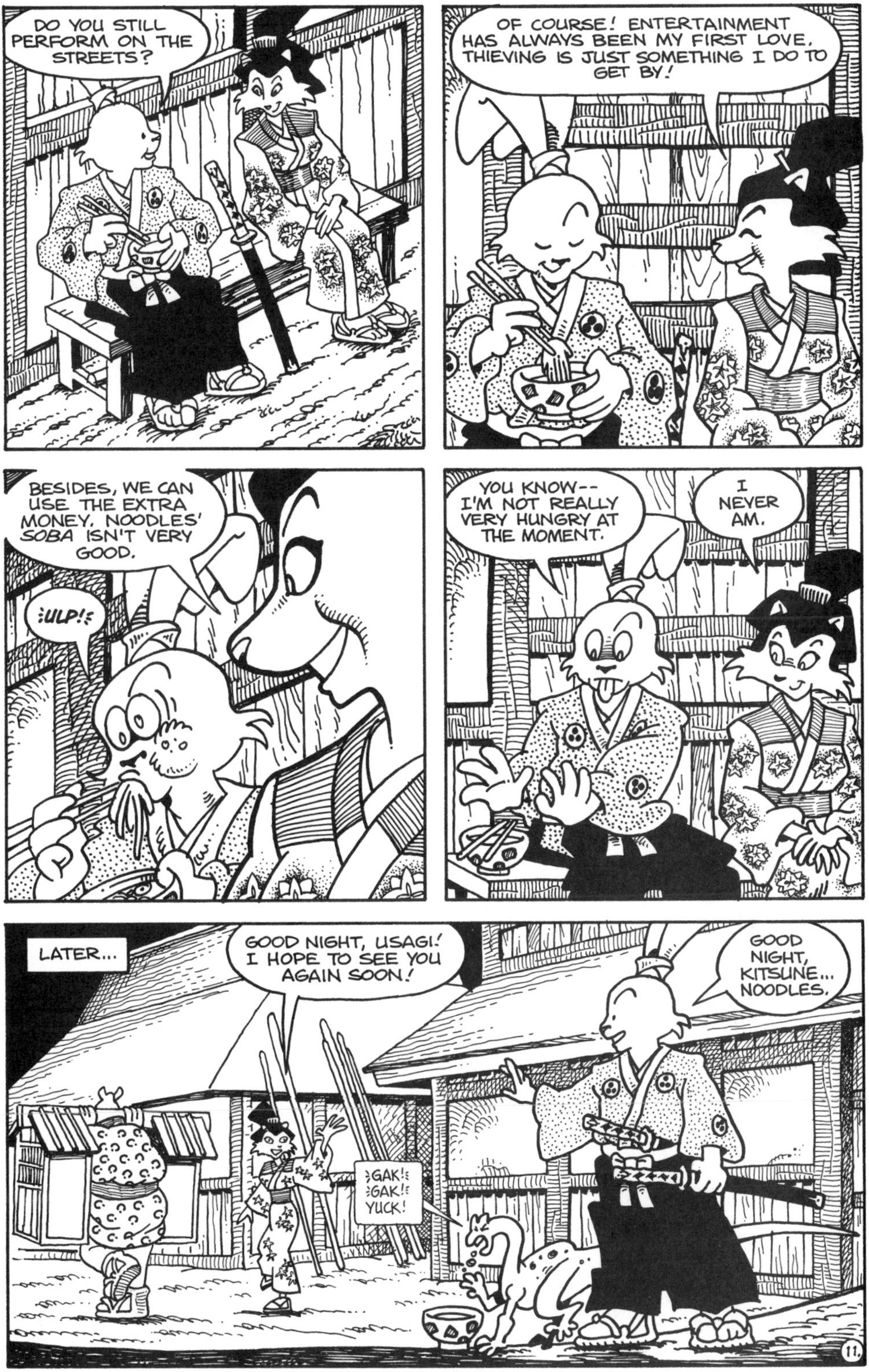
DO YOU STILL PERFORM ON THE STREETS?
OF COURSE! ENTERTAINMENT HAS ALWAYS BEEN MY FIRST LOVE, THIEVING IS JUST SOMETHING I DO TO GET BY!
BESIDES, WE CAN USE THE EXTRA MONEY. NOODLES' SOBA ISN'T VERY GOOD.
ULP!
YOU KNOW-- I'M NOT REALLY VERY HUNGRY AT THE MOMENT.
I NEVER AM.
LATER...
GOOD NIGHT, USAGI! I HOPE TO SEE YOU AGAIN SOON!
GOOD NIGHT, KITSUNE... NOODLES.
GAK! GAK! YUCK!
11.

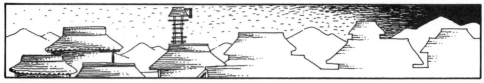

"THEN THE HERO LEAPED OVER THE MOUNTAIN PEAKS...

"...WHERE HE DASHED ALONG THE DRAGON'S BACK...

"...AND SCALED THE HEIGHTS TO HEAVEN...

"...THEN PLUNGED INTO THE VOID...

"...AND FINALLY DESCENDED ONTO THE FIRMAMENT."

70

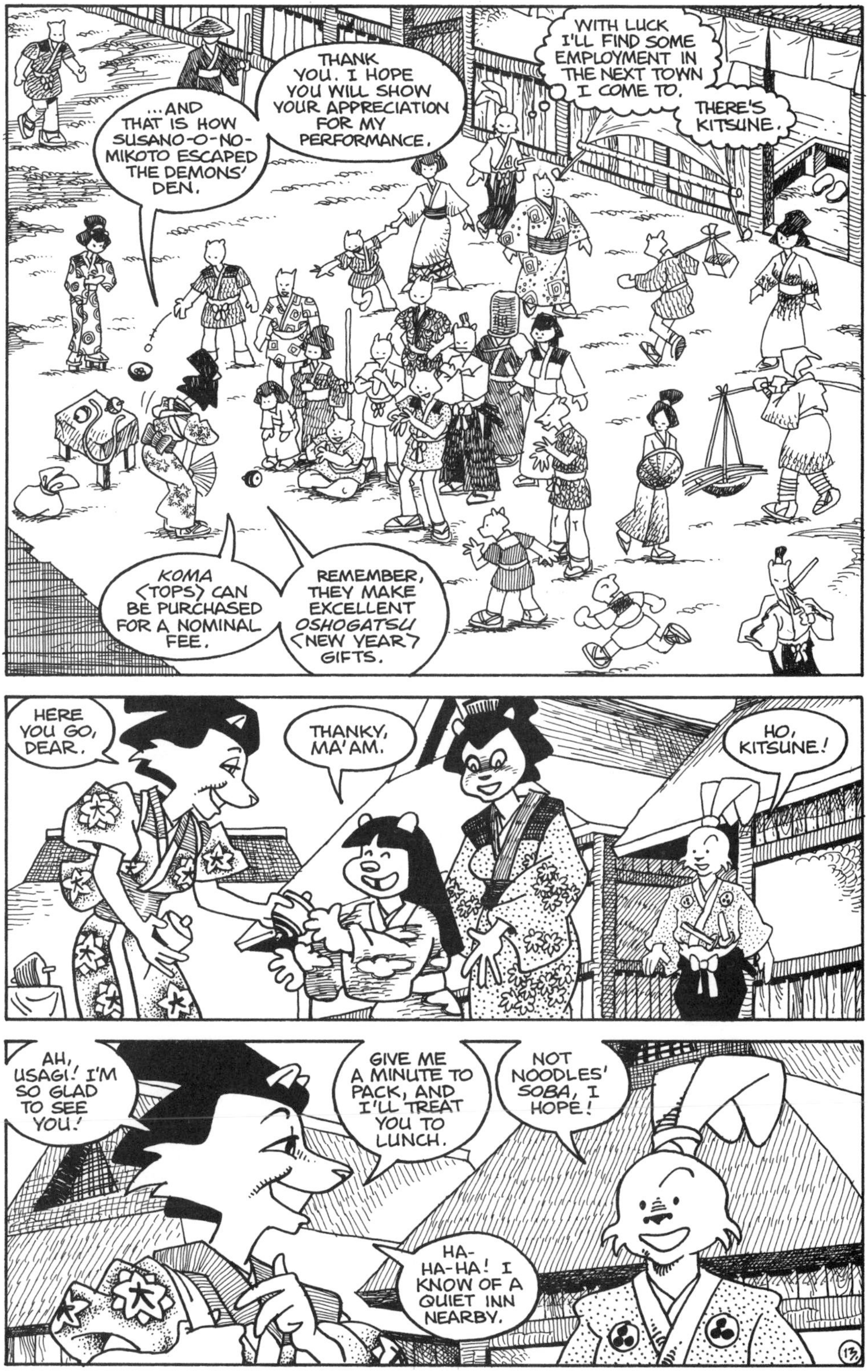
...AND THAT IS HOW SUSANO-O-NO-MIKOTO ESCAPED THE DEMONS' DEN.
THANK YOU. I HOPE YOU WILL SHOW YOUR APPRECIATION FOR MY PERFORMANCE.
WITH LUCK I'LL FIND SOME EMPLOYMENT IN THE NEXT TOWN I COME TO.
THERE'S KITSUNE.
KOMA <TOPS> CAN BE PURCHASED FOR A NOMINAL FEE.
REMEMBER, THEY MAKE EXCELLENT *OSHOGATSU* <NEW YEAR> GIFTS.
HERE YOU GO, DEAR.
THANKY, MA'AM.
HO, KITSUNE!
AH, USAGI! I'M SO GLAD TO SEE YOU!
GIVE ME A MINUTE TO PACK, AND I'LL TREAT YOU TO LUNCH.
NOT NOODLES' *SOBA*, I HOPE!
HA-HA-HA! I KNOW OF A QUIET INN NEARBY.
13

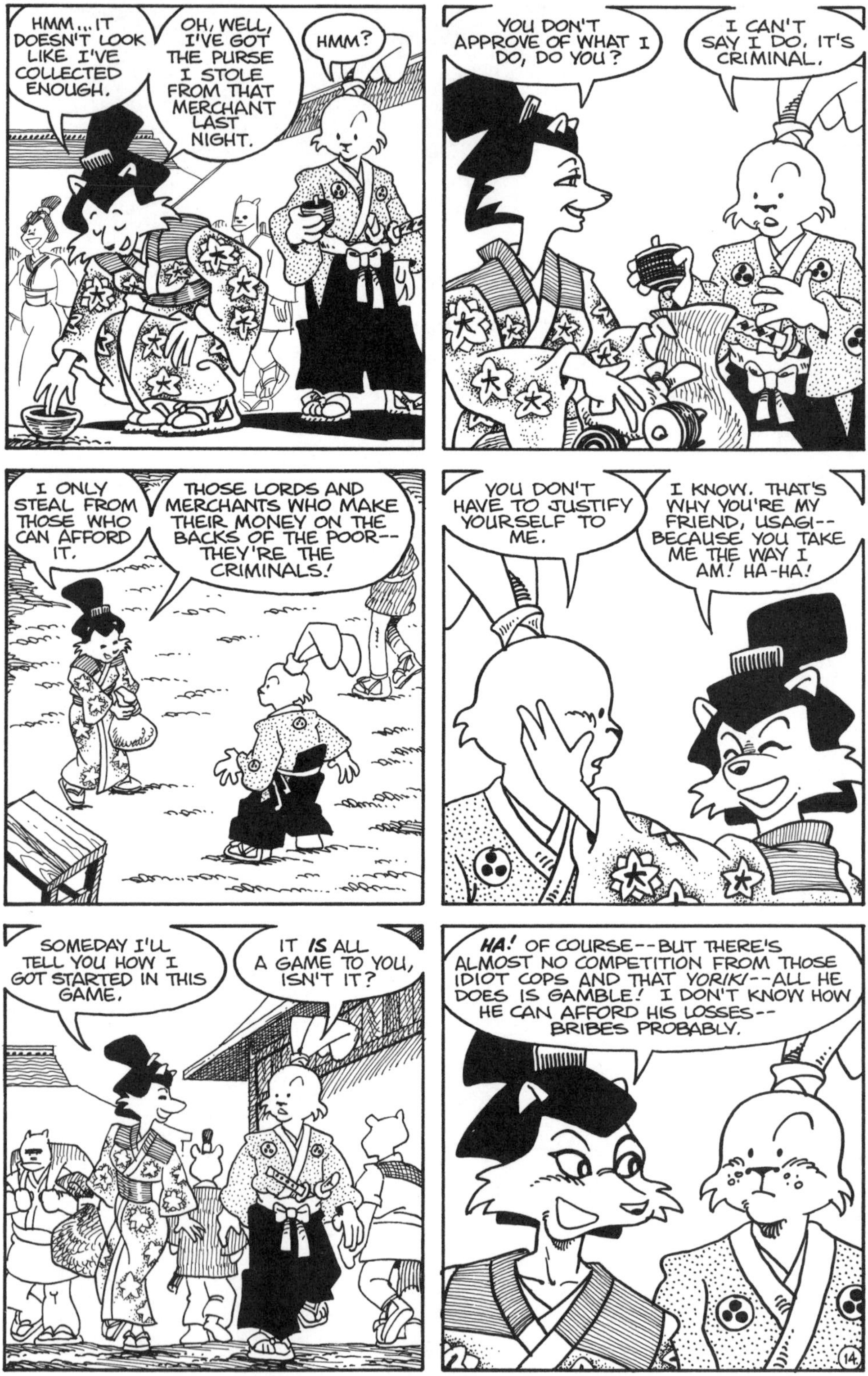
HMM... IT DOESN'T LOOK LIKE I'VE COLLECTED ENOUGH.
OH, WELL, I'VE GOT THE PURSE I STOLE FROM THAT MERCHANT LAST NIGHT.
HMM?
YOU DON'T APPROVE OF WHAT I DO, DO YOU?
I CAN'T SAY I DO. IT'S CRIMINAL.
I ONLY STEAL FROM THOSE WHO CAN AFFORD IT.
THOSE LORDS AND MERCHANTS WHO MAKE THEIR MONEY ON THE BACKS OF THE POOR-- THEY'RE THE CRIMINALS!
YOU DON'T HAVE TO JUSTIFY YOURSELF TO ME.
I KNOW. THAT'S WHY YOU'RE MY FRIEND, USAGI-- BECAUSE YOU TAKE ME THE WAY I AM! HA-HA!
SOMEDAY I'LL TELL YOU HOW I GOT STARTED IN THIS GAME.
IT IS ALL A GAME TO YOU, ISN'T IT?
HA! OF COURSE--BUT THERE'S ALMOST NO COMPETITION FROM THOSE IDIOT COPS AND THAT YORIKI--ALL HE DOES IS GAMBLE! I DON'T KNOW HOW HE CAN AFFORD HIS LOSSES-- BRIBES PROBABLY.
14.

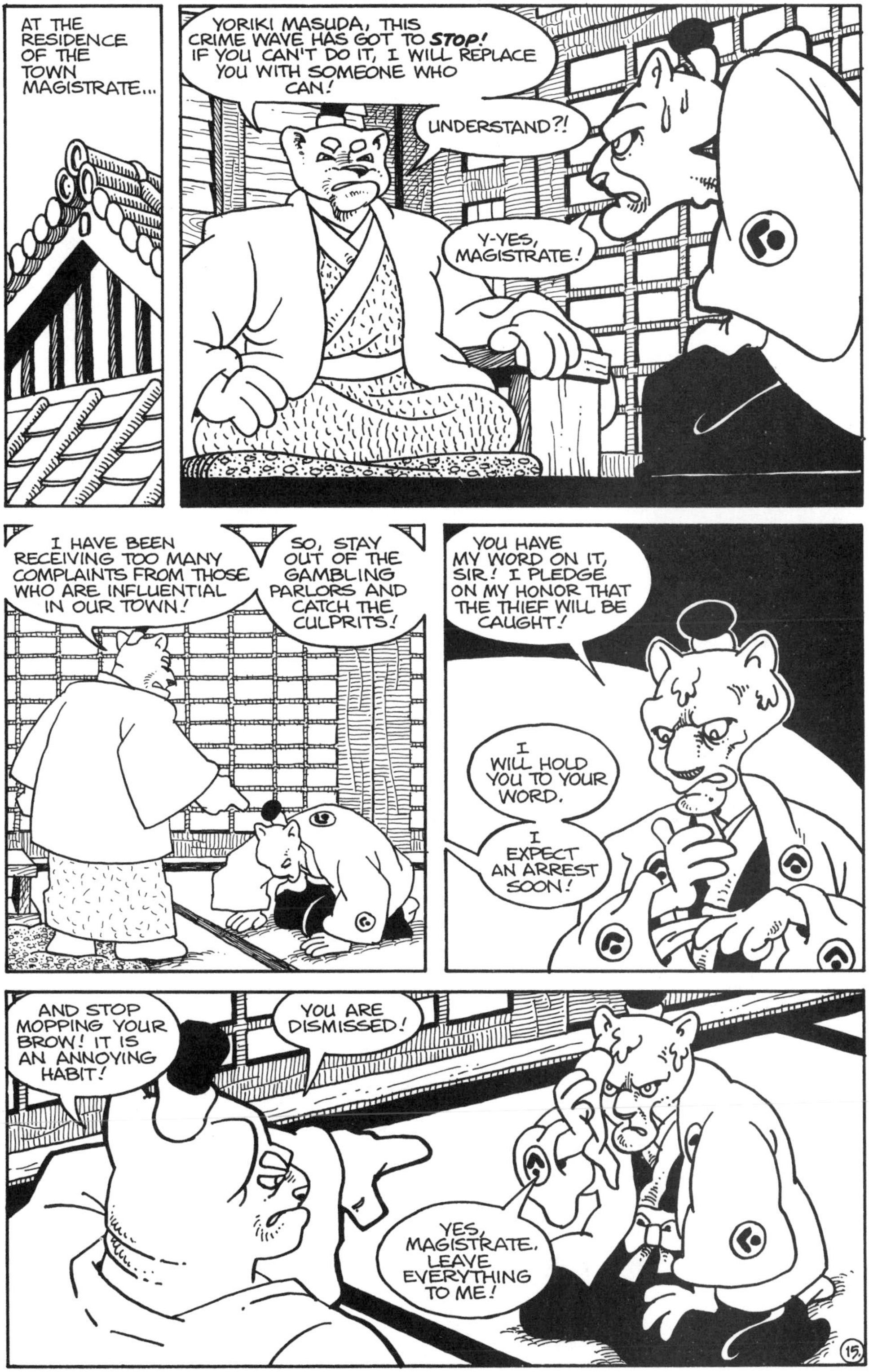
AT THE RESIDENCE OF THE TOWN MAGISTRATE...
YORIKI MASUDA, THIS CRIME WAVE HAS GOT TO STOP! IF YOU CAN'T DO IT, I WILL REPLACE YOU WITH SOMEONE WHO CAN!
UNDERSTAND?!
Y-YES, MAGISTRATE!
I HAVE BEEN RECEIVING TOO MANY COMPLAINTS FROM THOSE WHO ARE INFLUENTIAL IN OUR TOWN!
SO, STAY OUT OF THE GAMBLING PARLORS AND CATCH THE CULPRITS!
YOU HAVE MY WORD ON IT, SIR! I PLEDGE ON MY HONOR THAT THE THIEF WILL BE CAUGHT!
I WILL HOLD YOU TO YOUR WORD.
I EXPECT AN ARREST SOON!
AND STOP MOPPING YOUR BROW! IT IS AN ANNOYING HABIT!
YOU ARE DISMISSED!
YES, MAGISTRATE. LEAVE EVERYTHING TO ME!
15

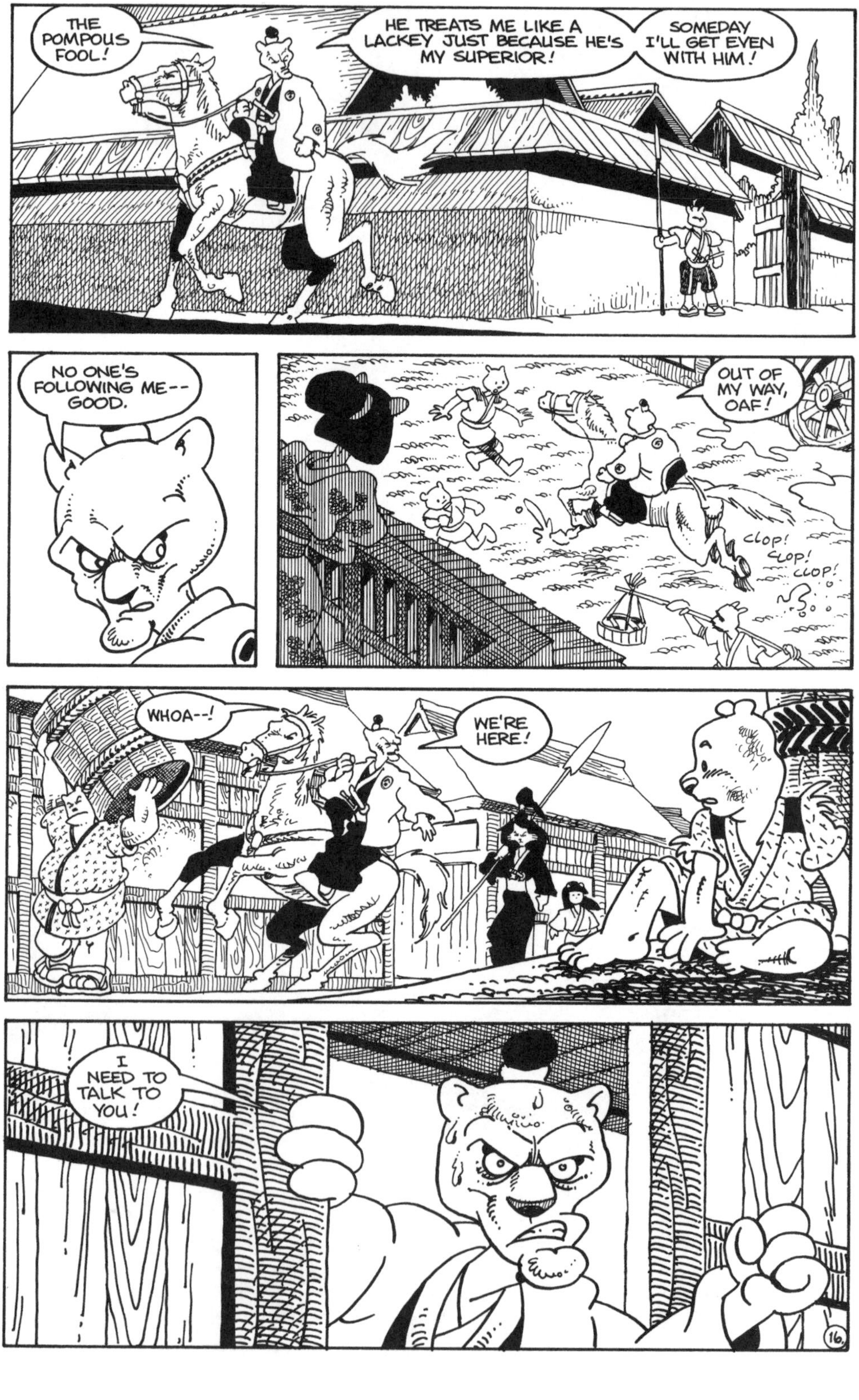
THE POMPOUS FOOL!
HE TREATS ME LIKE A LACKEY JUST BECAUSE HE'S MY SUPERIOR!
SOMEDAY I'LL GET EVEN WITH HIM!
NO ONE'S FOLLOWING ME-- GOOD.
OUT OF MY WAY, OAF!
CLOP! CLOP! CLOP!
WHOA--!
WE'RE HERE!
I NEED TO TALK TO YOU!
16

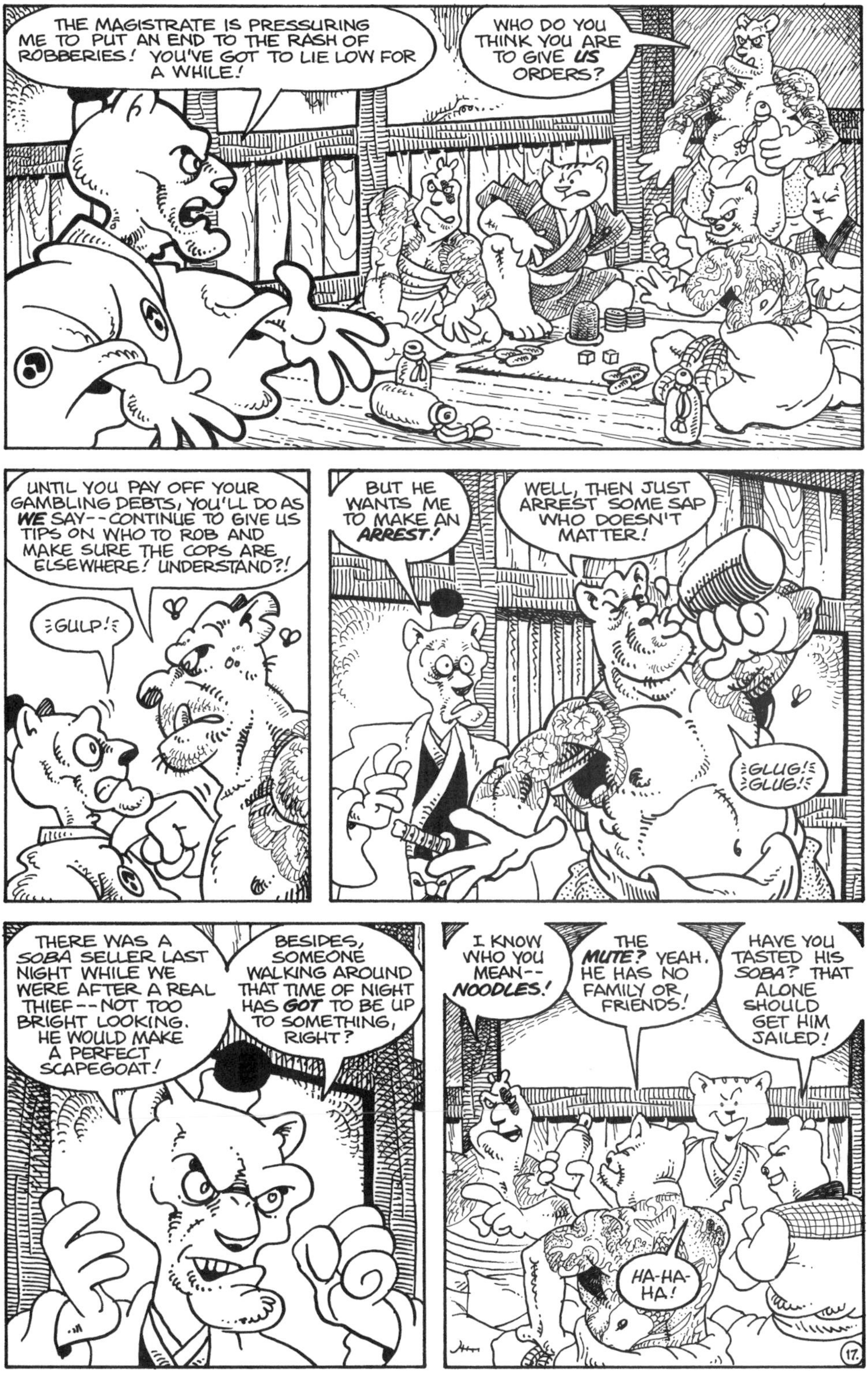
THE MAGISTRATE IS PRESSURING ME TO PUT AN END TO THE RASH OF ROBBERIES! YOU'VE GOT TO LIE LOW FOR A WHILE!
WHO DO YOU THINK YOU ARE TO GIVE US ORDERS?
UNTIL YOU PAY OFF YOUR GAMBLING DEBTS, YOU'LL DO AS WE SAY--CONTINUE TO GIVE US TIPS ON WHO TO ROB AND MAKE SURE THE COPS ARE ELSEWHERE! UNDERSTAND?!
GULP!
BUT HE WANTS ME TO MAKE AN ARREST!
WELL, THEN JUST ARREST SOME SAP WHO DOESN'T MATTER!
GLUG! GLUG!
THERE WAS A SOBA SELLER LAST NIGHT WHILE WE WERE AFTER A REAL THIEF--NOT TOO BRIGHT LOOKING. HE WOULD MAKE A PERFECT SCAPEGOAT!
BESIDES, SOMEONE WALKING AROUND THAT TIME OF NIGHT HAS GOT TO BE UP TO SOMETHING, RIGHT?
I KNOW WHO YOU MEAN-- NOODLES!
THE MUTE? YEAH. HE HAS NO FAMILY OR FRIENDS!
HAVE YOU TASTED HIS SOBA? THAT ALONE SHOULD GET HIM JAILED!
HA-HA-HA!
17.

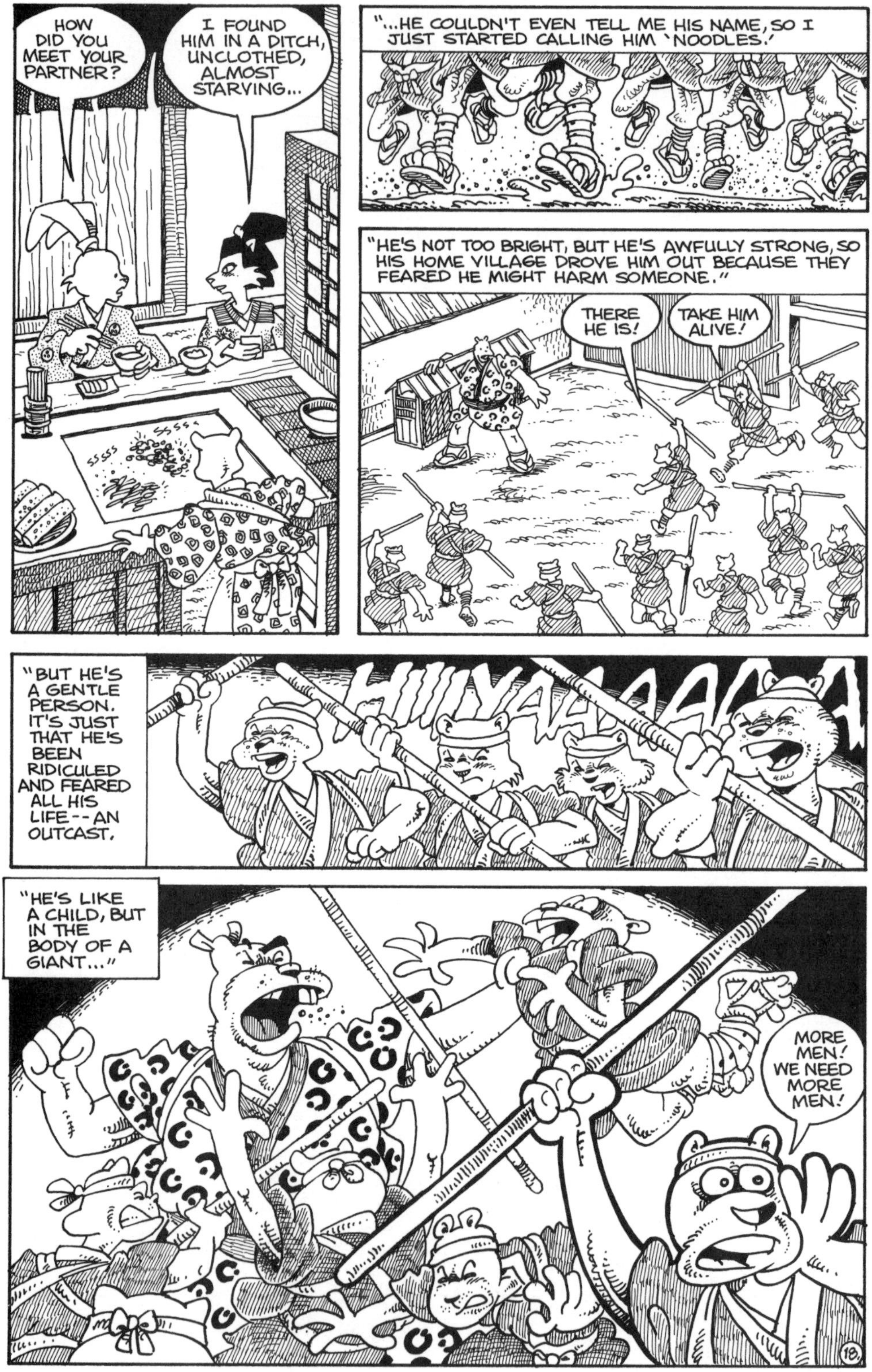
HOW DID YOU MEET YOUR PARTNER?
I FOUND HIM IN A DITCH, UNCLOTHED, ALMOST STARVING...
"...HE COULDN'T EVEN TELL ME HIS NAME, SO I JUST STARTED CALLING HIM 'NOODLES.'
"HE'S NOT TOO BRIGHT, BUT HE'S AWFULLY STRONG, SO HIS HOME VILLAGE DROVE HIM OUT BECAUSE THEY FEARED HE MIGHT HARM SOMEONE."
THERE HE IS!
TAKE HIM ALIVE!
"BUT HE'S A GENTLE PERSON. IT'S JUST THAT HE'S BEEN RIDICULED AND FEARED ALL HIS LIFE--AN OUTCAST.
HIIIYAAAAAAA
"HE'S LIKE A CHILD, BUT IN THE BODY OF A GIANT..."
MORE MEN! WE NEED MORE MEN!
18

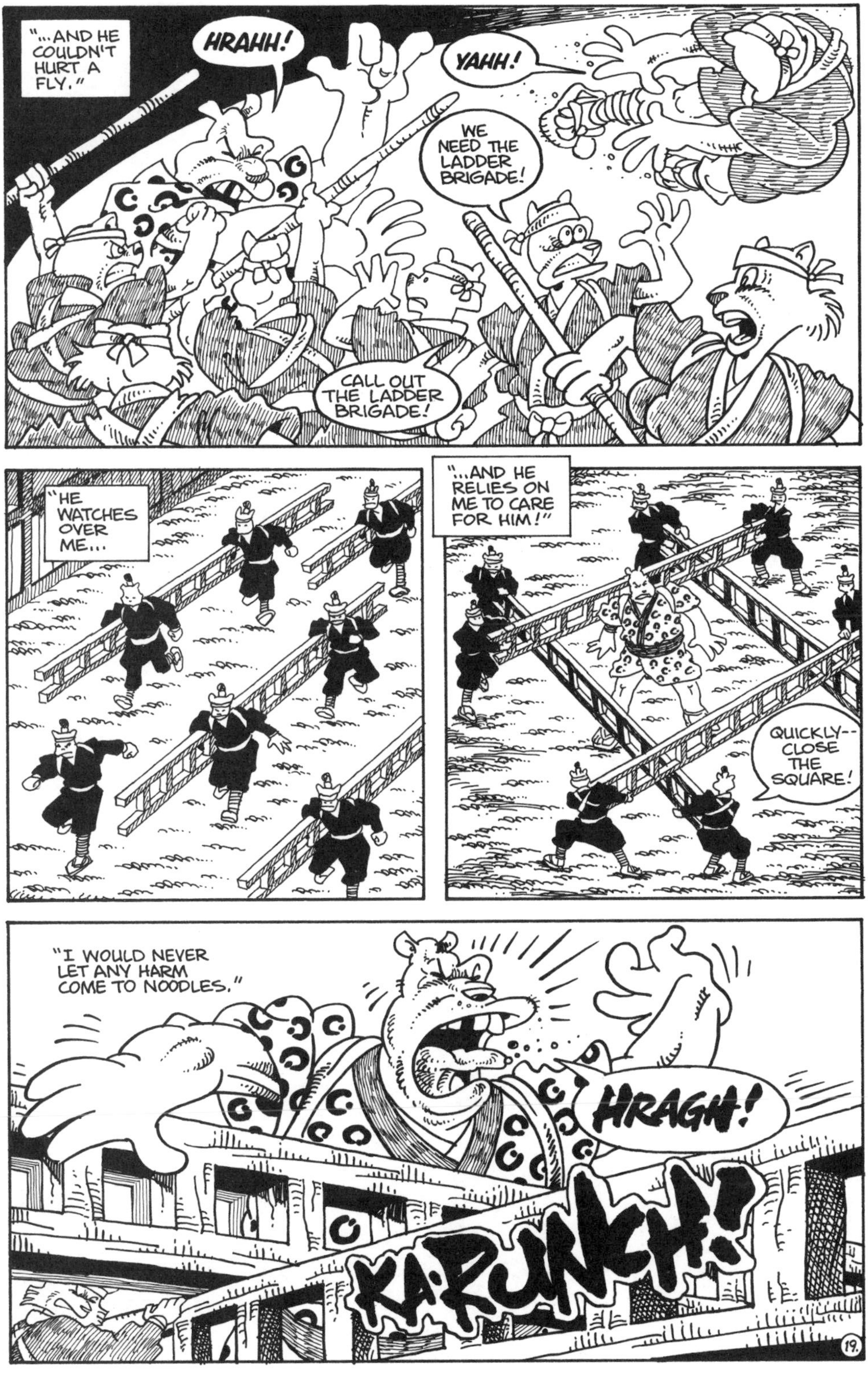
"...AND HE COULDN'T HURT A FLY."
HRAHH!
YAHH!
WE NEED THE LADDER BRIGADE!
CALL OUT THE LADDER BRIGADE!
"HE WATCHES OVER ME...
"...AND HE RELIES ON ME TO CARE FOR HIM!"
QUICKLY-- CLOSE THE SQUARE!
"I WOULD NEVER LET ANY HARM COME TO NOODLES."
HRAGH!
KA-RUNCH!
19.

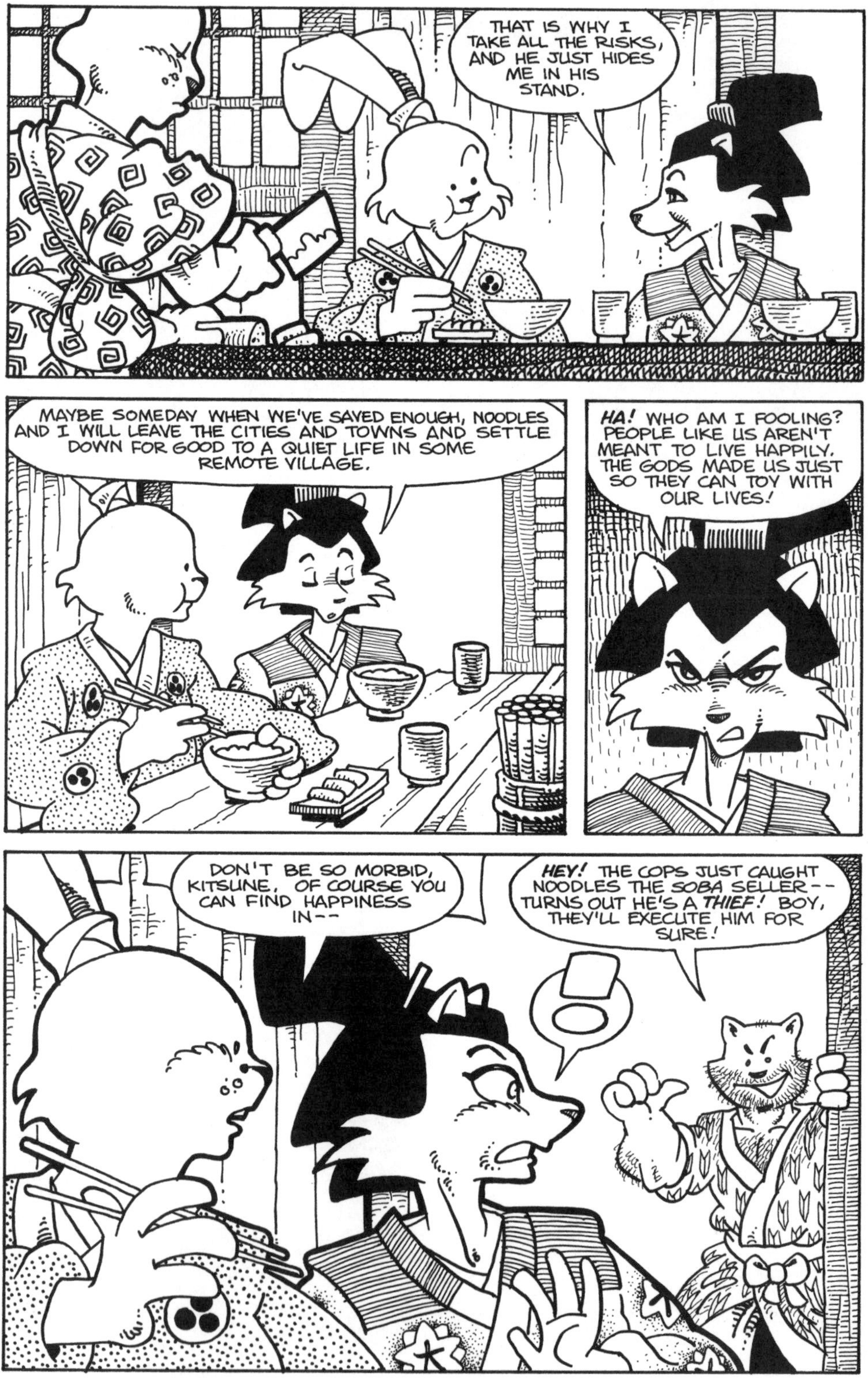
THAT IS WHY I TAKE ALL THE RISKS, AND HE JUST HIDES ME IN HIS STAND.
MAYBE SOMEDAY WHEN WE'VE SAVED ENOUGH, NOODLES AND I WILL LEAVE THE CITIES AND TOWNS AND SETTLE DOWN FOR GOOD TO A QUIET LIFE IN SOME REMOTE VILLAGE.
HA! WHO AM I FOOLING? PEOPLE LIKE US AREN'T MEANT TO LIVE HAPPILY. THE GODS MADE US JUST SO THEY CAN TOY WITH OUR LIVES!
DON'T BE SO MORBID, KITSUNE, OF COURSE YOU CAN FIND HAPPINESS IN--
HEY! THE COPS JUST CAUGHT NOODLES THE SOBA SELLER-- TURNS OUT HE'S A THIEF! BOY, THEY'LL EXECUTE HIM FOR SURE!

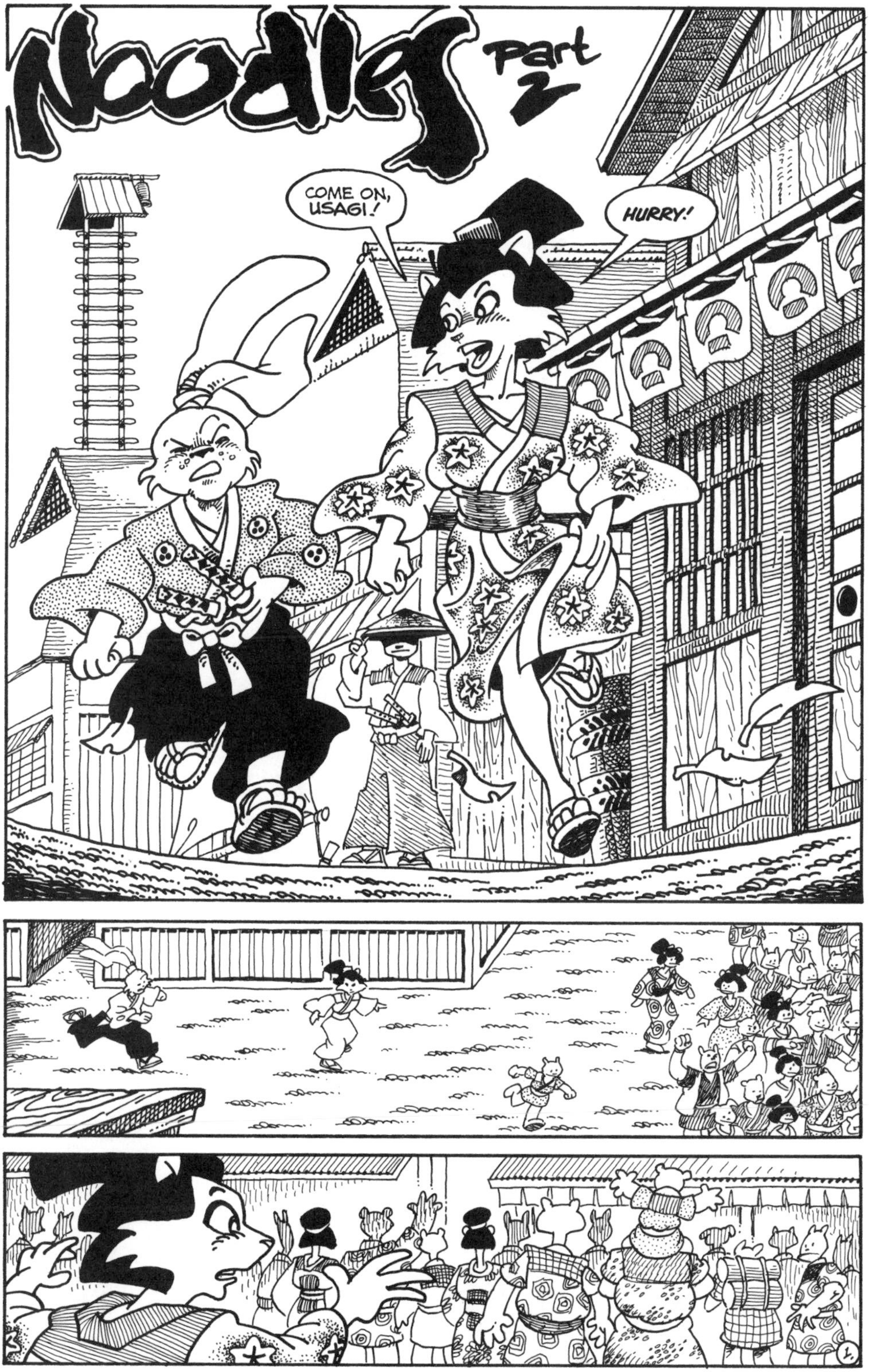
Noodles Part 2
COME ON, USAGI!
HURRY!

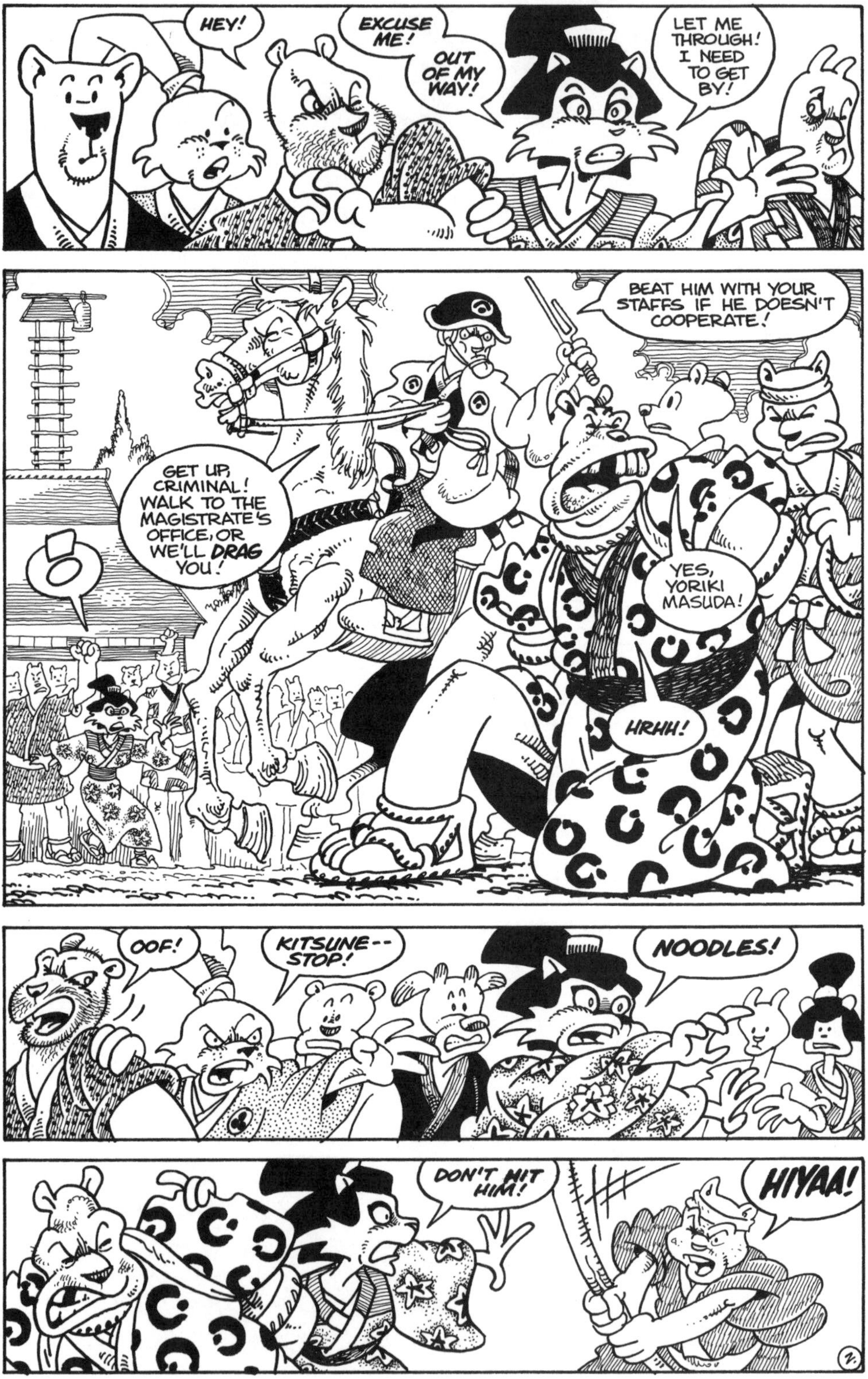
HEY!
EXCUSE ME!
OUT OF MY WAY!
LET ME THROUGH! I NEED TO GET BY!
BEAT HIM WITH YOUR STAFFS IF HE DOESN'T COOPERATE!
GET UP, CRIMINAL! WALK TO THE MAGISTRATE'S OFFICE, OR WE'LL DRAG YOU!
YES, YORIKI MASUDA!
HRHH!
OOF!
KITSUNE-- STOP!
NOODLES!
DON'T HIT HIM!
HIYAA!

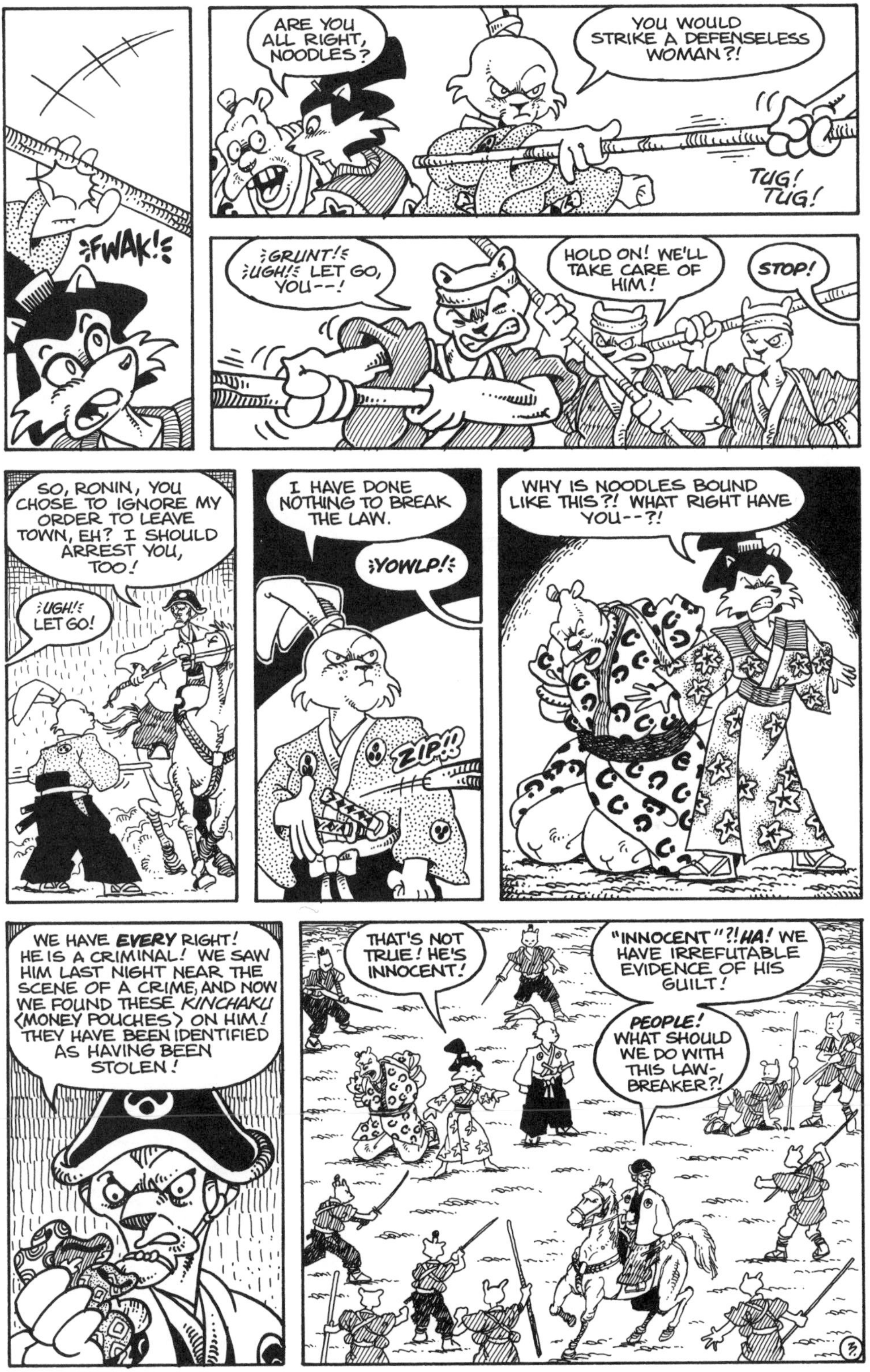
FWAK!
ARE YOU ALL RIGHT, NOODLES?
YOU WOULD STRIKE A DEFENSELESS WOMAN?!
TUG! TUG!
GRUNT! UGH! LET GO, YOU--!
HOLD ON! WE'LL TAKE CARE OF HIM!
STOP!
SO, RONIN, YOU CHOSE TO IGNORE MY ORDER TO LEAVE TOWN, EH? I SHOULD ARREST YOU, TOO!
UGH! LET GO!
I HAVE DONE NOTHING TO BREAK THE LAW.
YOWLP!
ZIP!!
WHY IS NOODLES BOUND LIKE THIS?! WHAT RIGHT HAVE YOU--?!
WE HAVE EVERY RIGHT! HE IS A CRIMINAL! WE SAW HIM LAST NIGHT NEAR THE SCENE OF A CRIME, AND NOW WE FOUND THESE KINCHAKU (MONEY POUCHES) ON HIM! THEY HAVE BEEN IDENTIFIED AS HAVING BEEN STOLEN!
THAT'S NOT TRUE! HE'S INNOCENT!
"INNOCENT"?! HA! WE HAVE IRREFUTABLE EVIDENCE OF HIS GUILT!
PEOPLE! WHAT SHOULD WE DO WITH THIS LAW-BREAKER?!
3

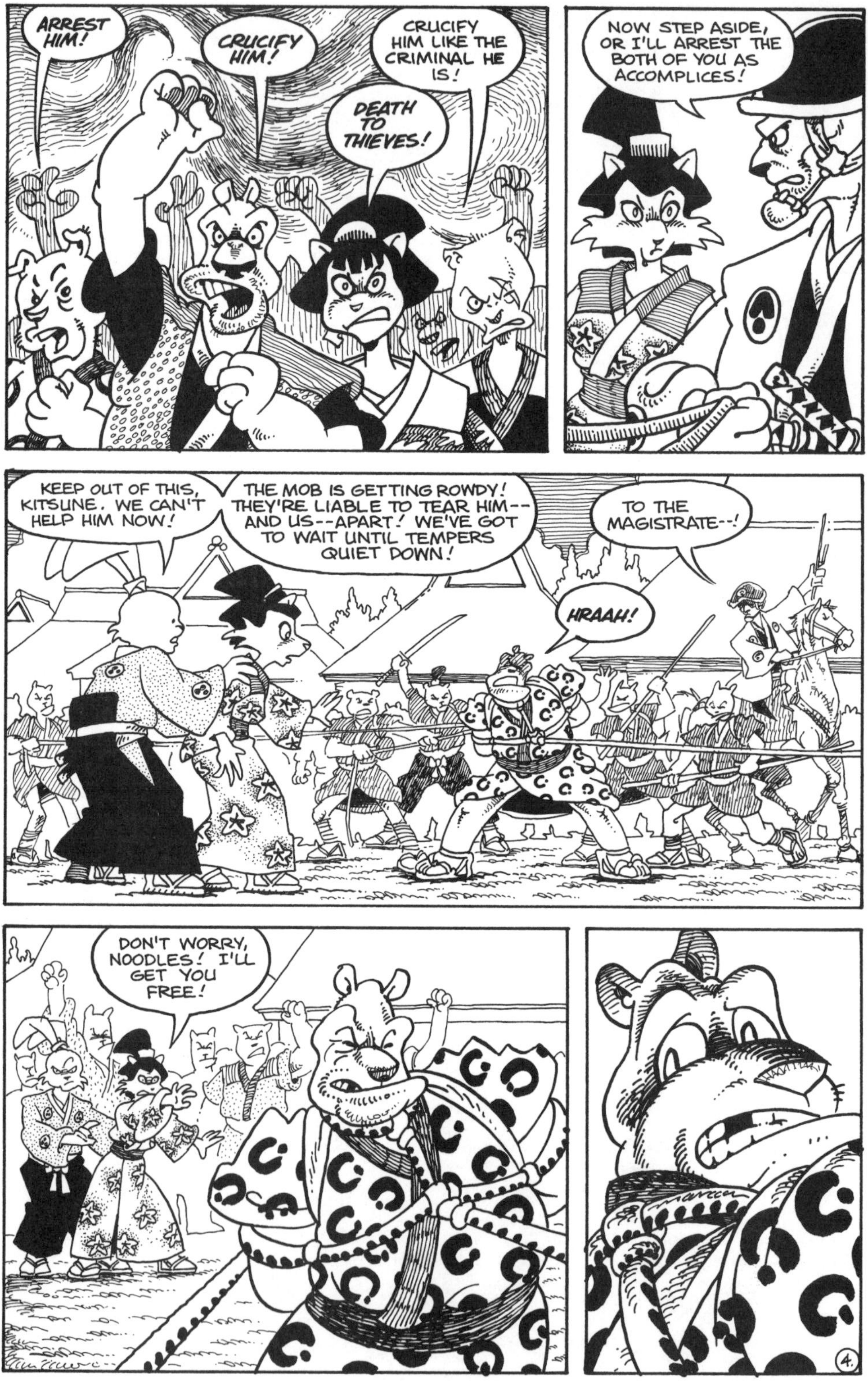
ARREST HIM!
CRUCIFY HIM!
CRUCIFY HIM LIKE THE CRIMINAL HE IS!
DEATH TO THIEVES!
NOW STEP ASIDE, OR I'LL ARREST THE BOTH OF YOU AS ACCOMPLICES!
KEEP OUT OF THIS, KITSUNE. WE CAN'T HELP HIM NOW!
THE MOB IS GETTING ROWDY! THEY'RE LIABLE TO TEAR HIM--AND US--APART! WE'VE GOT TO WAIT UNTIL TEMPERS QUIET DOWN!
TO THE MAGISTRATE--!
HRAAH!
DON'T WORRY, NOODLES! I'LL GET YOU FREE!
4.

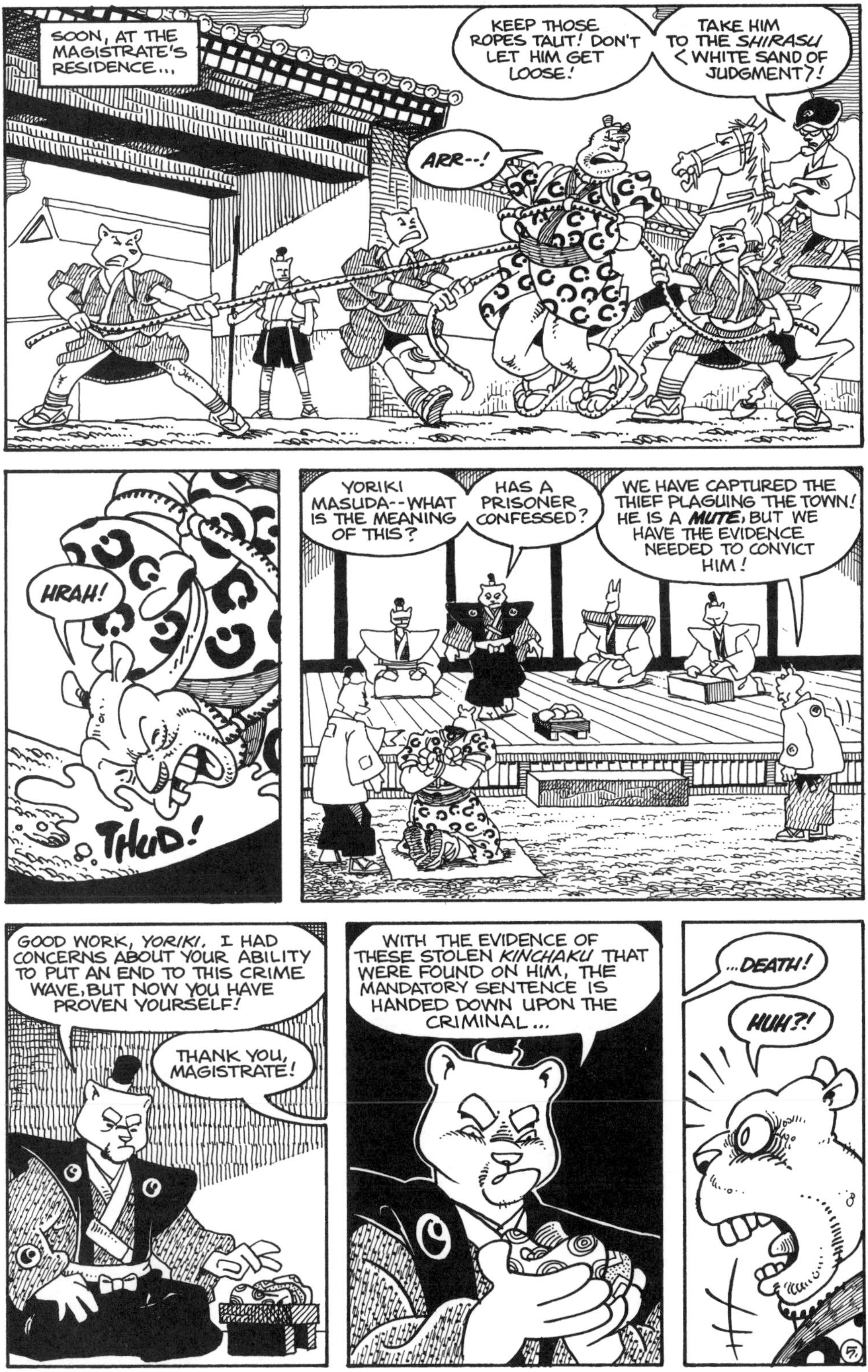
SOON, AT THE MAGISTRATE'S RESIDENCE...
KEEP THOSE ROPES TAUT! DON'T LET HIM GET LOOSE!
TAKE HIM TO THE SHIRASU <WHITE SAND OF JUDGMENT>!
ARR--!
HRAH!
THUD!
YORIKI MASUDA--WHAT IS THE MEANING OF THIS?
HAS A PRISONER CONFESSED?
WE HAVE CAPTURED THE THIEF PLAGUING THE TOWN! HE IS A MUTE, BUT WE HAVE THE EVIDENCE NEEDED TO CONVICT HIM!
GOOD WORK, YORIKI. I HAD CONCERNS ABOUT YOUR ABILITY TO PUT AN END TO THIS CRIME WAVE, BUT NOW YOU HAVE PROVEN YOURSELF!
THANK YOU, MAGISTRATE!
WITH THE EVIDENCE OF THESE STOLEN KINCHAKU THAT WERE FOUND ON HIM, THE MANDATORY SENTENCE IS HANDED DOWN UPON THE CRIMINAL...
...DEATH!
HUH?!

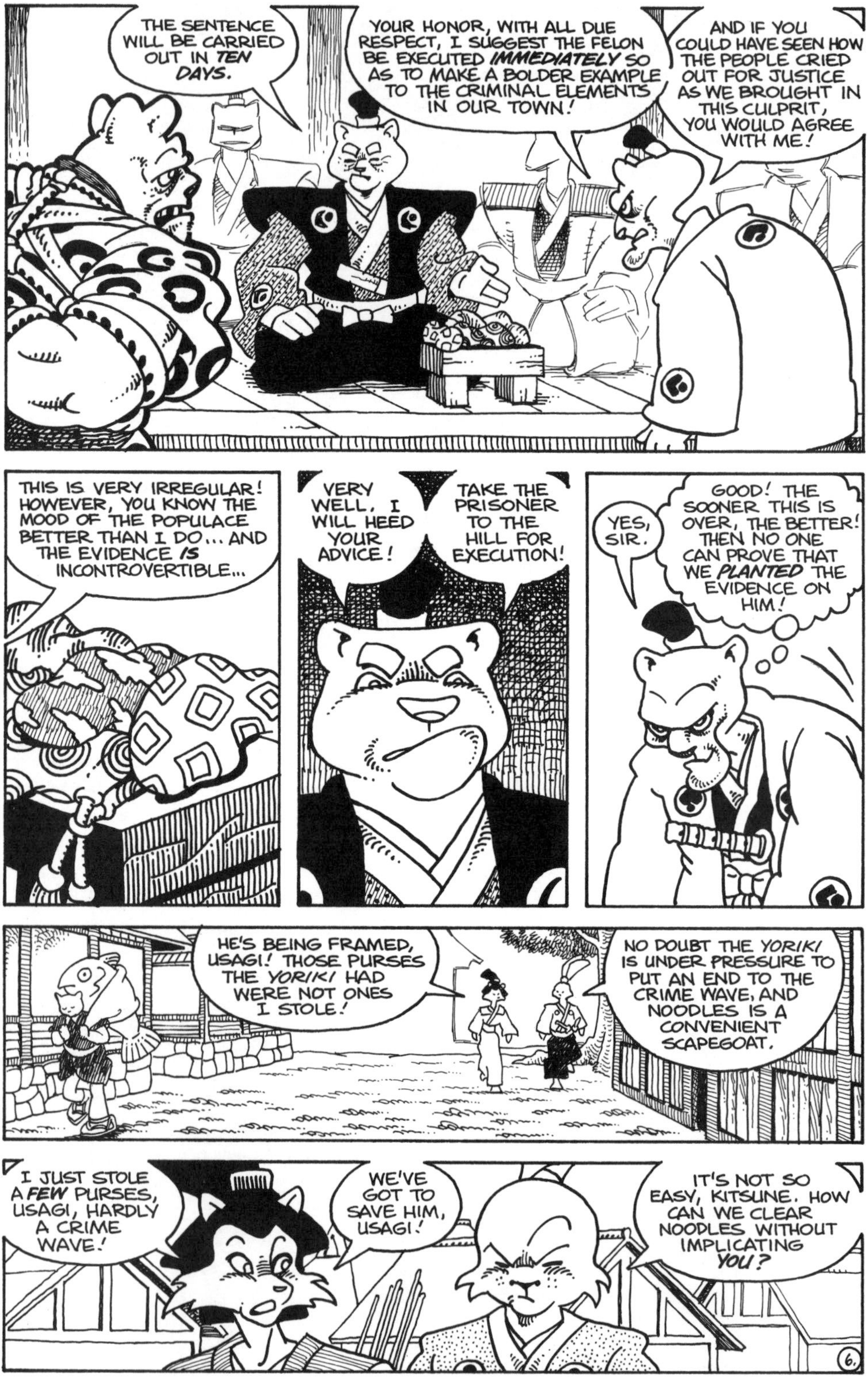
THE SENTENCE WILL BE CARRIED OUT IN TEN DAYS.
YOUR HONOR, WITH ALL DUE RESPECT, I SUGGEST THE FELON BE EXECUTED IMMEDIATELY SO AS TO MAKE A BOLDER EXAMPLE TO THE CRIMINAL ELEMENTS IN OUR TOWN!
AND IF YOU COULD HAVE SEEN HOW THE PEOPLE CRIED OUT FOR JUSTICE AS WE BROUGHT IN THIS CULPRIT, YOU WOULD AGREE WITH ME!
THIS IS VERY IRREGULAR! HOWEVER, YOU KNOW THE MOOD OF THE POPULACE BETTER THAN I DO... AND THE EVIDENCE IS INCONTROVERTIBLE...
VERY WELL, I WILL HEED YOUR ADVICE!
TAKE THE PRISONER TO THE HILL FOR EXECUTION!
YES, SIR.
GOOD! THE SOONER THIS IS OVER, THE BETTER! THEN NO ONE CAN PROVE THAT WE PLANTED THE EVIDENCE ON HIM!
HE'S BEING FRAMED, USAGI! THOSE PURSES THE YORIKI HAD WERE NOT ONES I STOLE!
NO DOUBT THE YORIKI IS UNDER PRESSURE TO PUT AN END TO THE CRIME WAVE, AND NOODLES IS A CONVENIENT SCAPEGOAT.
I JUST STOLE A FEW PURSES, USAGI, HARDLY A CRIME WAVE!
WE'VE GOT TO SAVE HIM, USAGI!
IT'S NOT SO EASY, KITSUNE. HOW CAN WE CLEAR NOODLES WITHOUT IMPLICATING YOU?
6.

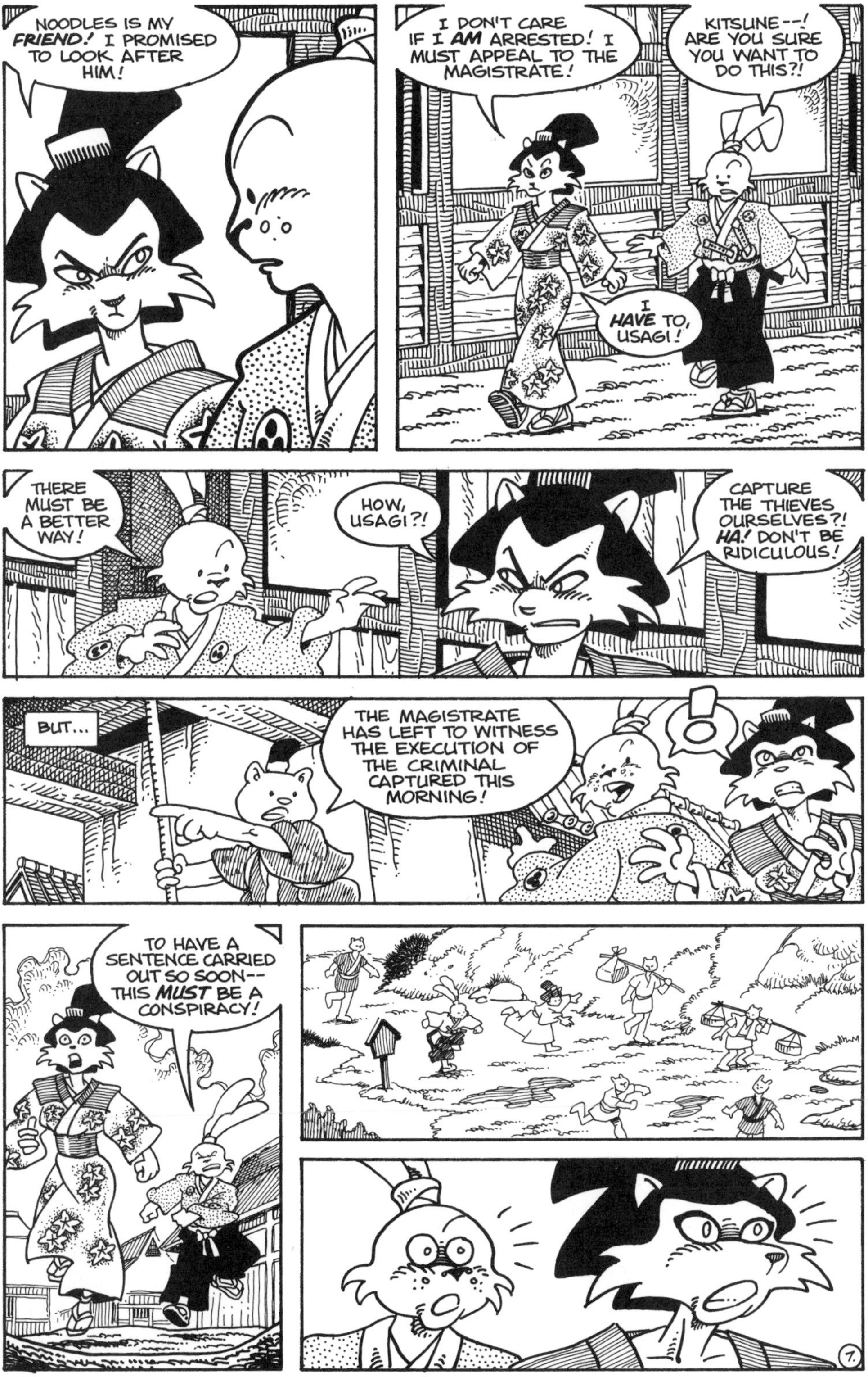
NOODLES IS MY FRIEND! I PROMISED TO LOOK AFTER HIM!
I DON'T CARE IF I AM ARRESTED! I MUST APPEAL TO THE MAGISTRATE!
KITSUNE--! ARE YOU SURE YOU WANT TO DO THIS?!
I HAVE TO, USAGI!
THERE MUST BE A BETTER WAY!
HOW, USAGI?!
CAPTURE THE THIEVES OURSELVES?! HA! DON'T BE RIDICULOUS!
BUT...
THE MAGISTRATE HAS LEFT TO WITNESS THE EXECUTION OF THE CRIMINAL CAPTURED THIS MORNING!
!
TO HAVE A SENTENCE CARRIED OUT SO SOON-- THIS MUST BE A CONSPIRACY!
7.

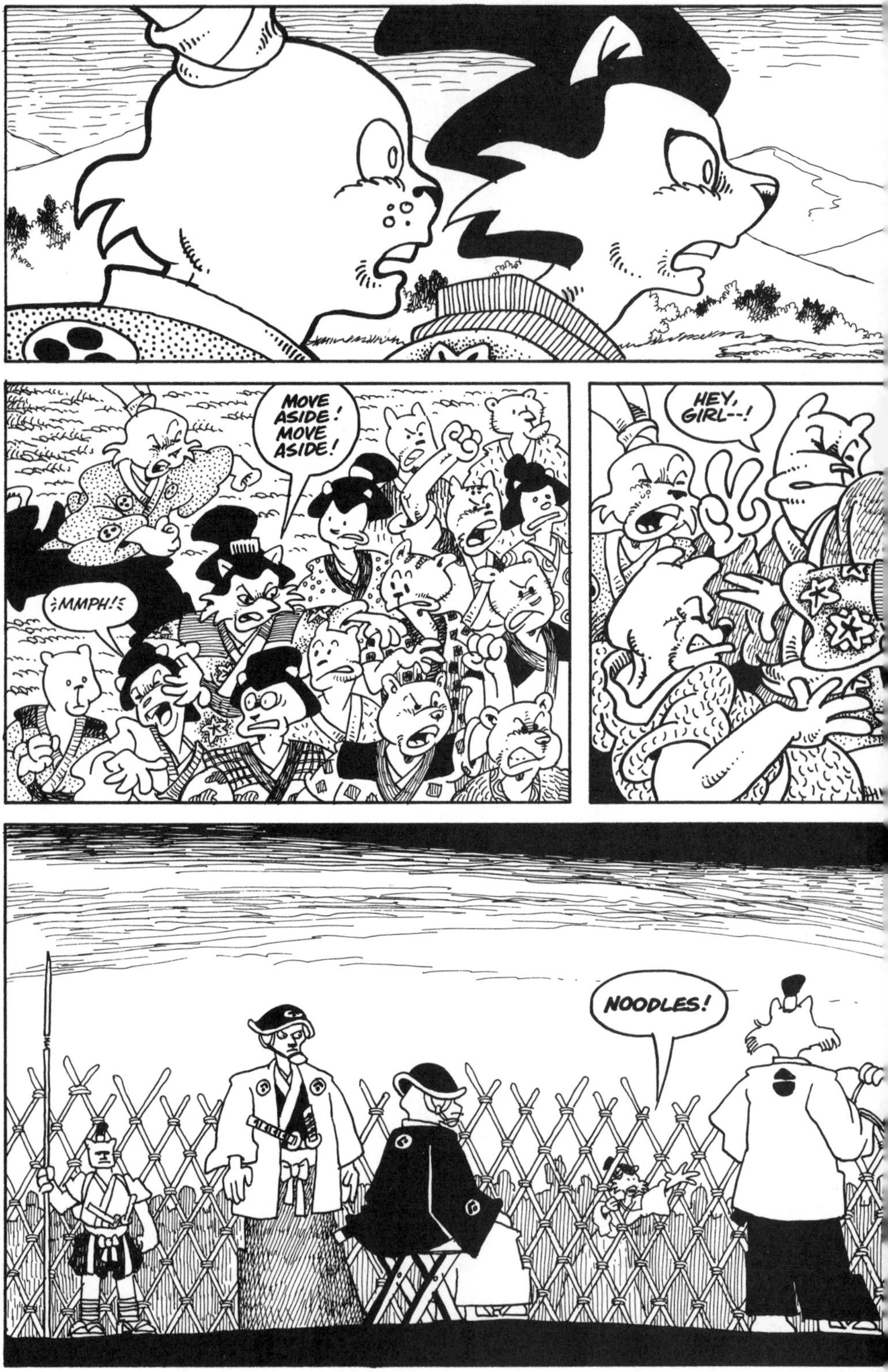
MOVE ASIDE! MOVE ASIDE!
MMPH!
HEY, GIRL--!
NOODLES!

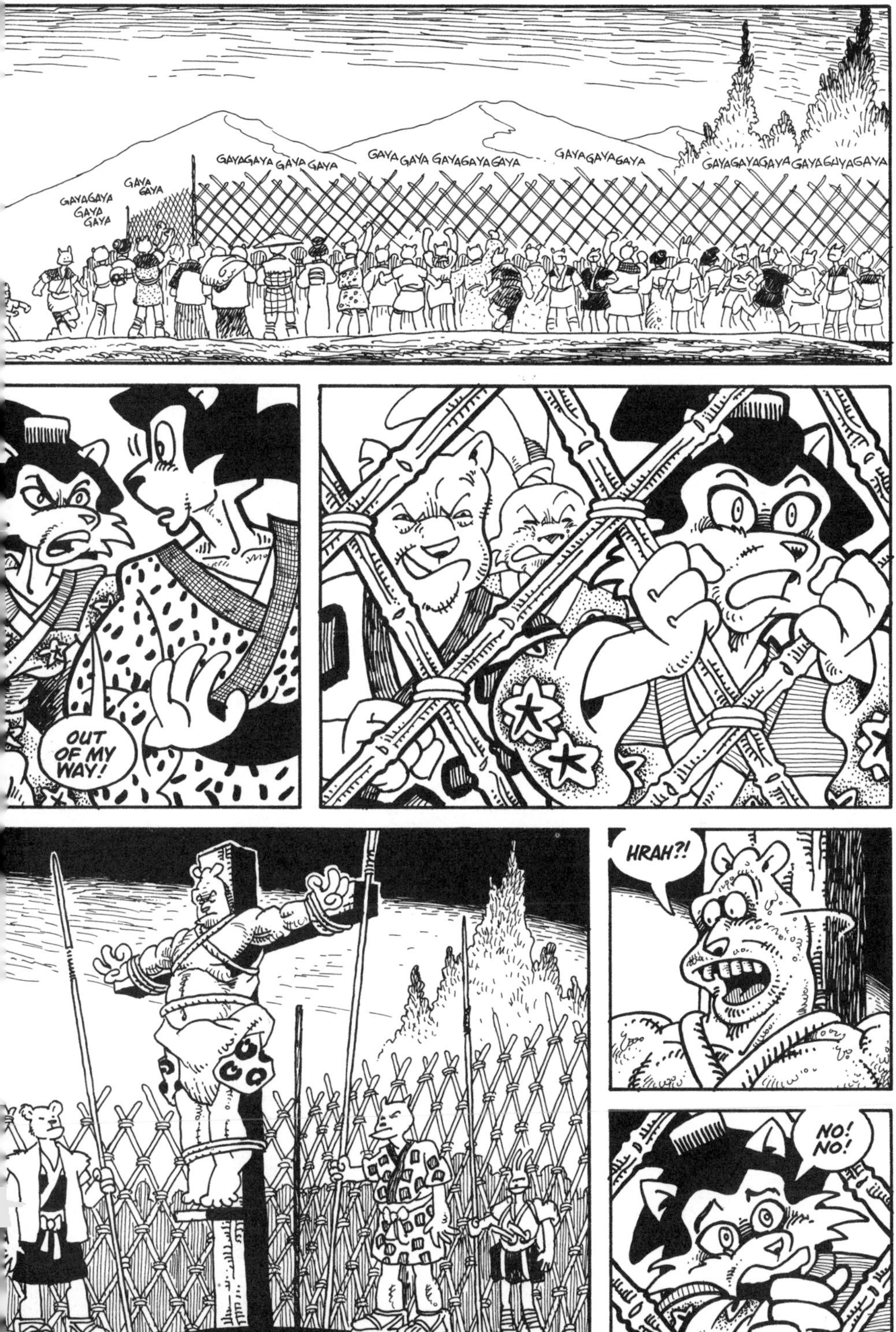
GAYAGAYA GAYA GAYA
GAYA GAYA
GAYAGAYA GAYA GAYA
GAYA GAYA GAYAGAYAGAYA
GAYAGAYAGAYA
GAYAGAYAGAYA GAYAGAYAGAYA
OUT OF MY WAY!
HRAH?!
NO! NO!
9.

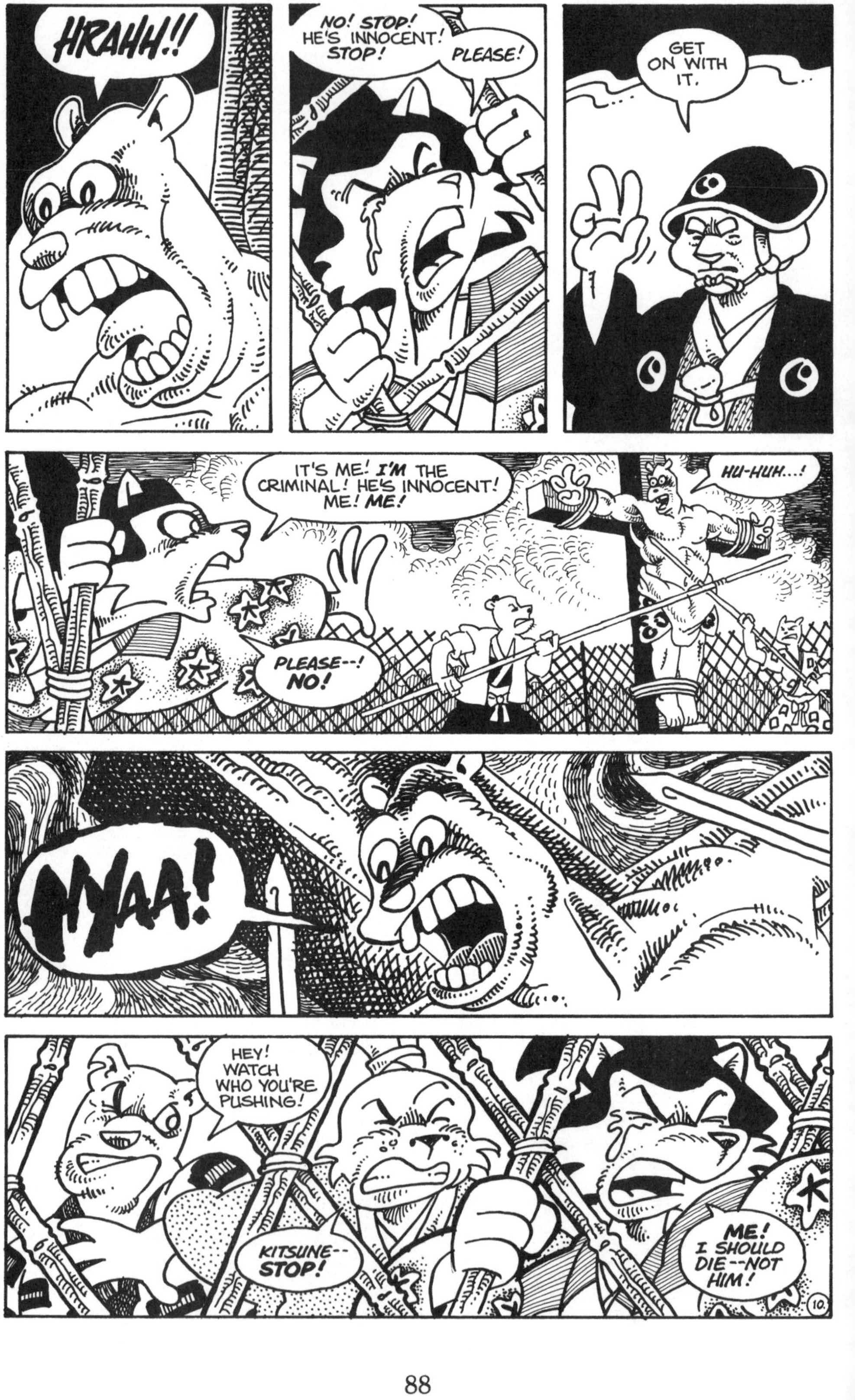
HRAHH!!
NO! STOP! HE'S INNOCENT! STOP!
PLEASE!
GET ON WITH IT.
IT'S ME! I'M THE CRIMINAL! HE'S INNOCENT! ME! ME!
HU-HUH...!
PLEASE--! NO!
HYAA!
HEY! WATCH WHO YOU'RE PUSHING!
KITSUNE-- STOP!
ME! I SHOULD DIE--NOT HIM!
10.

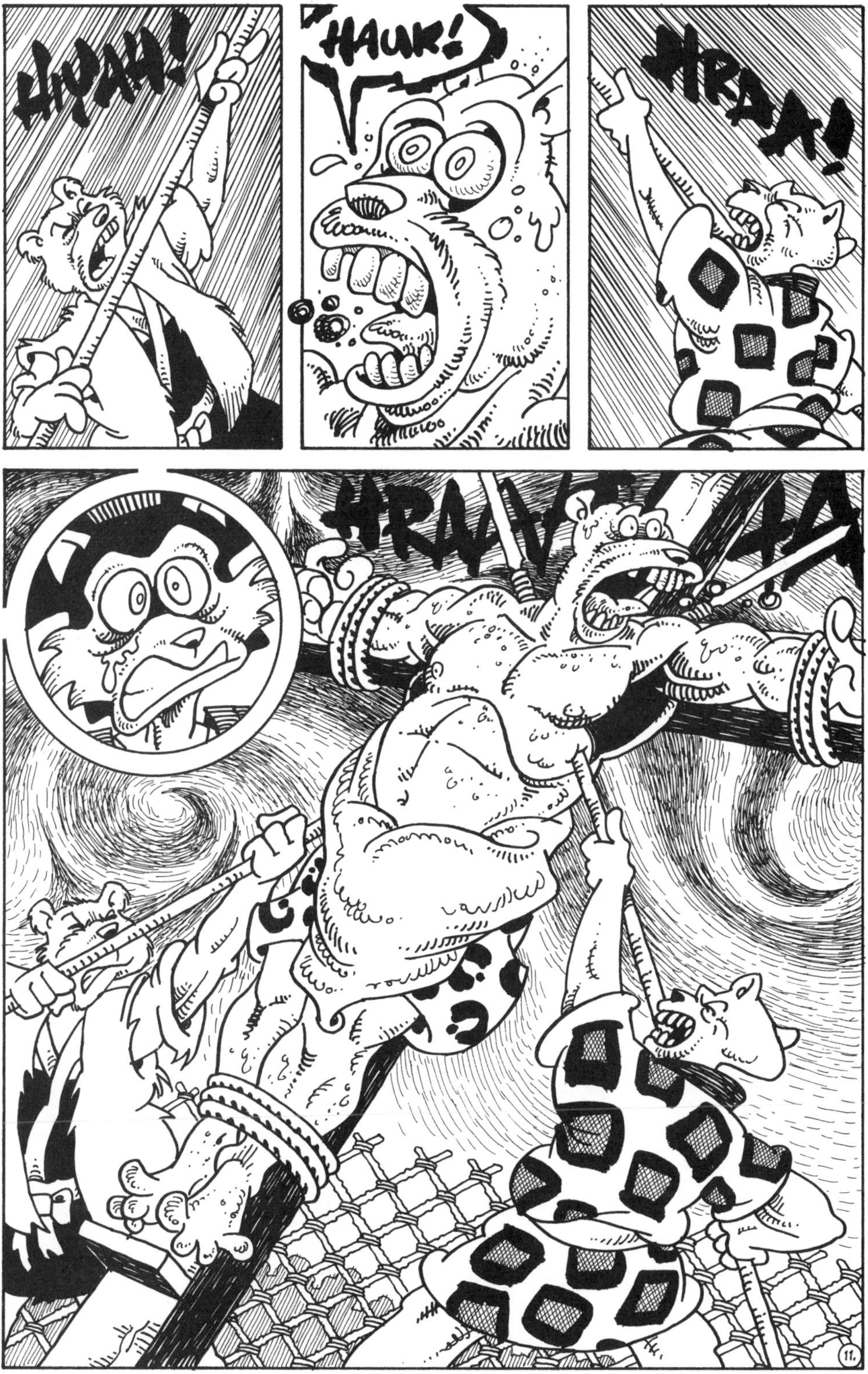
HIYAH!
HAUK!
HRAA!
11.

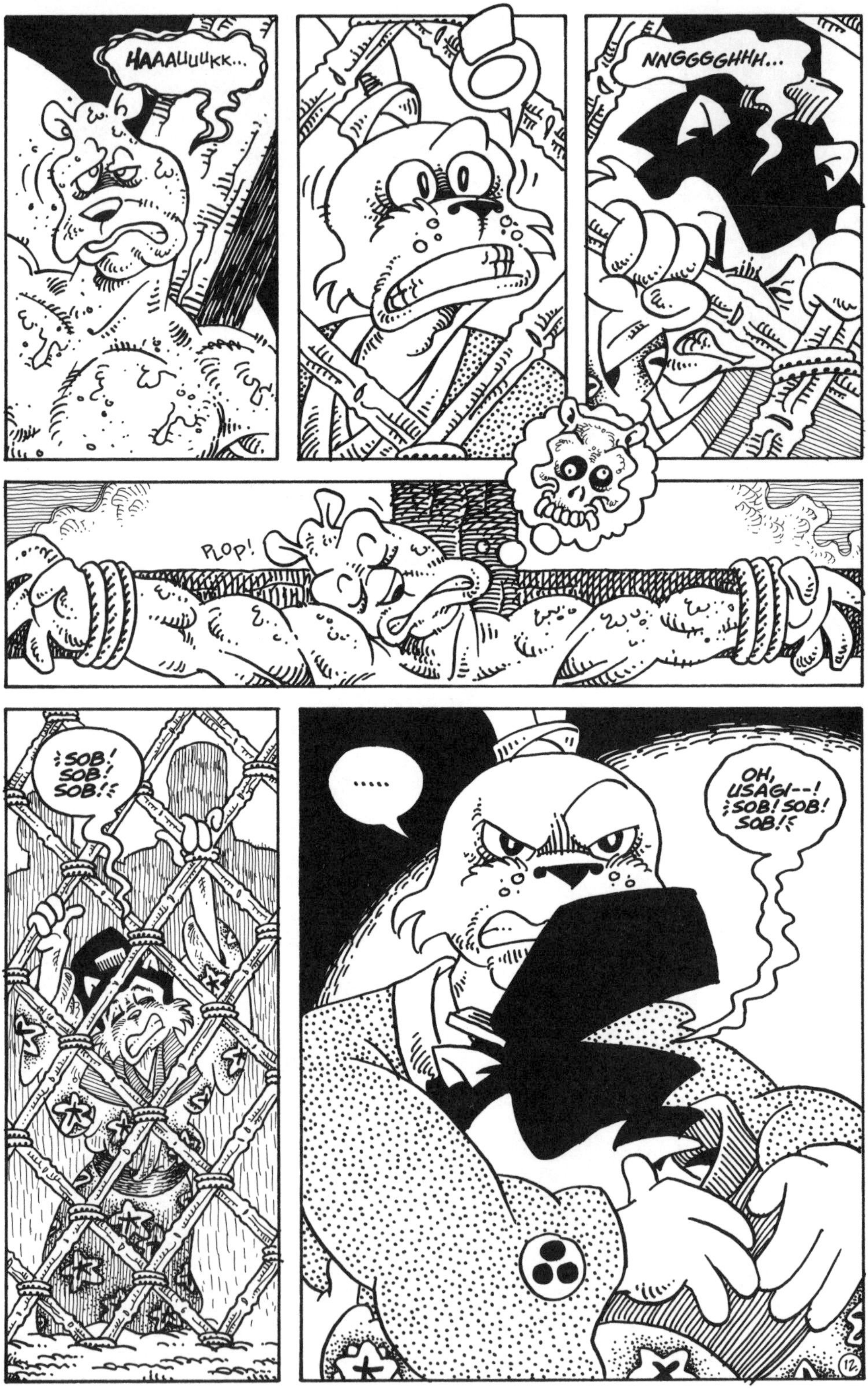
HAAAUUUKK...
NNGGGGHHH...
PLOP!
SOB! SOB! SOB!
.....
OH, USAGI--! SOB! SOB! SOB!
12.

...IT'S GETTING LATE. WE HAD BEST BE GOING.

HE TRUSTED ME, USAGI, AND I DIDN'T SAVE HIM...

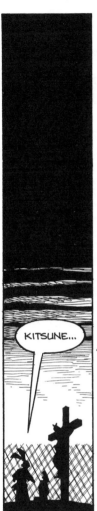

KITSUNE...

THAT RONIN IS STILL THERE! WHAT IS HIS INTEREST IN A COMMON SOBA SELLER?

HE'S GOING TO BE TROUBLE--I KNOW IT!

IF HE WEREN'T SUCH A SKILLED SWORDSMAN--

...I DIDN'T SAVE HIM.

HEY, PARTNER!

EH--?!

WHAT ARE YOU DOING HERE?! IF THE MAGISTRATE SAW ME TALKING TO YOU GAMBLERS--

HA! DON'T WORRY, PAL!

WE'LL MAKE THIS SHORT!

13.

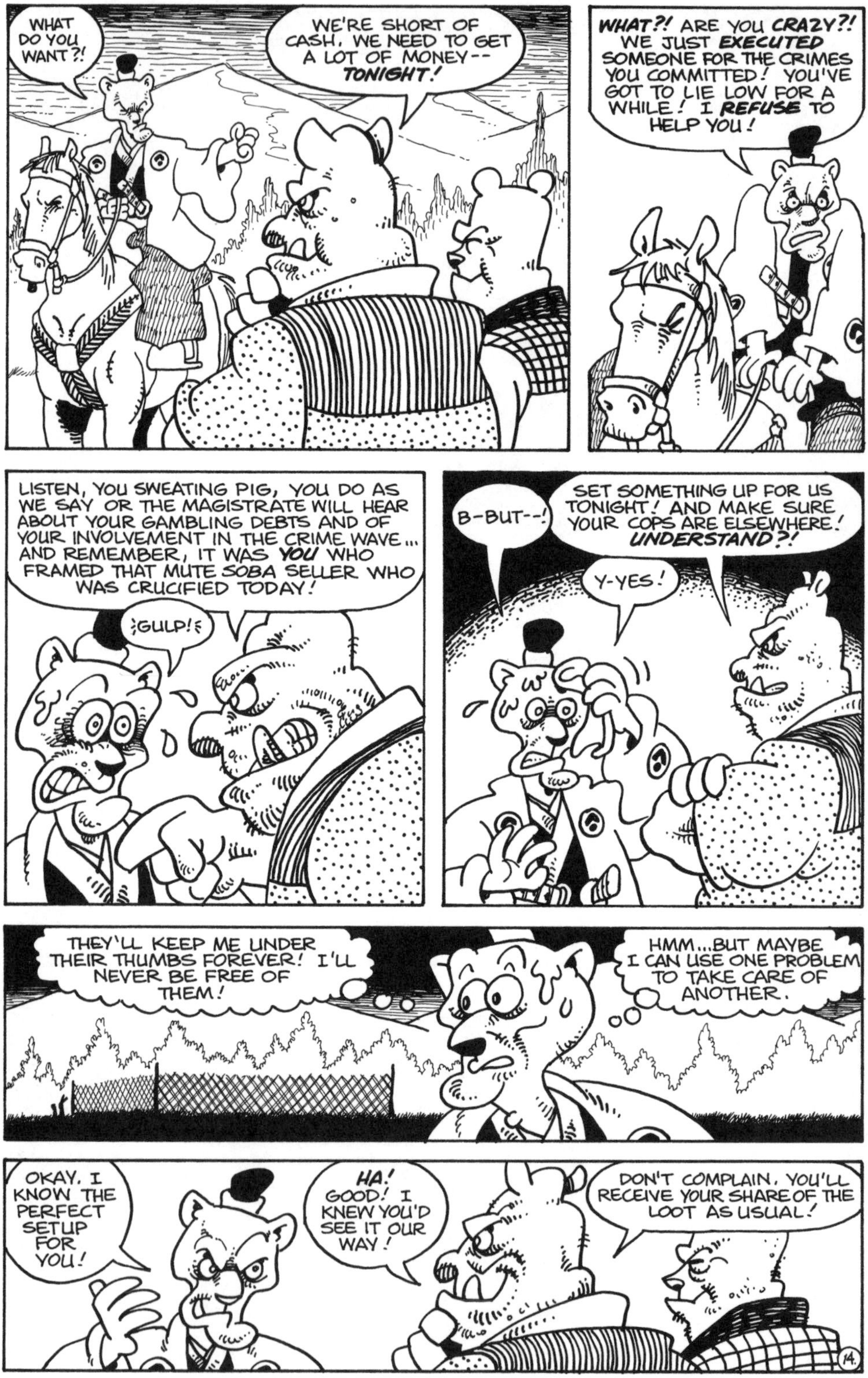
WHAT DO YOU WANT?!
WE'RE SHORT OF CASH. WE NEED TO GET A LOT OF MONEY-- TONIGHT!
WHAT?! ARE YOU CRAZY?! WE JUST EXECUTED SOMEONE FOR THE CRIMES YOU COMMITTED! YOU'VE GOT TO LIE LOW FOR A WHILE! I REFUSE TO HELP YOU!
LISTEN, YOU SWEATING PIG, YOU DO AS WE SAY OR THE MAGISTRATE WILL HEAR ABOUT YOUR GAMBLING DEBTS AND OF YOUR INVOLVEMENT IN THE CRIME WAVE... AND REMEMBER, IT WAS YOU WHO FRAMED THAT MUTE SOBA SELLER WHO WAS CRUCIFIED TODAY!
GULP!
B-BUT--!
SET SOMETHING UP FOR US TONIGHT! AND MAKE SURE YOUR COPS ARE ELSEWHERE! UNDERSTAND?!
Y-YES!
THEY'LL KEEP ME UNDER THEIR THUMBS FOREVER! I'LL NEVER BE FREE OF THEM!
HMM...BUT MAYBE I CAN USE ONE PROBLEM TO TAKE CARE OF ANOTHER.
OKAY. I KNOW THE PERFECT SETUP FOR YOU!
HA! GOOD! I KNEW YOU'D SEE IT OUR WAY!
DON'T COMPLAIN. YOU'LL RECEIVE YOUR SHARE OF THE LOOT AS USUAL!
14.

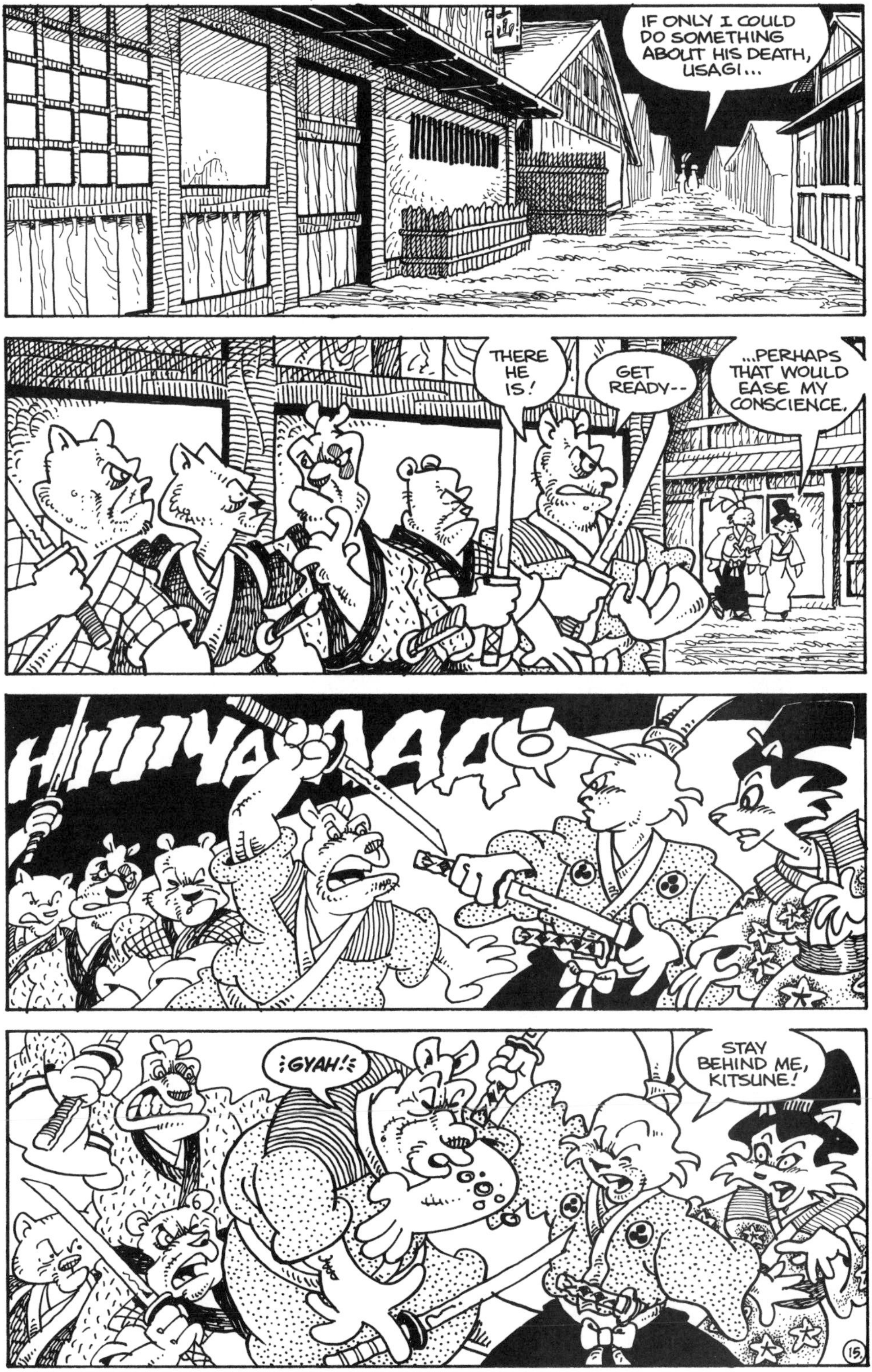
IF ONLY I COULD DO SOMETHING ABOUT HIS DEATH, USAGI...
THERE HE IS!
GET READY--
...PERHAPS THAT WOULD EASE MY CONSCIENCE.
HIIIYAAAA!
GYAH!
STAY BEHIND ME, KITSUNE!
15

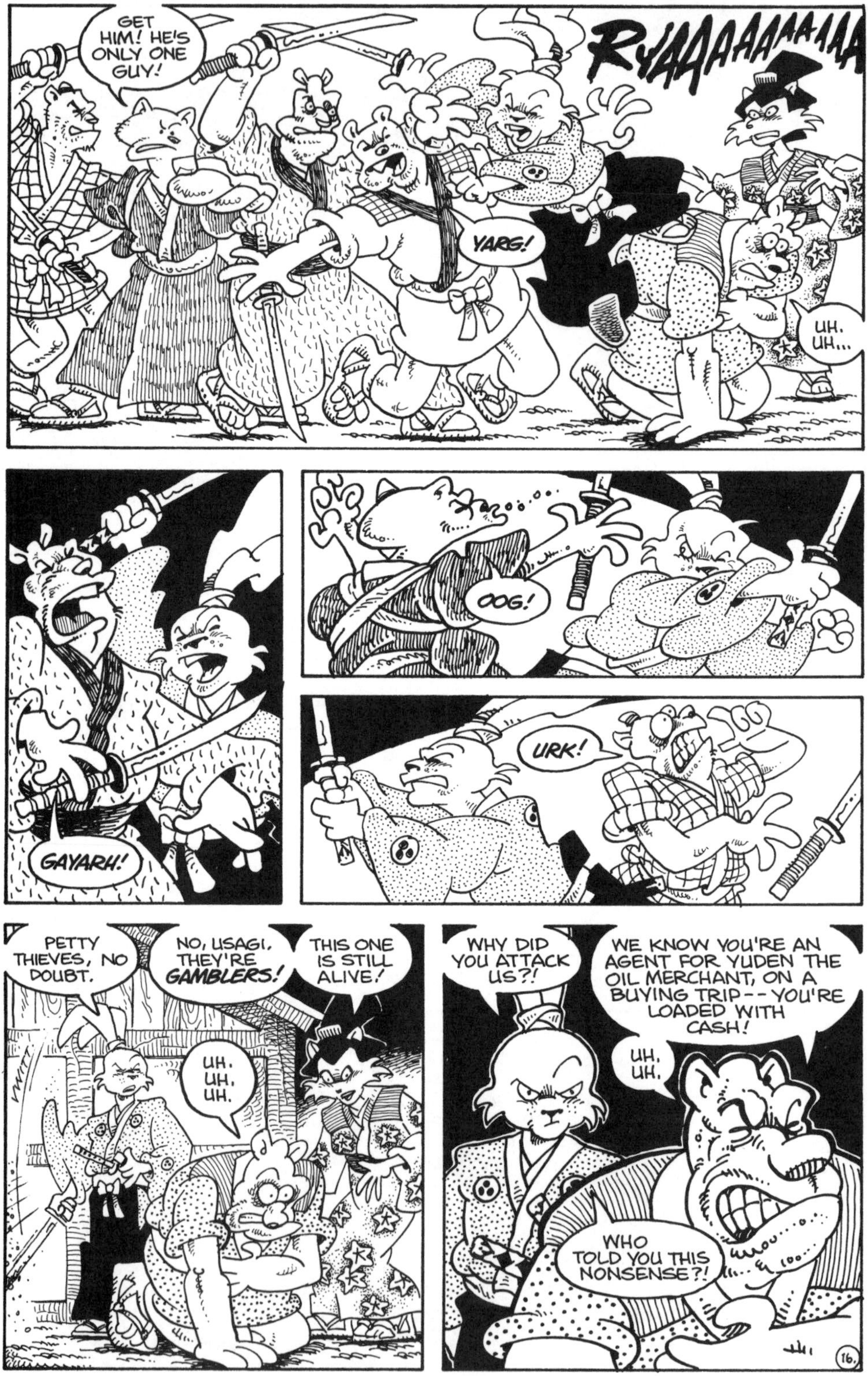
GET HIM! HE'S ONLY ONE GUY!
RYAAAAAAAAAA
YARG!
UH. UH...
GAYARH!
OOG!
URK!
PETTY THIEVES, NO DOUBT.
NO, USAGI. THEY'RE GAMBLERS!
THIS ONE IS STILL ALIVE!
UH. UH. UH.
WHY DID YOU ATTACK US?!
WE KNOW YOU'RE AN AGENT FOR YUDEN THE OIL MERCHANT, ON A BUYING TRIP-- YOU'RE LOADED WITH CASH!
UH. UH.
WHO TOLD YOU THIS NONSENSE?!
16.

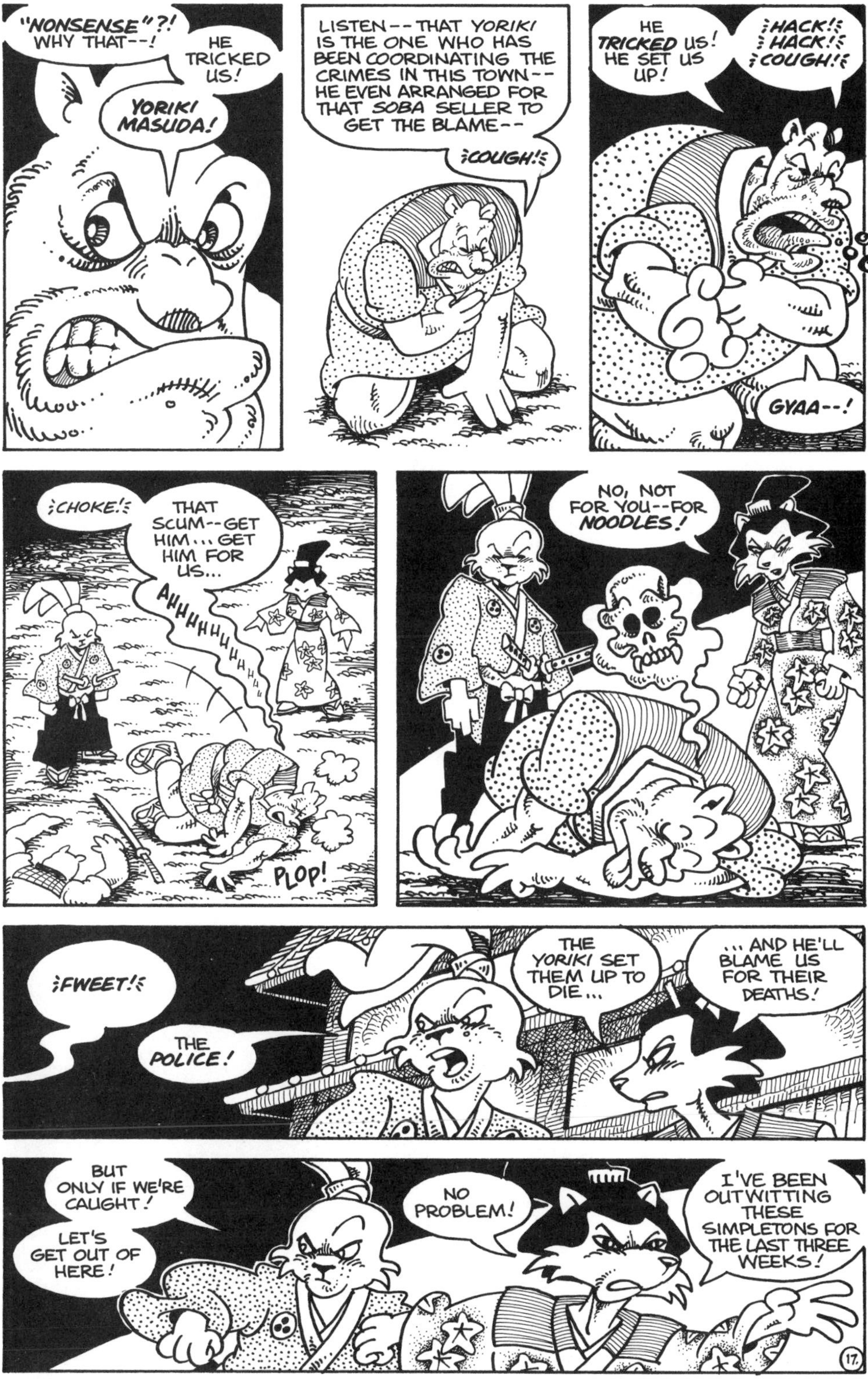
"NONSENSE"?! WHY THAT--!
HE TRICKED US!
YORIKI MASUDA!
LISTEN--THAT YORIKI IS THE ONE WHO HAS BEEN COORDINATING THE CRIMES IN THIS TOWN--HE EVEN ARRANGED FOR THAT SOBA SELLER TO GET THE BLAME--
COUGH!
HE TRICKED US! HE SET US UP!
HACK! HACK! COUGH!
GYAA--!
CHOKE!
THAT SCUM--GET HIM... GET HIM FOR US...
AHHHHHHHHHHHH
PLOP!
NO, NOT FOR YOU--FOR NOODLES!
FWEET!
THE POLICE!
THE YORIKI SET THEM UP TO DIE...
...AND HE'LL BLAME US FOR THEIR DEATHS!
BUT ONLY IF WE'RE CAUGHT!
LET'S GET OUT OF HERE!
NO PROBLEM!
I'VE BEEN OUTWITTING THESE SIMPLETONS FOR THE LAST THREE WEEKS!
17

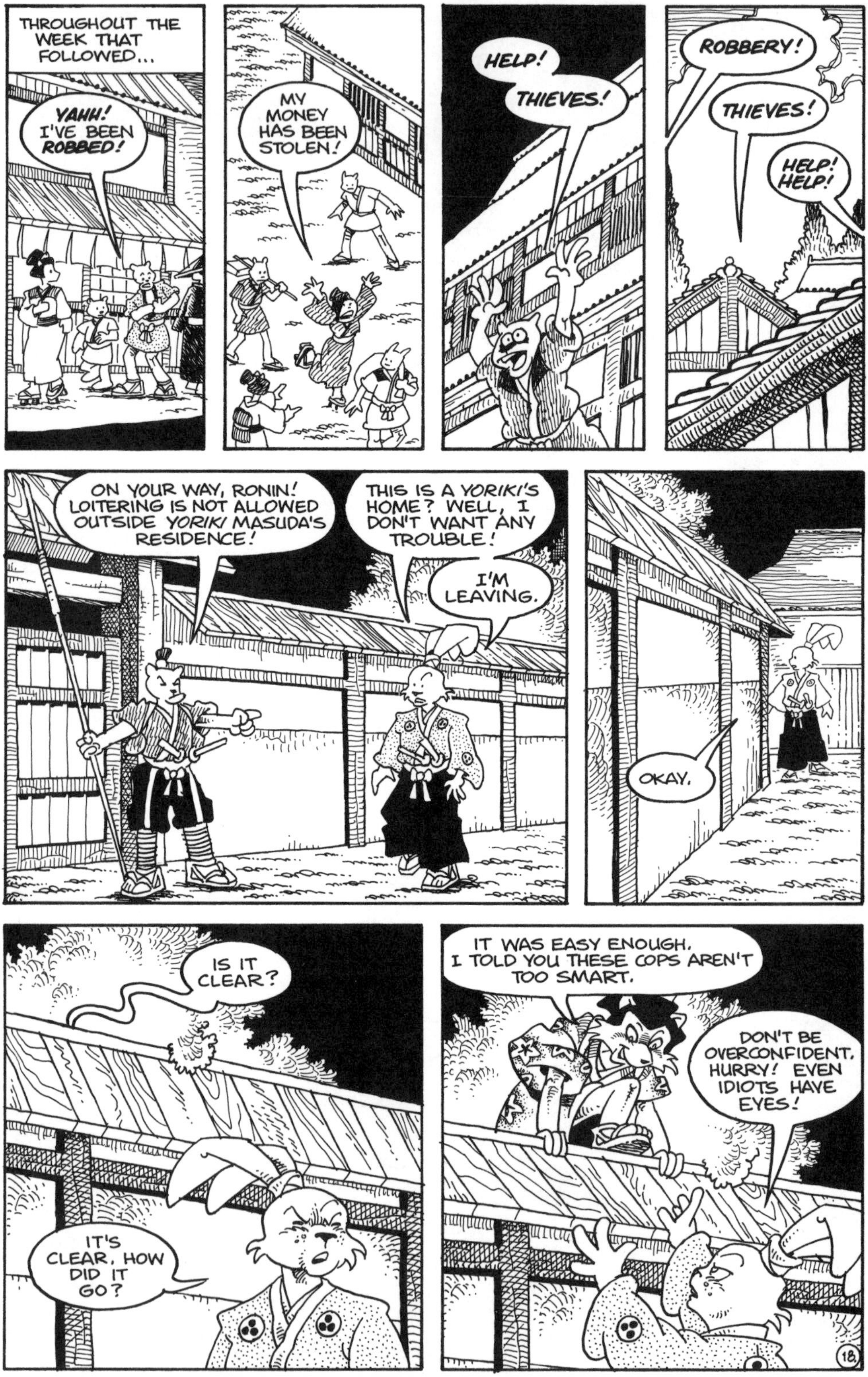
THROUGHOUT THE WEEK THAT FOLLOWED...
YAHH! I'VE BEEN ROBBED!
MY MONEY HAS BEEN STOLEN!
HELP!
THIEVES!
ROBBERY!
THIEVES!
HELP! HELP!
ON YOUR WAY, RONIN! LOITERING IS NOT ALLOWED OUTSIDE YORIKI MASUDA'S RESIDENCE!
THIS IS A YORIKI'S HOME? WELL, I DON'T WANT ANY TROUBLE!
I'M LEAVING.
OKAY.
IS IT CLEAR?
IT'S CLEAR, HOW DID IT GO?
IT WAS EASY ENOUGH. I TOLD YOU THESE COPS AREN'T TOO SMART.
DON'T BE OVERCONFIDENT. HURRY! EVEN IDIOTS HAVE EYES!
18

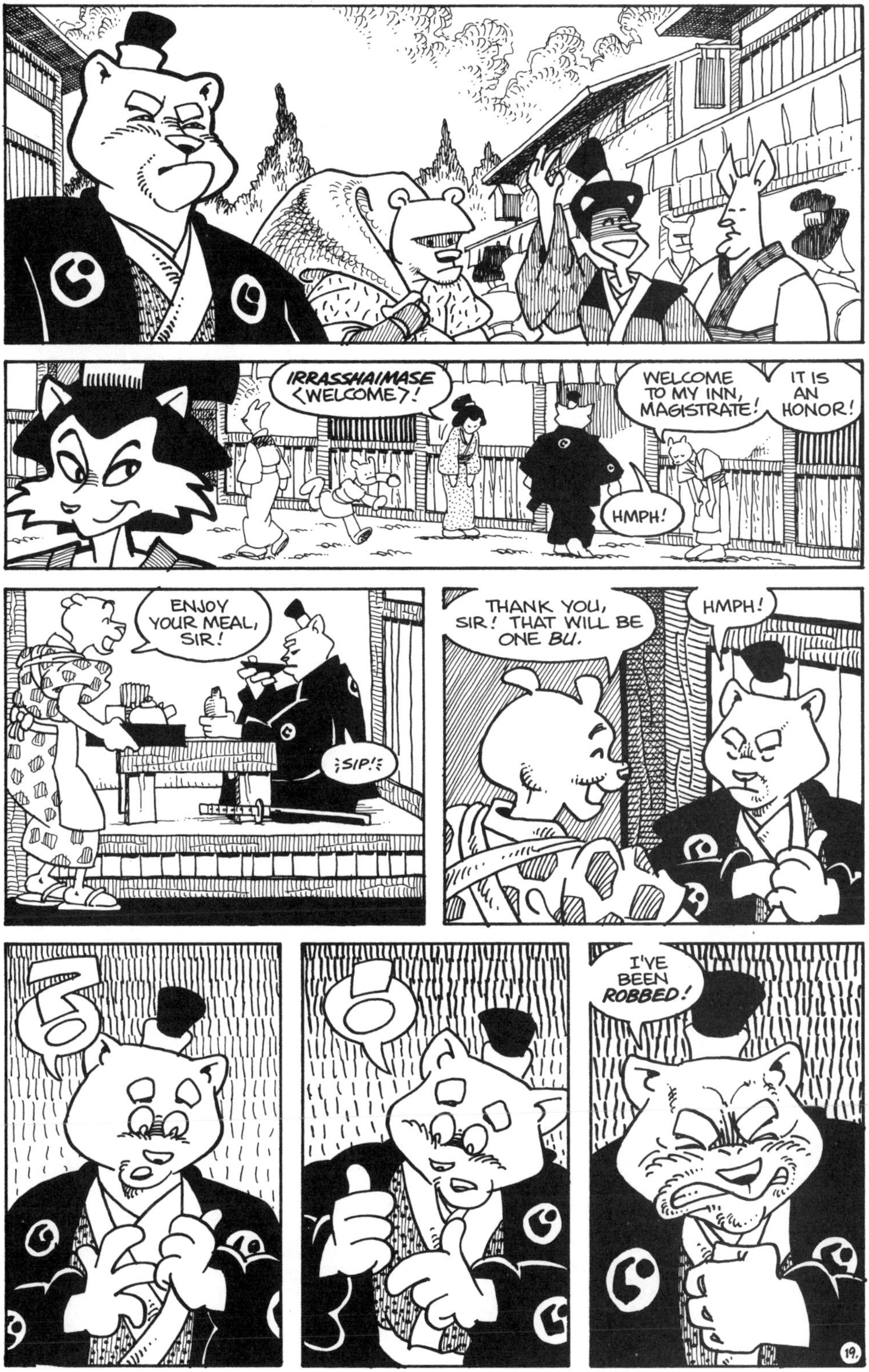
IRRASSHAIMASE <WELCOME>!
WELCOME TO MY INN, MAGISTRATE!
IT IS AN HONOR!
HMPH!
ENJOY YOUR MEAL, SIR!
SIP!
THANK YOU, SIR! THAT WILL BE ONE BU.
HMPH!
I'VE BEEN ROBBED!
19

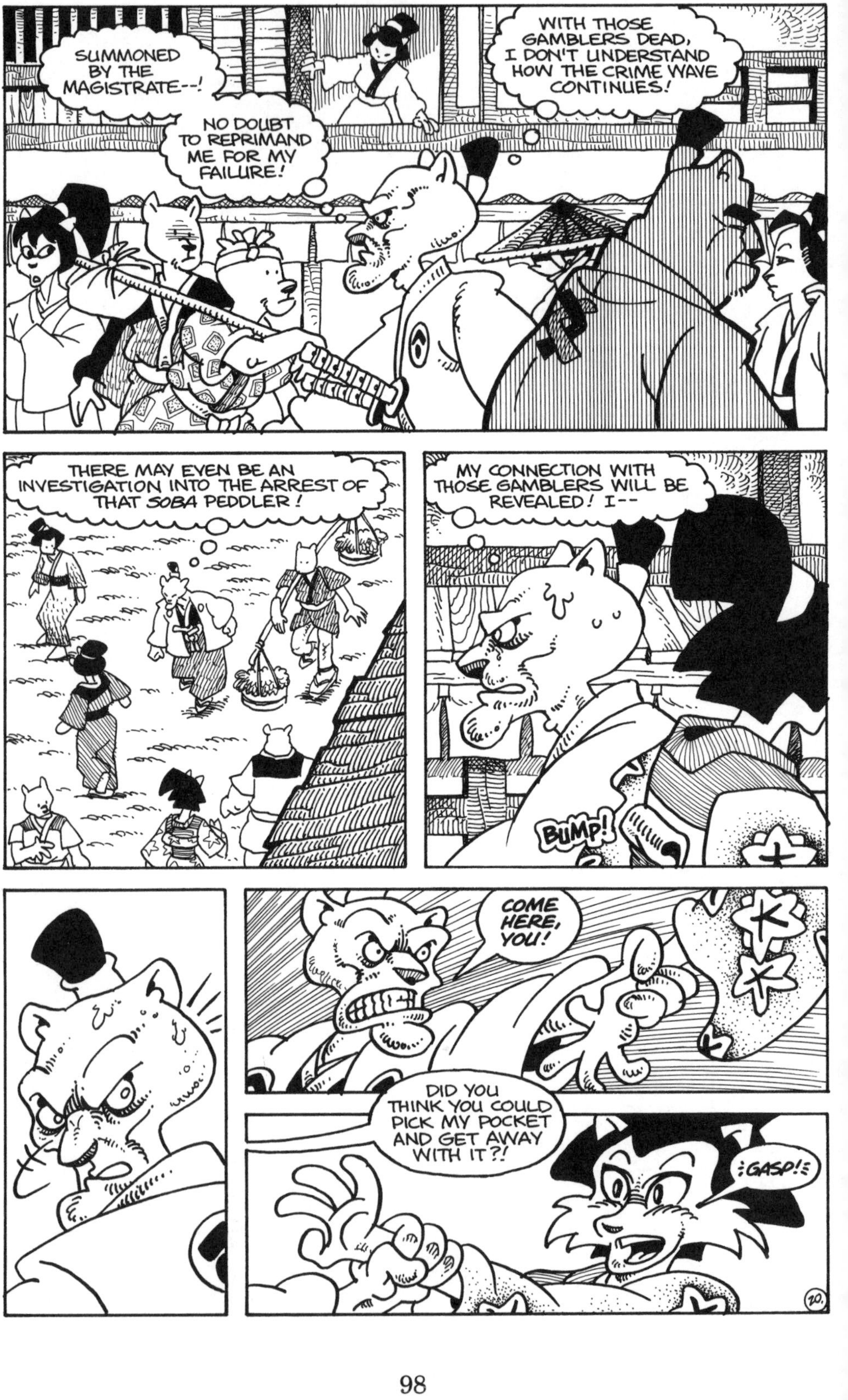
SUMMONED BY THE MAGISTRATE--!
NO DOUBT TO REPRIMAND ME FOR MY FAILURE!
WITH THOSE GAMBLERS DEAD, I DON'T UNDERSTAND HOW THE CRIME WAVE CONTINUES!
THERE MAY EVEN BE AN INVESTIGATION INTO THE ARREST OF THAT SOBA PEDDLER!
MY CONNECTION WITH THOSE GAMBLERS WILL BE REVEALED! I--
BUMP!
COME HERE, YOU!
DID YOU THINK YOU COULD PICK MY POCKET AND GET AWAY WITH IT?!
GASP!
20.

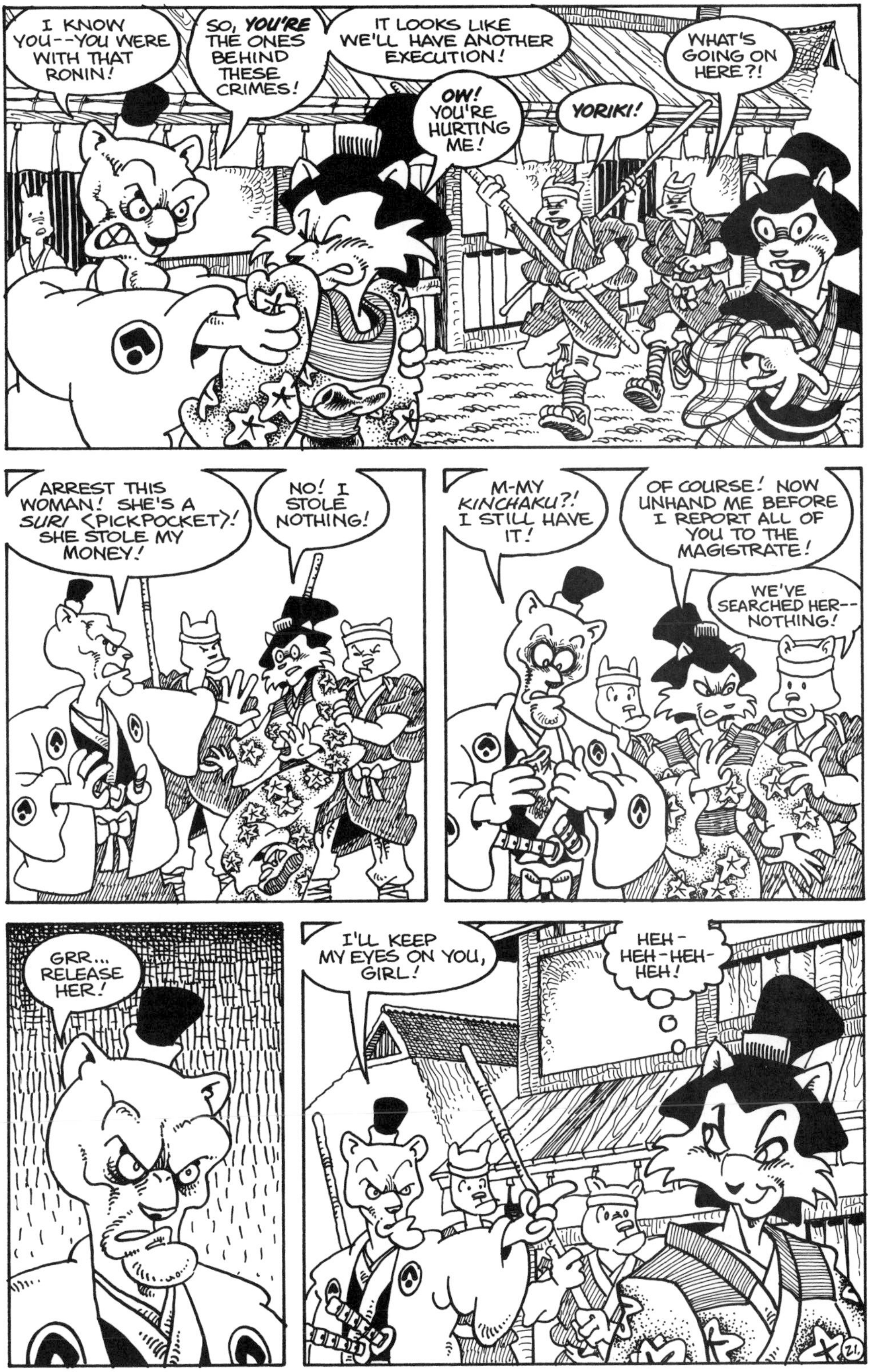

I KNOW YOU--YOU WERE WITH THAT RONIN!
SO, *YOU'RE* THE ONES BEHIND THESE CRIMES!
IT LOOKS LIKE WE'LL HAVE ANOTHER EXECUTION!
OW! YOU'RE HURTING ME!
YORIKI!
WHAT'S GOING ON HERE?!
ARREST THIS WOMAN! SHE'S A *SURI* <PICKPOCKET>! SHE STOLE MY MONEY!
NO! I STOLE NOTHING!
M-MY *KINCHAKU*?! I STILL HAVE IT!
OF COURSE! NOW UNHAND ME BEFORE I REPORT ALL OF YOU TO THE MAGISTRATE!
WE'VE SEARCHED HER-- NOTHING!
GRR... RELEASE HER!
I'LL KEEP MY EYES ON YOU, GIRL!
HEH-HEH-HEH-HEH!
21.

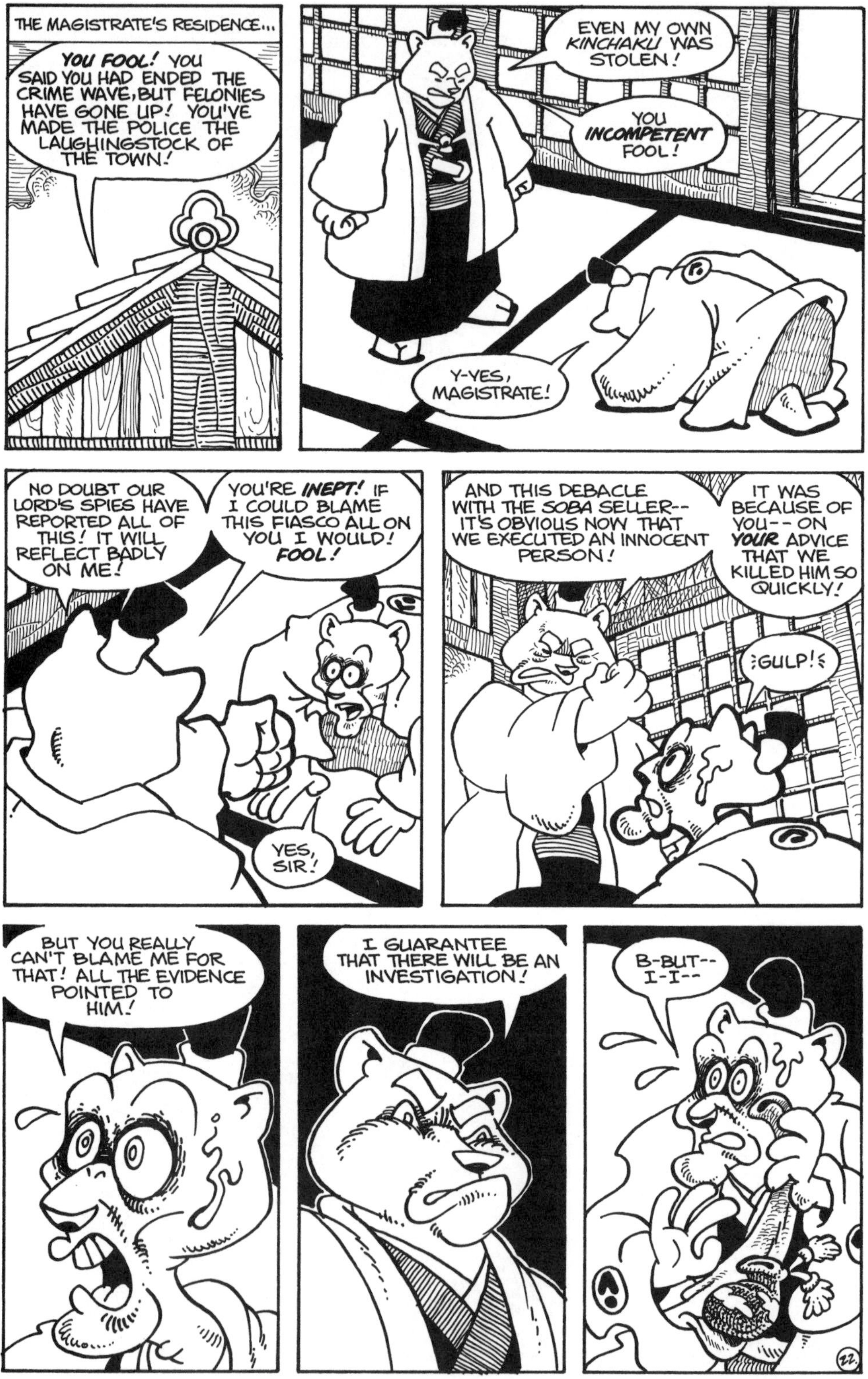

THE MAGISTRATE'S RESIDENCE...
YOU FOOL! YOU SAID YOU HAD ENDED THE CRIME WAVE, BUT FELONIES HAVE GONE UP! YOU'VE MADE THE POLICE THE LAUGHINGSTOCK OF THE TOWN!
EVEN MY OWN KINCHAKU WAS STOLEN!
YOU INCOMPETENT FOOL!
Y-YES, MAGISTRATE!
NO DOUBT OUR LORD'S SPIES HAVE REPORTED ALL OF THIS! IT WILL REFLECT BADLY ON ME!
YOU'RE INEPT! IF I COULD BLAME THIS FIASCO ALL ON YOU I WOULD! FOOL!
YES, SIR!
AND THIS DEBACLE WITH THE SOBA SELLER-- IT'S OBVIOUS NOW THAT WE EXECUTED AN INNOCENT PERSON!
IT WAS BECAUSE OF YOU-- ON YOUR ADVICE THAT WE KILLED HIM SO QUICKLY!
GULP!
BUT YOU REALLY CAN'T BLAME ME FOR THAT! ALL THE EVIDENCE POINTED TO HIM!
I GUARANTEE THAT THERE WILL BE AN INVESTIGATION!
B-BUT-- I-I--
22.

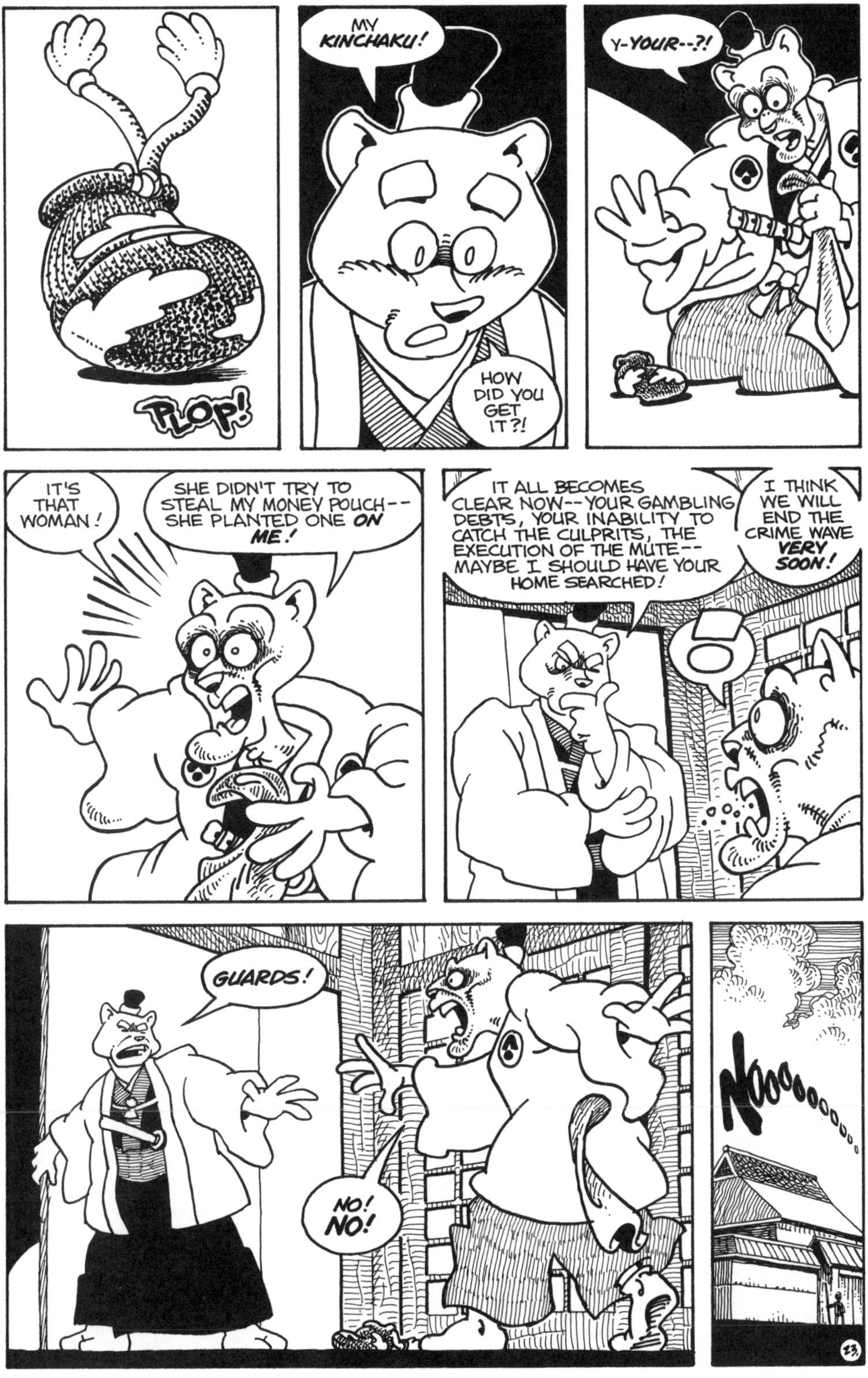
PLOP!
MY KINCHAKU!
HOW DID YOU GET IT?!
Y-YOUR--?!
IT'S THAT WOMAN!
SHE DIDN'T TRY TO STEAL MY MONEY POUCH-- SHE PLANTED ONE ON ME!
IT ALL BECOMES CLEAR NOW--YOUR GAMBLING DEBTS, YOUR INABILITY TO CATCH THE CULPRITS, THE EXECUTION OF THE MUTE-- MAYBE I SHOULD HAVE YOUR HOME SEARCHED!
I THINK WE WILL END THE CRIME WAVE VERY SOON!
GUARDS!
NO! NO!
NOOOOOOOOO
23

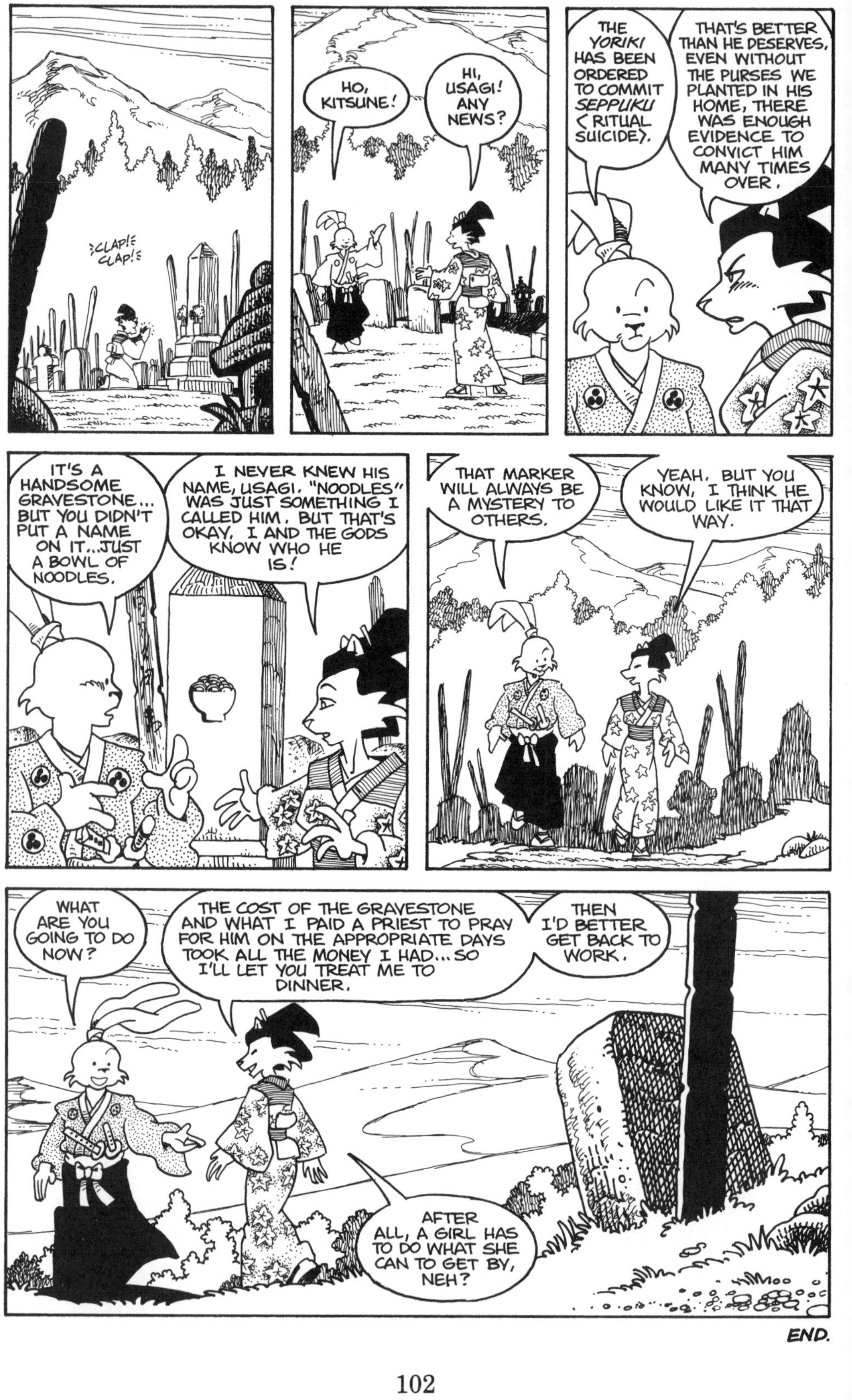
CLAP! CLAP!
HO, KITSUNE!
HI, USAGI! ANY NEWS?
THE *YORIKI* HAS BEEN ORDERED TO COMMIT *SEPPUKU* <RITUAL SUICIDE>.
THAT'S BETTER THAN HE DESERVES. EVEN WITHOUT THE PURSES WE PLANTED IN HIS HOME, THERE WAS ENOUGH EVIDENCE TO CONVICT HIM MANY TIMES OVER.
IT'S A HANDSOME GRAVESTONE... BUT YOU DIDN'T PUT A NAME ON IT...JUST A BOWL OF NOODLES.
I NEVER KNEW HIS NAME, USAGI. "NOODLES" WAS JUST SOMETHING I CALLED HIM. BUT THAT'S OKAY. I AND THE GODS KNOW WHO HE IS!
THAT MARKER WILL ALWAYS BE A MYSTERY TO OTHERS.
YEAH. BUT YOU KNOW, I THINK HE WOULD LIKE IT THAT WAY.
WHAT ARE YOU GOING TO DO NOW?
THE COST OF THE GRAVESTONE AND WHAT I PAID A PRIEST TO PRAY FOR HIM ON THE APPROPRIATE DAYS TOOK ALL THE MONEY I HAD...SO I'LL LET YOU TREAT ME TO DINNER.
THEN I'D BETTER GET BACK TO WORK.
AFTER ALL, A GIRL HAS TO DO WHAT SHE CAN TO GET BY, NEH?

END.

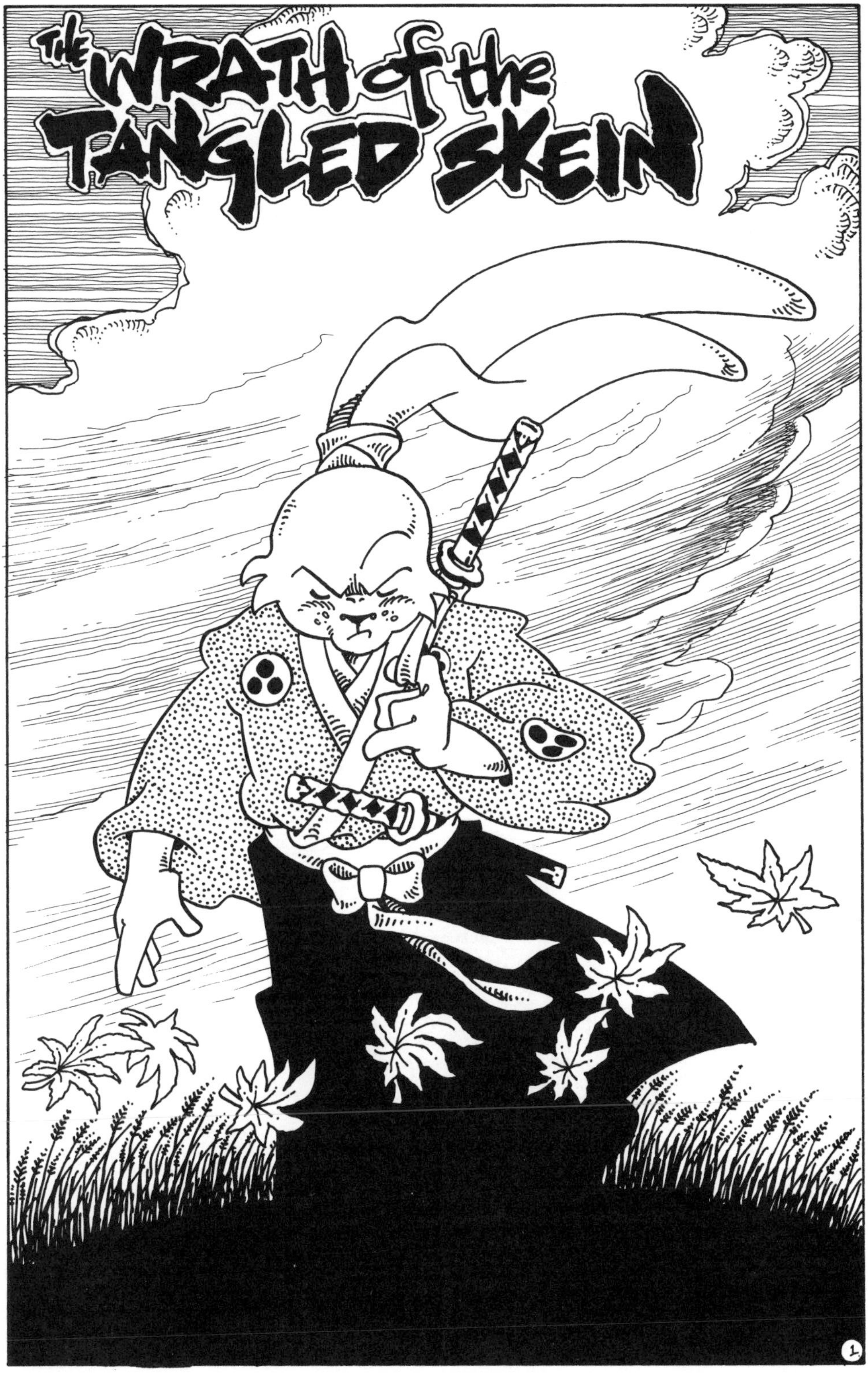
THE WRATH of the TANGLED SKEIN
1

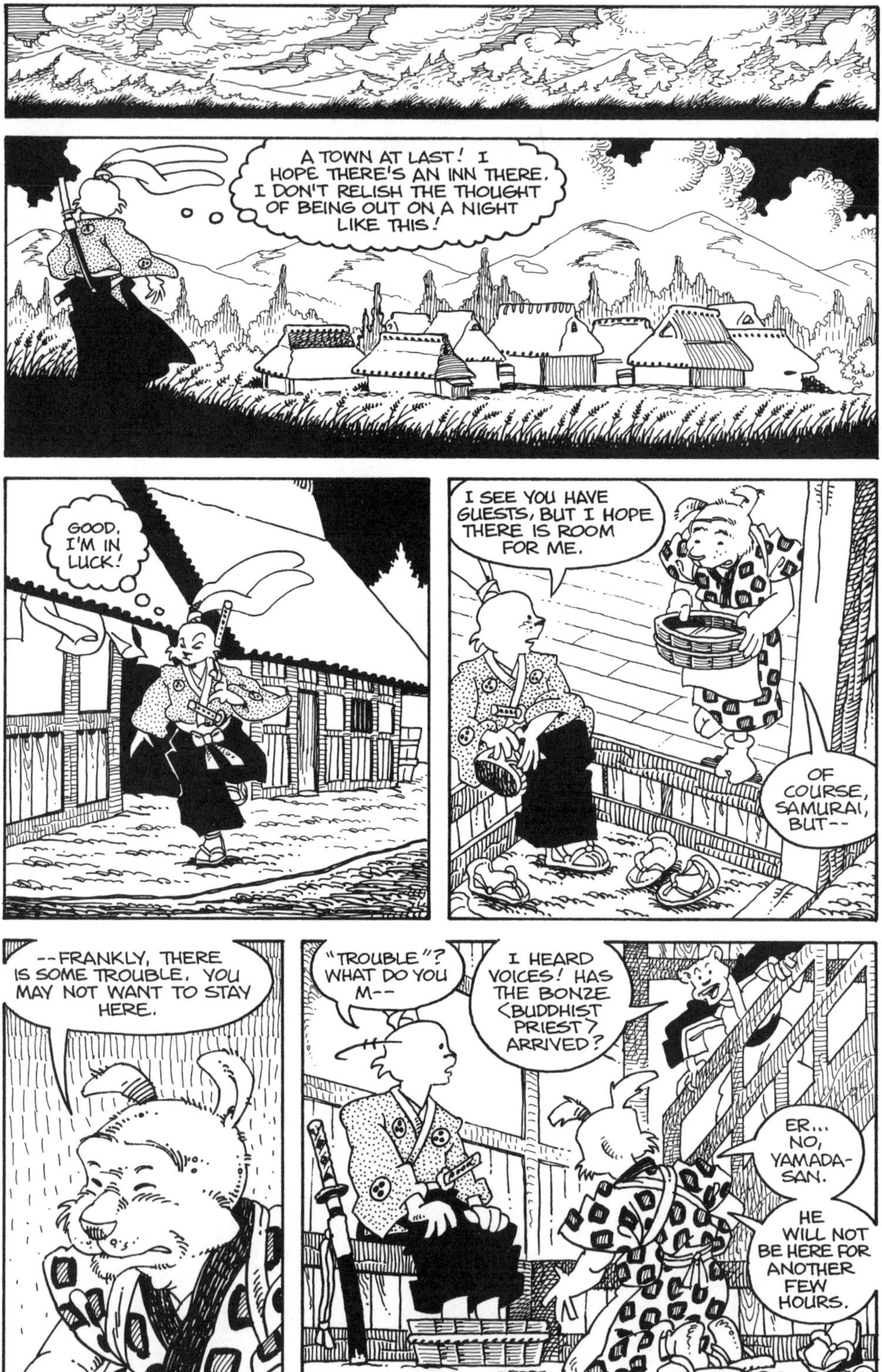
A TOWN AT LAST! I HOPE THERE'S AN INN THERE. I DON'T RELISH THE THOUGHT OF BEING OUT ON A NIGHT LIKE THIS!
GOOD, I'M IN LUCK!
I SEE YOU HAVE GUESTS, BUT I HOPE THERE IS ROOM FOR ME.
OF COURSE, SAMURAI, BUT--
--FRANKLY, THERE IS SOME TROUBLE. YOU MAY NOT WANT TO STAY HERE.
"TROUBLE"? WHAT DO YOU M--
I HEARD VOICES! HAS THE BONZE <BUDDHIST PRIEST> ARRIVED?
ER... NO, YAMADA-SAN.
HE WILL NOT BE HERE FOR ANOTHER FEW HOURS.
2.

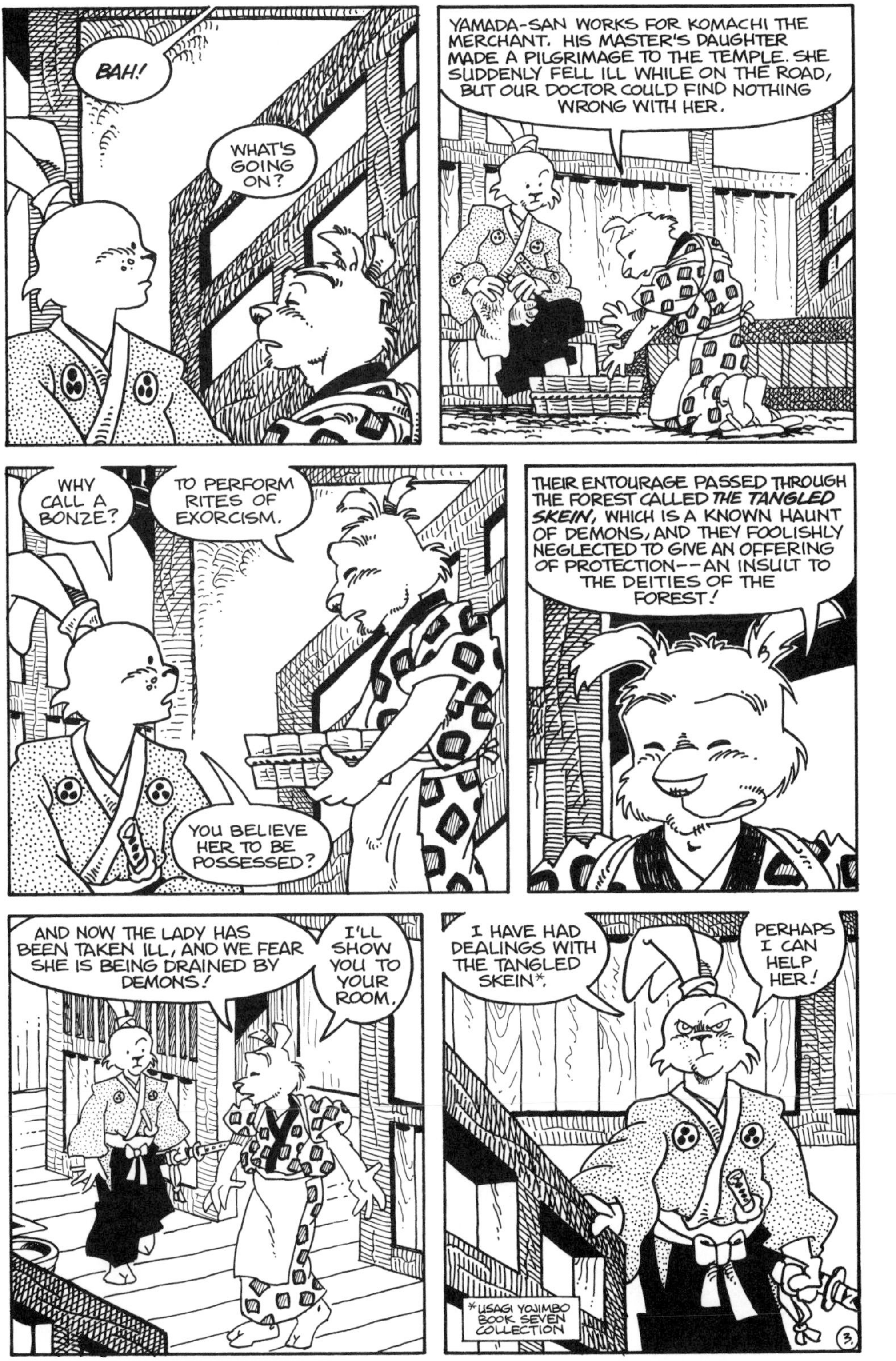
BAH!
WHAT'S GOING ON?
YAMADA-SAN WORKS FOR KOMACHI THE MERCHANT. HIS MASTER'S DAUGHTER MADE A PILGRIMAGE TO THE TEMPLE. SHE SUDDENLY FELL ILL WHILE ON THE ROAD, BUT OUR DOCTOR COULD FIND NOTHING WRONG WITH HER.
WHY CALL A BONZE?
TO PERFORM RITES OF EXORCISM.
YOU BELIEVE HER TO BE POSSESSED?
THEIR ENTOURAGE PASSED THROUGH THE FOREST CALLED THE TANGLED SKEIN, WHICH IS A KNOWN HAUNT OF DEMONS, AND THEY FOOLISHLY NEGLECTED TO GIVE AN OFFERING OF PROTECTION--AN INSULT TO THE DEITIES OF THE FOREST!
AND NOW THE LADY HAS BEEN TAKEN ILL, AND WE FEAR SHE IS BEING DRAINED BY DEMONS!
I'LL SHOW YOU TO YOUR ROOM.
I HAVE HAD DEALINGS WITH THE TANGLED SKEIN*.
PERHAPS I CAN HELP HER!
*USAGI YOJIMBO BOOK SEVEN COLLECTION
3

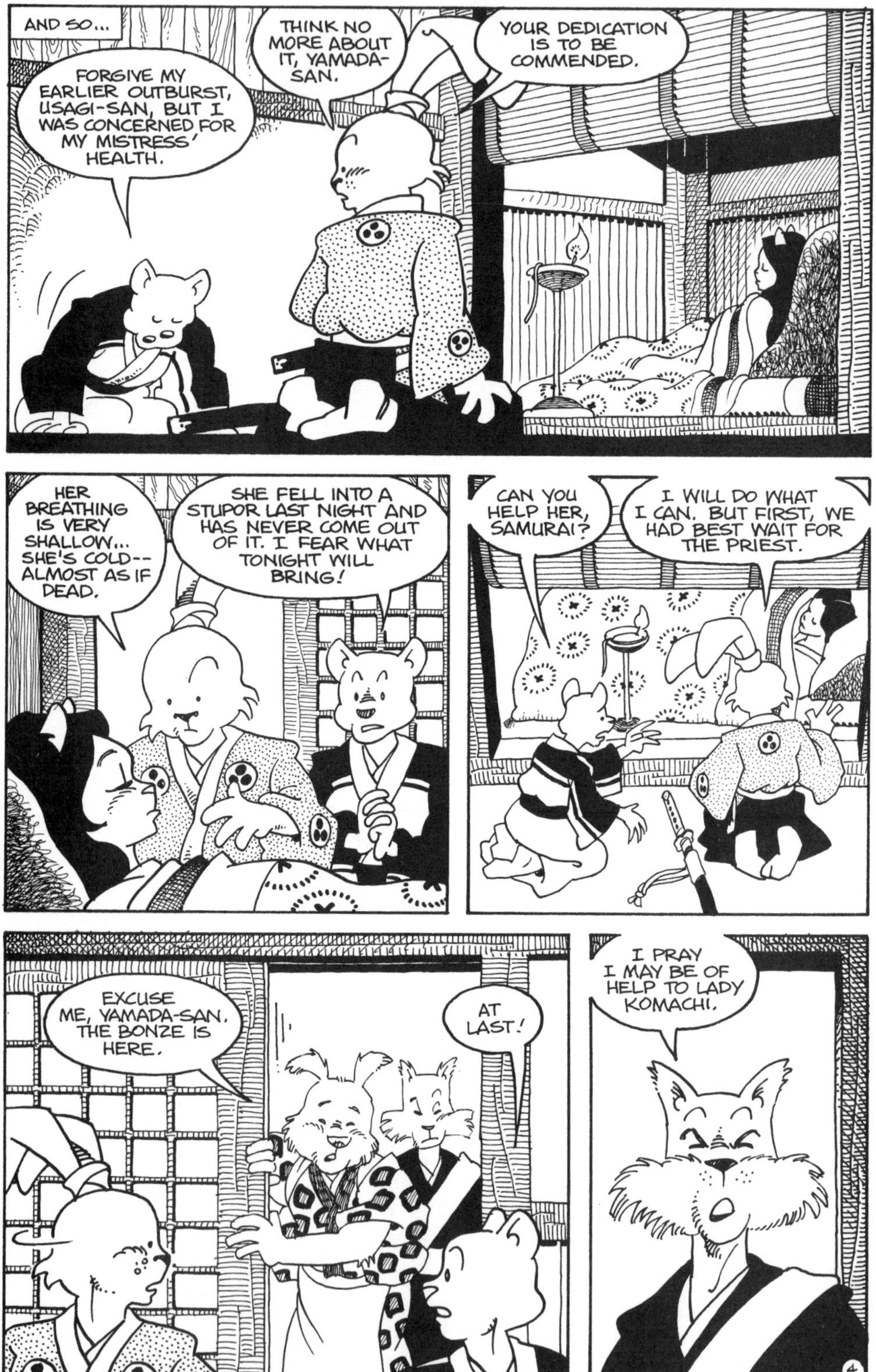
AND SO...
FORGIVE MY EARLIER OUTBURST, USAGI-SAN, BUT I WAS CONCERNED FOR MY MISTRESS' HEALTH.
THINK NO MORE ABOUT IT, YAMADA-SAN.
YOUR DEDICATION IS TO BE COMMENDED.
HER BREATHING IS VERY SHALLOW... SHE'S COLD-- ALMOST AS IF DEAD.
SHE FELL INTO A STUPOR LAST NIGHT AND HAS NEVER COME OUT OF IT. I FEAR WHAT TONIGHT WILL BRING!
CAN YOU HELP HER, SAMURAI?
I WILL DO WHAT I CAN. BUT FIRST, WE HAD BEST WAIT FOR THE PRIEST.
EXCUSE ME, YAMADA-SAN. THE BONZE IS HERE.
AT LAST!
I PRAY I MAY BE OF HELP TO LADY KOMACHI.
4.

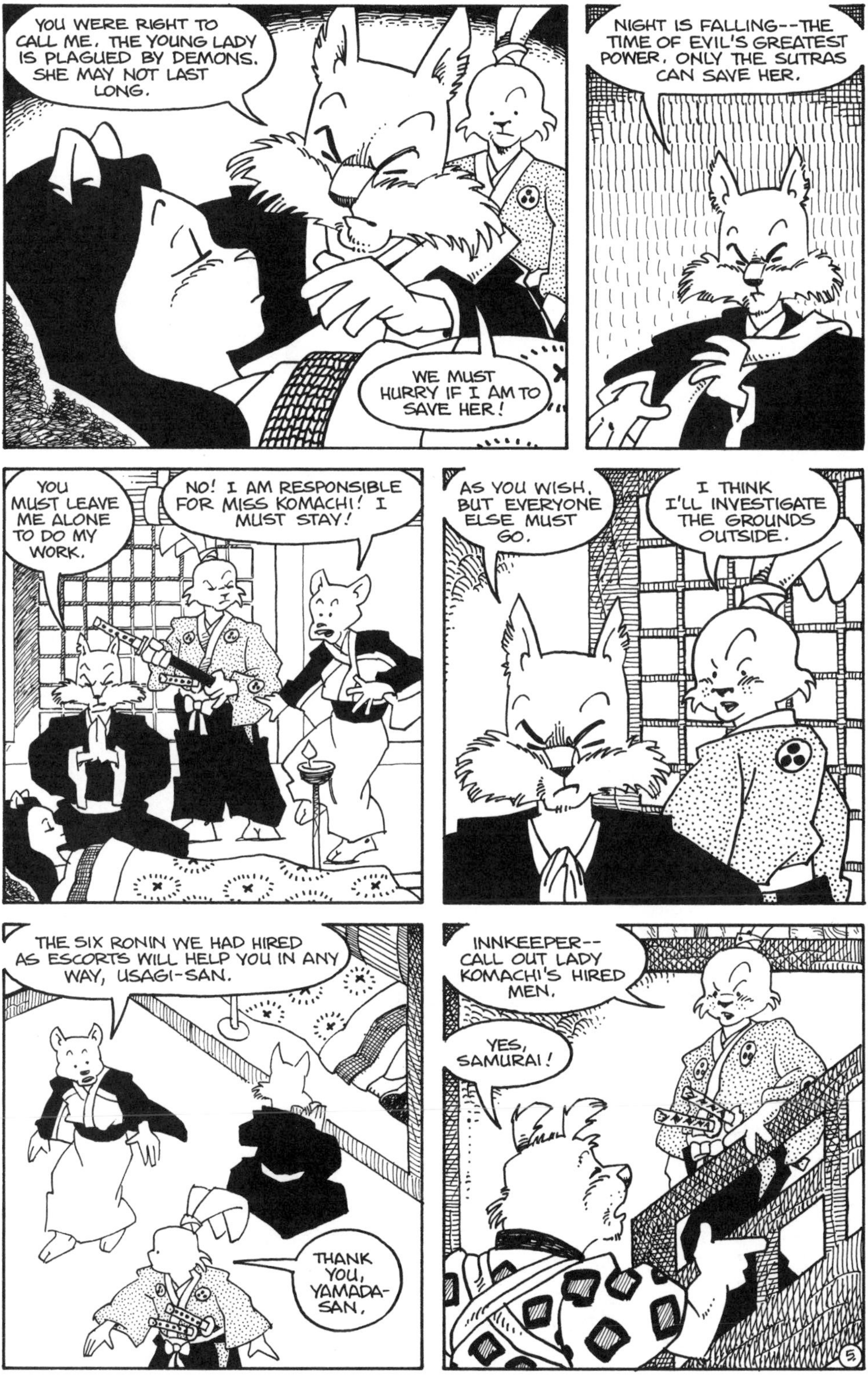
YOU WERE RIGHT TO CALL ME. THE YOUNG LADY IS PLAGUED BY DEMONS. SHE MAY NOT LAST LONG.
WE MUST HURRY IF I AM TO SAVE HER!
NIGHT IS FALLING--THE TIME OF EVIL'S GREATEST POWER. ONLY THE SUTRAS CAN SAVE HER.
YOU MUST LEAVE ME ALONE TO DO MY WORK.
NO! I AM RESPONSIBLE FOR MISS KOMACHI! I MUST STAY!
AS YOU WISH, BUT EVERYONE ELSE MUST GO.
I THINK I'LL INVESTIGATE THE GROUNDS OUTSIDE.
THE SIX RONIN WE HAD HIRED AS ESCORTS WILL HELP YOU IN ANY WAY, USAGI-SAN.
THANK YOU, YAMADA-SAN.
INNKEEPER--CALL OUT LADY KOMACHI'S HIRED MEN.
YES, SAMURAI!
5

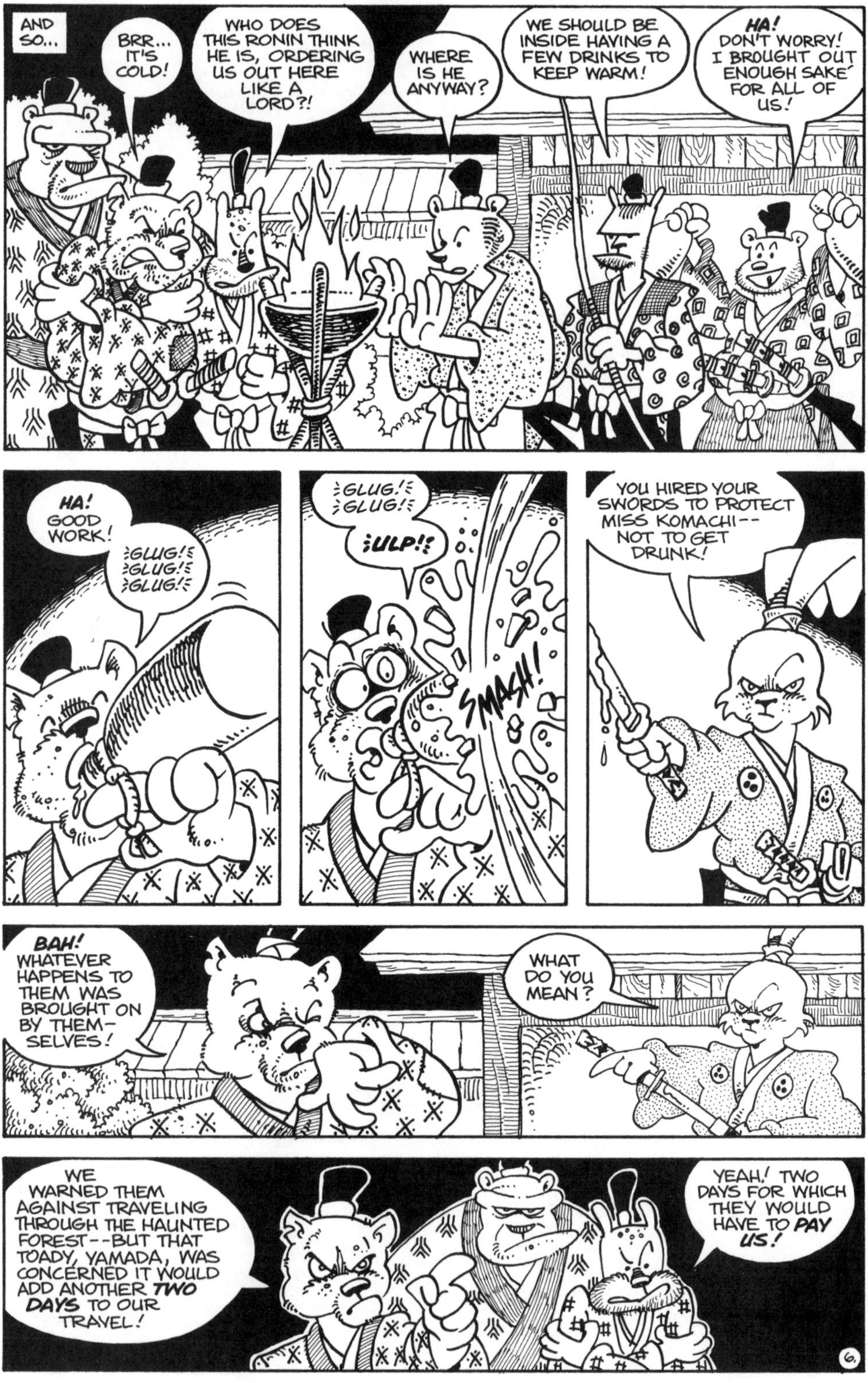
AND SO...
BRR... IT'S COLD!
WHO DOES THIS RONIN THINK HE IS, ORDERING US OUT HERE LIKE A LORD?!
WHERE IS HE ANYWAY?
WE SHOULD BE INSIDE HAVING A FEW DRINKS TO KEEP WARM!
HA! DON'T WORRY! I BROUGHT OUT ENOUGH SAKÉ FOR ALL OF US!
HA! GOOD WORK!
GLUG! GLUG! GLUG!
GLUG! GLUG!
ULP!!
SMASH!
YOU HIRED YOUR SWORDS TO PROTECT MISS KOMACHI-- NOT TO GET DRUNK!
BAH! WHATEVER HAPPENS TO THEM WAS BROUGHT ON BY THEM-SELVES!
WHAT DO YOU MEAN?
WE WARNED THEM AGAINST TRAVELING THROUGH THE HAUNTED FOREST--BUT THAT TOADY, YAMADA, WAS CONCERNED IT WOULD ADD ANOTHER TWO DAYS TO OUR TRAVEL!
YEAH! TWO DAYS FOR WHICH THEY WOULD HAVE TO PAY US!
6.

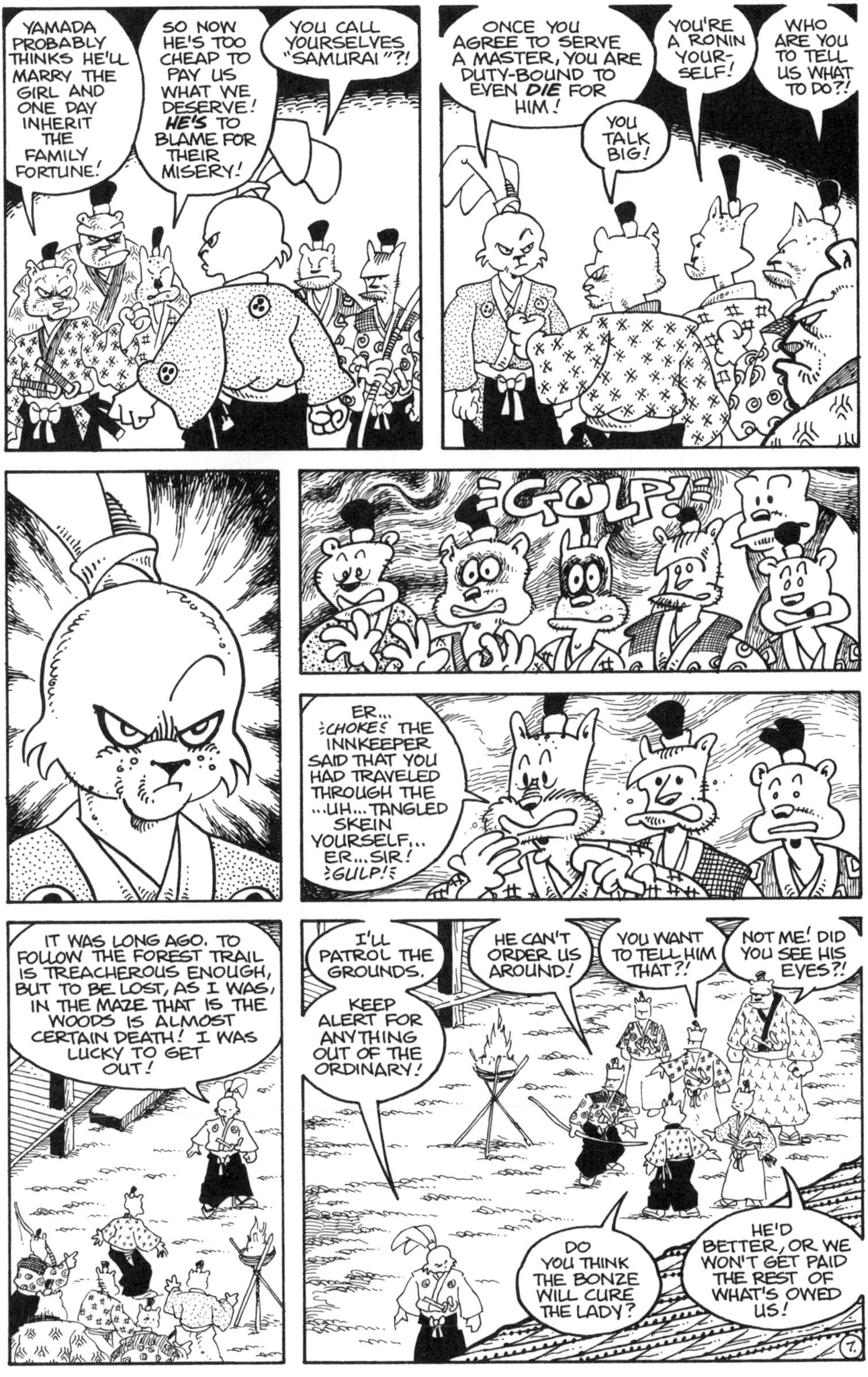
YAMADA PROBABLY THINKS HE'LL MARRY THE GIRL AND ONE DAY INHERIT THE FAMILY FORTUNE!
SO NOW HE'S TOO CHEAP TO PAY US WHAT WE DESERVE! HE'S TO BLAME FOR THEIR MISERY!
YOU CALL YOURSELVES "SAMURAI"?!
ONCE YOU AGREE TO SERVE A MASTER, YOU ARE DUTY-BOUND TO EVEN DIE FOR HIM!
YOU TALK BIG!
YOU'RE A RONIN YOURSELF!
WHO ARE YOU TO TELL US WHAT TO DO?!
GULP!
ER... CHOKE THE INNKEEPER SAID THAT YOU HAD TRAVELED THROUGH THE ...UH... TANGLED SKEIN YOURSELF... ER...SIR! GULP!
IT WAS LONG AGO. TO FOLLOW THE FOREST TRAIL IS TREACHEROUS ENOUGH, BUT TO BE LOST, AS I WAS, IN THE MAZE THAT IS THE WOODS IS ALMOST CERTAIN DEATH! I WAS LUCKY TO GET OUT!
I'LL PATROL THE GROUNDS.
KEEP ALERT FOR ANYTHING OUT OF THE ORDINARY!
HE CAN'T ORDER US AROUND!
YOU WANT TO TELL HIM THAT?!
NOT ME! DID YOU SEE HIS EYES?!
DO YOU THINK THE BONZE WILL CURE THE LADY?
HE'D BETTER, OR WE WON'T GET PAID THE REST OF WHAT'S OWED US!
7.

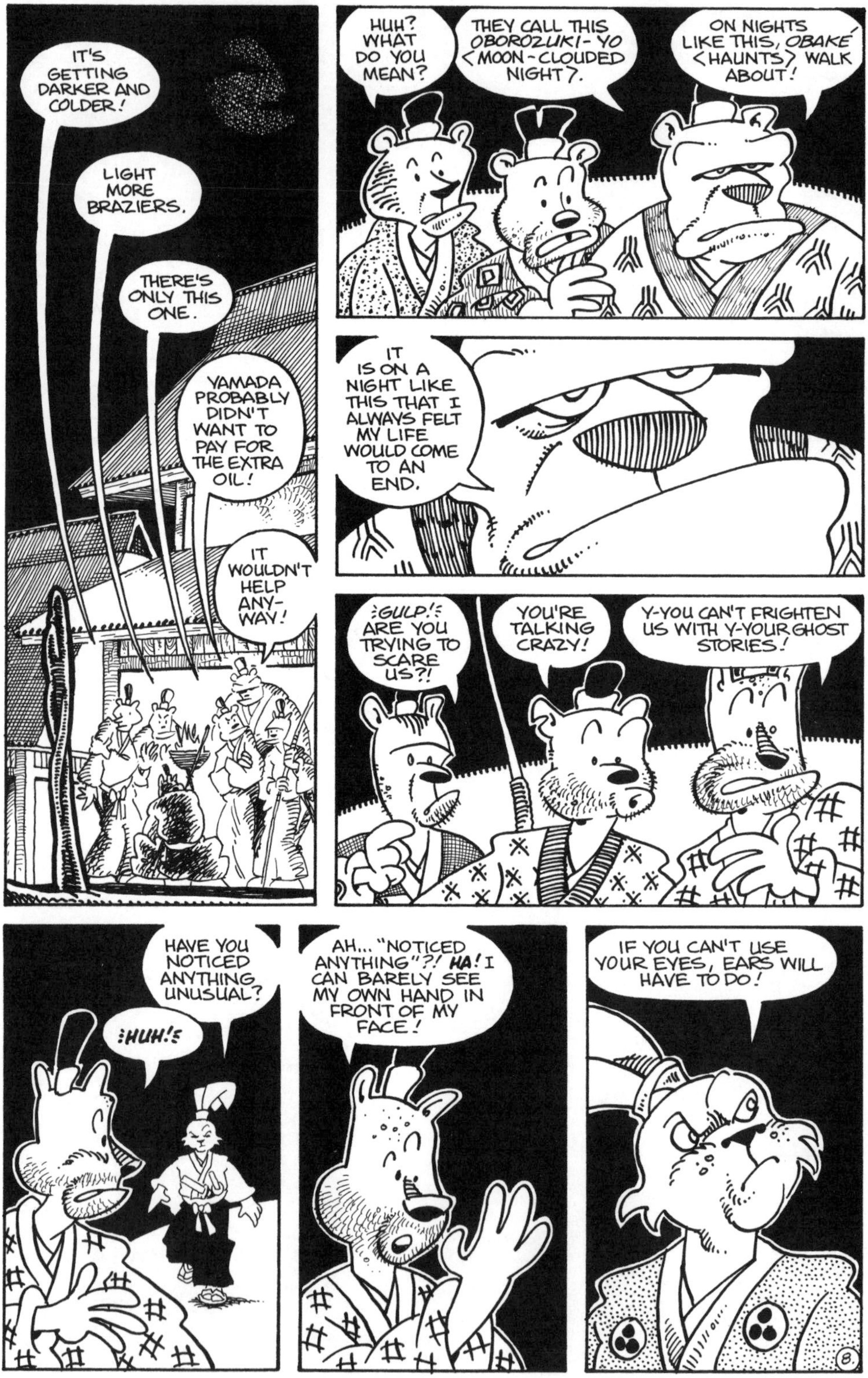

IT'S GETTING DARKER AND COLDER!
LIGHT MORE BRAZIERS.
THERE'S ONLY THIS ONE.
YAMADA PROBABLY DIDN'T WANT TO PAY FOR THE EXTRA OIL!
IT WOULDN'T HELP ANY-WAY!
HUH? WHAT DO YOU MEAN?
THEY CALL THIS OBOROZUKI-YO <MOON-CLOUDED NIGHT>.
ON NIGHTS LIKE THIS, OBAKE <HAUNTS> WALK ABOUT!
IT IS ON A NIGHT LIKE THIS THAT I ALWAYS FELT MY LIFE WOULD COME TO AN END.
GULP! ARE YOU TRYING TO SCARE US?!
YOU'RE TALKING CRAZY!
Y-YOU CAN'T FRIGHTEN US WITH Y-YOUR GHOST STORIES!
HAVE YOU NOTICED ANYTHING UNUSUAL?
HUH!
AH... "NOTICED ANYTHING"?! HA! I CAN BARELY SEE MY OWN HAND IN FRONT OF MY FACE!
IF YOU CAN'T USE YOUR EYES, EARS WILL HAVE TO DO!
8.

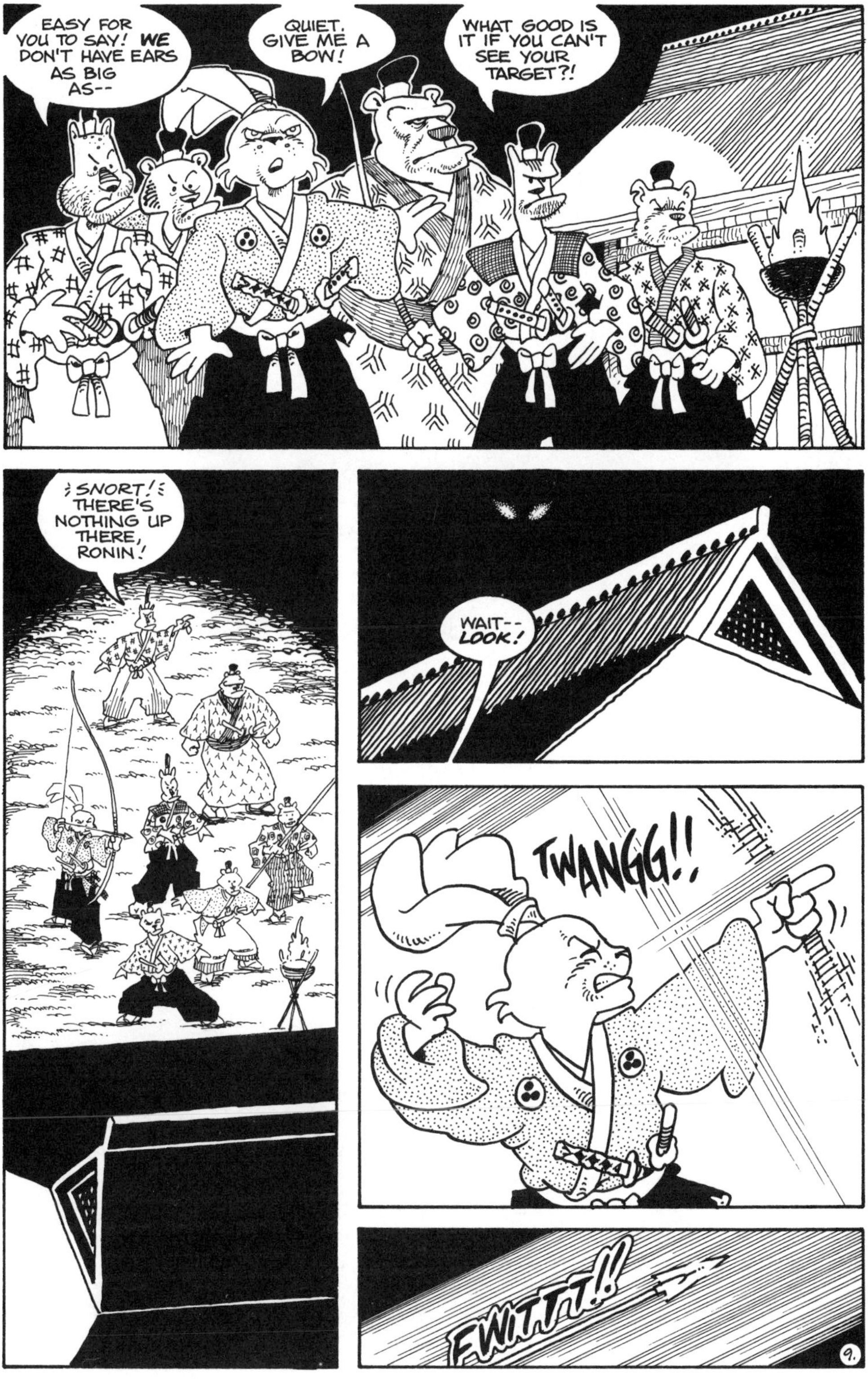
EASY FOR YOU TO SAY! WE DON'T HAVE EARS AS BIG AS--
QUIET. GIVE ME A BOW!
WHAT GOOD IS IT IF YOU CAN'T SEE YOUR TARGET?!
SNORT! THERE'S NOTHING UP THERE, RONIN!
WAIT-- LOOK!
TWANGG!!
FWITTTT!!
9.

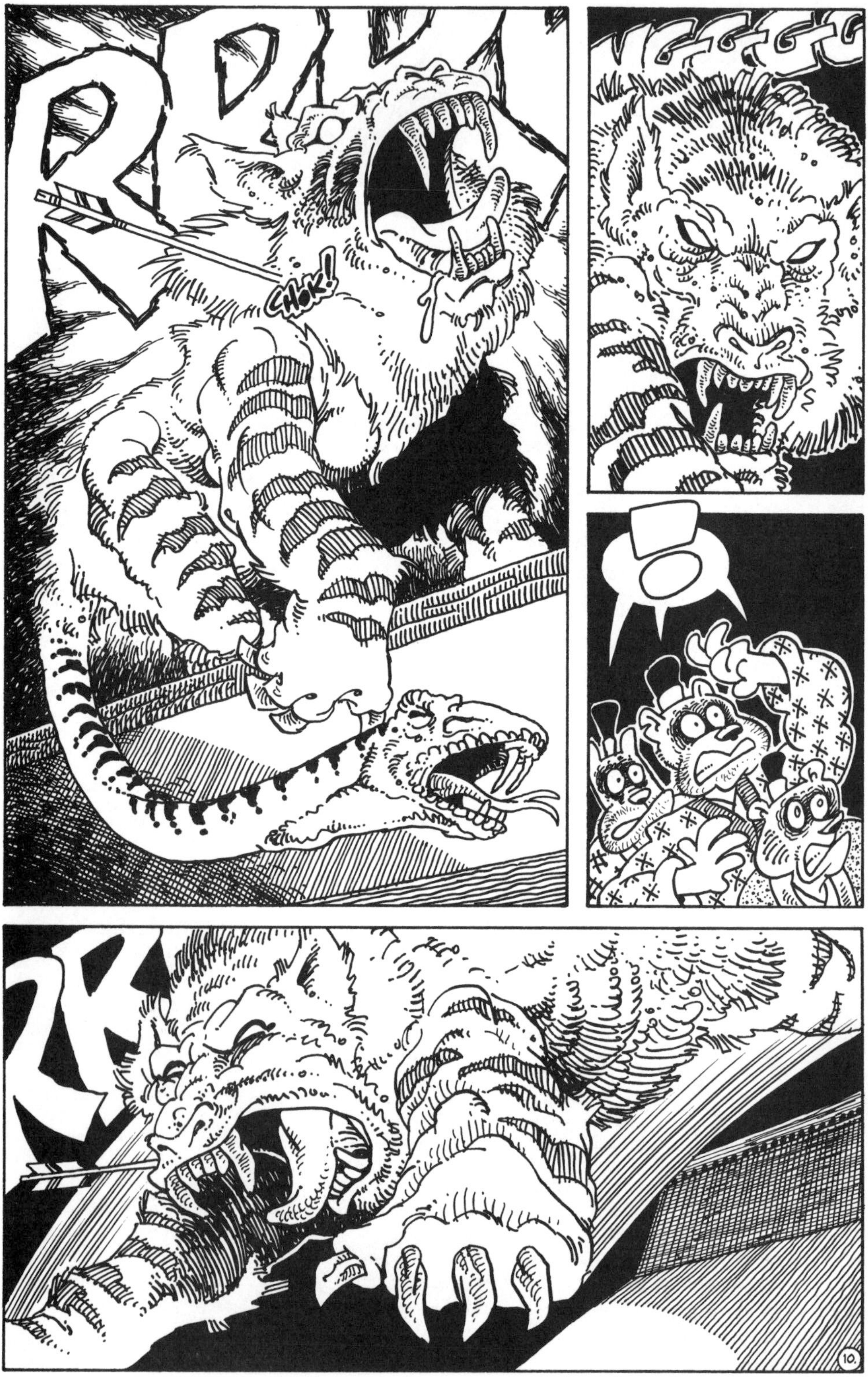
CHOK!
!
10.

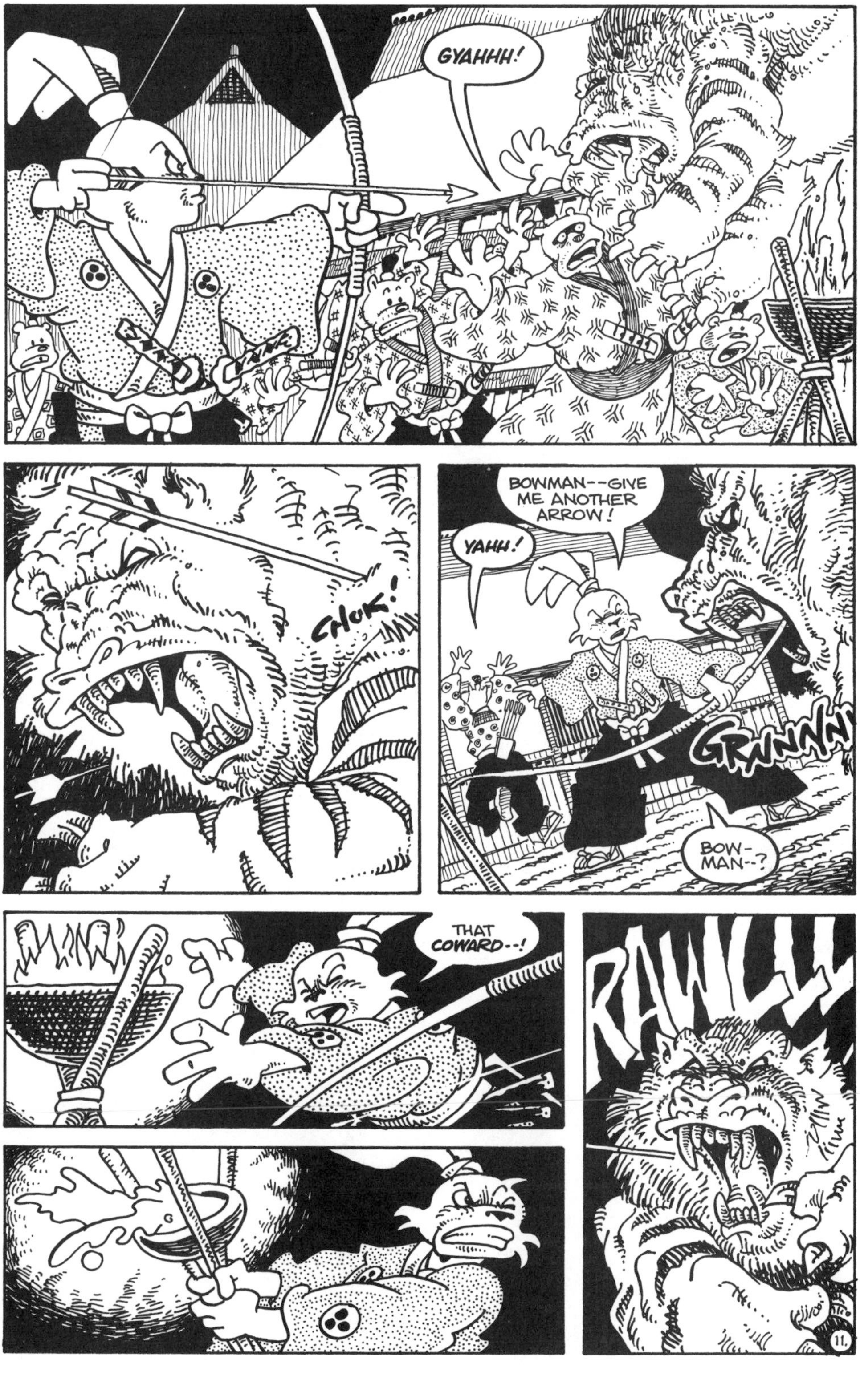
GYAHHH!
CHUK!
BOWMAN--GIVE ME ANOTHER ARROW!
YAHH!
GRNNNN
BOW-MAN--?
THAT COWARD--!
RAWLL
11.

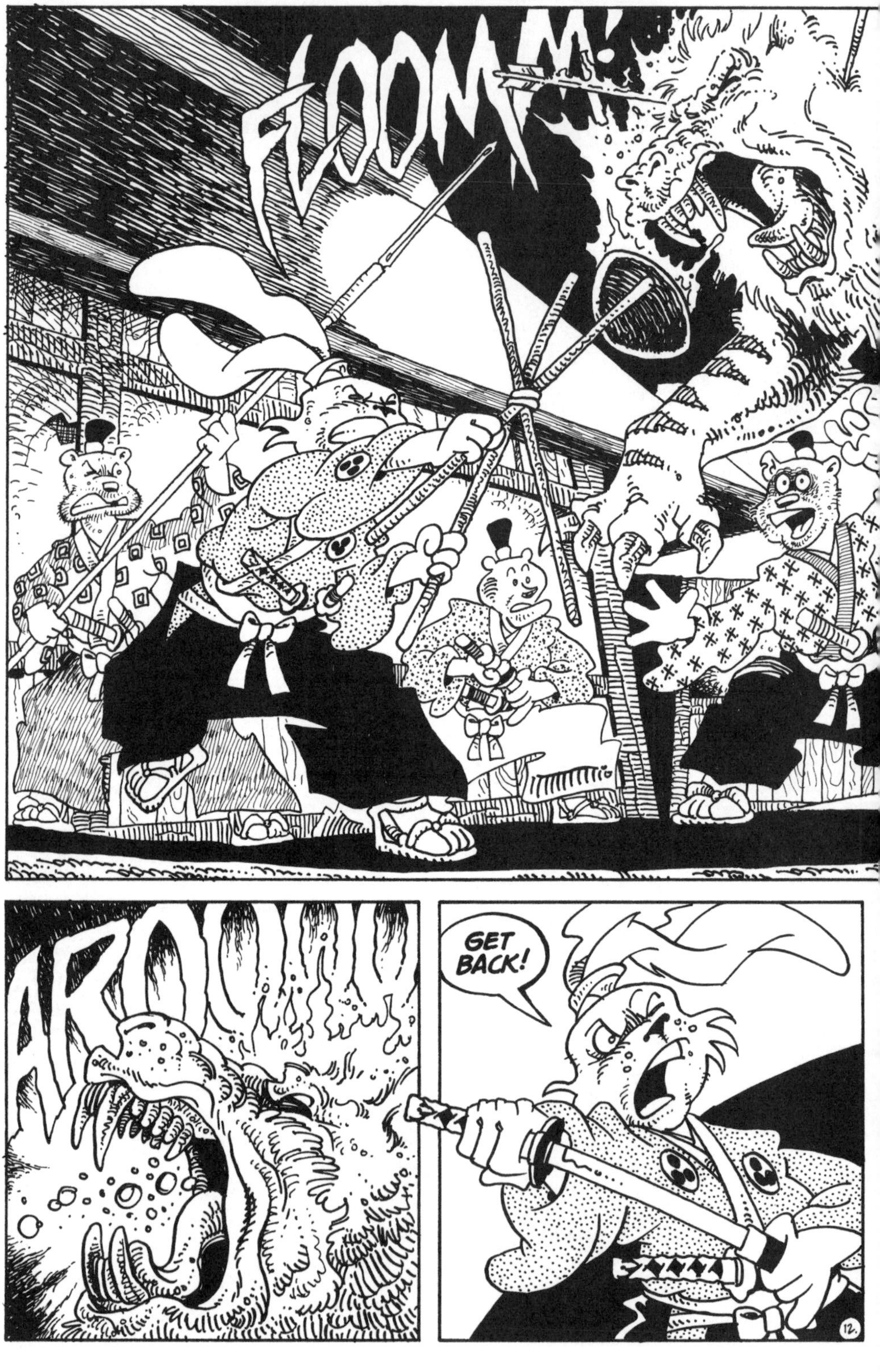
FLOOMM!
AROOOO
GET BACK!
12.

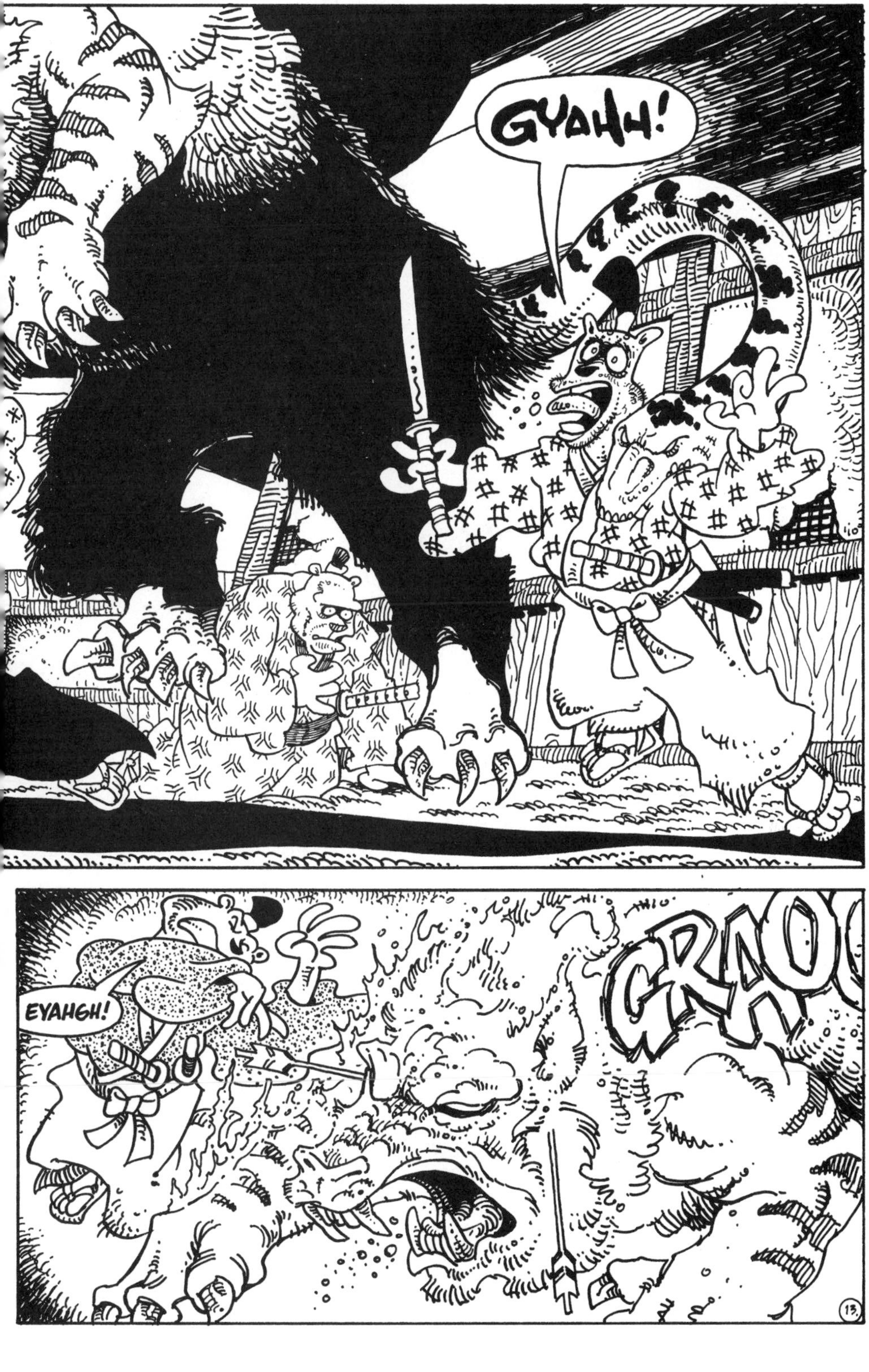
GYAHH!
EYAHGH!
GRAO

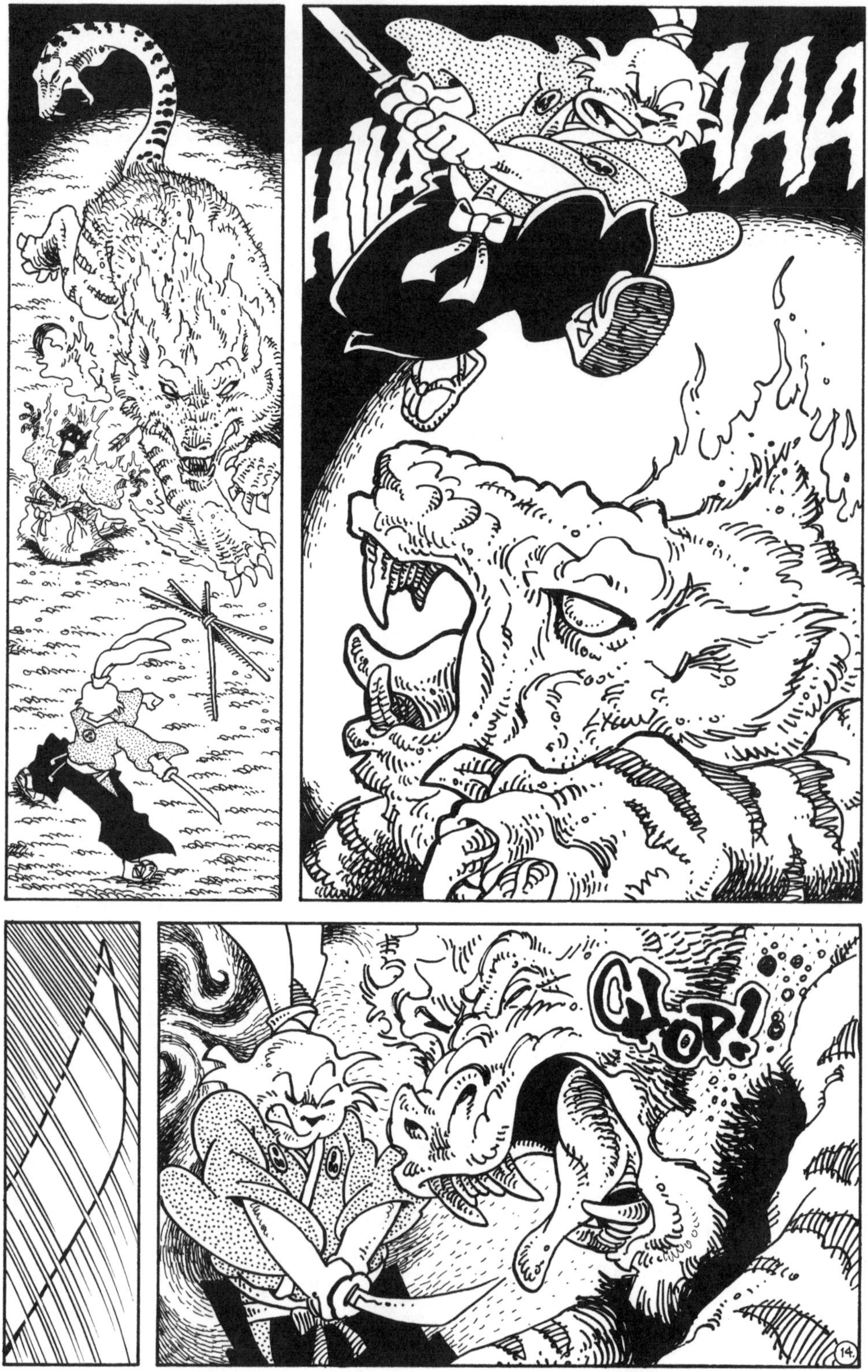
HIAAAA
CHOP!
14.

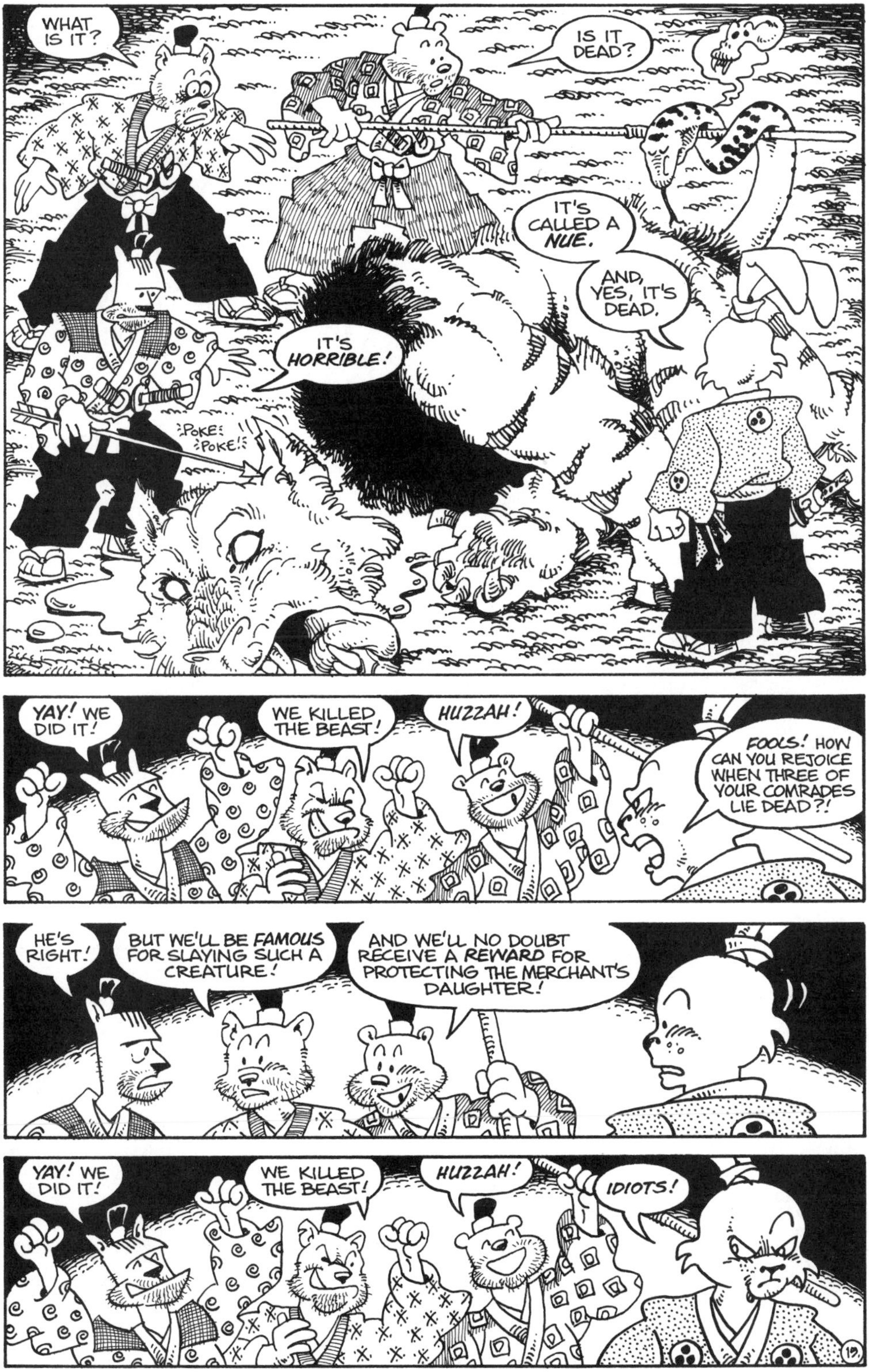
WHAT IS IT?
IS IT DEAD?
IT'S CALLED A NUE.
AND, YES, IT'S DEAD.
IT'S HORRIBLE!
POKE POKE
YAY! WE DID IT!
WE KILLED THE BEAST!
HUZZAH!
FOOLS! HOW CAN YOU REJOICE WHEN THREE OF YOUR COMRADES LIE DEAD?!
HE'S RIGHT!
BUT WE'LL BE FAMOUS FOR SLAYING SUCH A CREATURE!
AND WE'LL NO DOUBT RECEIVE A REWARD FOR PROTECTING THE MERCHANT'S DAUGHTER!
YAY! WE DID IT!
WE KILLED THE BEAST!
HUZZAH!
IDIOTS!
19

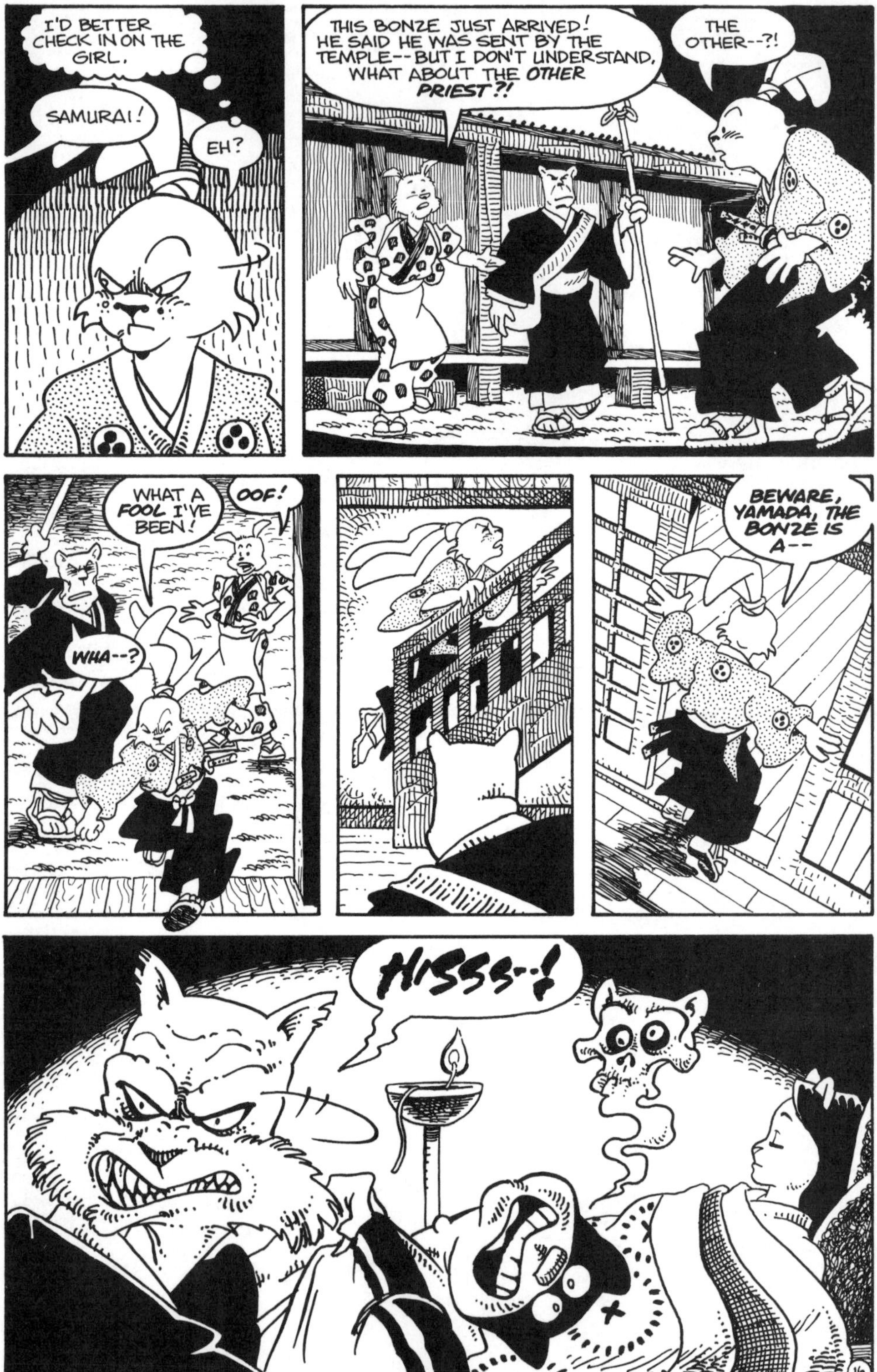
I'D BETTER CHECK IN ON THE GIRL.
SAMURAI!
EH?
THIS BONZE JUST ARRIVED! HE SAID HE WAS SENT BY THE TEMPLE--BUT I DON'T UNDERSTAND, WHAT ABOUT THE OTHER PRIEST?!
THE OTHER--?!
WHAT A FOOL I'VE BEEN!
OOF!
WHA--?
BEWARE, YAMADA, THE BONZE IS A--
HISSS--!
16.

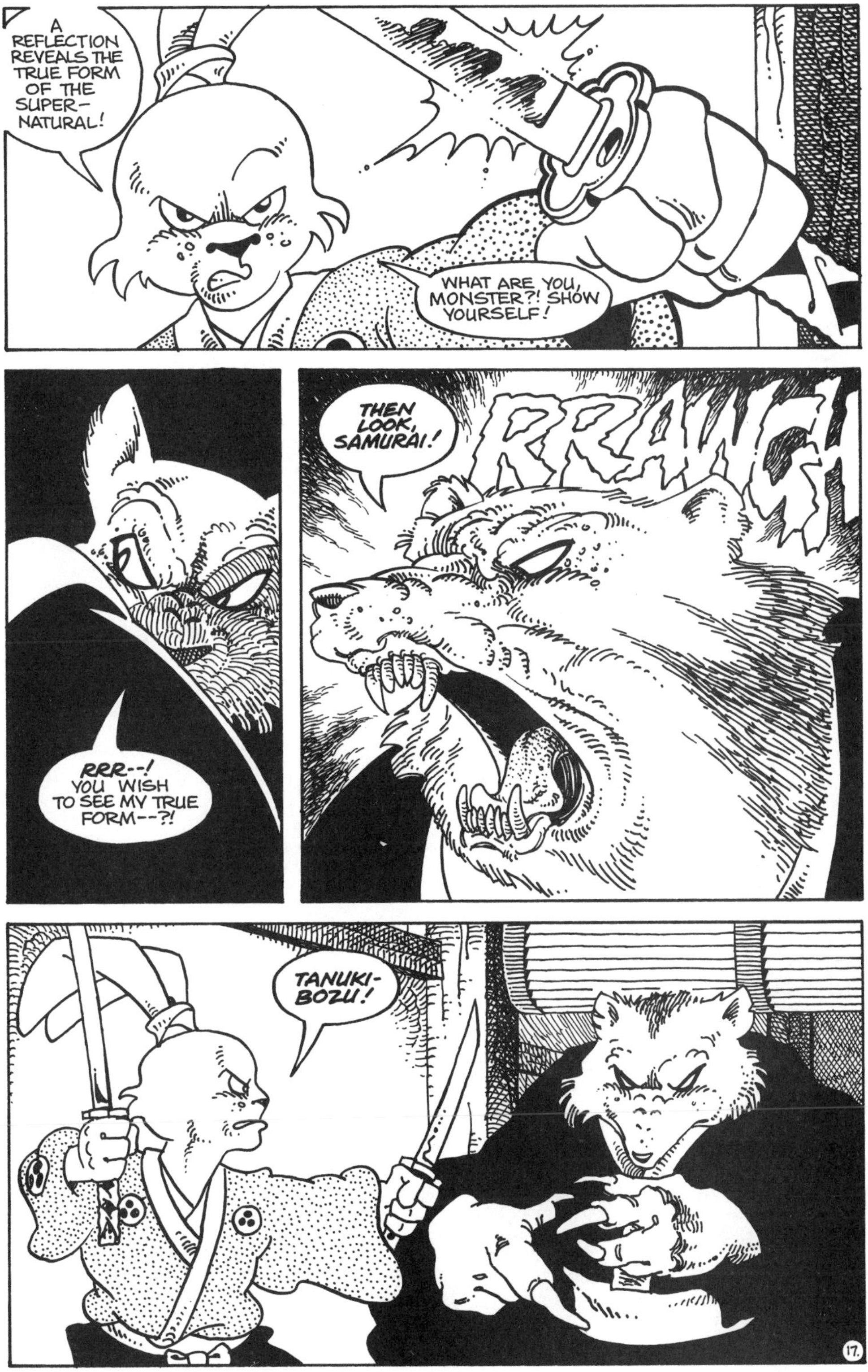
A REFLECTION REVEALS THE TRUE FORM OF THE SUPER-NATURAL!
WHAT ARE YOU, MONSTER?! SHOW YOURSELF!
RRR--! YOU WISH TO SEE MY TRUE FORM--?!
THEN LOOK, SAMURAI!
RRAUGH
TANUKI-BOZU!
17.

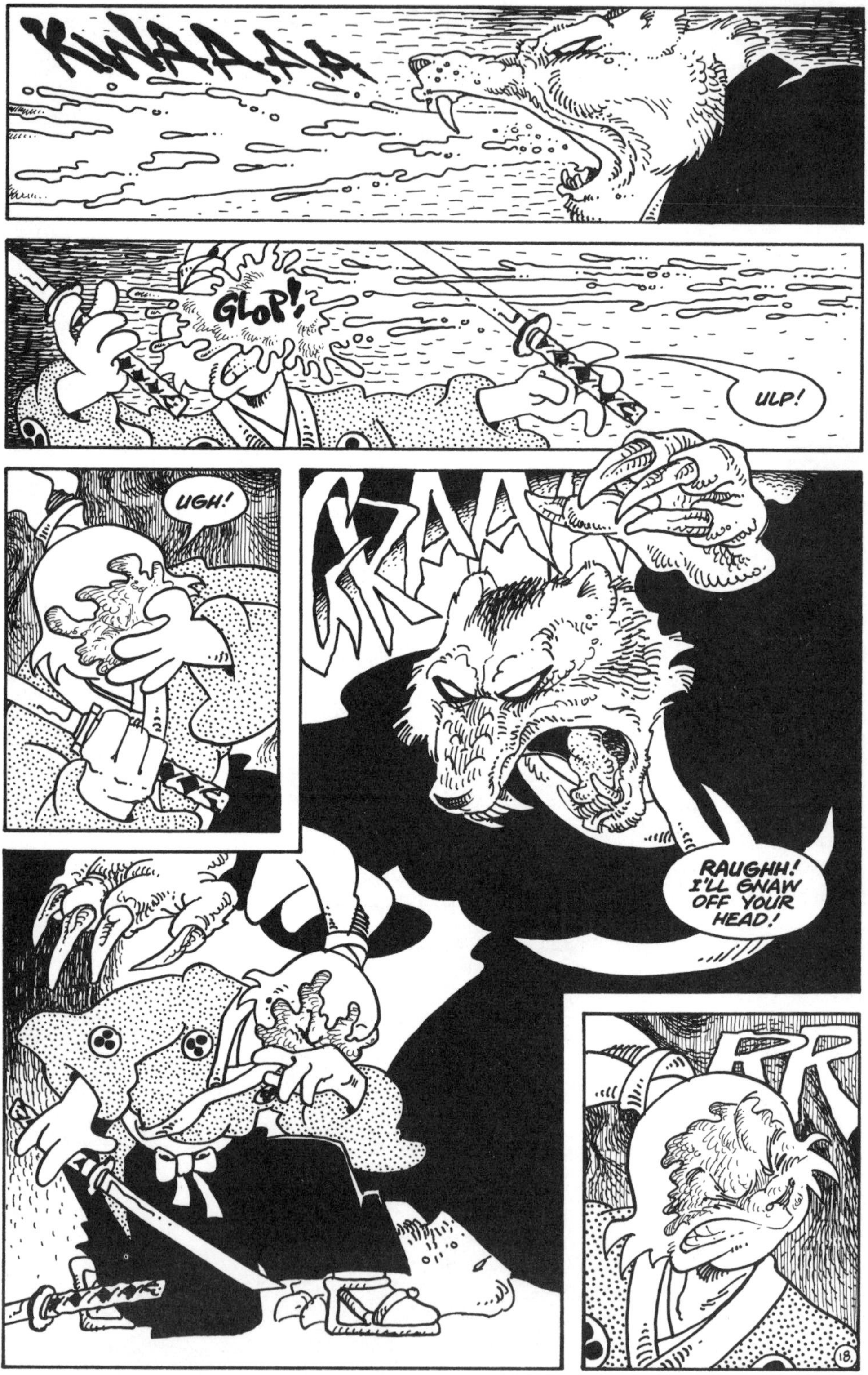
KWRAAAA
GLOP!
ULP!
UGH!
KRAA
RAUGHH! I'LL GNAW OFF YOUR HEAD!
RR
18

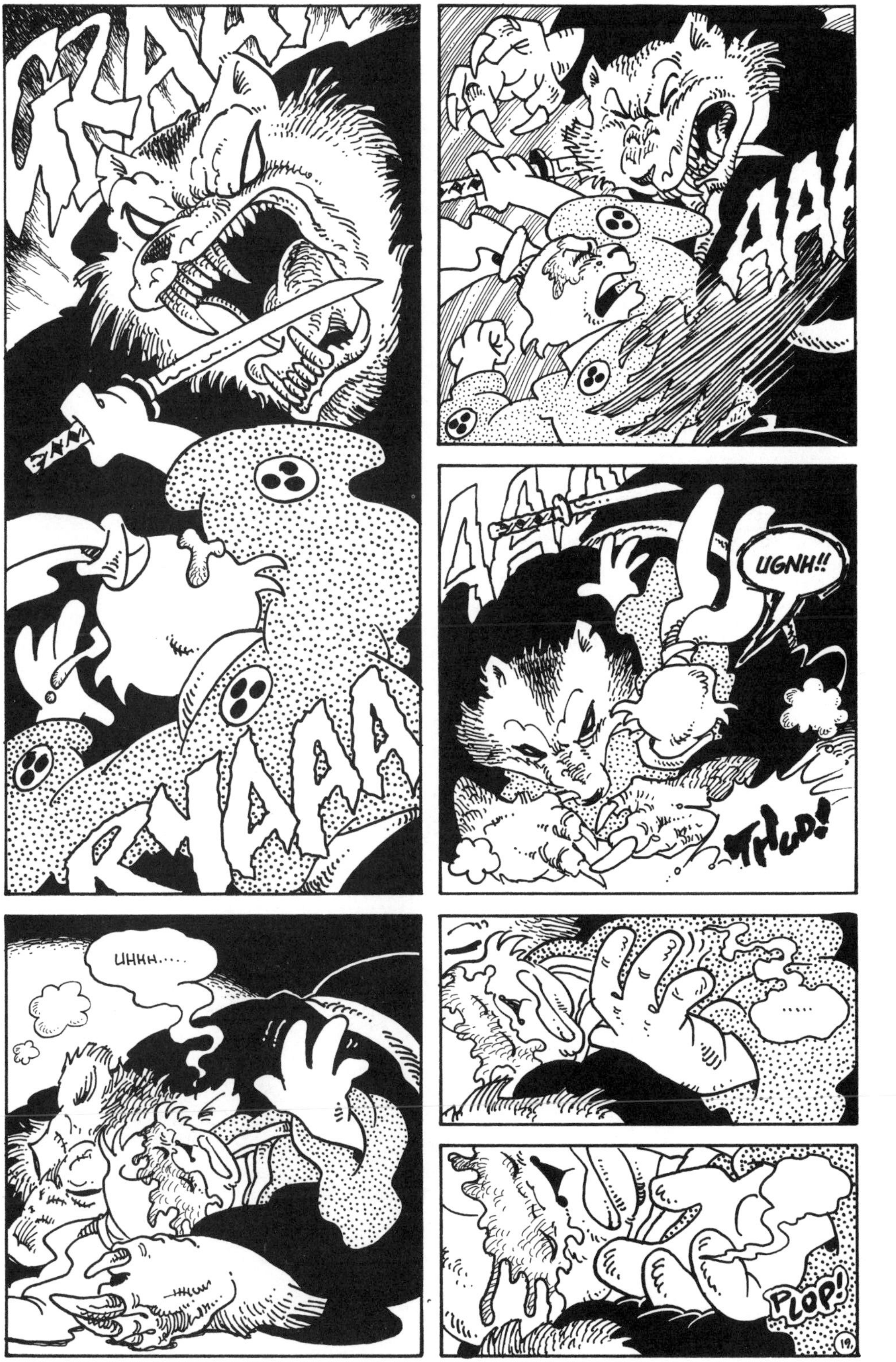
UGNH!!
THUD!
UHHH....
.....
PLOP!

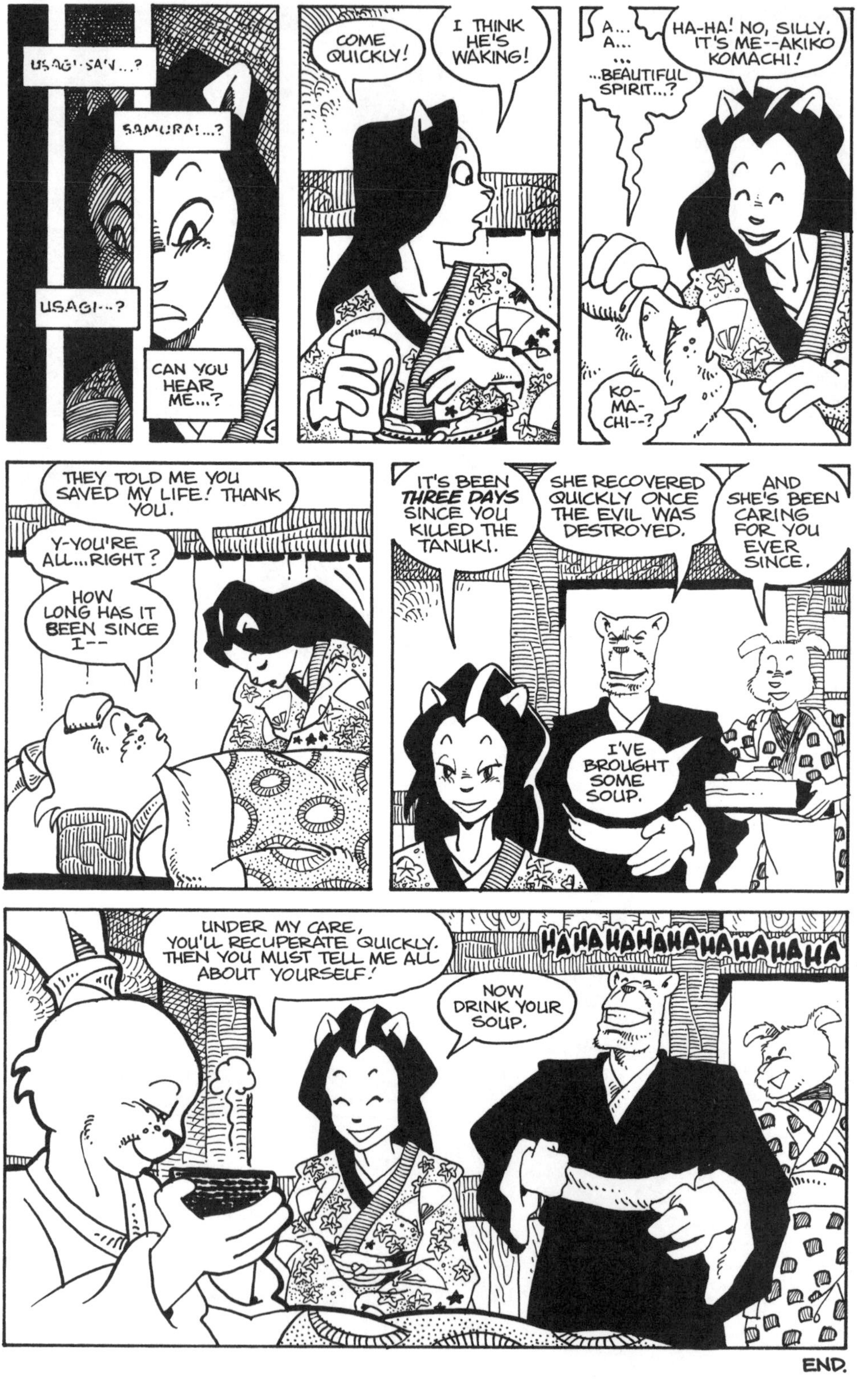
USAGI-SAN...?
SAMURAI...?
USAGI--?
CAN YOU HEAR ME...?
COME QUICKLY!
I THINK HE'S WAKING!
A... A... ... ...BEAUTIFUL SPIRIT...?
HA-HA! NO, SILLY. IT'S ME--AKIKO KOMACHI!
KO-MA-CHI--?
THEY TOLD ME YOU SAVED MY LIFE! THANK YOU.
Y-YOU'RE ALL...RIGHT?
HOW LONG HAS IT BEEN SINCE I--
IT'S BEEN THREE DAYS SINCE YOU KILLED THE TANUKI.
SHE RECOVERED QUICKLY ONCE THE EVIL WAS DESTROYED.
AND SHE'S BEEN CARING FOR YOU EVER SINCE.
I'VE BROUGHT SOME SOUP.
UNDER MY CARE, YOU'LL RECUPERATE QUICKLY. THEN YOU MUST TELL ME ALL ABOUT YOURSELF!
NOW DRINK YOUR SOUP.
HAHAHAHAHAHAHAHAHA
END.

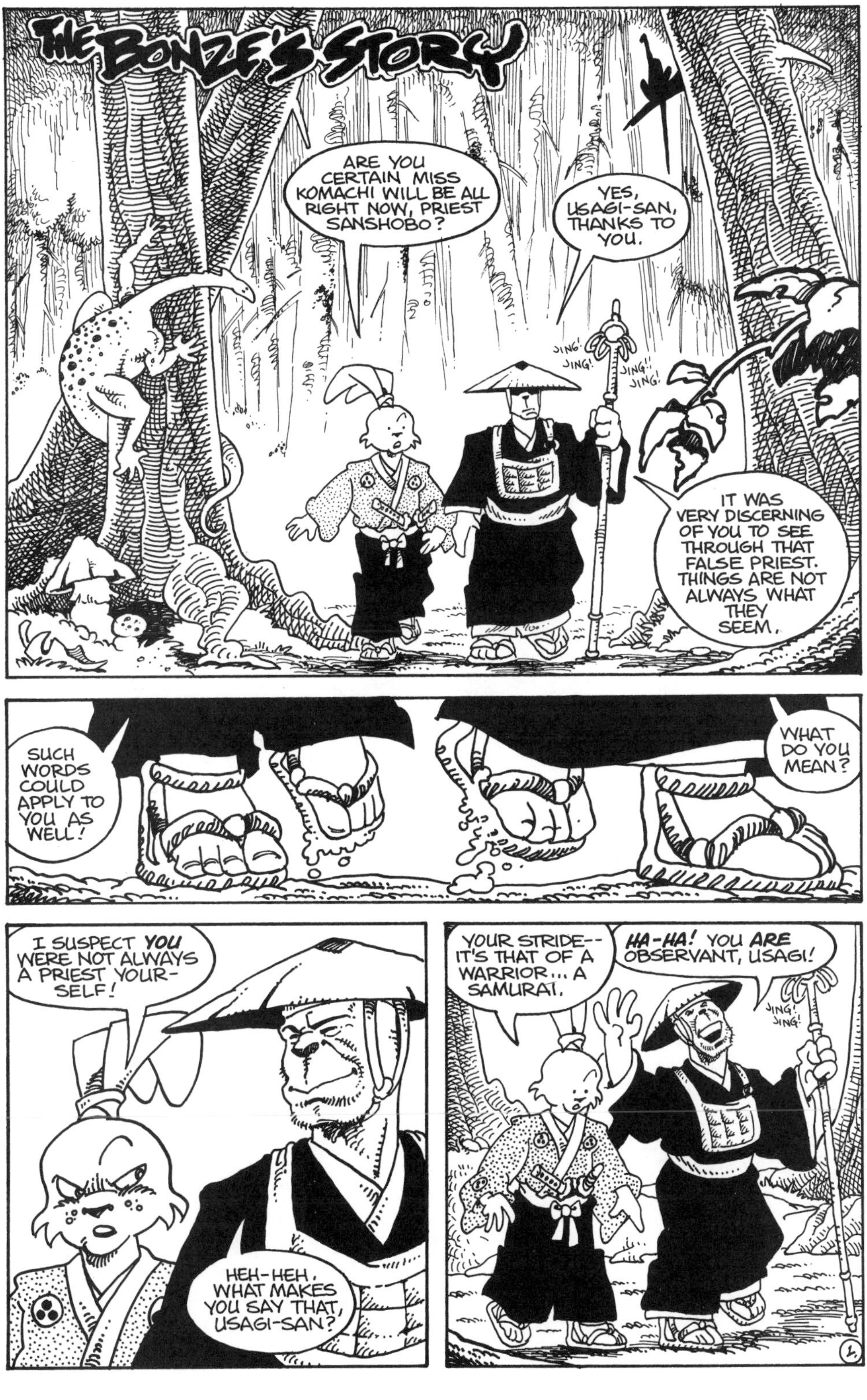
THE BONZE'S STORY
ARE YOU CERTAIN MISS KOMACHI WILL BE ALL RIGHT NOW, PRIEST SANSHOBO?
YES, USAGI-SAN, THANKS TO YOU.
JING! JING! JING!! JING!
IT WAS VERY DISCERNING OF YOU TO SEE THROUGH THAT FALSE PRIEST. THINGS ARE NOT ALWAYS WHAT THEY SEEM.
SUCH WORDS COULD APPLY TO YOU AS WELL!
WHAT DO YOU MEAN?
I SUSPECT YOU WERE NOT ALWAYS A PRIEST YOUR-SELF!
HEH-HEH, WHAT MAKES YOU SAY THAT, USAGI-SAN?
YOUR STRIDE-- IT'S THAT OF A WARRIOR... A SAMURAI.
HA-HA! YOU ARE OBSERVANT, USAGI!
JING! JING!
1

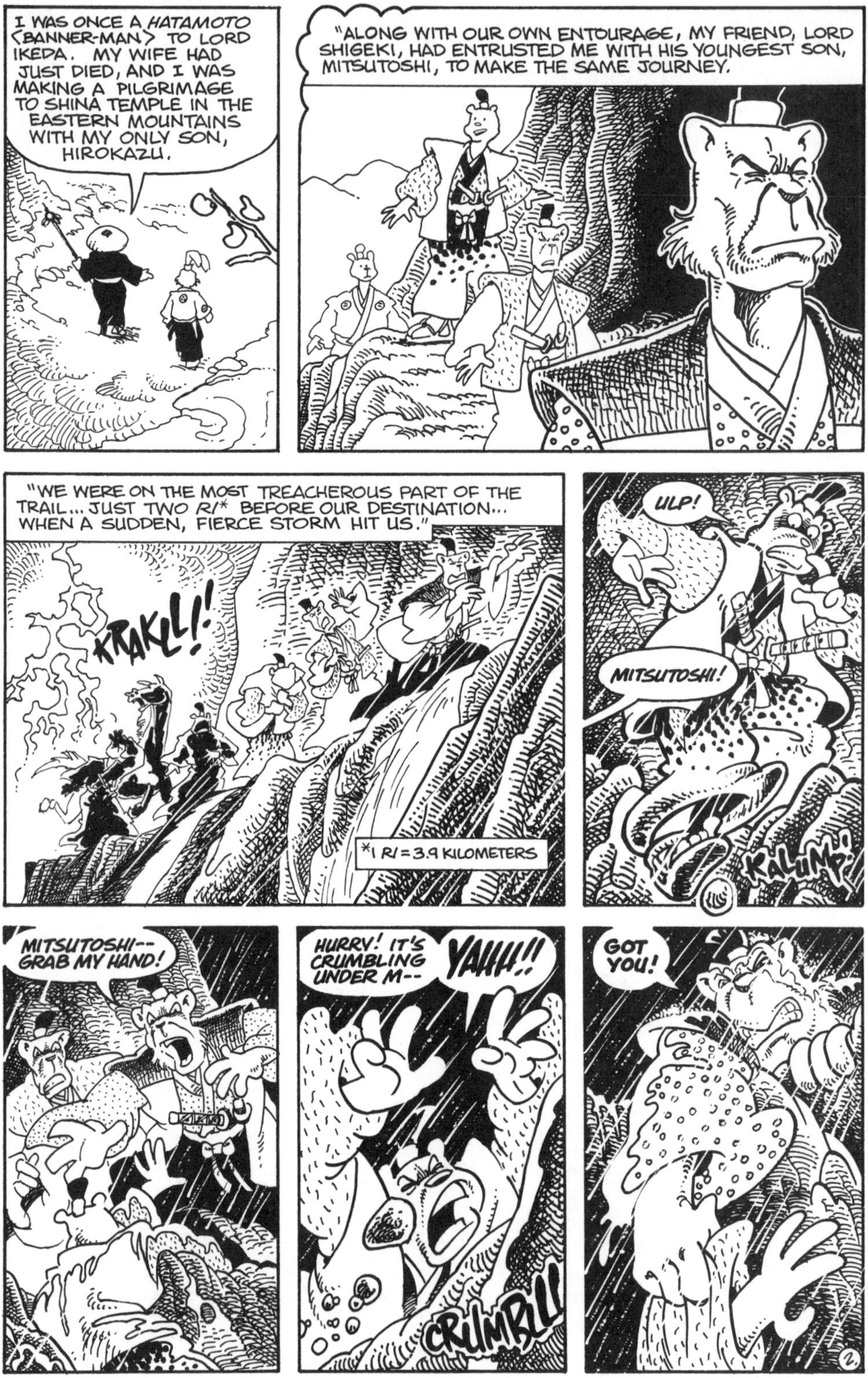
I WAS ONCE A HATAMOTO (BANNER-MAN) TO LORD IKEDA. MY WIFE HAD JUST DIED, AND I WAS MAKING A PILGRIMAGE TO SHINA TEMPLE IN THE EASTERN MOUNTAINS WITH MY ONLY SON, HIROKAZU.
"ALONG WITH OUR OWN ENTOURAGE, MY FRIEND, LORD SHIGEKI, HAD ENTRUSTED ME WITH HIS YOUNGEST SON, MITSUTOSHI, TO MAKE THE SAME JOURNEY.
"WE WERE ON THE MOST TREACHEROUS PART OF THE TRAIL... JUST TWO RI* BEFORE OUR DESTINATION... WHEN A SUDDEN, FIERCE STORM HIT US."
KRAKLL!!
*1 RI = 3.9 KILOMETERS
ULP!
MITSUTOSHI!
KALUMP!
MITSUTOSHI-- GRAB MY HAND!
HURRY! IT'S CRUMBLING UNDER M--
YAHH!!
CRUMBLL!
GOT YOU!
2.

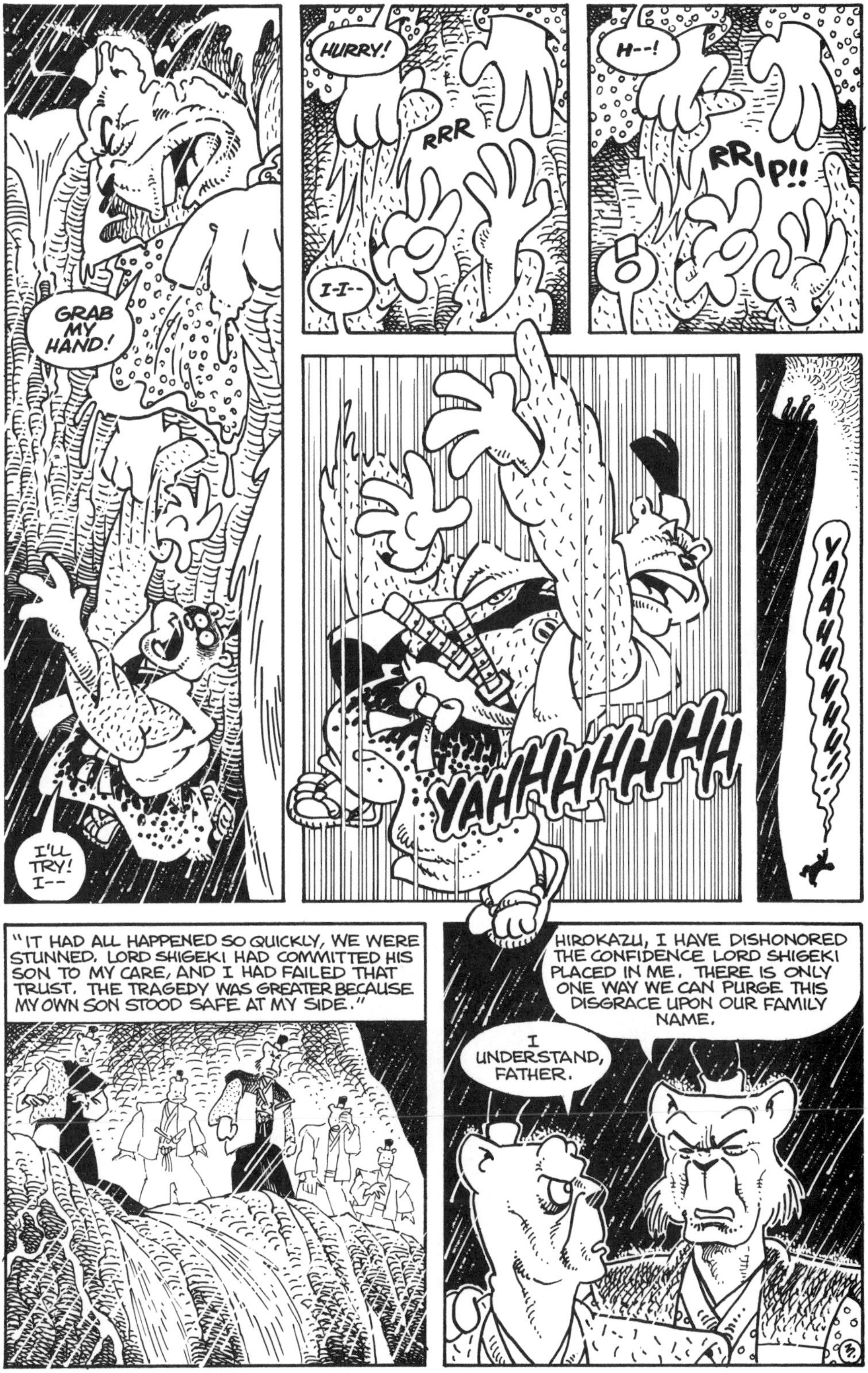
GRAB MY HAND!
I'LL TRY! I--
HURRY!
RRR
I-I--
H--!
RRIP!!
!
YAHHHHHHHH
YAAHHHHHHH!
"IT HAD ALL HAPPENED SO QUICKLY, WE WERE STUNNED. LORD SHIGEKI HAD COMMITTED HIS SON TO MY CARE, AND I HAD FAILED THAT TRUST. THE TRAGEDY WAS GREATER BECAUSE MY OWN SON STOOD SAFE AT MY SIDE."
HIROKAZU, I HAVE DISHONORED THE CONFIDENCE LORD SHIGEKI PLACED IN ME. THERE IS ONLY ONE WAY WE CAN PURGE THIS DISGRACE UPON OUR FAMILY NAME.
I UNDERSTAND, FATHER.

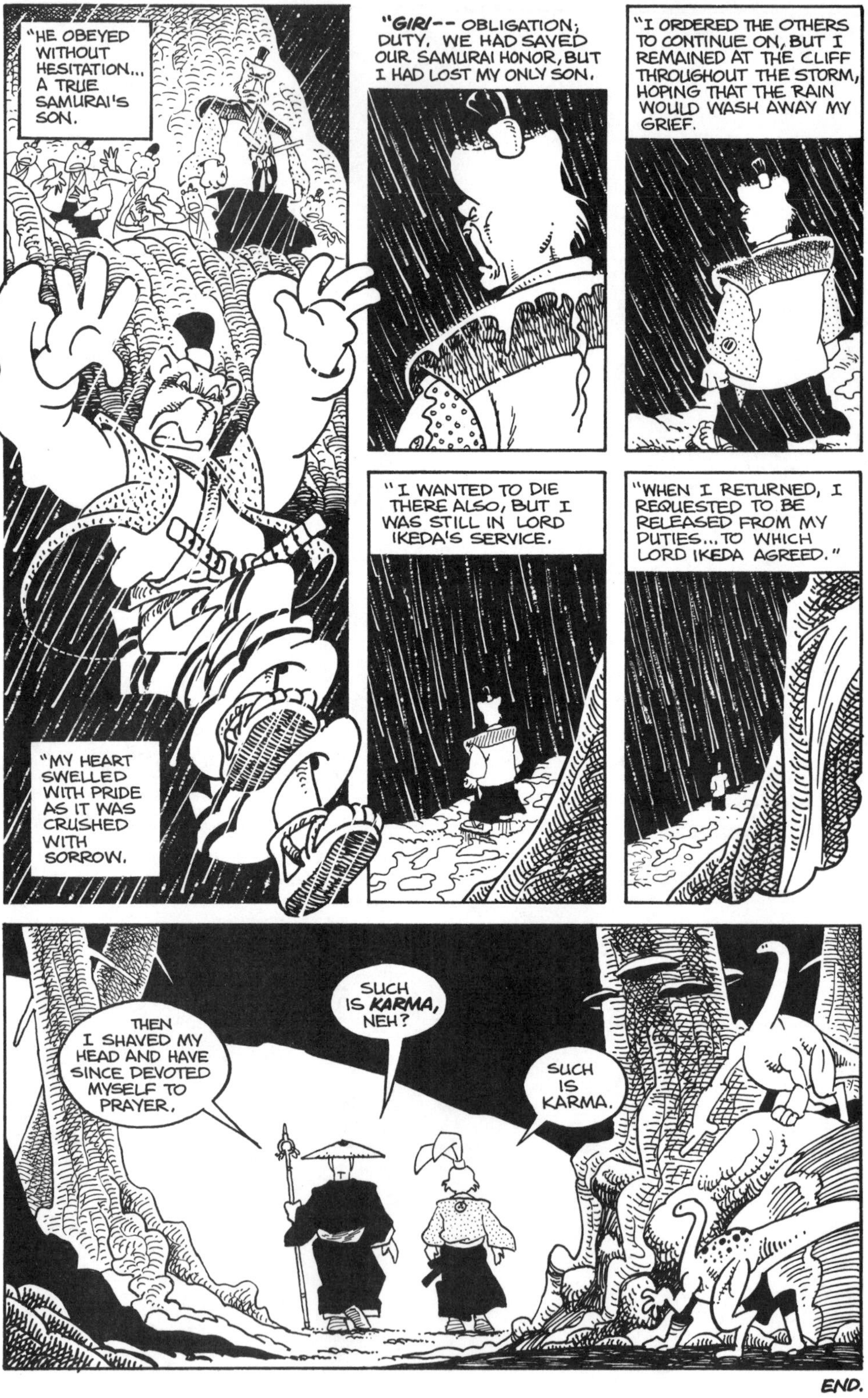
"HE OBEYED WITHOUT HESITATION... A TRUE SAMURAI'S SON.
"MY HEART SWELLED WITH PRIDE AS IT WAS CRUSHED WITH SORROW.
"GIRI-- OBLIGATION; DUTY. WE HAD SAVED OUR SAMURAI HONOR, BUT I HAD LOST MY ONLY SON.
"I ORDERED THE OTHERS TO CONTINUE ON, BUT I REMAINED AT THE CLIFF THROUGHOUT THE STORM, HOPING THAT THE RAIN WOULD WASH AWAY MY GRIEF.
"I WANTED TO DIE THERE ALSO, BUT I WAS STILL IN LORD IKEDA'S SERVICE.
"WHEN I RETURNED, I REQUESTED TO BE RELEASED FROM MY DUTIES... TO WHICH LORD IKEDA AGREED."
THEN I SHAVED MY HEAD AND HAVE SINCE DEVOTED MYSELF TO PRAYER.
SUCH IS KARMA, NEH?
SUCH IS KARMA.
END.

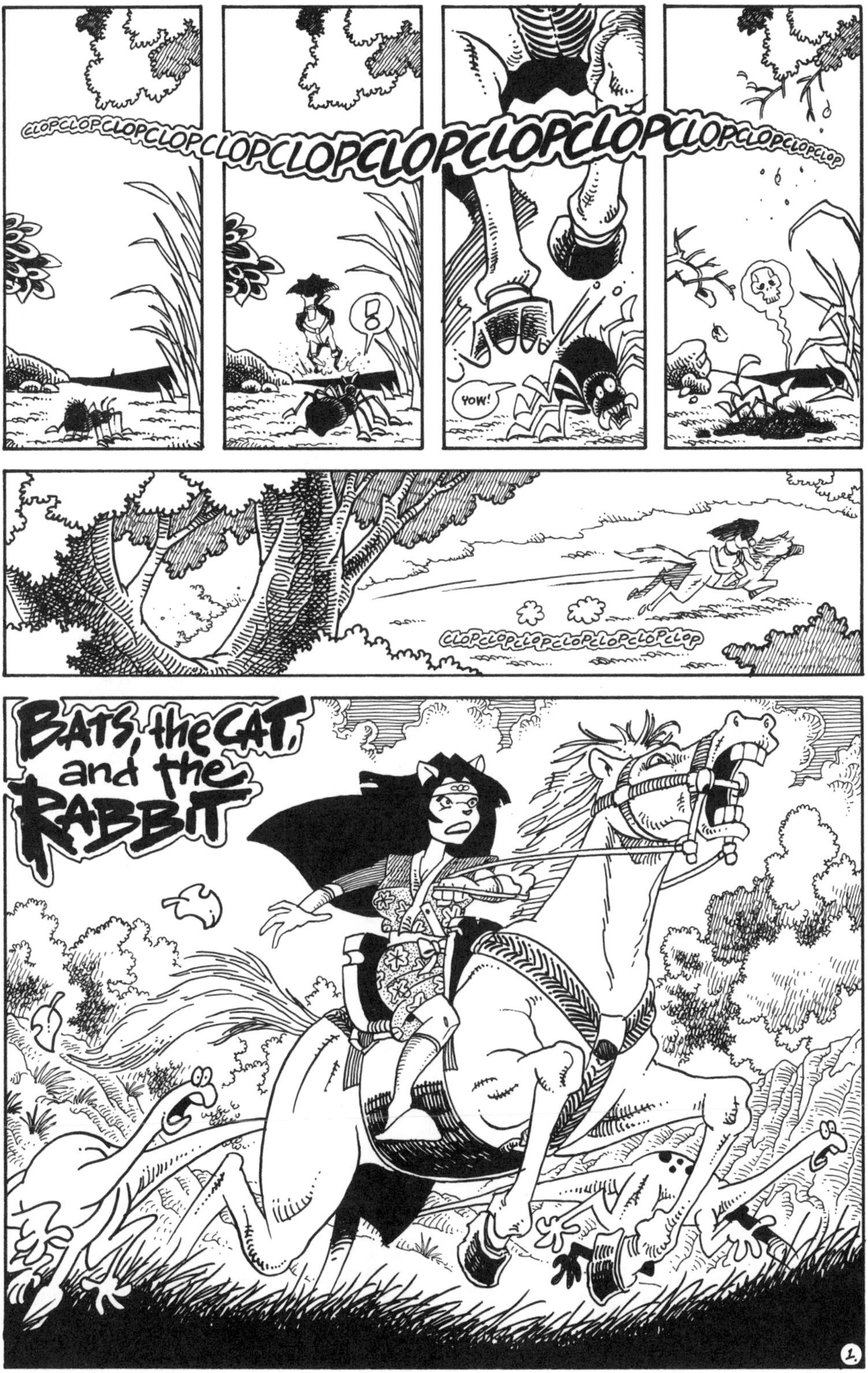

CLOPCLOPCLOPCLOPCLOPCLOPCLOPCLOPCLOPCLOPCLOPCLOPCLOP
!
YOW!
CLOPCLOPCLOPCLOPCLOPCLOPCLOP
BATS, the CAT, and the RABBIT
1.

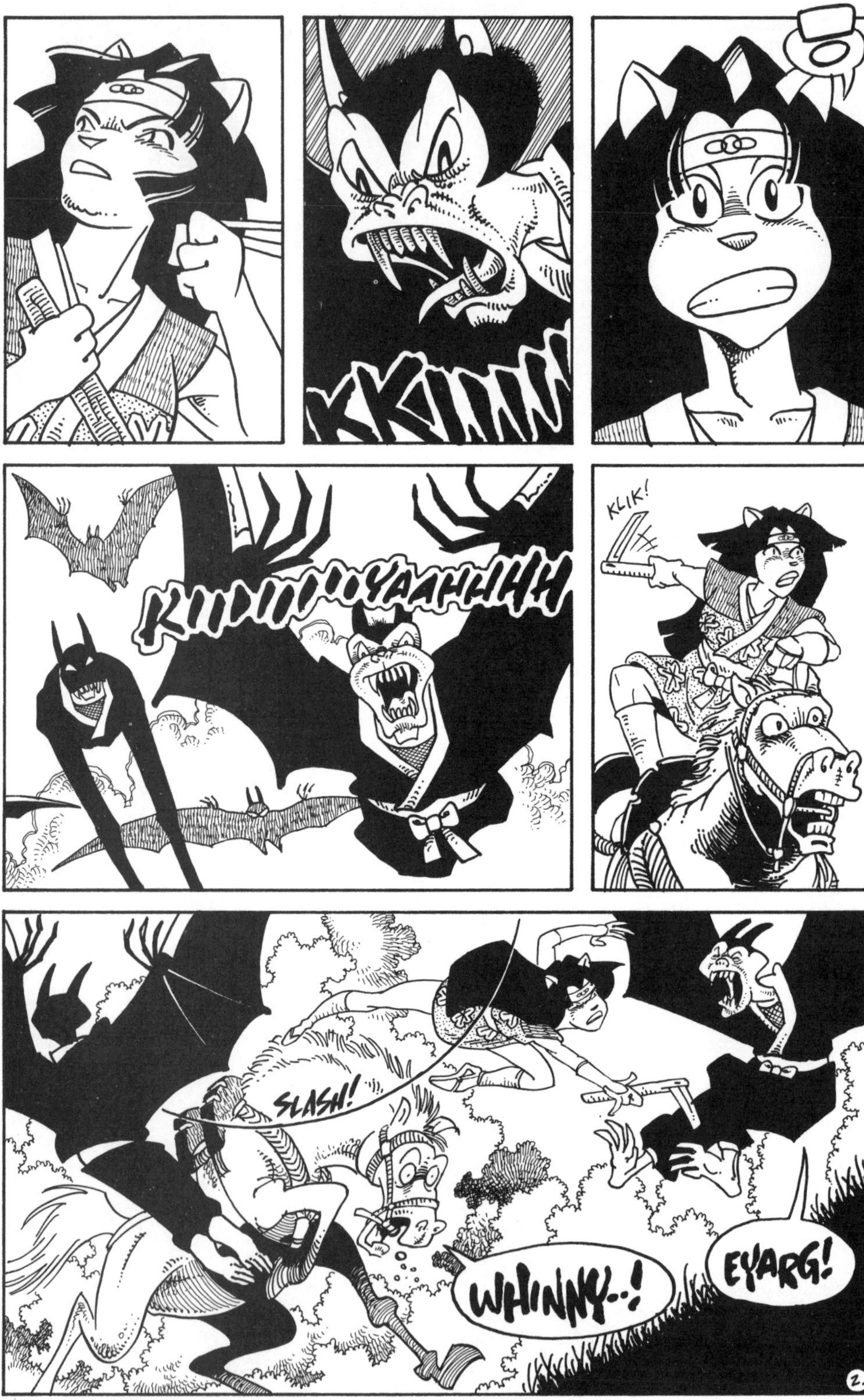
KIIIIIIYAAHHHH
KLIK!
SLASH!
WHINNY..!
EYARG!
2.

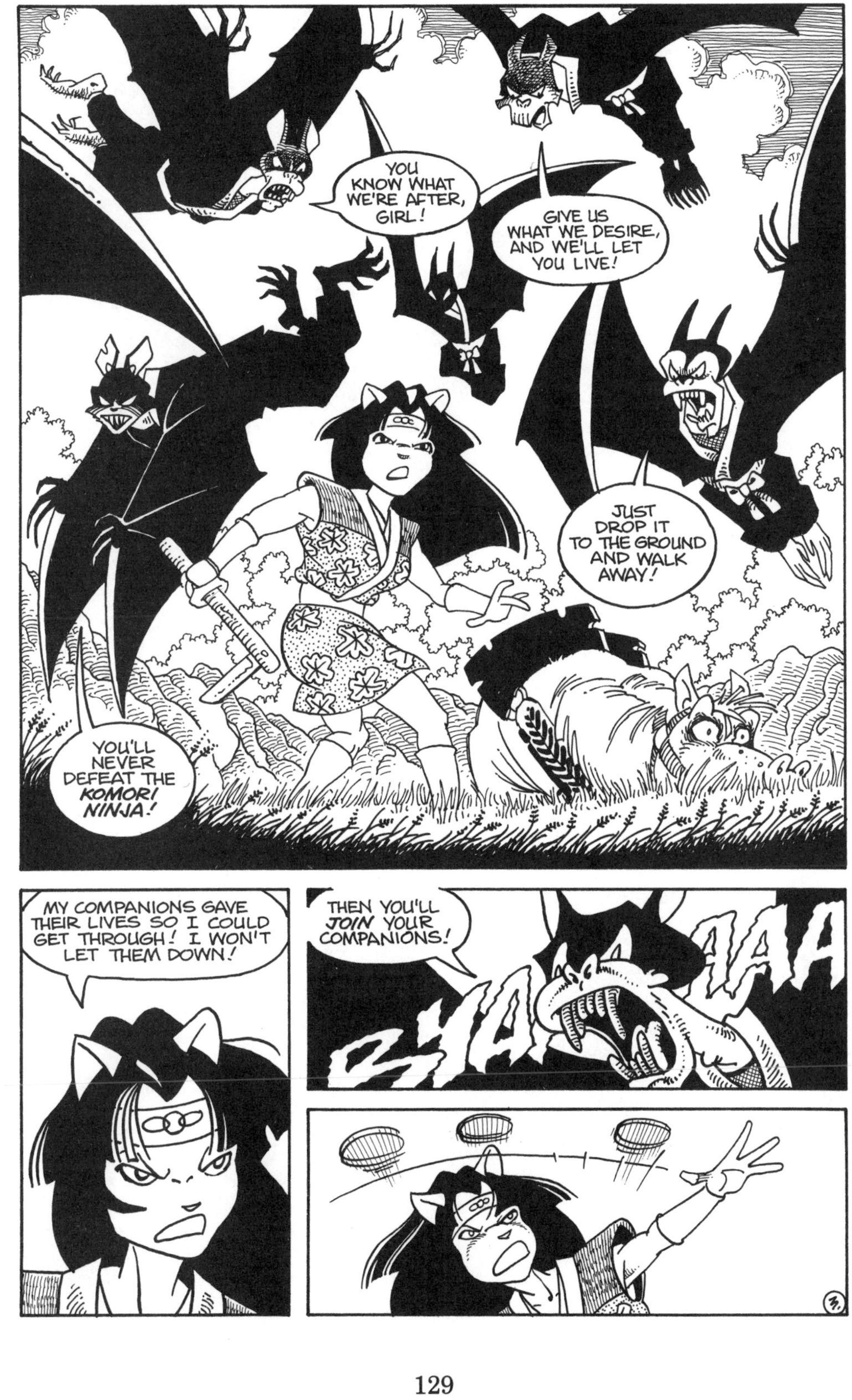
YOU KNOW WHAT WE'RE AFTER, GIRL!
GIVE US WHAT WE DESIRE, AND WE'LL LET YOU LIVE!
JUST DROP IT TO THE GROUND AND WALK AWAY!
YOU'LL NEVER DEFEAT THE *KOMORI NINJA*!
MY COMPANIONS GAVE THEIR LIVES SO I COULD GET THROUGH! I WON'T LET THEM DOWN!
THEN YOU'LL *JOIN* YOUR COMPANIONS!

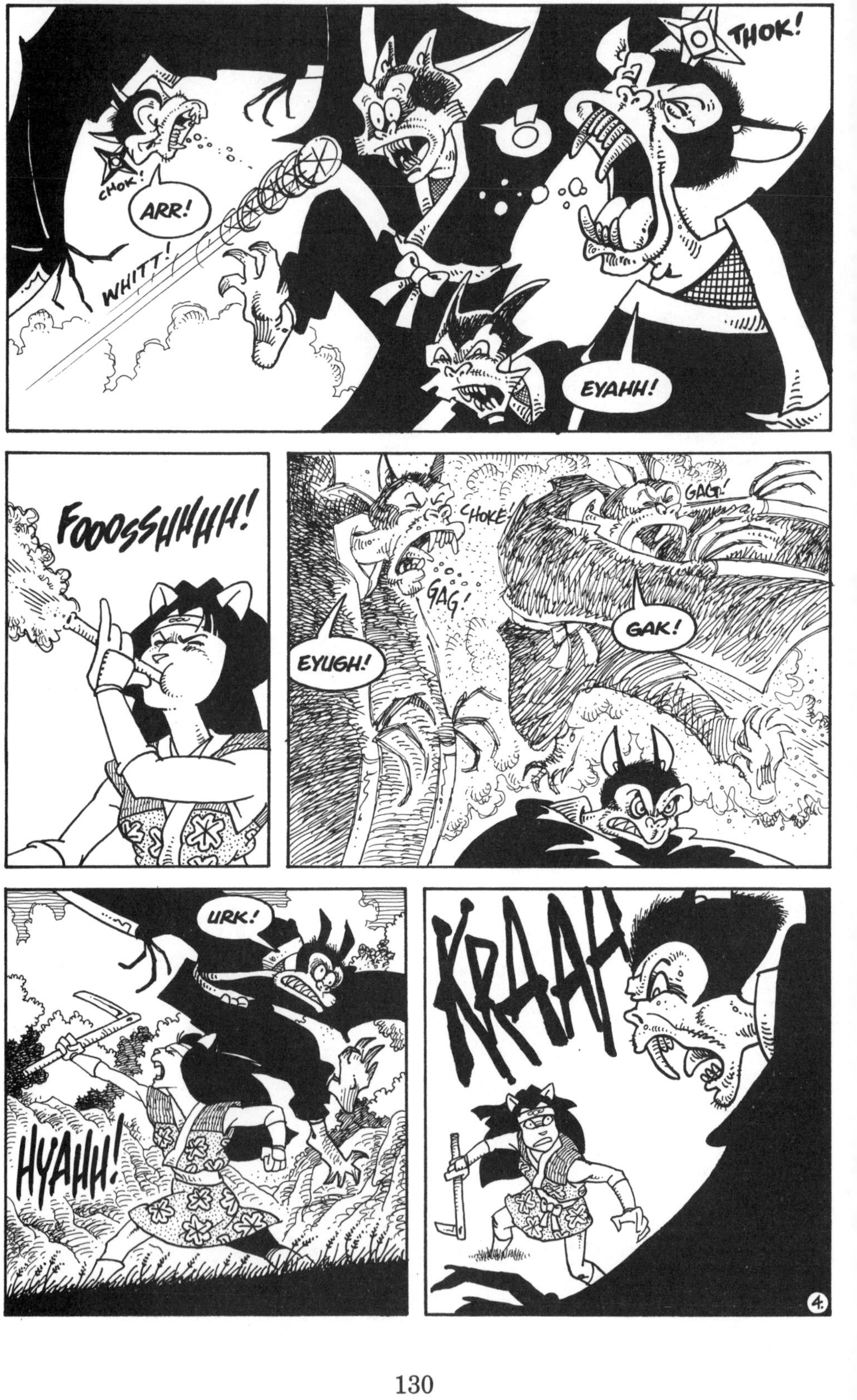
CHOK!
ARR!
WHITT!
THOK!
EYAHH!
FOOOSSHHHH!
CHOKE!
GAG!
GAG!
EYUGH!
GAK!
URK!
HYAHH!
KRAAH
4.

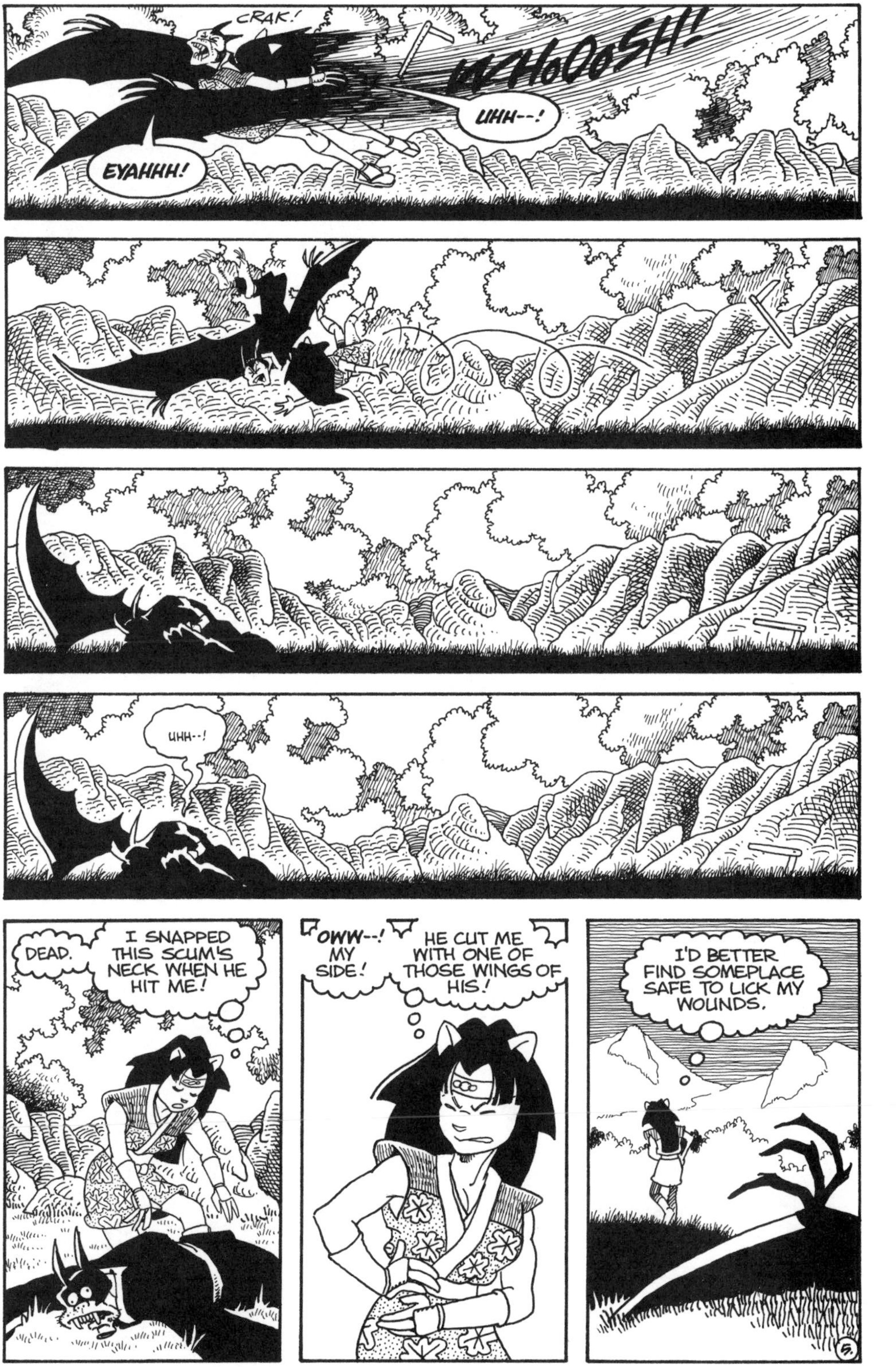
CRAK!
WHOOOSH!
UHH--!
EYAHHH!
UHH--!
DEAD.
I SNAPPED THIS SCUM'S NECK WHEN HE HIT ME!
OWW--! MY SIDE!
HE CUT ME WITH ONE OF THOSE WINGS OF HIS!
I'D BETTER FIND SOMEPLACE SAFE TO LICK MY WOUNDS.
5.

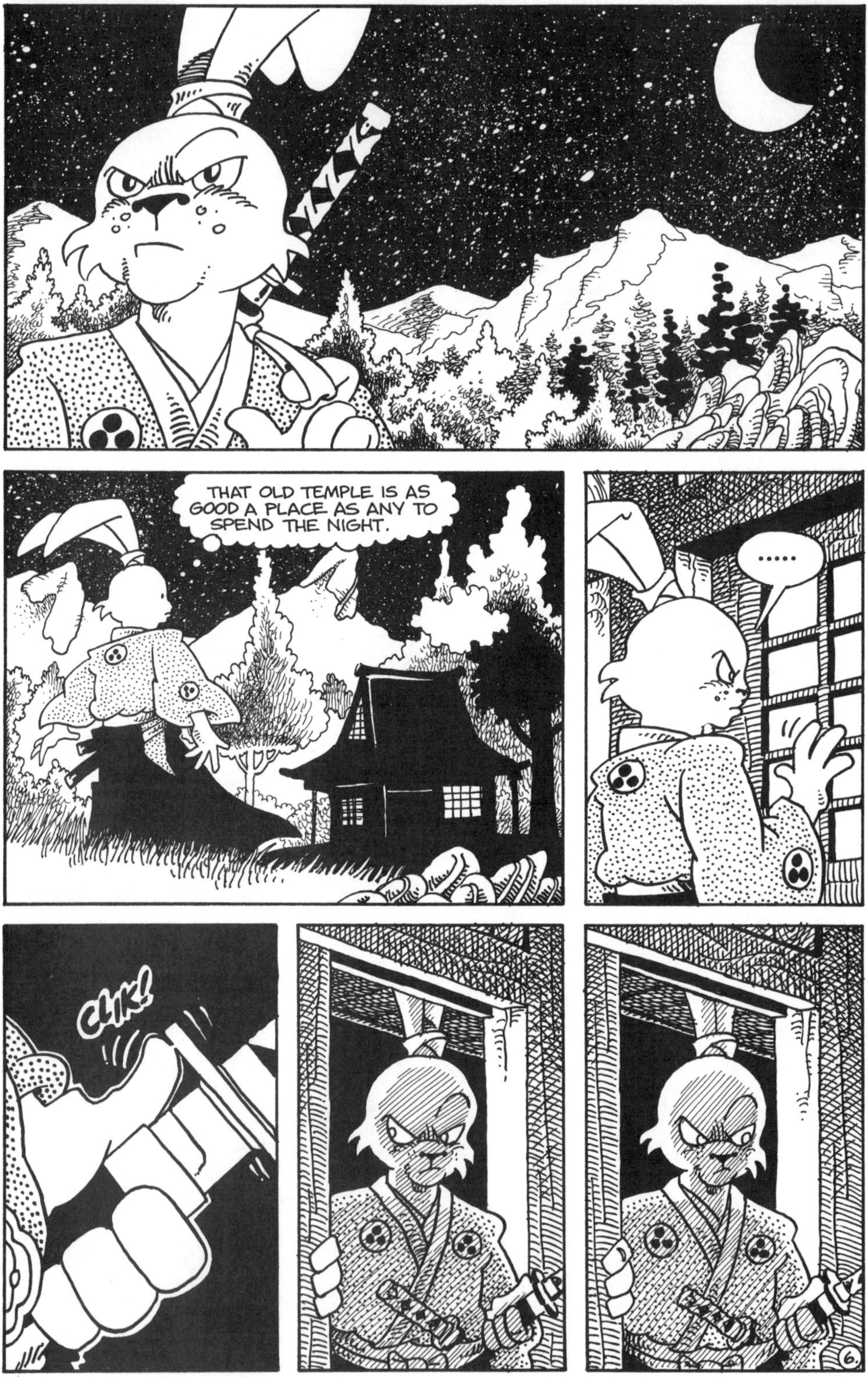
THAT OLD TEMPLE IS AS GOOD A PLACE AS ANY TO SPEND THE NIGHT.
......
CLIK!
6.

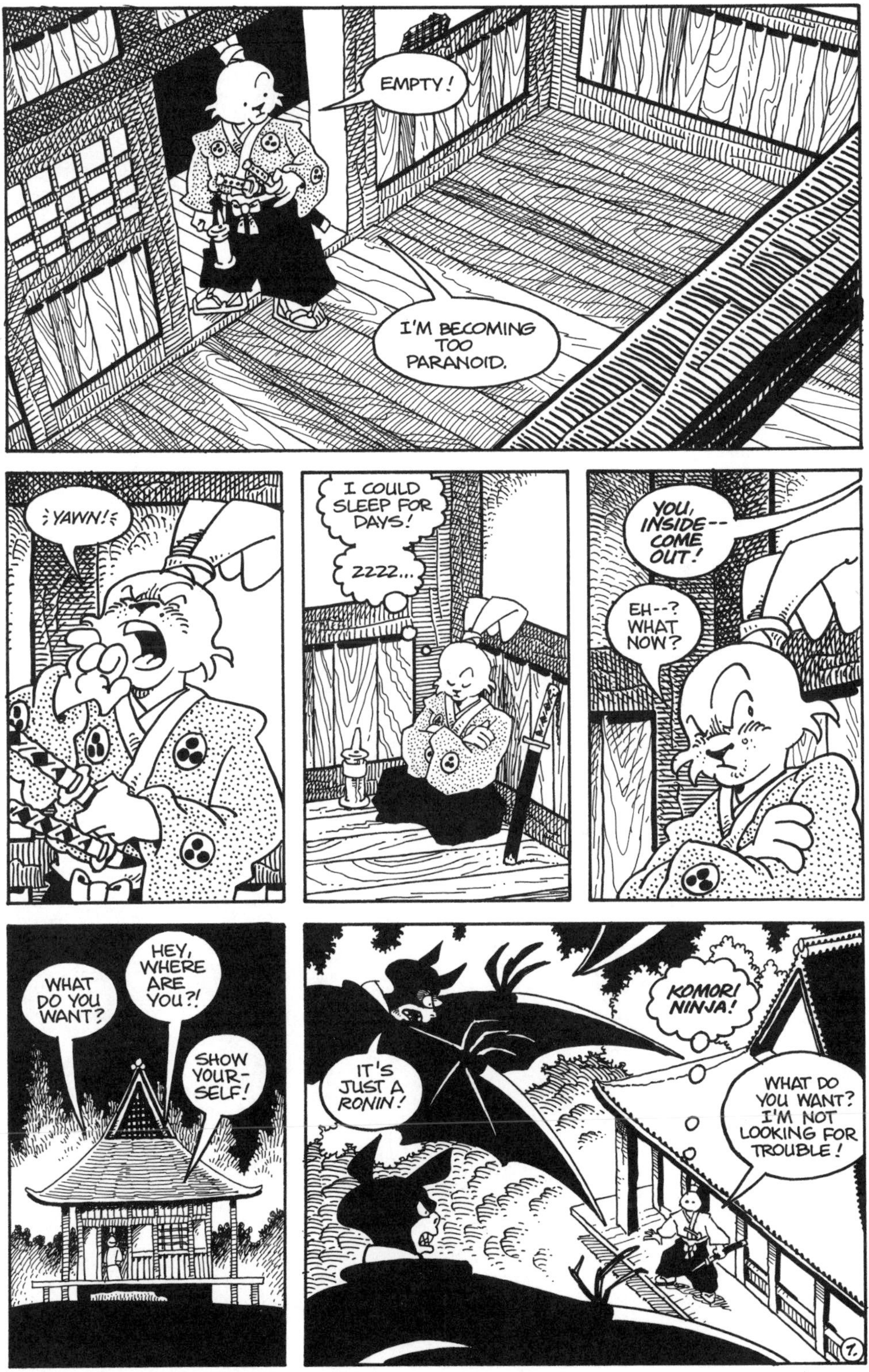
EMPTY!
I'M BECOMING TOO PARANOID.
YAWN!
I COULD SLEEP FOR DAYS!
ZZZZ...
YOU, INSIDE-- COME OUT!
EH--? WHAT NOW?
WHAT DO YOU WANT?
HEY, WHERE ARE YOU?!
SHOW YOURSELF!
IT'S JUST A RONIN!
KOMORI NINJA!
WHAT DO YOU WANT? I'M NOT LOOKING FOR TROUBLE!
7.

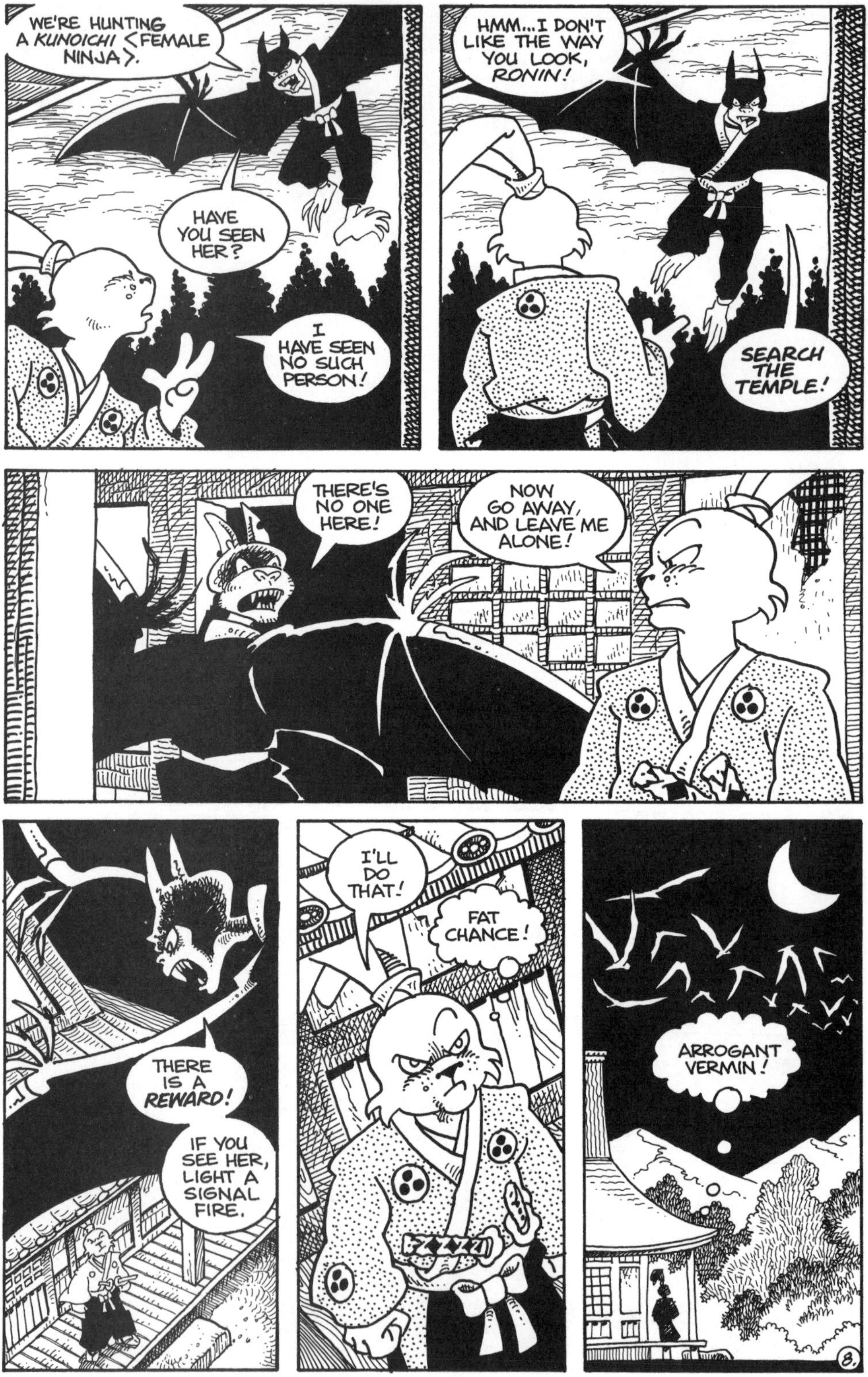
WE'RE HUNTING A KUNOICHI <FEMALE NINJA>.
HAVE YOU SEEN HER?
I HAVE SEEN NO SUCH PERSON!
HMM...I DON'T LIKE THE WAY YOU LOOK, RONIN!
SEARCH THE TEMPLE!
THERE'S NO ONE HERE!
NOW GO AWAY, AND LEAVE ME ALONE!
THERE IS A REWARD!
IF YOU SEE HER, LIGHT A SIGNAL FIRE.
I'LL DO THAT!
FAT CHANCE!
ARROGANT VERMIN!
8.

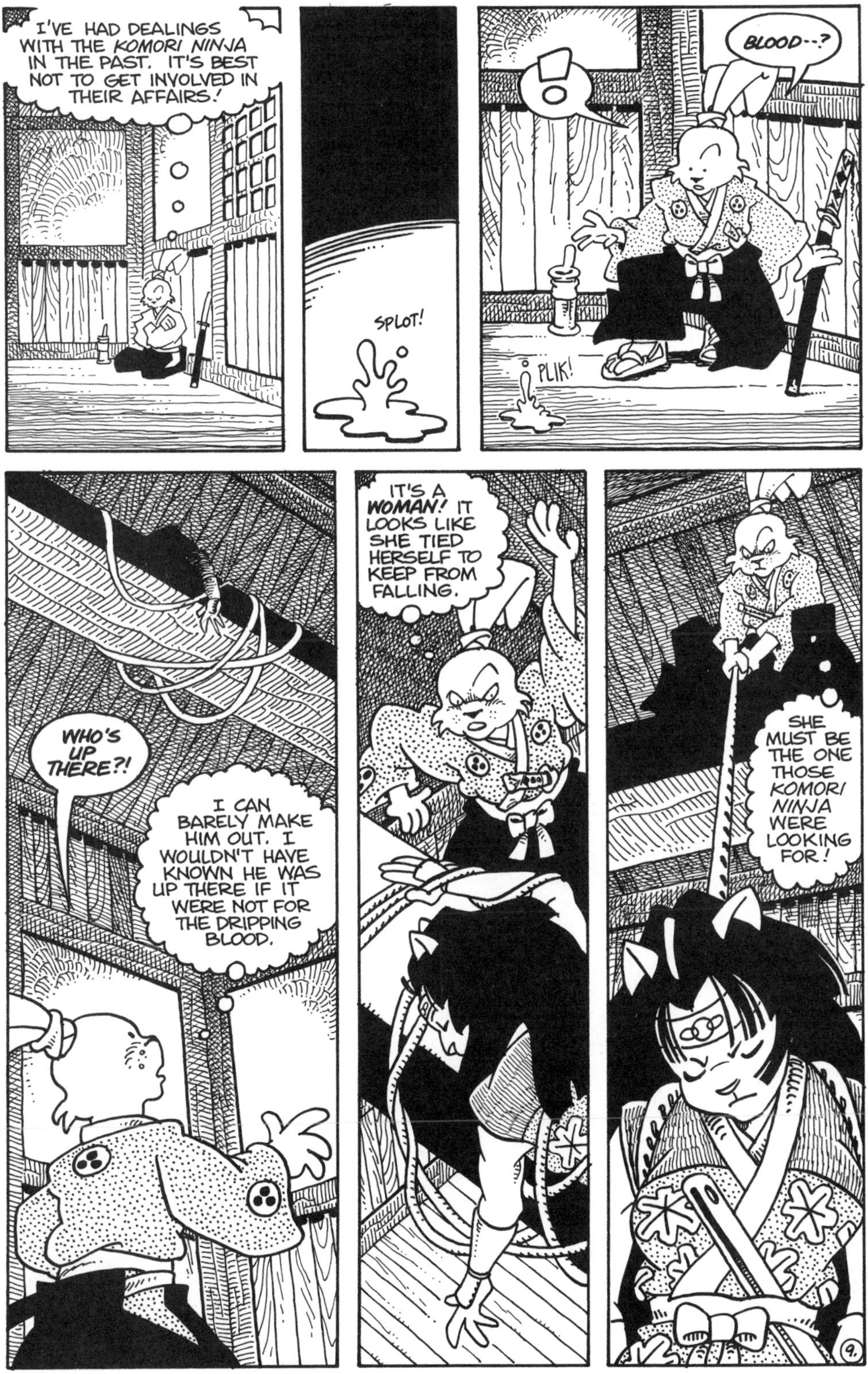

I'VE HAD DEALINGS WITH THE KOMORI NINJA IN THE PAST. IT'S BEST NOT TO GET INVOLVED IN THEIR AFFAIRS!
SPLOT!
!
BLOOD--?
PLIK!
WHO'S UP THERE?!
I CAN BARELY MAKE HIM OUT. I WOULDN'T HAVE KNOWN HE WAS UP THERE IF IT WERE NOT FOR THE DRIPPING BLOOD.
IT'S A WOMAN! IT LOOKS LIKE SHE TIED HERSELF TO KEEP FROM FALLING.
SHE MUST BE THE ONE THOSE KOMORI NINJA WERE LOOKING FOR!
9.

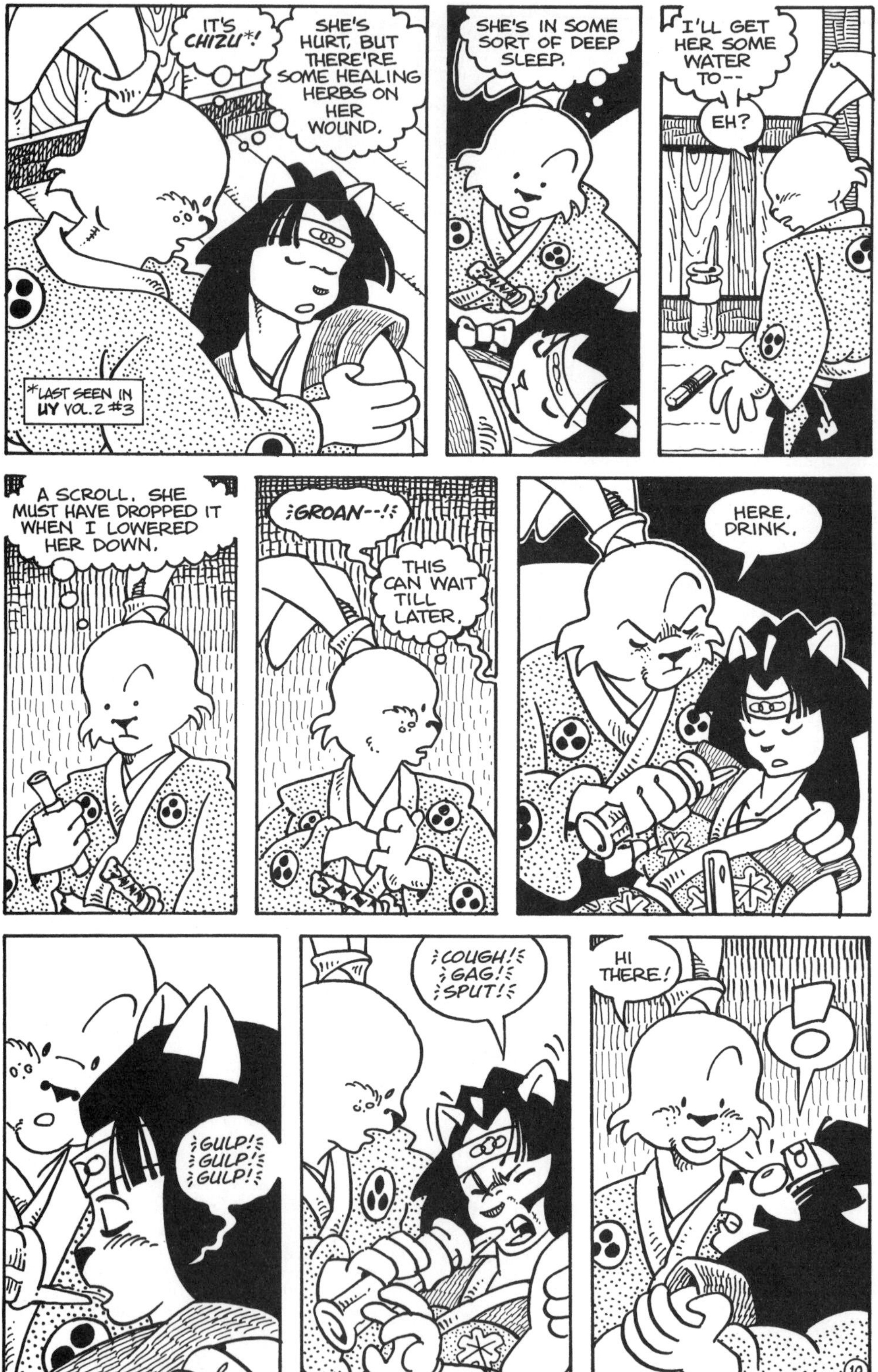
IT'S CHIZU*!
SHE'S HURT, BUT THERE'RE SOME HEALING HERBS ON HER WOUND.
*LAST SEEN IN UY VOL. 2 #3
SHE'S IN SOME SORT OF DEEP SLEEP.
I'LL GET HER SOME WATER TO--
EH?
A SCROLL. SHE MUST HAVE DROPPED IT WHEN I LOWERED HER DOWN.
GROAN--!
THIS CAN WAIT TILL LATER.
HERE. DRINK.
GULP! GULP! GULP!
COUGH! GAG! SPUT!
HI THERE!
!
10

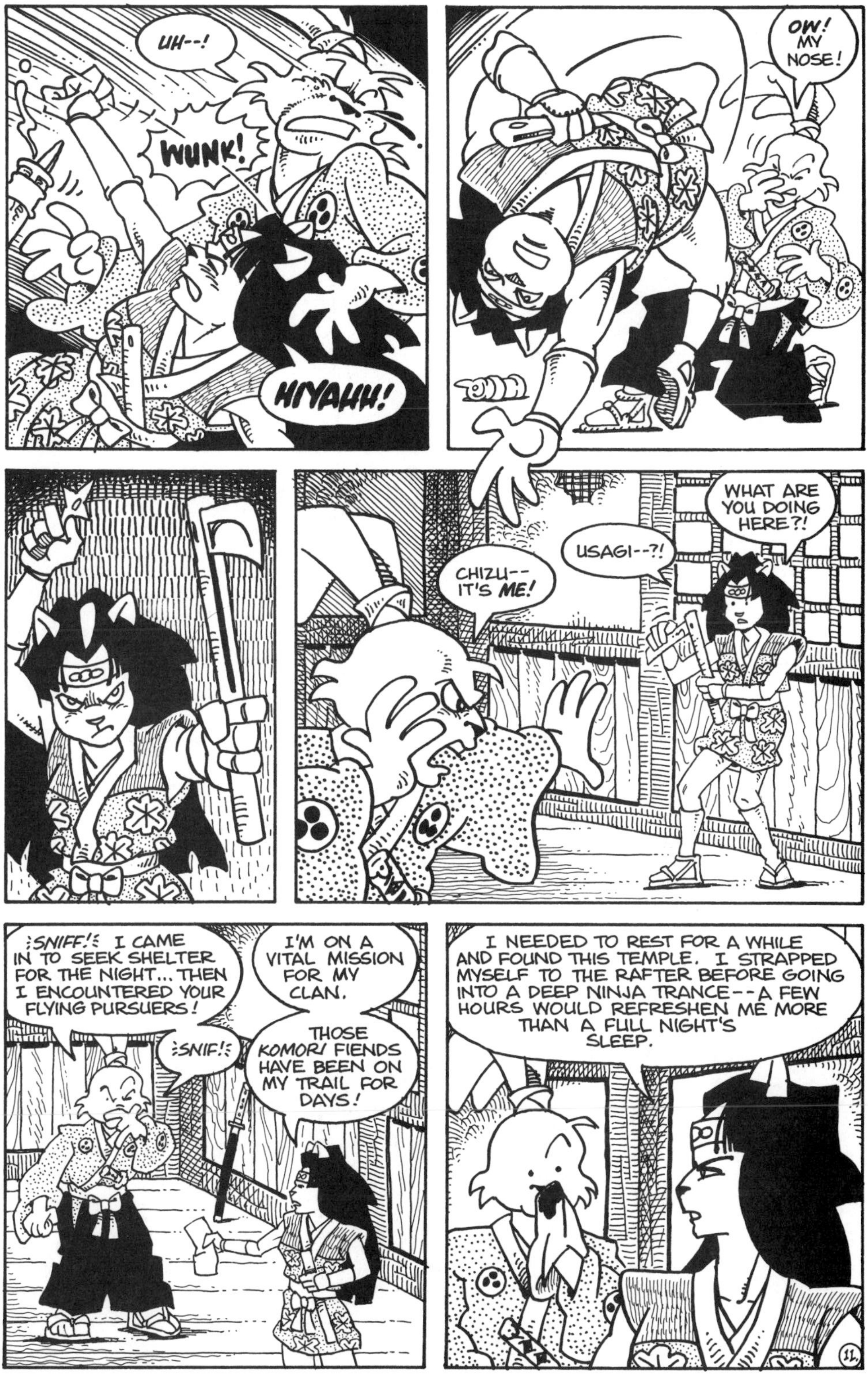
UH--!
WUNK!
HIYAHH!
OW! MY NOSE!
CHIZU-- IT'S ME!
USAGI--?!
WHAT ARE YOU DOING HERE?!
:SNIFF!: I CAME IN TO SEEK SHELTER FOR THE NIGHT... THEN I ENCOUNTERED YOUR FLYING PURSUERS!
:SNIF!:
I'M ON A VITAL MISSION FOR MY CLAN.
THOSE KOMORI FIENDS HAVE BEEN ON MY TRAIL FOR DAYS!
I NEEDED TO REST FOR A WHILE AND FOUND THIS TEMPLE. I STRAPPED MYSELF TO THE RAFTER BEFORE GOING INTO A DEEP NINJA TRANCE--A FEW HOURS WOULD REFRESHEN ME MORE THAN A FULL NIGHT'S SLEEP.
11.

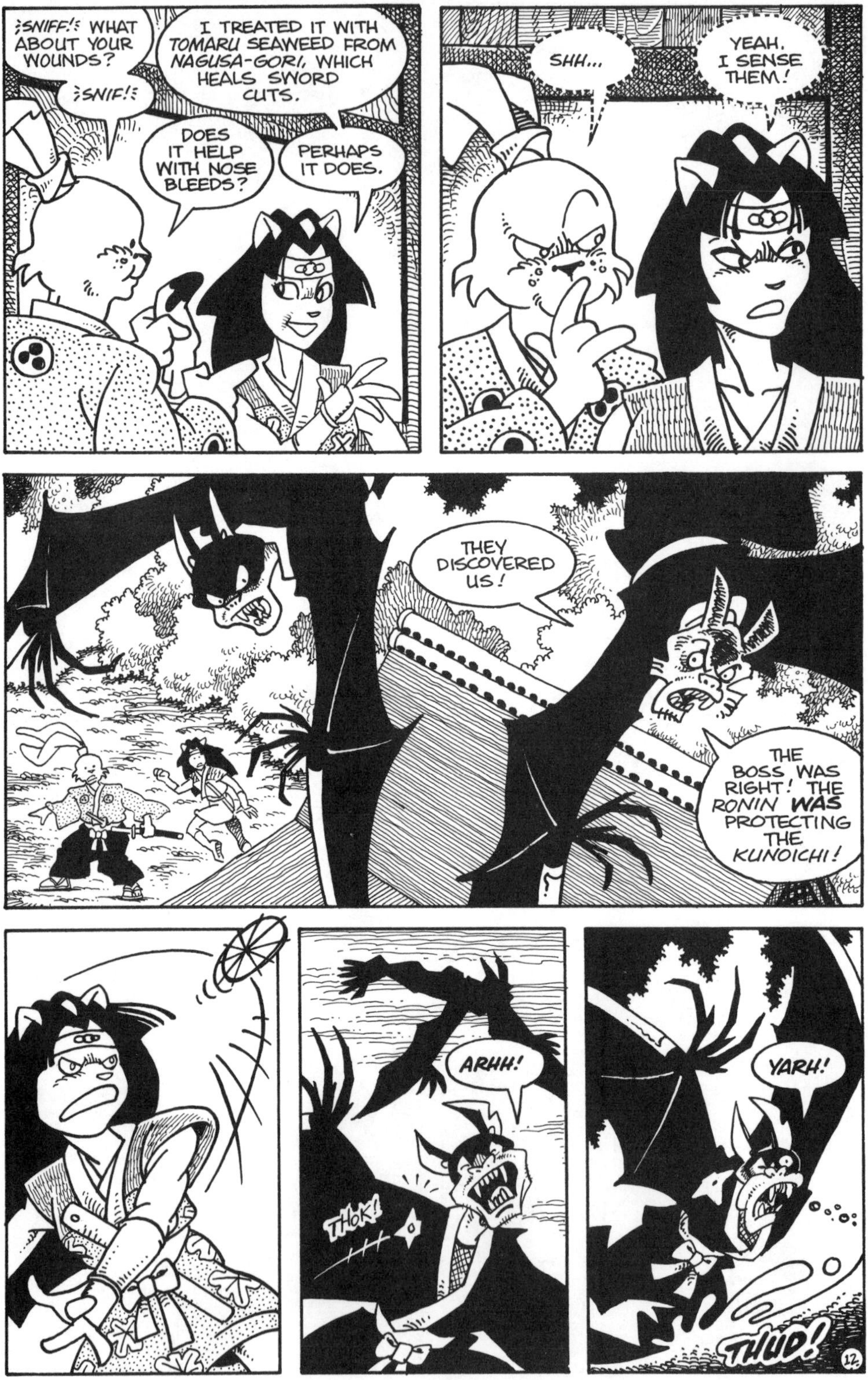

SNIFF! WHAT ABOUT YOUR WOUNDS?
SNIF!
I TREATED IT WITH TOMARU SEAWEED FROM NAGUSA-GORI, WHICH HEALS SWORD CUTS.
DOES IT HELP WITH NOSE BLEEDS?
PERHAPS IT DOES.
SHH...
YEAH, I SENSE THEM!
THEY DISCOVERED US!
THE BOSS WAS RIGHT! THE RONIN WAS PROTECTING THE KUNOICHI!
ARHH!
THOK!
YARH!
THUD!
12

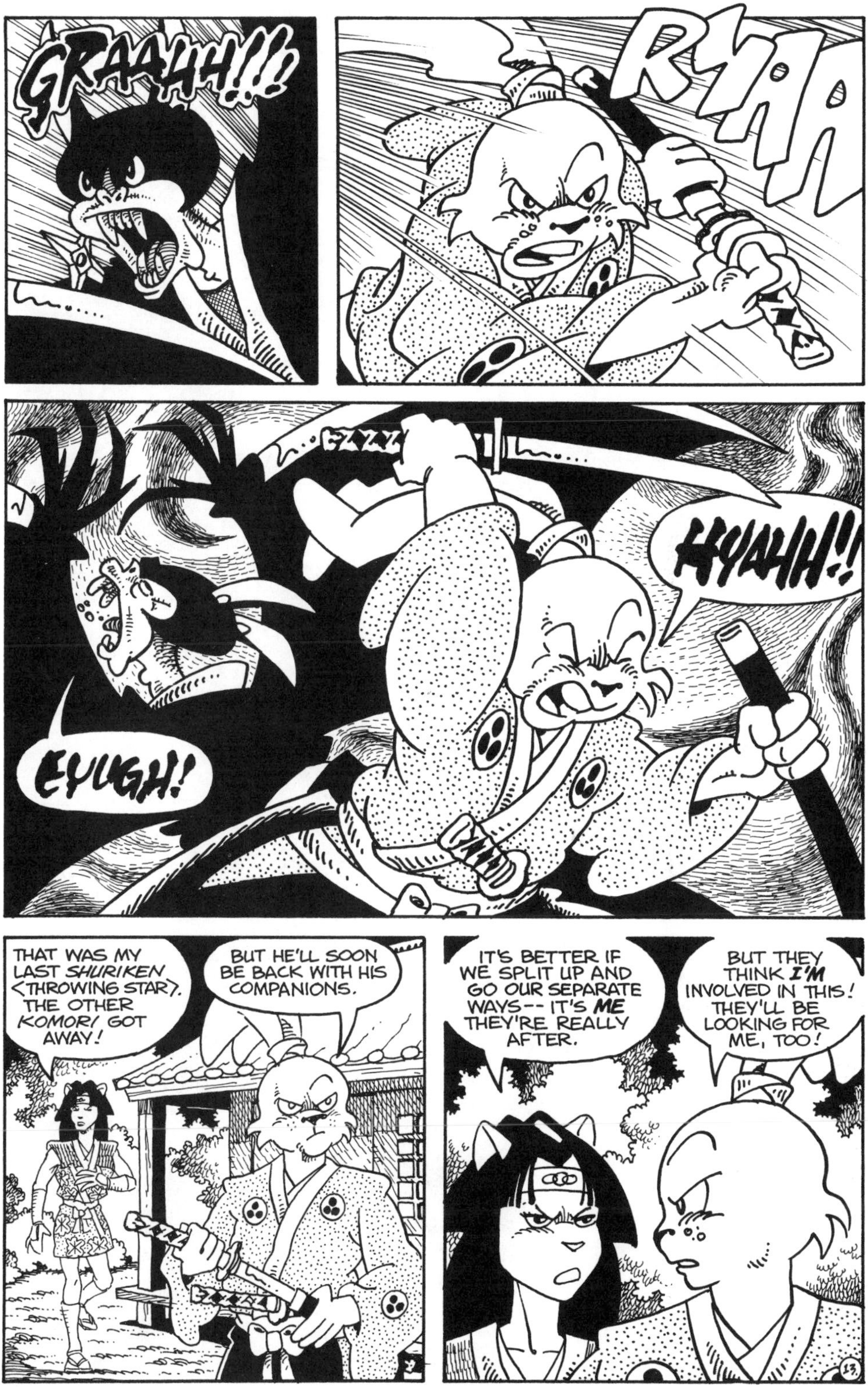
GRAAHH!!!
RYAA
HYAHH!!
EYUGH!
THAT WAS MY LAST *SHURIKEN* <THROWING STAR>. THE OTHER *KOMORI* GOT AWAY!
BUT HE'LL SOON BE BACK WITH HIS COMPANIONS.
IT'S BETTER IF WE SPLIT UP AND GO OUR SEPARATE WAYS-- IT'S ***ME*** THEY'RE REALLY AFTER.
BUT THEY THINK ***I'M*** INVOLVED IN THIS! THEY'LL BE LOOKING FOR ME, TOO!

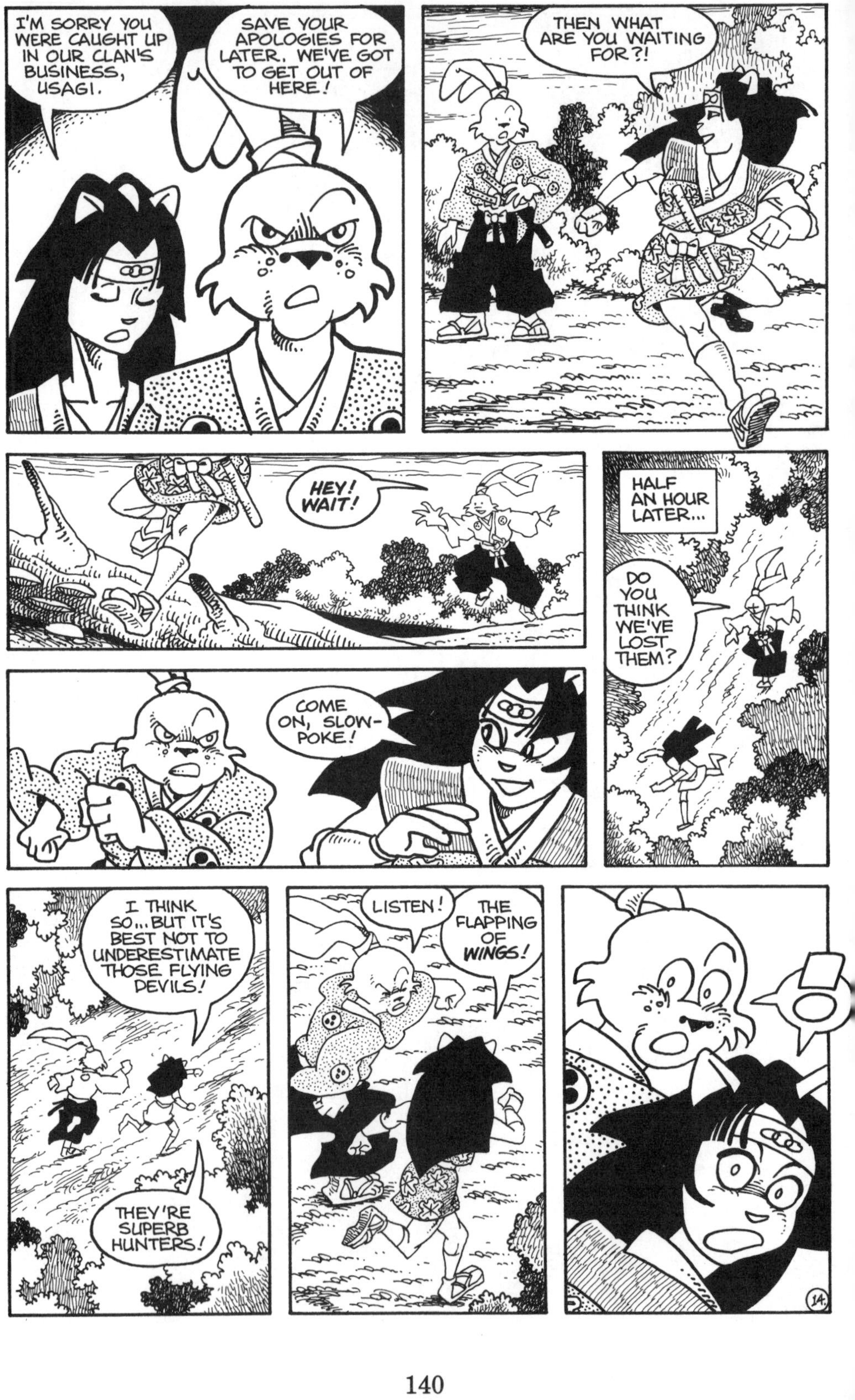
I'M SORRY YOU WERE CAUGHT UP IN OUR CLAN'S BUSINESS, USAGI.
SAVE YOUR APOLOGIES FOR LATER. WE'VE GOT TO GET OUT OF HERE!
THEN WHAT ARE YOU WAITING FOR?!
HEY! WAIT!
COME ON, SLOW-POKE!
HALF AN HOUR LATER...
DO YOU THINK WE'VE LOST THEM?
I THINK SO... BUT IT'S BEST NOT TO UNDERESTIMATE THOSE FLYING DEVILS!
THEY'RE SUPERB HUNTERS!
LISTEN!
THE FLAPPING OF WINGS!
14.

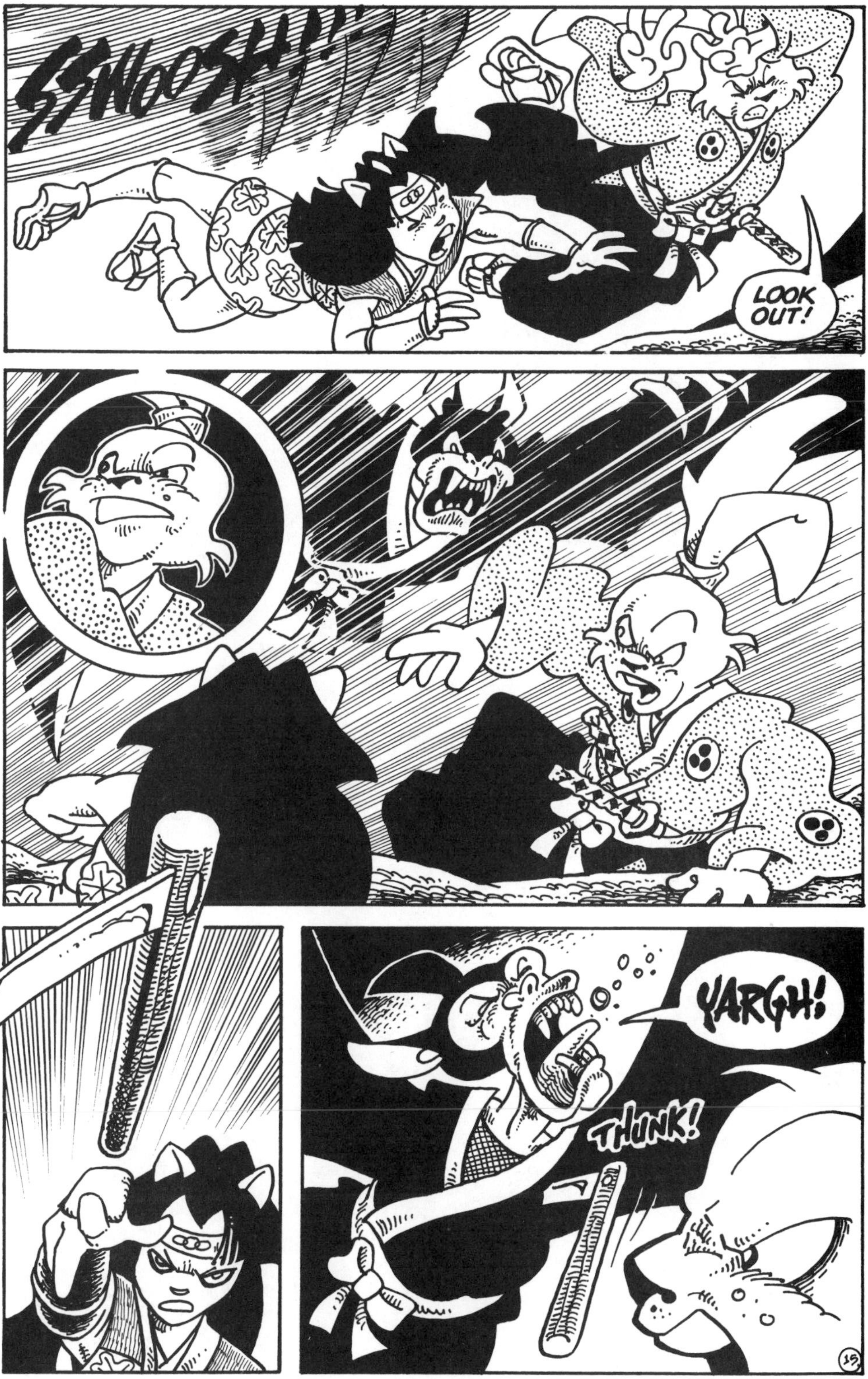
SSWOOSH!!
LOOK OUT!
YARGH!
THUNK!
15

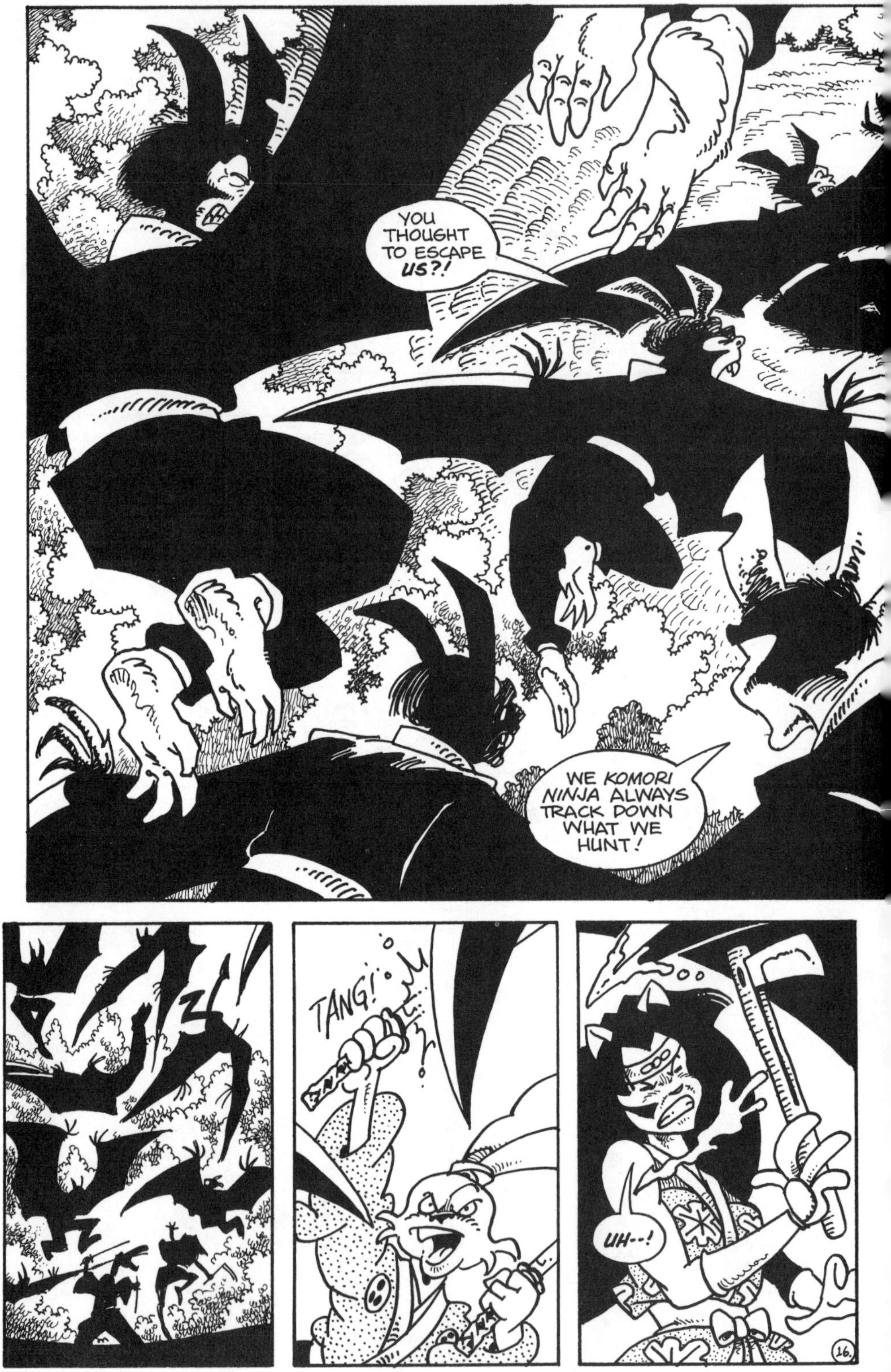
YOU THOUGHT TO ESCAPE US?!
WE KOMORI NINJA ALWAYS TRACK DOWN WHAT WE HUNT!
TANG!
UH--!
16.

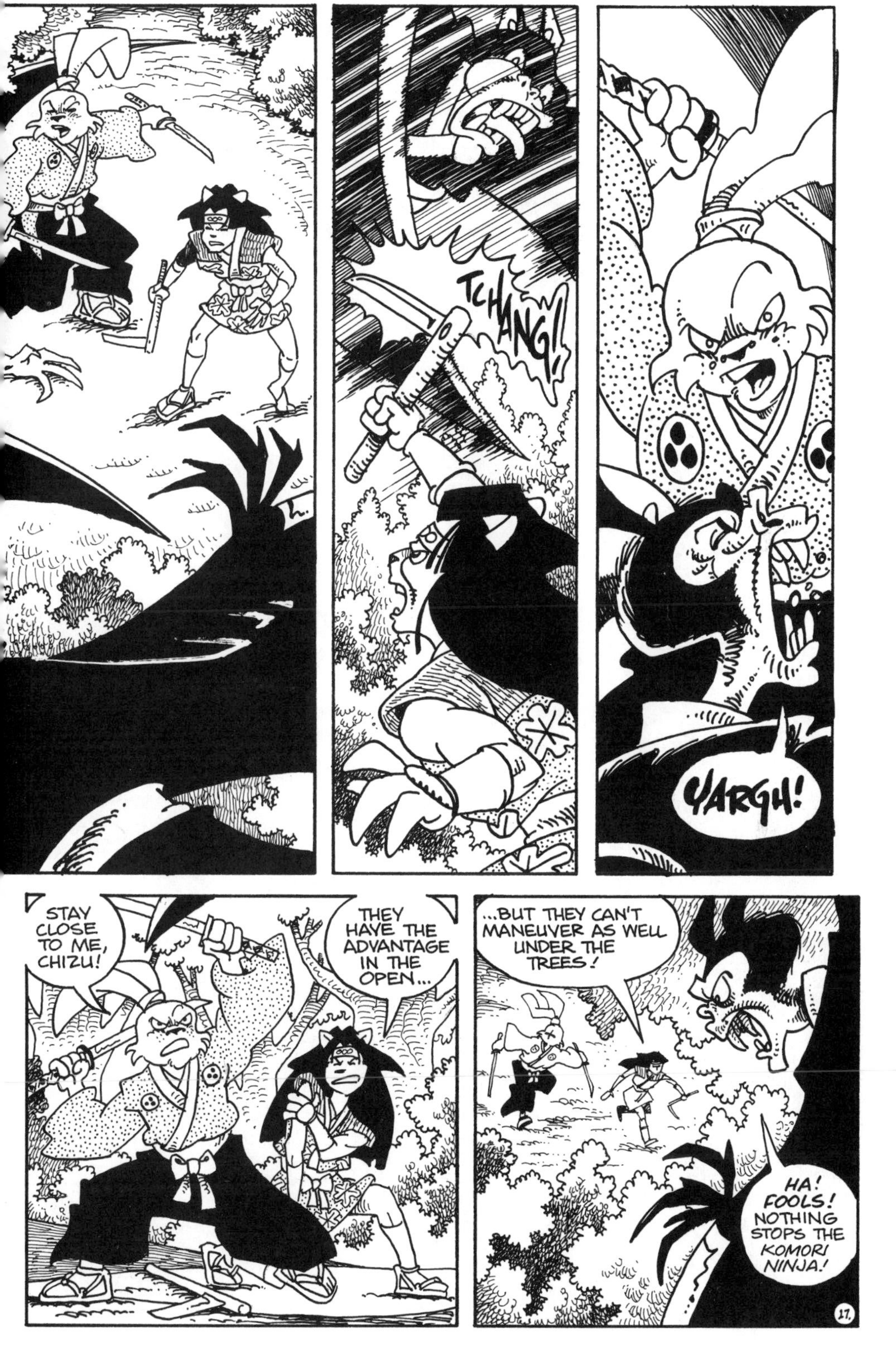
TCHANG!!
YARGH!
STAY CLOSE TO ME, CHIZU!
THEY HAVE THE ADVANTAGE IN THE OPEN...
...BUT THEY CAN'T MANEUVER AS WELL UNDER THE TREES!
HA! FOOLS! NOTHING STOPS THE KOMORI NINJA!
17.

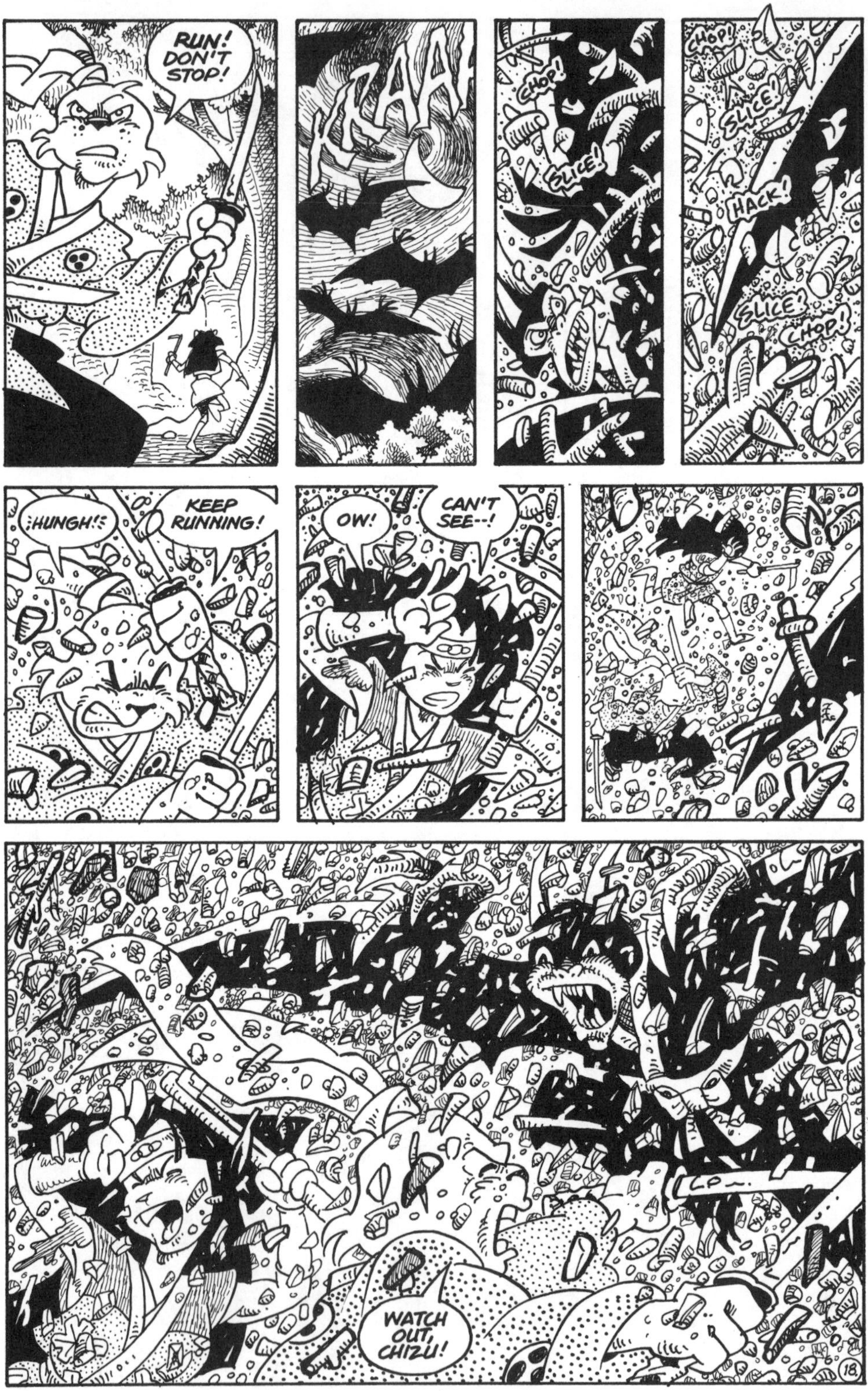
RUN! DON'T STOP!
KRAAA
CHOP!
SLICE!
CHOP!
SLICE!
HACK!
SLICE!
CHOP!
HUNGH!
KEEP RUNNING!
OW!
CAN'T SEE--!
WATCH OUT, CHIZU!
18

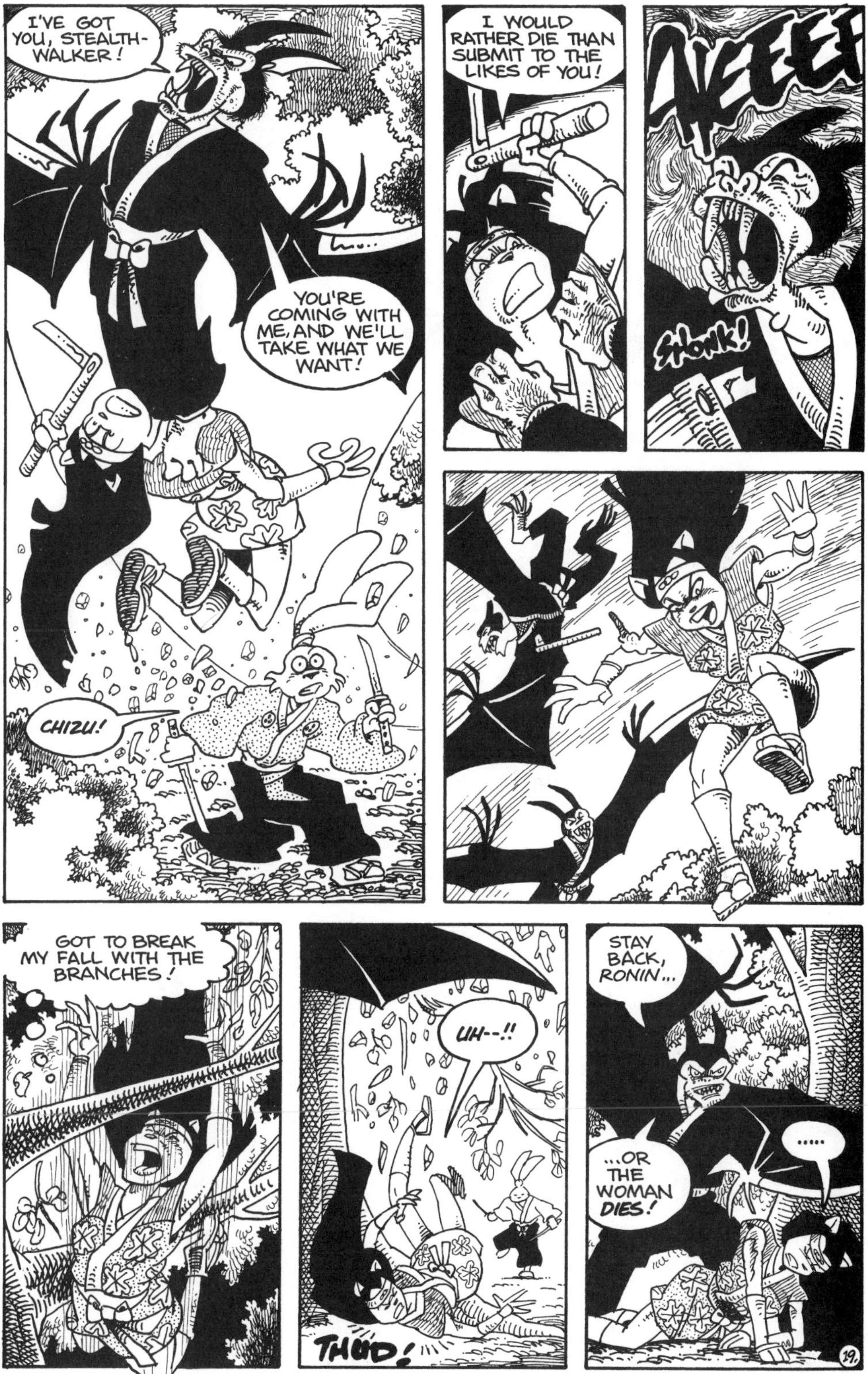
I'VE GOT YOU, STEALTH-WALKER!
YOU'RE COMING WITH ME, AND WE'LL TAKE WHAT WE WANT!
CHIZU!
I WOULD RATHER DIE THAN SUBMIT TO THE LIKES OF YOU!
AIEEEE
SHONK!
GOT TO BREAK MY FALL WITH THE BRANCHES!
UH--!!
THUD!
STAY BACK, RONIN...
...OR THE WOMAN DIES!
.....
19.

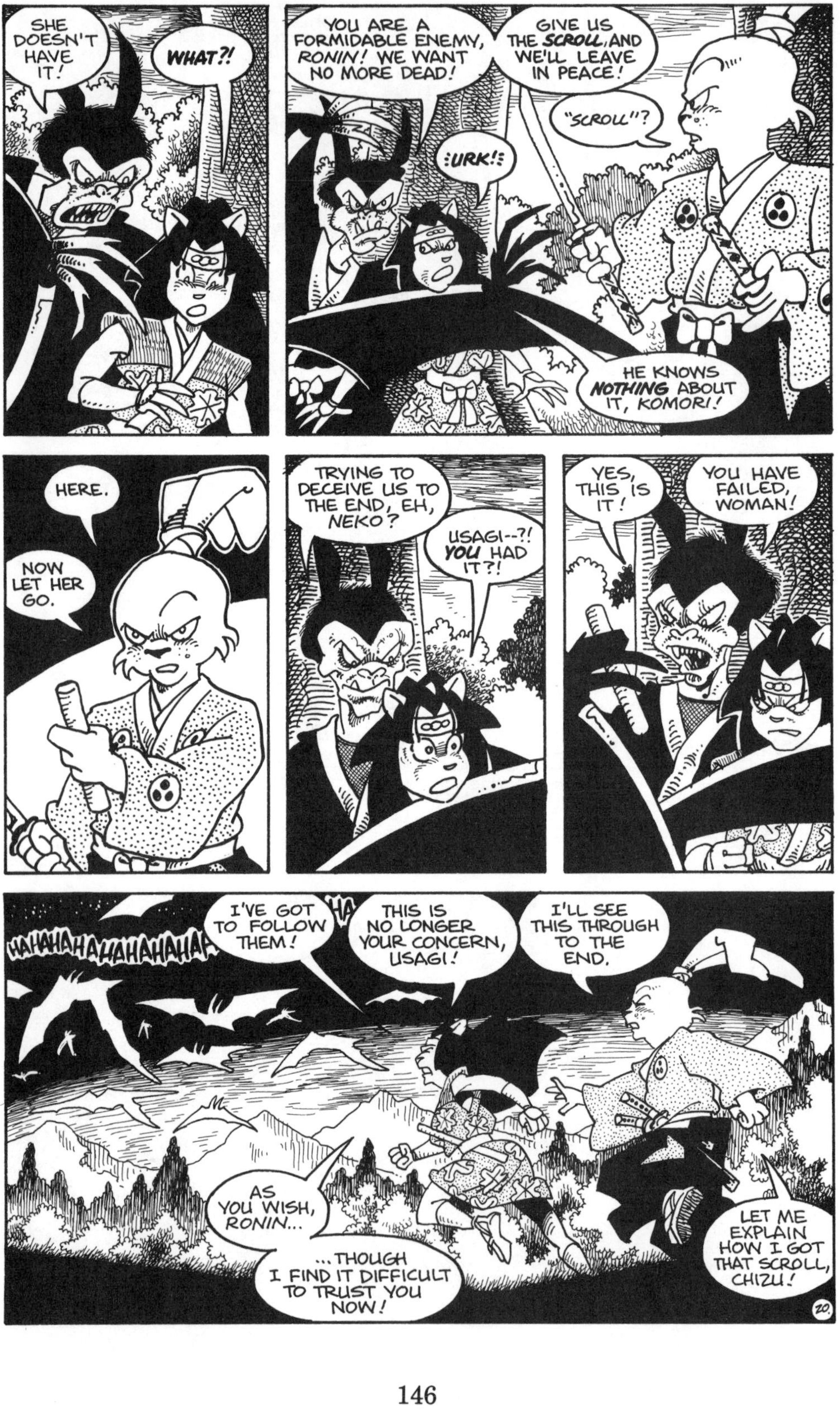
SHE DOESN'T HAVE IT!
WHAT?!
YOU ARE A FORMIDABLE ENEMY, RONIN! WE WANT NO MORE DEAD!
GIVE US THE SCROLL, AND WE'LL LEAVE IN PEACE!
"SCROLL"?
URK!
HE KNOWS NOTHING ABOUT IT, KOMORI!
HERE.
NOW LET HER GO.
TRYING TO DECEIVE US TO THE END, EH, NEKO?
USAGI--?! YOU HAD IT?!
YES, THIS IS IT!
YOU HAVE FAILED, WOMAN!
HAHAHAHAHAHAHAHAHA
HA
I'VE GOT TO FOLLOW THEM!
THIS IS NO LONGER YOUR CONCERN, USAGI!
I'LL SEE THIS THROUGH TO THE END.
AS YOU WISH, RONIN...
...THOUGH I FIND IT DIFFICULT TO TRUST YOU NOW!
LET ME EXPLAIN HOW I GOT THAT SCROLL, CHIZU!
20.

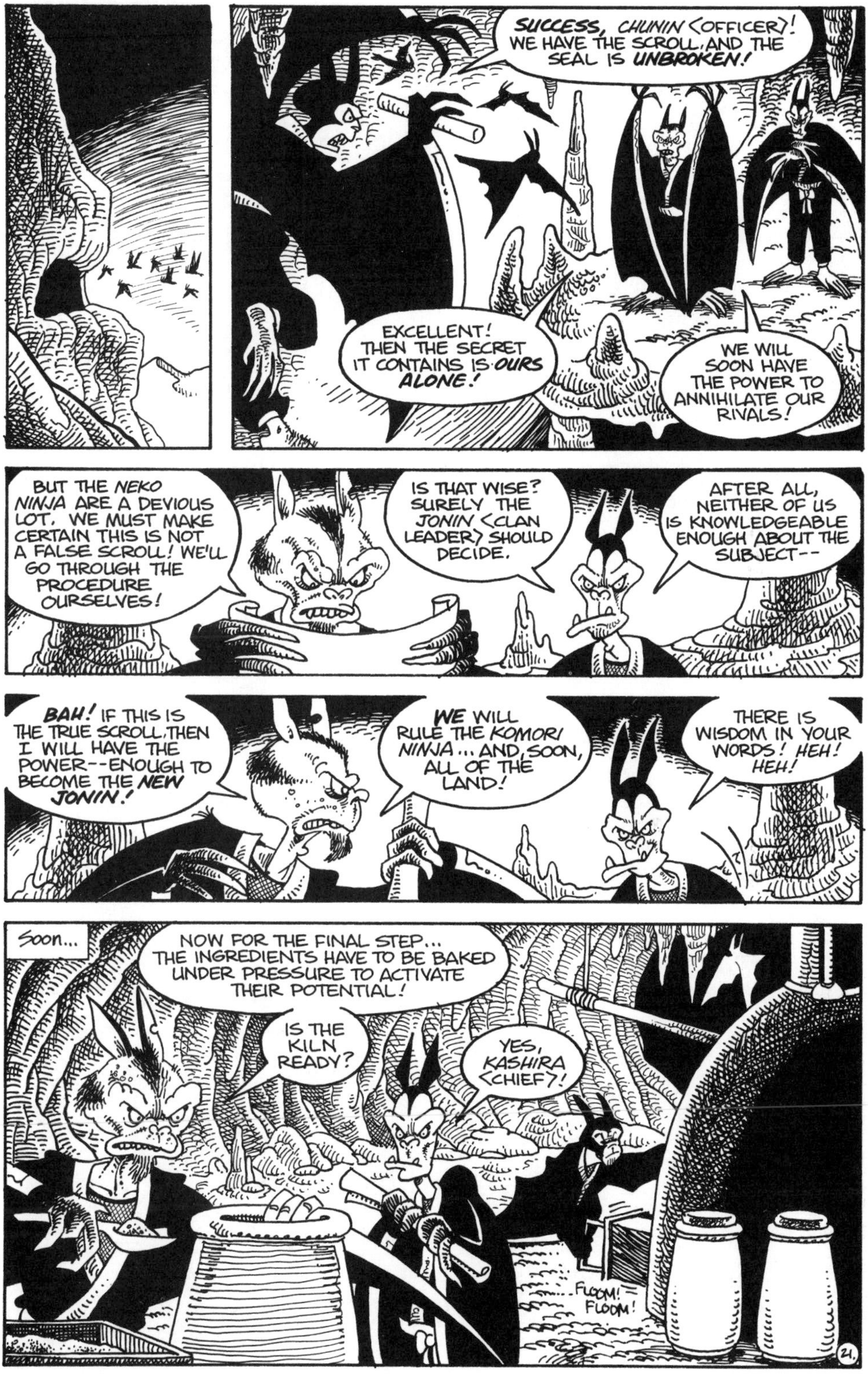
SUCCESS, CHUNIN <OFFICER>! WE HAVE THE SCROLL, AND THE SEAL IS UNBROKEN!
EXCELLENT! THEN THE SECRET IT CONTAINS IS OURS ALONE!
WE WILL SOON HAVE THE POWER TO ANNIHILATE OUR RIVALS!
BUT THE NEKO NINJA ARE A DEVIOUS LOT. WE MUST MAKE CERTAIN THIS IS NOT A FALSE SCROLL! WE'LL GO THROUGH THE PROCEDURE OURSELVES!
IS THAT WISE? SURELY THE JONIN <CLAN LEADER> SHOULD DECIDE.
AFTER ALL, NEITHER OF US IS KNOWLEDGEABLE ENOUGH ABOUT THE SUBJECT--
BAH! IF THIS IS THE TRUE SCROLL, THEN I WILL HAVE THE POWER--ENOUGH TO BECOME THE NEW JONIN!
WE WILL RULE THE KOMORI NINJA... AND, SOON, ALL OF THE LAND!
THERE IS WISDOM IN YOUR WORDS! HEH! HEH!
Soon...
NOW FOR THE FINAL STEP... THE INGREDIENTS HAVE TO BE BAKED UNDER PRESSURE TO ACTIVATE THEIR POTENTIAL!
IS THE KILN READY?
YES, KASHIRA <CHIEF>!
...FLOOM! FLOOM!
21.

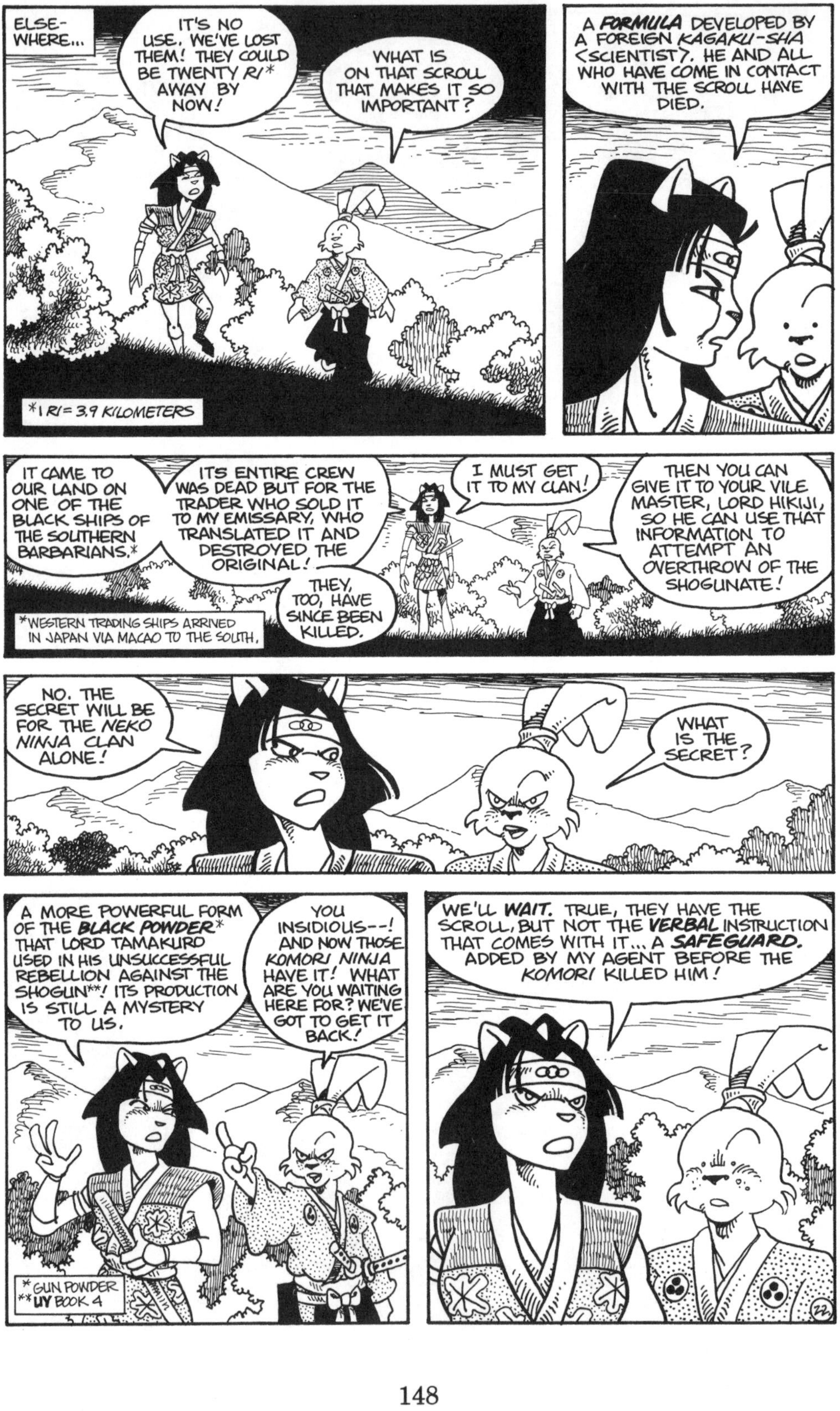
ELSE-WHERE...
IT'S NO USE. WE'VE LOST THEM! THEY COULD BE TWENTY *RI** AWAY BY NOW!
WHAT IS ON THAT SCROLL THAT MAKES IT SO IMPORTANT?
*1 RI = 3.9 KILOMETERS
A ***FORMULA*** DEVELOPED BY A FOREIGN *KAGAKU-SHA* <SCIENTIST>. HE AND ALL WHO HAVE COME IN CONTACT WITH THE SCROLL HAVE DIED.
IT CAME TO OUR LAND ON ONE OF THE BLACK SHIPS OF THE SOUTHERN BARBARIANS.*
ITS ENTIRE CREW WAS DEAD BUT FOR THE TRADER WHO SOLD IT TO MY EMISSARY, WHO TRANSLATED IT AND DESTROYED THE ORIGINAL!
THEY, TOO, HAVE SINCE BEEN KILLED.
*WESTERN TRADING SHIPS ARRIVED IN JAPAN VIA MACAO TO THE SOUTH.
I MUST GET IT TO MY CLAN!
THEN YOU CAN GIVE IT TO YOUR VILE MASTER, LORD HIKIJI, SO HE CAN USE THAT INFORMATION TO ATTEMPT AN OVERTHROW OF THE SHOGUNATE!
NO. THE SECRET WILL BE FOR THE *NEKO NINJA* CLAN ALONE!
WHAT IS THE SECRET?
A MORE POWERFUL FORM OF THE ***BLACK POWDER**** THAT LORD TAMAKURO USED IN HIS UNSUCCESSFUL REBELLION AGAINST THE SHOGUN**! ITS PRODUCTION IS STILL A MYSTERY TO US.
YOU INSIDIOUS--! AND NOW THOSE *KOMORI NINJA* HAVE IT! WHAT ARE YOU WAITING HERE FOR? WE'VE GOT TO GET IT BACK!
*GUN POWDER
****UY** BOOK 4
WE'LL ***WAIT.*** TRUE, THEY HAVE THE SCROLL, BUT NOT THE ***VERBAL*** INSTRUCTION THAT COMES WITH IT... A ***SAFEGUARD.*** ADDED BY MY AGENT BEFORE THE *KOMORI* KILLED HIM!
22

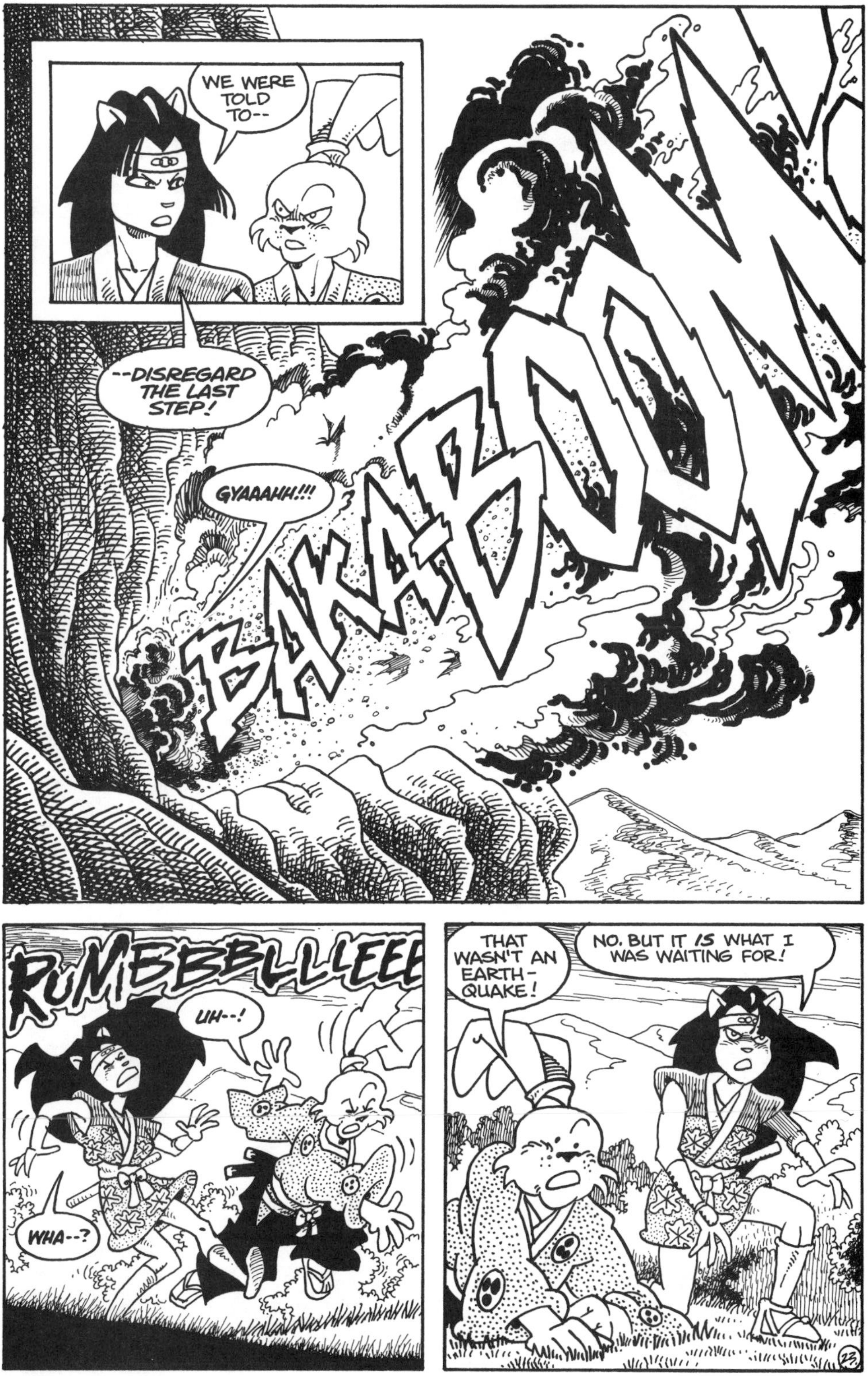
WE WERE TOLD TO--
--DISREGARD THE LAST STEP!
GYAAAHH!!!
BAKA-BOOM
RUMBBBLLLEEE
UH--!
WHA--?
THAT WASN'T AN EARTH-QUAKE!
NO. BUT IT IS WHAT I WAS WAITING FOR!
23

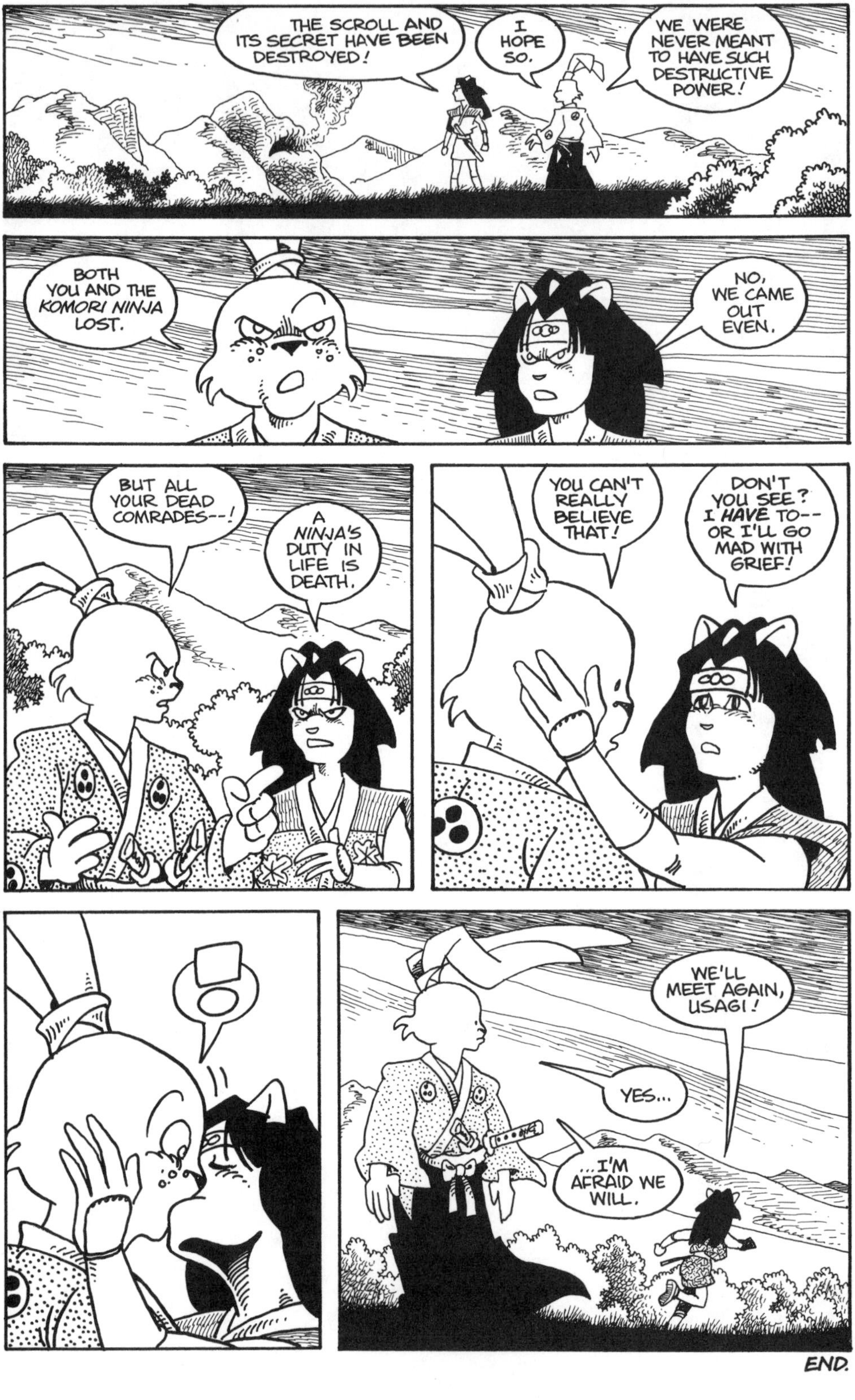
THE SCROLL AND ITS SECRET HAVE BEEN DESTROYED!
I HOPE SO.
WE WERE NEVER MEANT TO HAVE SUCH DESTRUCTIVE POWER!
BOTH YOU AND THE KOMORI NINJA LOST.
NO, WE CAME OUT EVEN.
BUT ALL YOUR DEAD COMRADES--!
A NINJA'S DUTY IN LIFE IS DEATH.
YOU CAN'T REALLY BELIEVE THAT!
DON'T YOU SEE? I HAVE TO--OR I'LL GO MAD WITH GRIEF!
WE'LL MEET AGAIN, USAGI!
YES...
...I'M AFRAID WE WILL.
END.

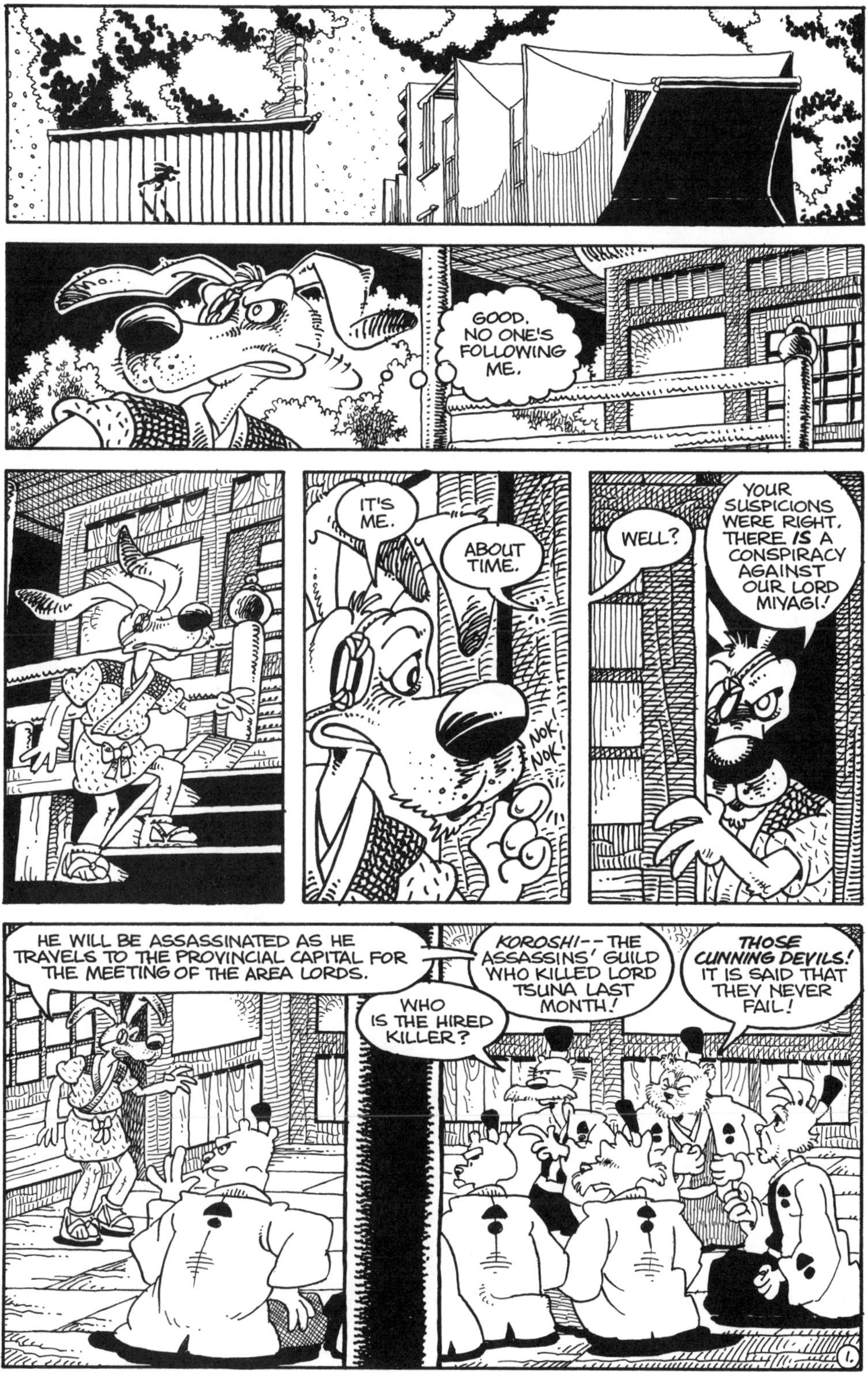
GOOD. NO ONE'S FOLLOWING ME.
IT'S ME.
ABOUT TIME.
NOK! NOK!
WELL?
YOUR SUSPICIONS WERE RIGHT. THERE IS A CONSPIRACY AGAINST OUR LORD MIYAGI!
HE WILL BE ASSASSINATED AS HE TRAVELS TO THE PROVINCIAL CAPITAL FOR THE MEETING OF THE AREA LORDS.
WHO IS THE HIRED KILLER?
KOROSHI-- THE ASSASSINS' GUILD WHO KILLED LORD TSUNA LAST MONTH!
THOSE CUNNING DEVILS! IT IS SAID THAT THEY NEVER FAIL!
1.

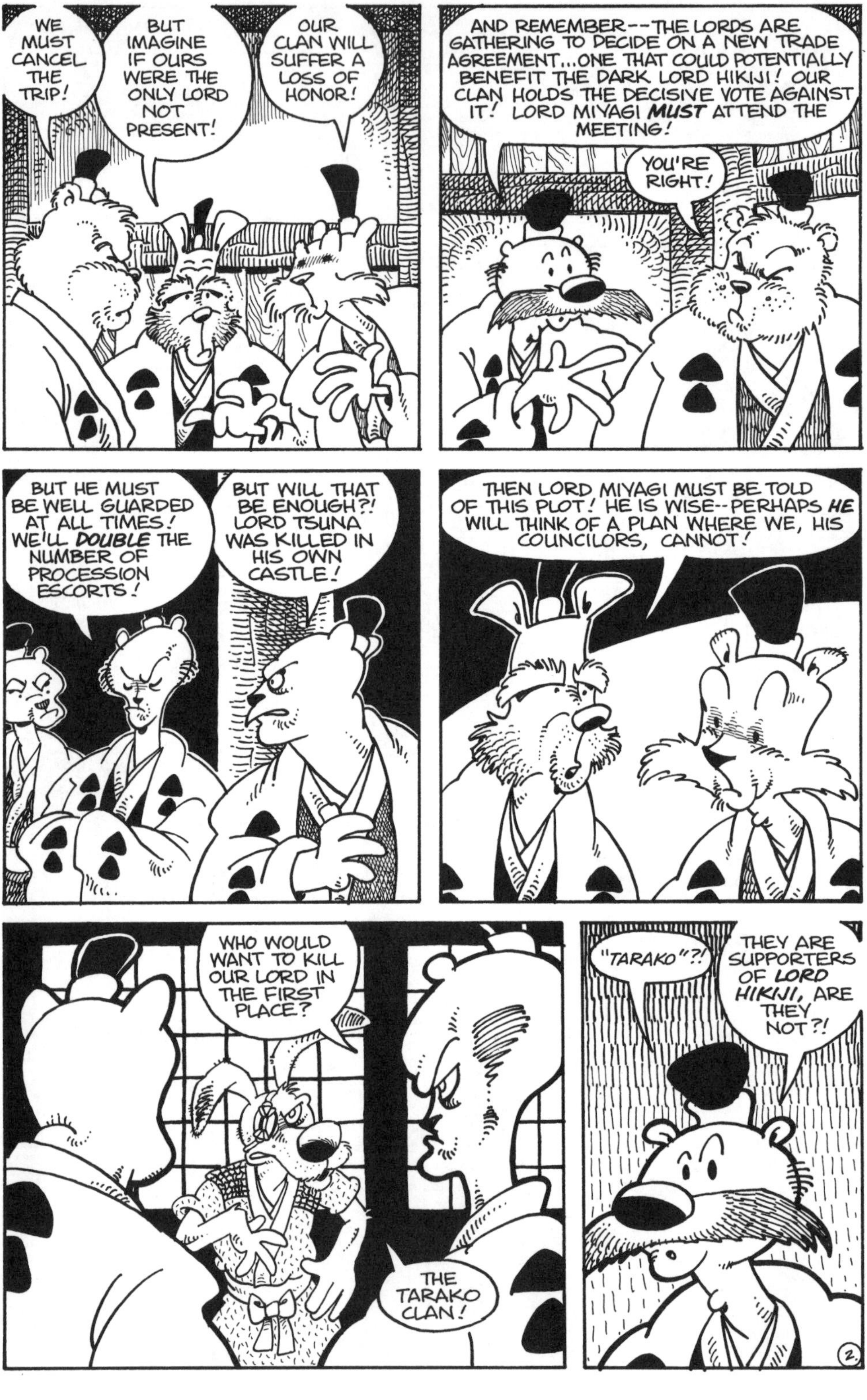
WE MUST CANCEL THE TRIP!
BUT IMAGINE IF OURS WERE THE ONLY LORD NOT PRESENT!
OUR CLAN WILL SUFFER A LOSS OF HONOR!
AND REMEMBER--THE LORDS ARE GATHERING TO DECIDE ON A NEW TRADE AGREEMENT...ONE THAT COULD POTENTIALLY BENEFIT THE DARK LORD HIKIJI! OUR CLAN HOLDS THE DECISIVE VOTE AGAINST IT! LORD MIYAGI MUST ATTEND THE MEETING!
YOU'RE RIGHT!
BUT HE MUST BE WELL GUARDED AT ALL TIMES! WE'LL DOUBLE THE NUMBER OF PROCESSION ESCORTS!
BUT WILL THAT BE ENOUGH?! LORD TSUNA WAS KILLED IN HIS OWN CASTLE!
THEN LORD MIYAGI MUST BE TOLD OF THIS PLOT! HE IS WISE--PERHAPS HE WILL THINK OF A PLAN WHERE WE, HIS COUNCILORS, CANNOT!
WHO WOULD WANT TO KILL OUR LORD IN THE FIRST PLACE?
THE TARAKO CLAN!
"TARAKO"?!
THEY ARE SUPPORTERS OF LORD HIKIJI, ARE THEY NOT?!
2.

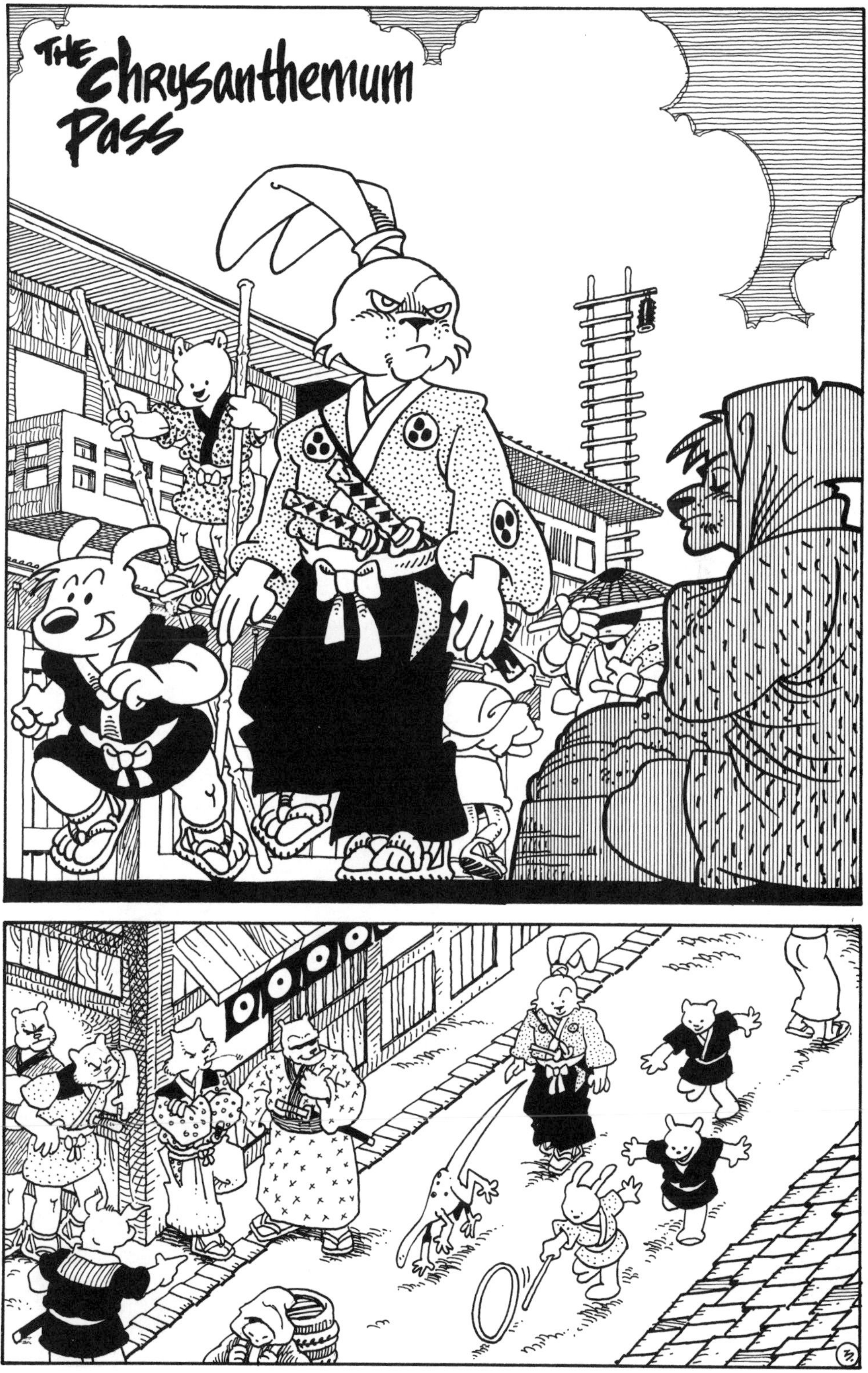
The Chrysanthemum Pass

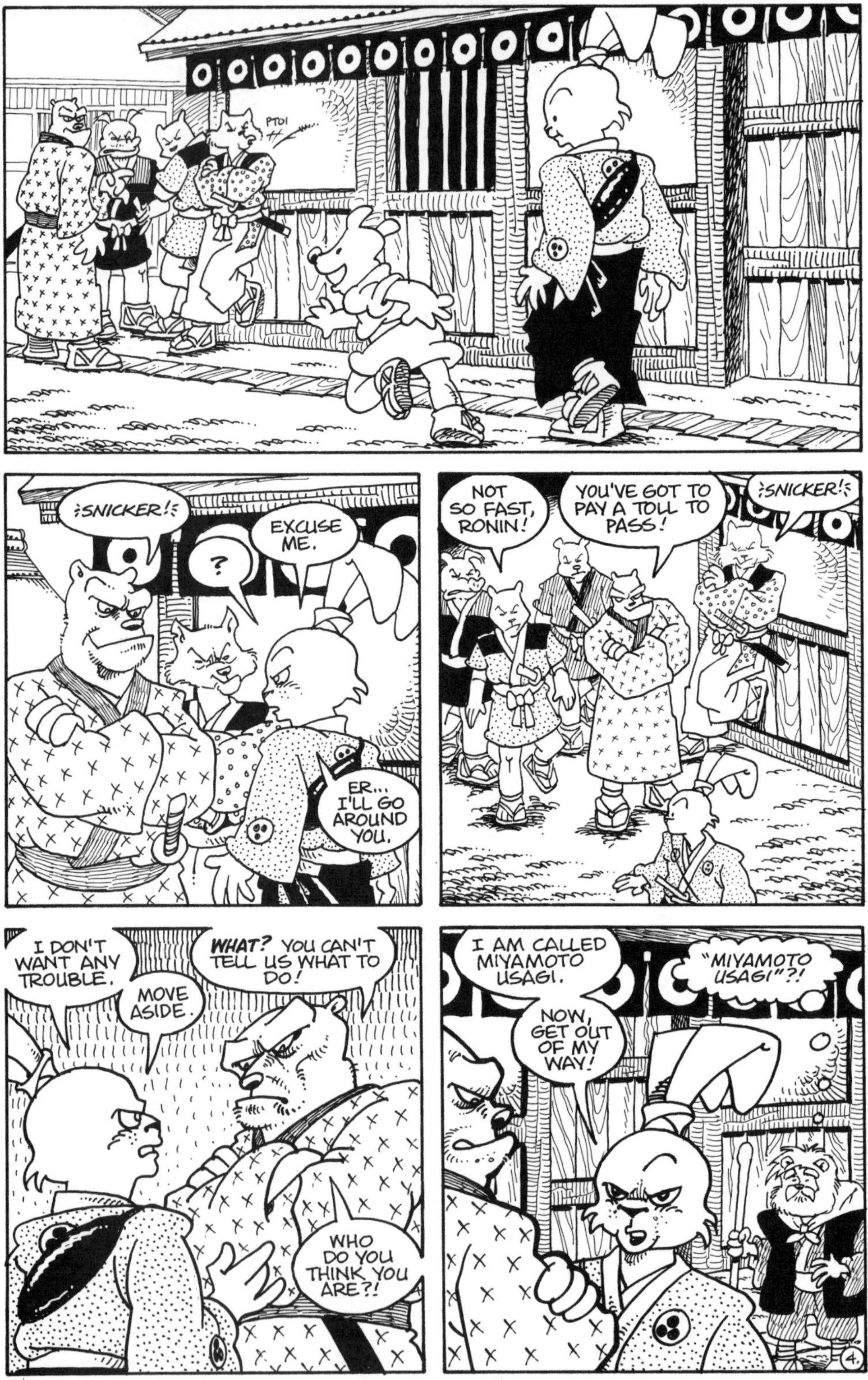
PTOI
¦SNICKER!¦
?
EXCUSE ME.
ER... I'LL GO AROUND YOU.
NOT SO FAST, RONIN!
YOU'VE GOT TO PAY A TOLL TO PASS!
¦SNICKER!¦
I DON'T WANT ANY TROUBLE.
MOVE ASIDE.
WHAT? YOU CAN'T TELL US WHAT TO DO!
WHO DO YOU THINK YOU ARE?!
I AM CALLED MIYAMOTO USAGI.
NOW, GET OUT OF MY WAY!
"MIYAMOTO USAGI"?!
4.

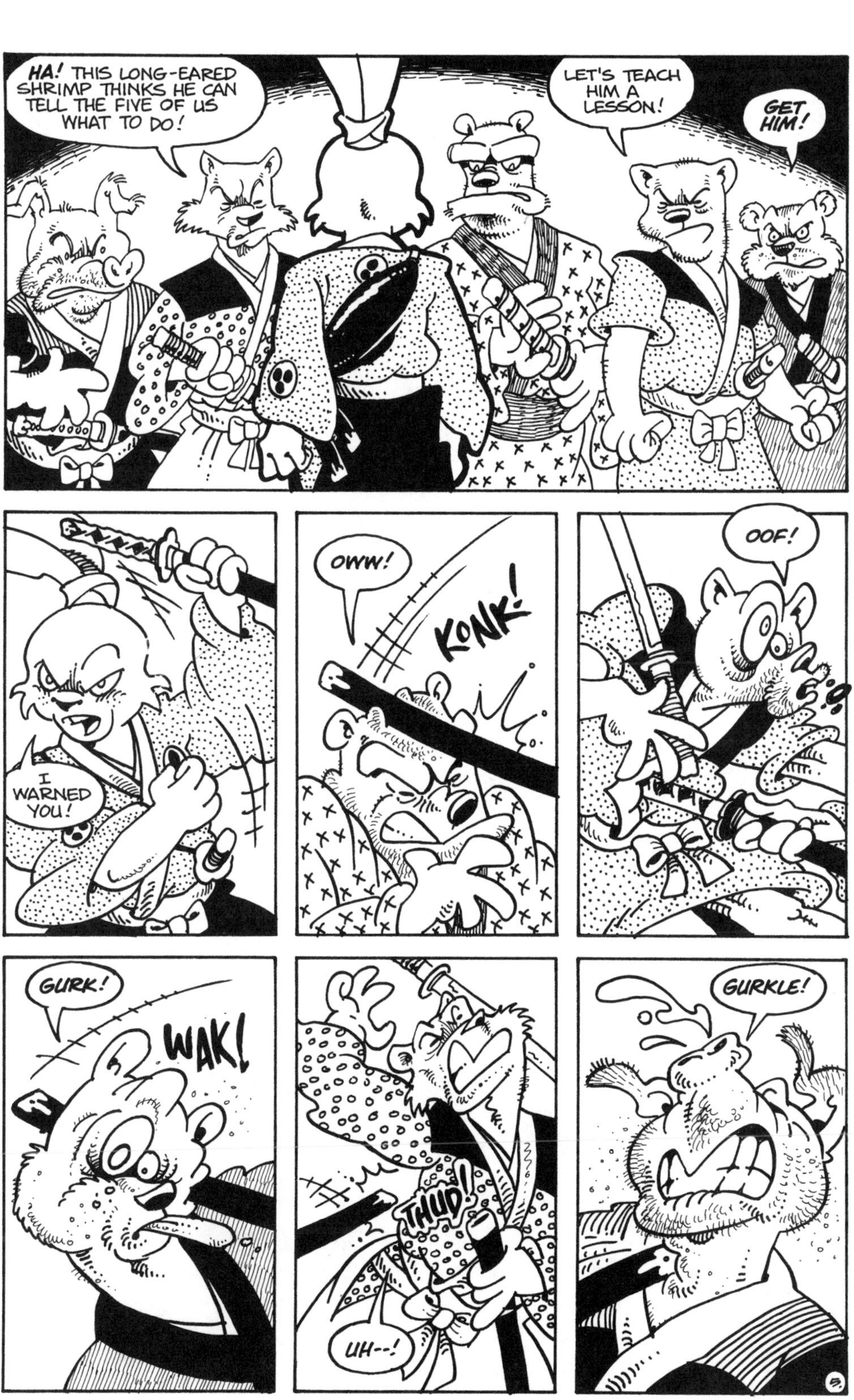
HA! THIS LONG-EARED SHRIMP THINKS HE CAN TELL THE FIVE OF US WHAT TO DO!
LET'S TEACH HIM A LESSON!
GET HIM!
I WARNED YOU!
OWW!
KONK!
OOF!
GURK!
WAK!
THUD!
UH--!
GURKLE!

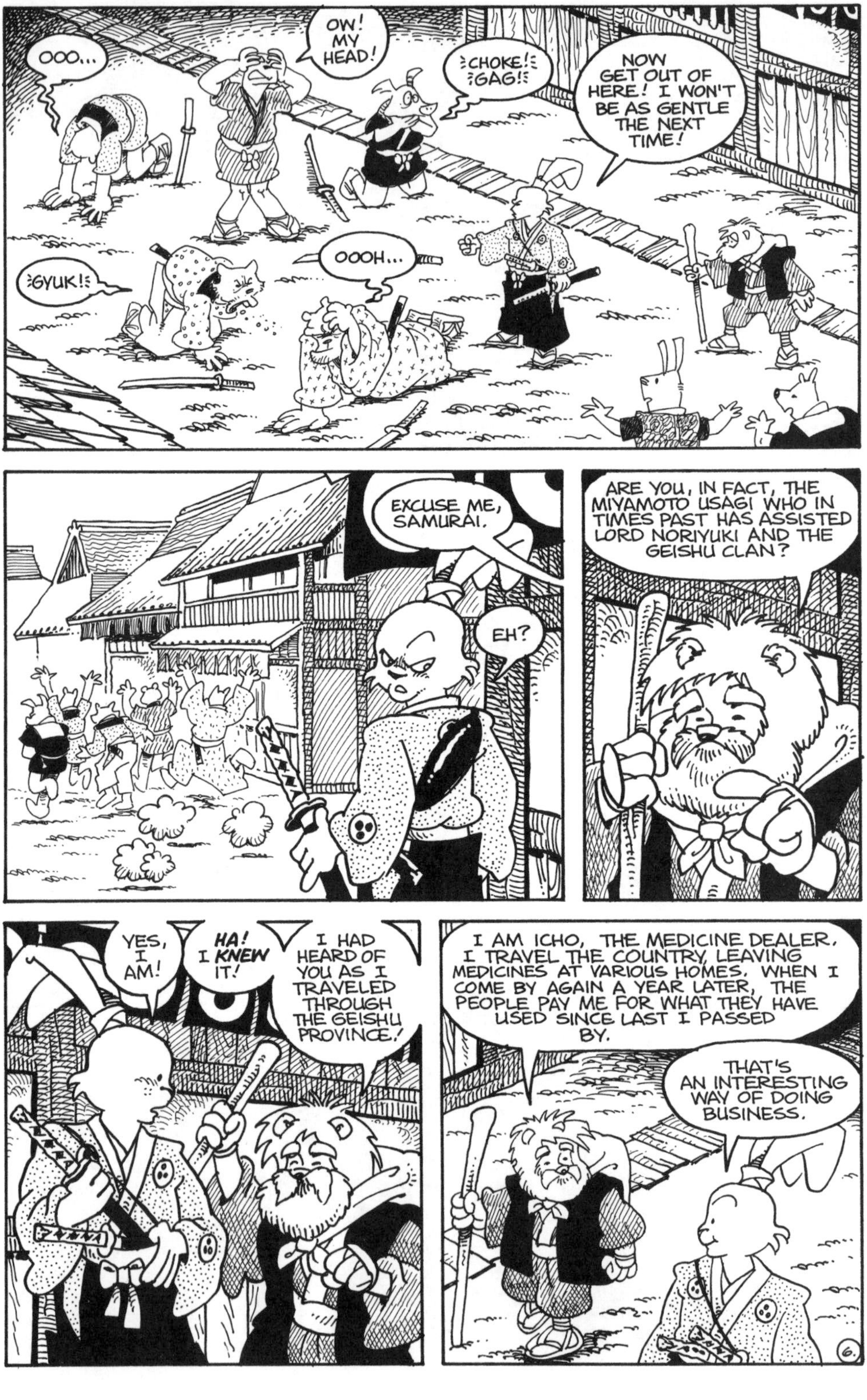
OOO...
OW! MY HEAD!
CHOKE! GAG!
NOW GET OUT OF HERE! I WON'T BE AS GENTLE THE NEXT TIME!
GYUK!
OOOH...
EXCUSE ME, SAMURAI.
EH?
ARE YOU, IN FACT, THE MIYAMOTO USAGI WHO IN TIMES PAST HAS ASSISTED LORD NORIYUKI AND THE GEISHU CLAN?
YES, I AM!
HA! I KNEW IT!
I HAD HEARD OF YOU AS I TRAVELED THROUGH THE GEISHU PROVINCE!
I AM ICHO, THE MEDICINE DEALER. I TRAVEL THE COUNTRY, LEAVING MEDICINES AT VARIOUS HOMES. WHEN I COME BY AGAIN A YEAR LATER, THE PEOPLE PAY ME FOR WHAT THEY HAVE USED SINCE LAST I PASSED BY.
THAT'S AN INTERESTING WAY OF DOING BUSINESS.
6.

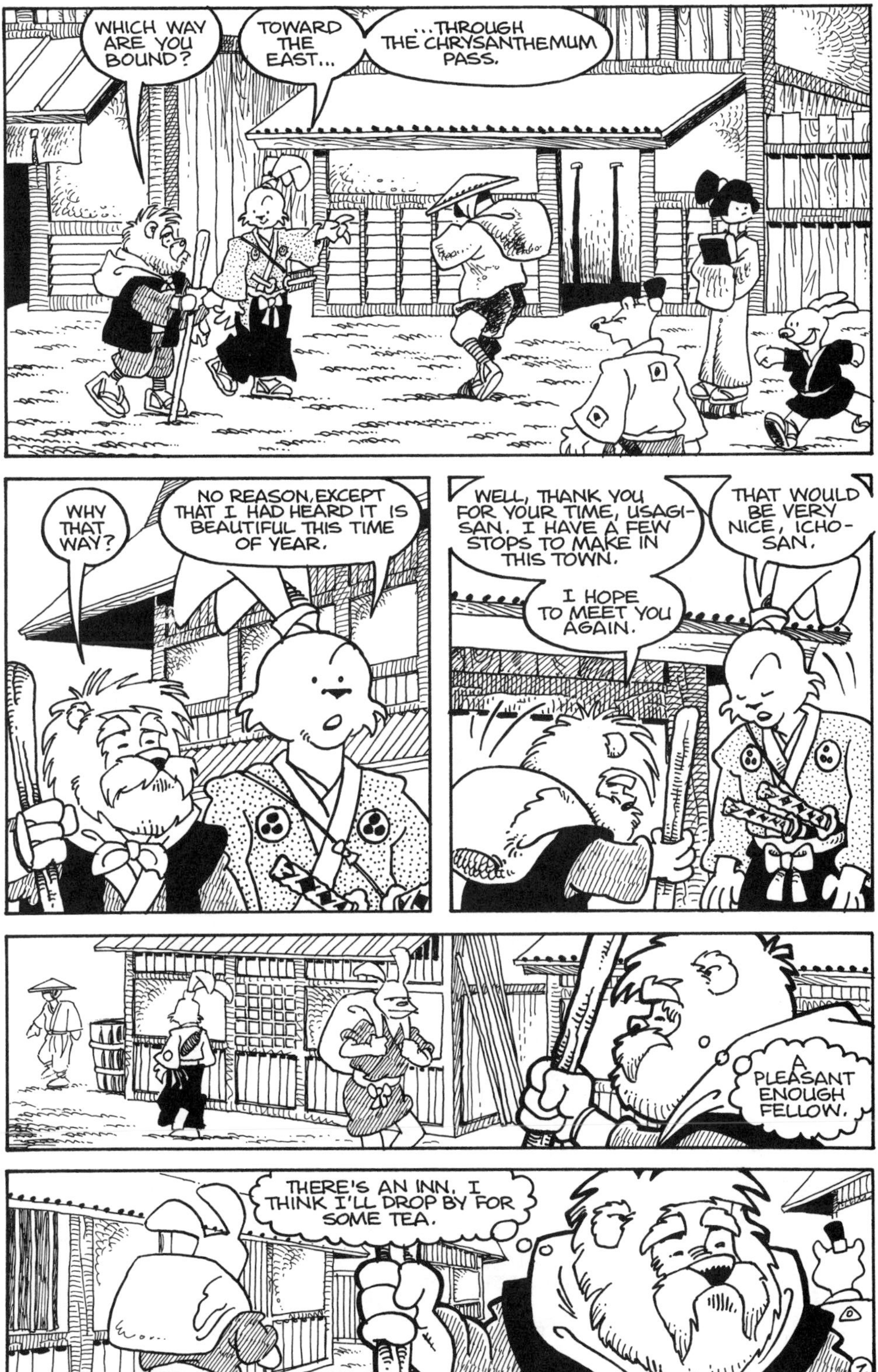
WHICH WAY ARE YOU BOUND?
TOWARD THE EAST...
...THROUGH THE CHRYSANTHEMUM PASS.
WHY THAT WAY?
NO REASON, EXCEPT THAT I HAD HEARD IT IS BEAUTIFUL THIS TIME OF YEAR.
WELL, THANK YOU FOR YOUR TIME, USAGI-SAN. I HAVE A FEW STOPS TO MAKE IN THIS TOWN.
I HOPE TO MEET YOU AGAIN.
THAT WOULD BE VERY NICE, ICHO-SAN.
A PLEASANT ENOUGH FELLOW.
THERE'S AN INN. I THINK I'LL DROP BY FOR SOME TEA.

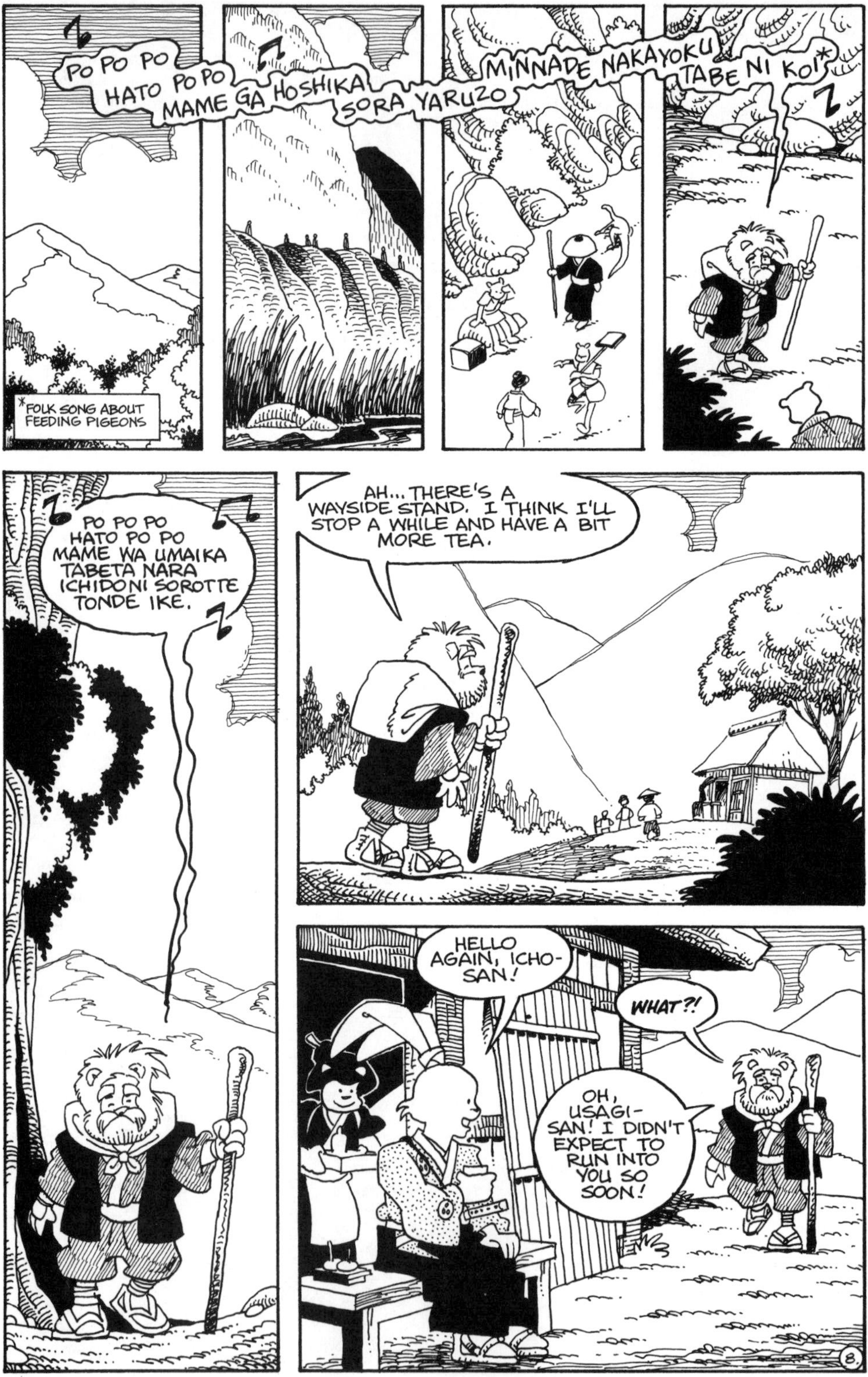
PO PO PO HATO PO PO MAME GA HOSHIKA SORA YARUZO MINNADE NAKAYOKU TABE NI KOI*
*FOLK SONG ABOUT FEEDING PIGEONS
PO PO PO HATO PO PO MAME WA UMAIKA TABETA NARA ICHIDONI SOROTTE TONDE IKE.
AH... THERE'S A WAYSIDE STAND. I THINK I'LL STOP A WHILE AND HAVE A BIT MORE TEA.
HELLO AGAIN, ICHO-SAN!
WHAT?!
OH, USAGI-SAN! I DIDN'T EXPECT TO RUN INTO YOU SO SOON!
8.

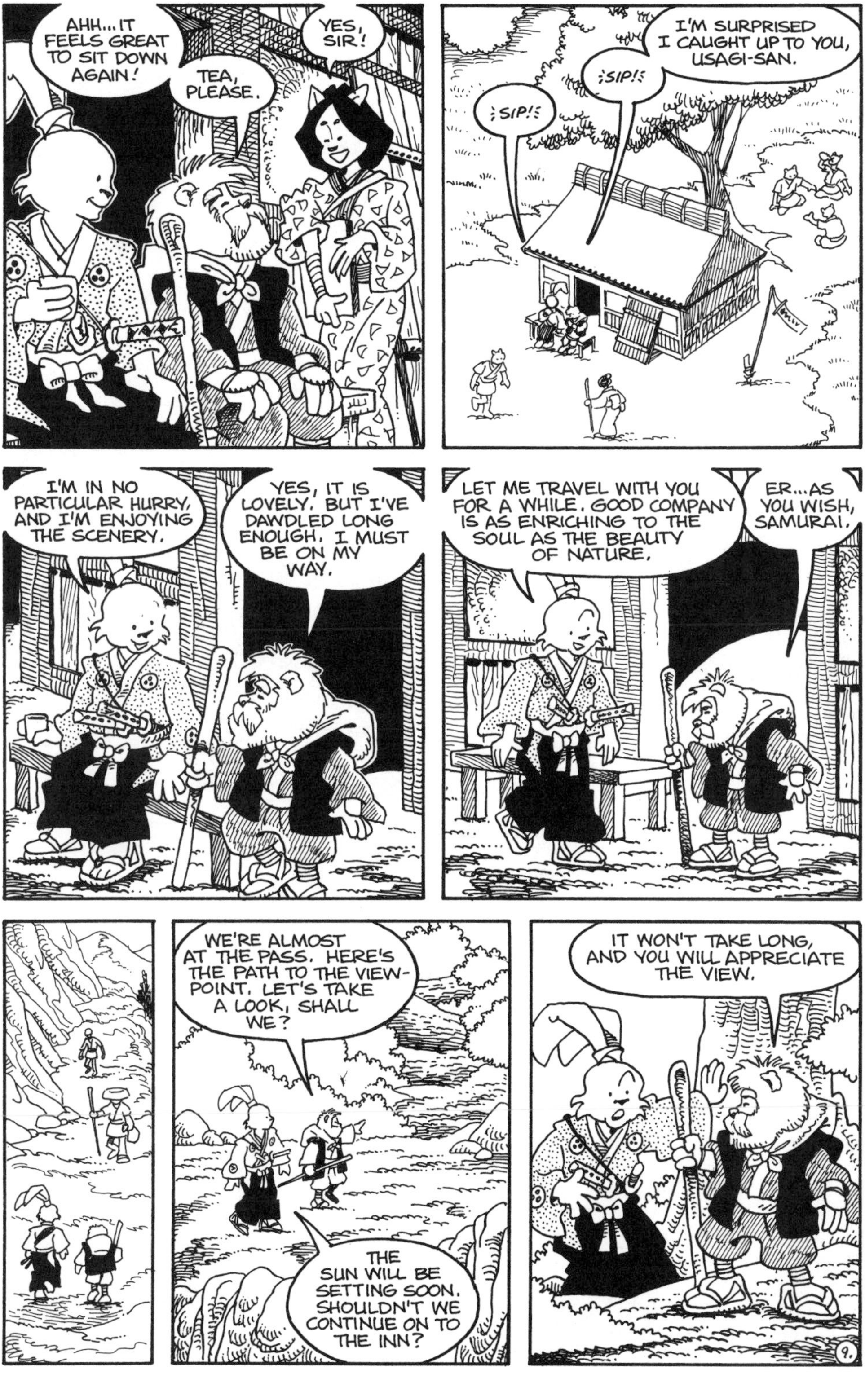
AHH... IT FEELS GREAT TO SIT DOWN AGAIN!
TEA, PLEASE.
YES, SIR!
;SIP!;
;SIP!;
I'M SURPRISED I CAUGHT UP TO YOU, USAGI-SAN.
I'M IN NO PARTICULAR HURRY, AND I'M ENJOYING THE SCENERY.
YES, IT IS LOVELY. BUT I'VE DAWDLED LONG ENOUGH. I MUST BE ON MY WAY.
LET ME TRAVEL WITH YOU FOR A WHILE. GOOD COMPANY IS AS ENRICHING TO THE SOUL AS THE BEAUTY OF NATURE.
ER...AS YOU WISH, SAMURAI.
WE'RE ALMOST AT THE PASS. HERE'S THE PATH TO THE VIEW-POINT. LET'S TAKE A LOOK, SHALL WE?
THE SUN WILL BE SETTING SOON. SHOULDN'T WE CONTINUE ON TO THE INN?
IT WON'T TAKE LONG, AND YOU WILL APPRECIATE THE VIEW.
9.

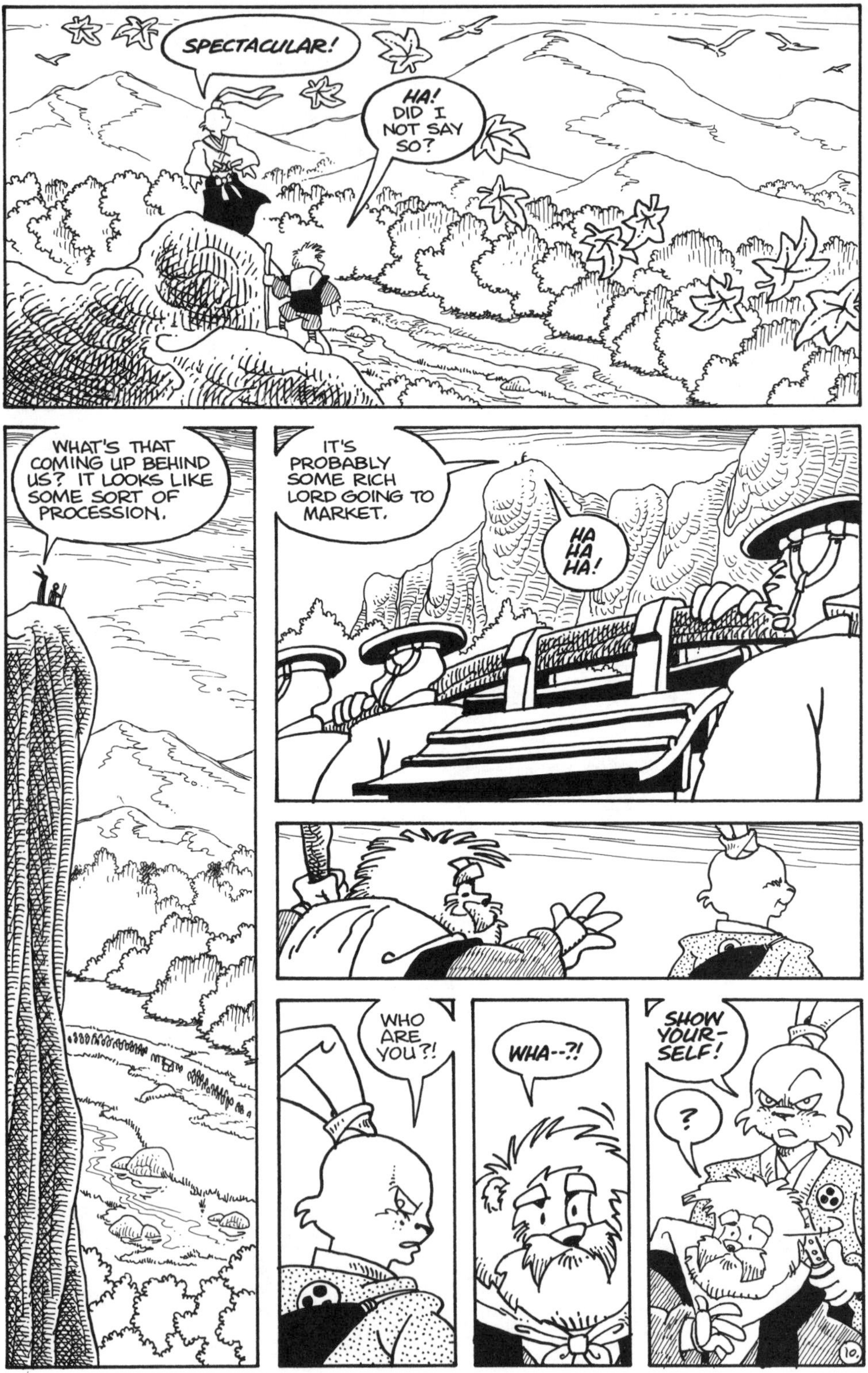
SPECTACULAR!
HA! DID I NOT SAY SO?
WHAT'S THAT COMING UP BEHIND US? IT LOOKS LIKE SOME SORT OF PROCESSION.
IT'S PROBABLY SOME RICH LORD GOING TO MARKET.
HA HA HA!
WHO ARE YOU?!
WHA--?!
SHOW YOUR-SELF!
?
10.

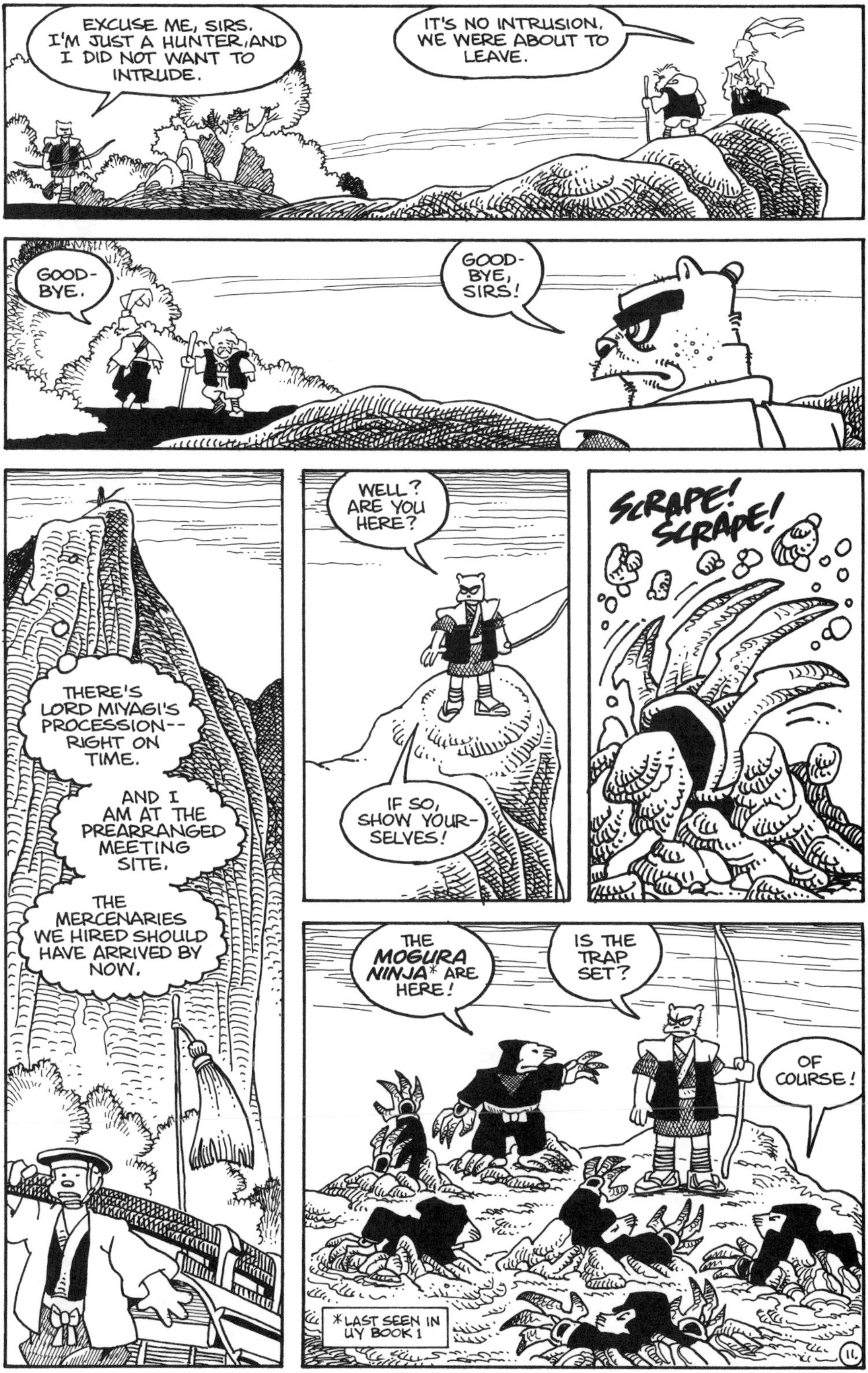
EXCUSE ME, SIRS. I'M JUST A HUNTER, AND I DID NOT WANT TO INTRUDE.
IT'S NO INTRUSION. WE WERE ABOUT TO LEAVE.
GOOD-BYE.
GOOD-BYE, SIRS!
THERE'S LORD MIYAGI'S PROCESSION-- RIGHT ON TIME.
AND I AM AT THE PREARRANGED MEETING SITE.
THE MERCENARIES WE HIRED SHOULD HAVE ARRIVED BY NOW.
WELL? ARE YOU HERE?
IF SO, SHOW YOUR-SELVES!
SCRAPE! SCRAPE!
THE MOGURA NINJA* ARE HERE!
IS THE TRAP SET?
OF COURSE!
*LAST SEEN IN UY BOOK 1
11.

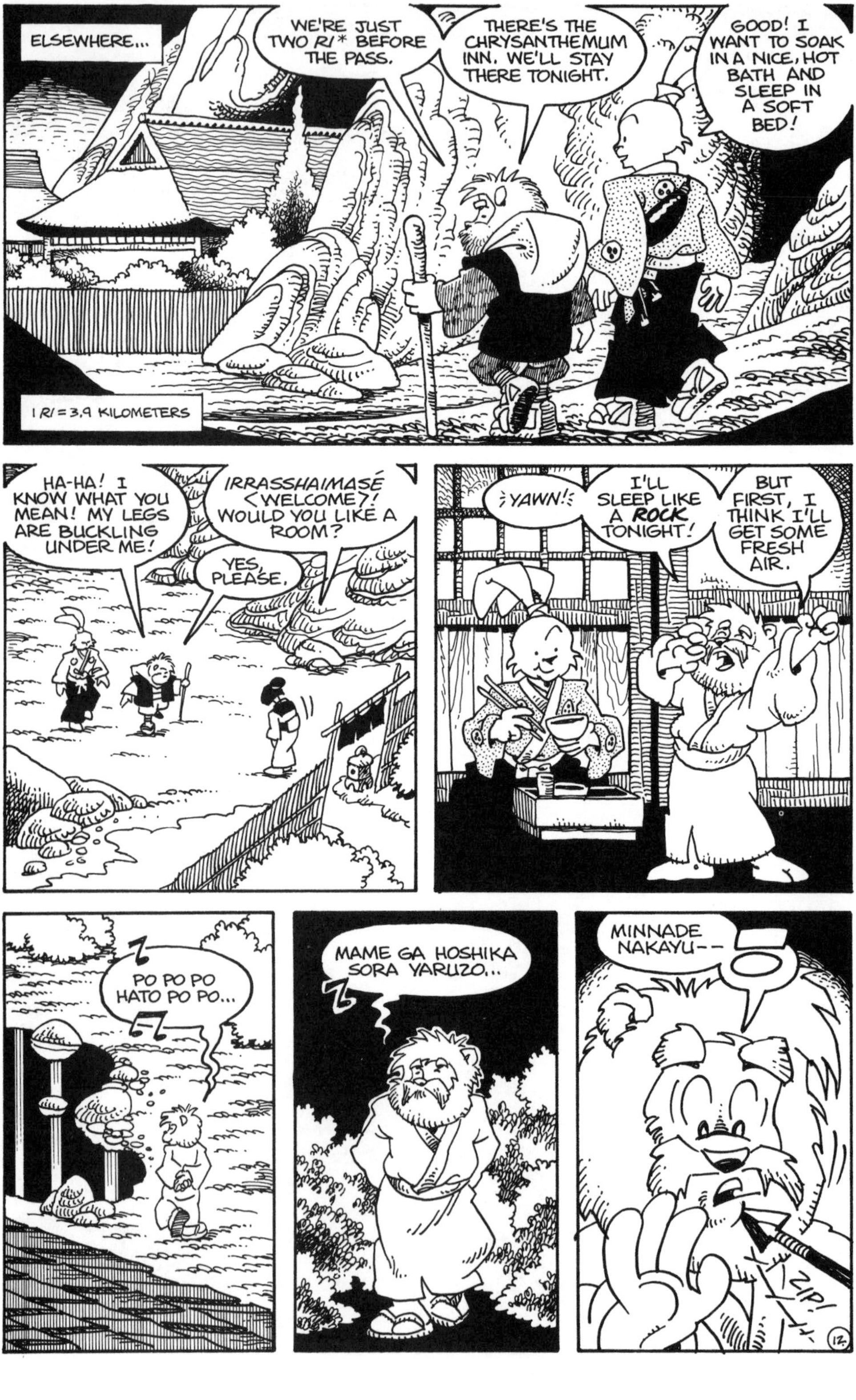
ELSEWHERE...
WE'RE JUST TWO RI* BEFORE THE PASS.
THERE'S THE CHRYSANTHEMUM INN. WE'LL STAY THERE TONIGHT.
GOOD! I WANT TO SOAK IN A NICE, HOT BATH AND SLEEP IN A SOFT BED!
1 RI = 3.9 KILOMETERS
HA-HA! I KNOW WHAT YOU MEAN! MY LEGS ARE BUCKLING UNDER ME!
IRRASSHAIMASÉ <WELCOME>! WOULD YOU LIKE A ROOM?
YES, PLEASE.
YAWN!
I'LL SLEEP LIKE A ROCK TONIGHT!
BUT FIRST, I THINK I'LL GET SOME FRESH AIR.
PO PO PO HATO PO PO...
MAME GA HOSHIKA SORA YARUZO...
MINNADE NAKAYU--
ZIP!
12

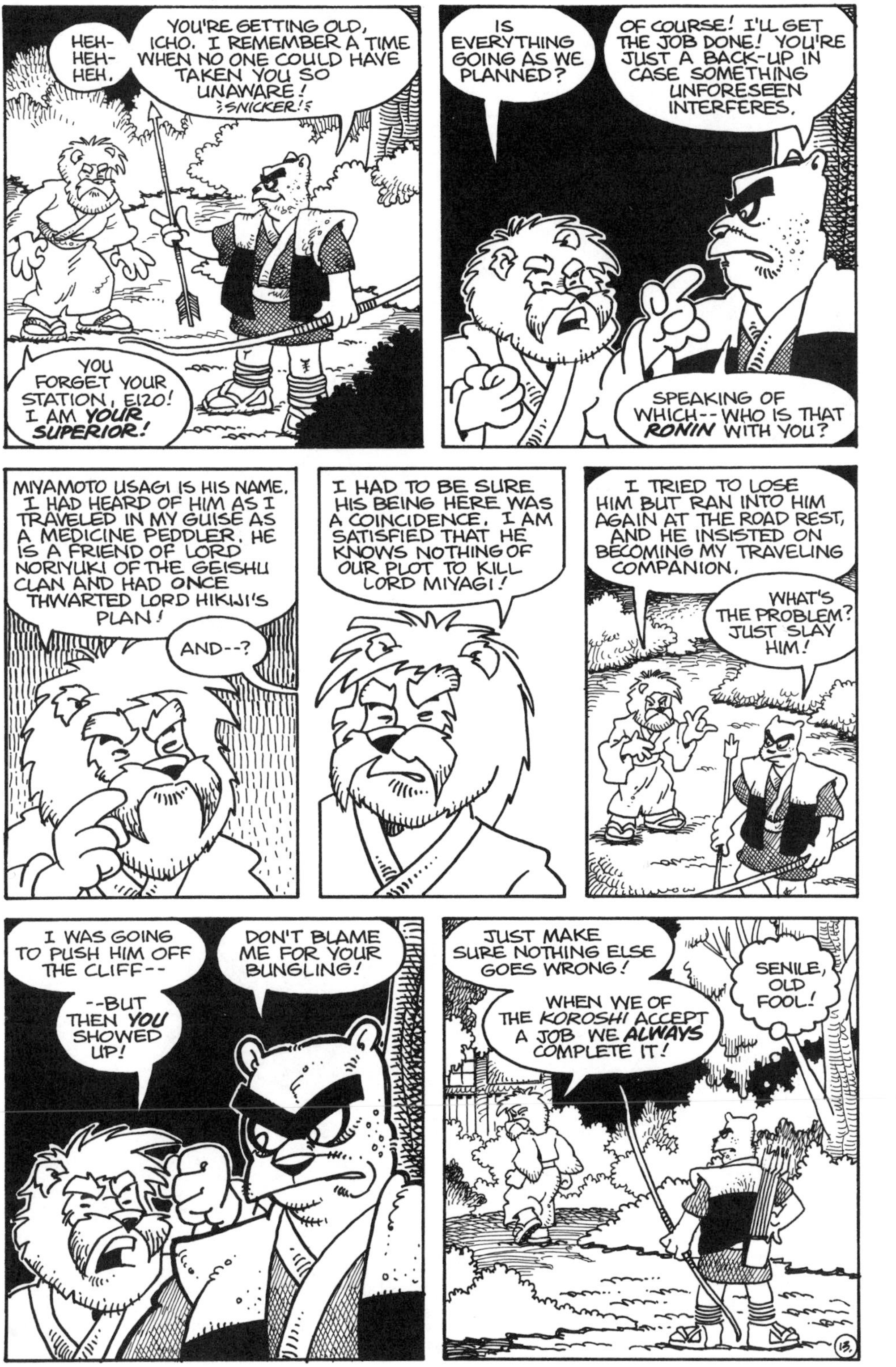
HEH-HEH-HEH.
YOU'RE GETTING OLD, ICHO. I REMEMBER A TIME WHEN NO ONE COULD HAVE TAKEN YOU SO UNAWARE!
SNICKER!
YOU FORGET YOUR STATION, EIZO! I AM YOUR SUPERIOR!
IS EVERYTHING GOING AS WE PLANNED?
OF COURSE! I'LL GET THE JOB DONE! YOU'RE JUST A BACK-UP IN CASE SOMETHING UNFORESEEN INTERFERES.
SPEAKING OF WHICH-- WHO IS THAT RONIN WITH YOU?
MIYAMOTO USAGI IS HIS NAME. I HAD HEARD OF HIM AS I TRAVELED IN MY GUISE AS A MEDICINE PEDDLER. HE IS A FRIEND OF LORD NORIYUKI OF THE GEISHU CLAN AND HAD ONCE THWARTED LORD HIKIJI'S PLAN!
AND--?
I HAD TO BE SURE HIS BEING HERE WAS A COINCIDENCE. I AM SATISFIED THAT HE KNOWS NOTHING OF OUR PLOT TO KILL LORD MIYAGI!
I TRIED TO LOSE HIM BUT RAN INTO HIM AGAIN AT THE ROAD REST, AND HE INSISTED ON BECOMING MY TRAVELING COMPANION.
WHAT'S THE PROBLEM? JUST SLAY HIM!
I WAS GOING TO PUSH HIM OFF THE CLIFF--
--BUT THEN YOU SHOWED UP!
DON'T BLAME ME FOR YOUR BUNGLING!
JUST MAKE SURE NOTHING ELSE GOES WRONG!
WHEN WE OF THE KOROSHI ACCEPT A JOB WE ALWAYS COMPLETE IT!
SENILE, OLD FOOL!
13

AH. THE RONIN IS ASLEEP. NOW IS THE CHANCE TO GET RID OF ANY DOUBTS ABOUT HIM!

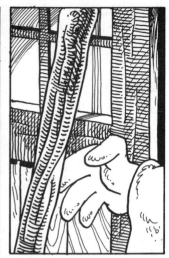

I'LL SHOW EIZO THAT I'M NOT TO BE TRIFLED WITH!

CLIK!

WHO'S THERE?!

OH, IT'S YOU, ICHO.

EXCUSE ME. I'M NOT USED TO HAVING A ROOM-MATE!

ER...THINK NOTHING OF IT, USAGI. I WAS...ER...JUST COMING BACK FROM MY WALK...

¡GULP!¡

HIS *DAIROKKAN* ⟨SIXTH SENSE⟩ IS TOO SHARP FOR HIM TO BE KILLED IN HIS SLEEP.

NO MATTER. HE'LL DIE WITH LORD MIYAGI TOMORROW!

14.

164

PO PO PO
HATO PO PO
MAME WA UMAIKA
TABETANARA
ICHIDO NI SOROTTE

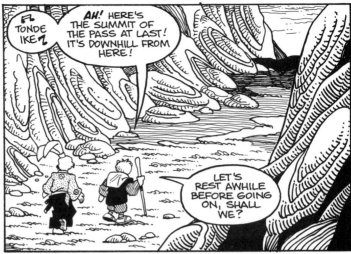

TONDE IKE

AH! HERE'S THE SUMMIT OF THE PASS AT LAST! IT'S DOWNHILL FROM HERE!

LET'S REST AWHILE BEFORE GOING ON, SHALL WE?

THERE'S THAT PROCESSION AGAIN. THEY MUST HAVE MADE CAMP JUST BELOW THE INN LAST NIGHT.

WE MAY AS WELL WAIT HERE AND LET THEM PASS US.

GOOD IDEA, USAGI.

HOLD THE PALANQUIN STEADY!

HEY! WHAT'S THAT?!

ARE YOU TRYING TO MAKE LORD MIYAGI SICK?

15.

165

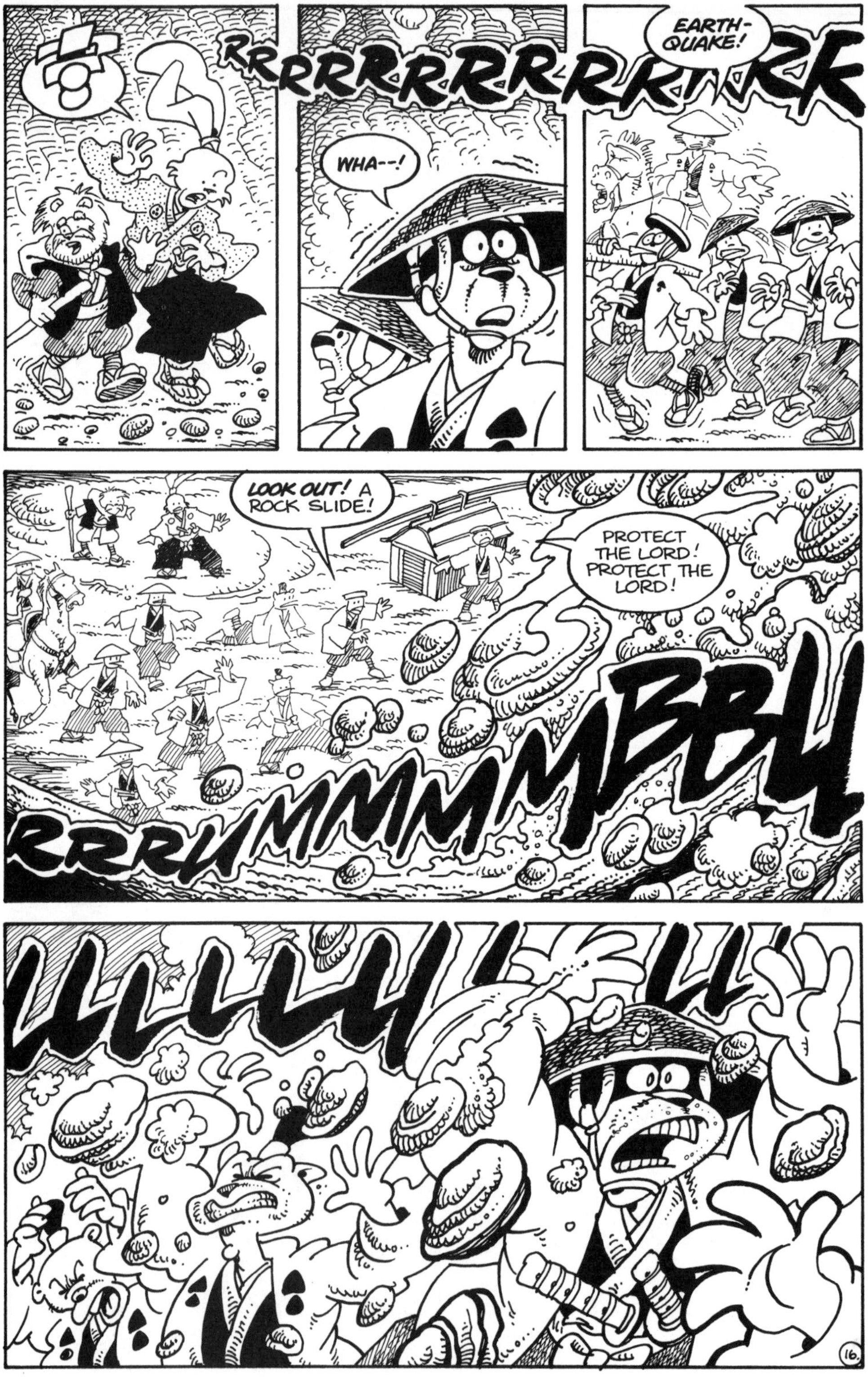
RRRRRRRRRRRRRRRK
WHA--!
EARTH-QUAKE!
LOOK OUT! A ROCK SLIDE!
PROTECT THE LORD! PROTECT THE LORD!
RRRUMMMMMBBU
ULLLLLLLL
16.

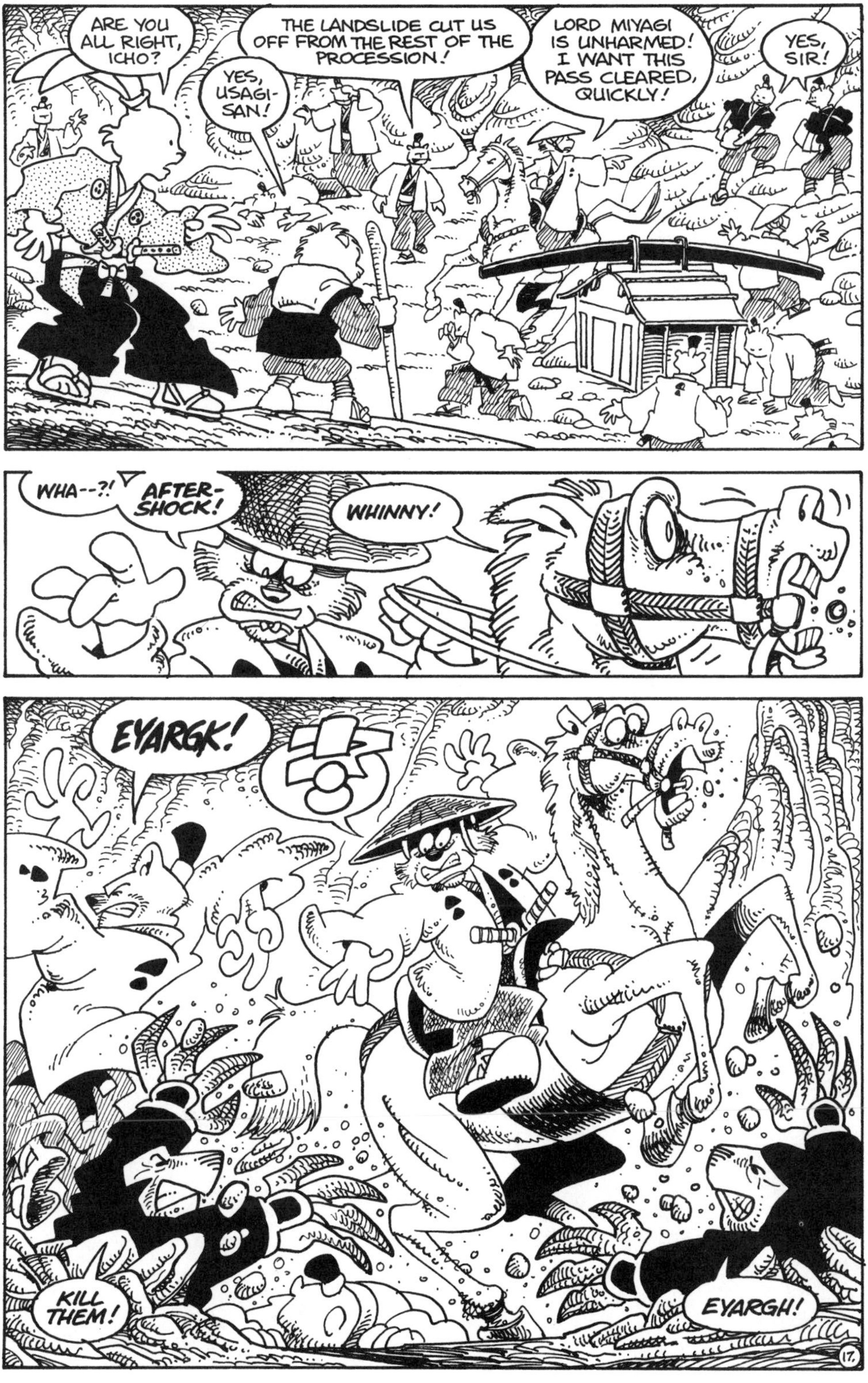

ARE YOU ALL RIGHT, ICHO?
YES, USAGI-SAN!
THE LANDSLIDE CUT US OFF FROM THE REST OF THE PROCESSION!
LORD MIYAGI IS UNHARMED! I WANT THIS PASS CLEARED, QUICKLY!
YES, SIR!
WHA--?!
AFTER-SHOCK!
WHINNY!
EYARGK!
KILL THEM!
EYARGH!
17.

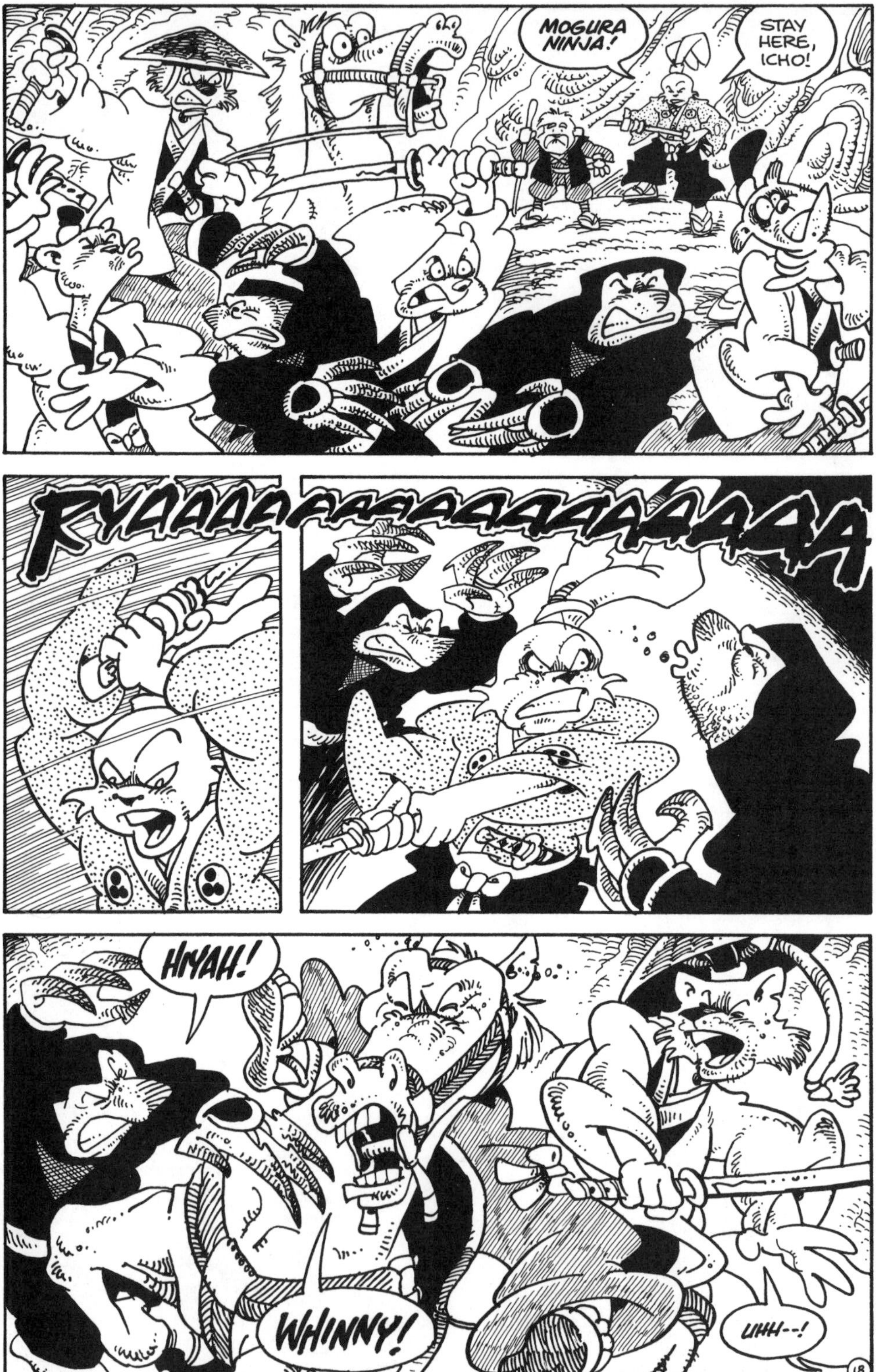
MOGURA NINJA!
STAY HERE, ICHO!
RYAAAAAAAAAAAAAAAAAA
HIYAH!
WHINNY!
UHH--!
18.

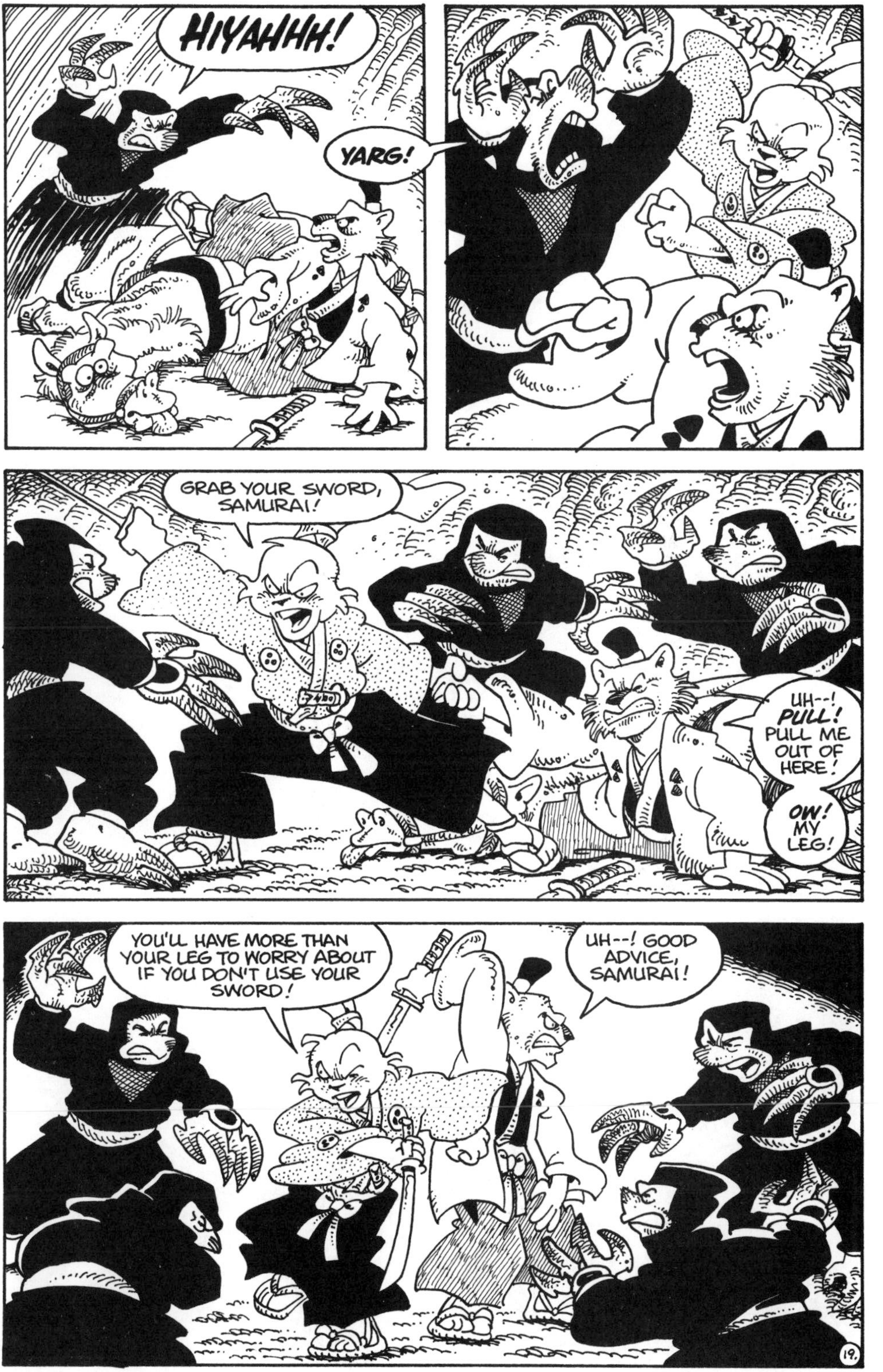
HIYAHHH!
YARG!
GRAB YOUR SWORD, SAMURAI!
UH--! PULL! PULL ME OUT OF HERE!
OW! MY LEG!
YOU'LL HAVE MORE THAN YOUR LEG TO WORRY ABOUT IF YOU DON'T USE YOUR SWORD!
UH--! GOOD ADVICE, SAMURAI!
19.

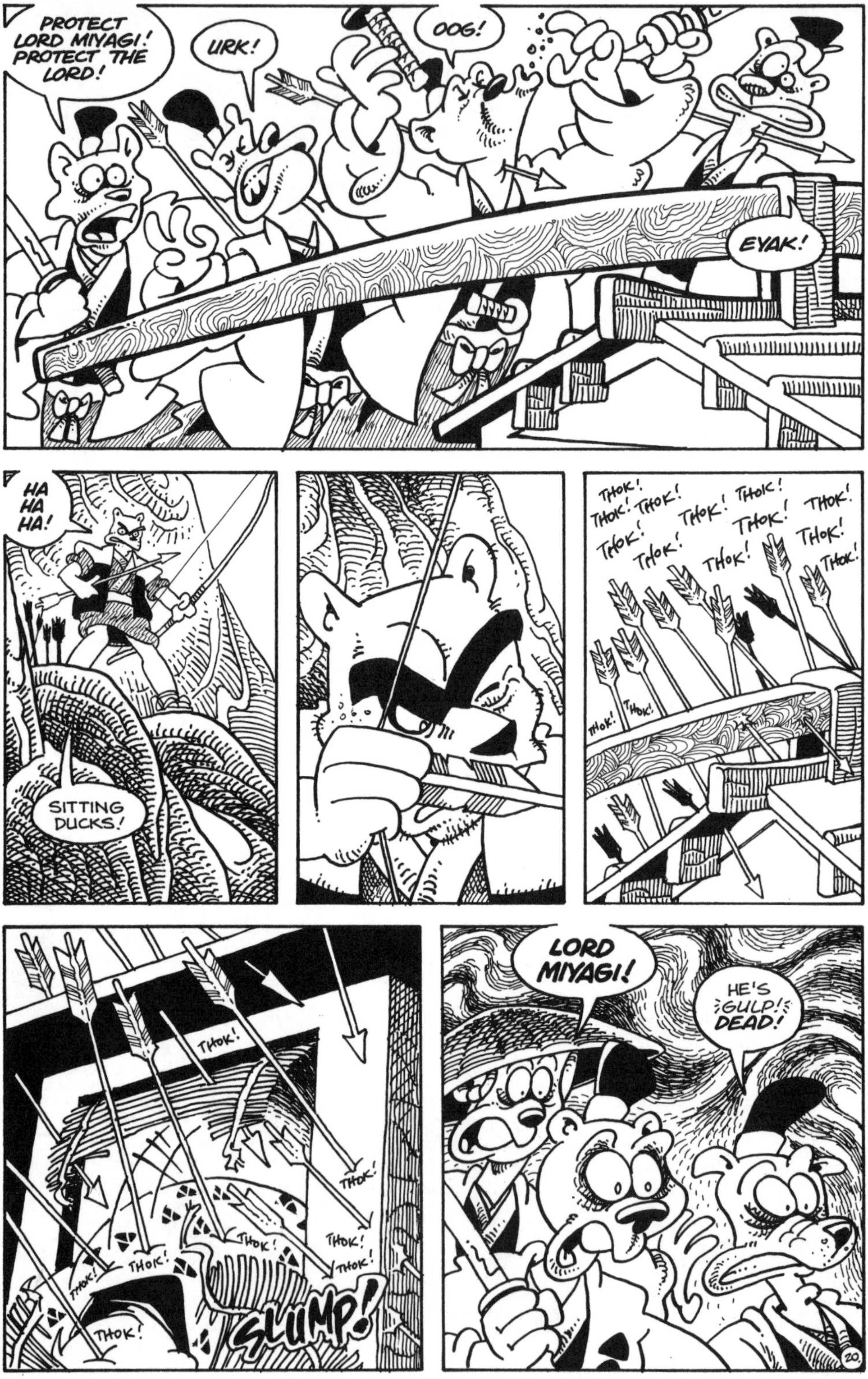
PROTECT LORD MIYAGI! PROTECT THE LORD!
URK!
OOG!
EYAK!
HA HA HA!
SITTING DUCKS!
THOK! THOK! THOK! THOK! THOK! THOK! THOK! THOK! THOK! THOK! THOK! THOK!
THOK! THOK!
THOK!
THOK!
THOK!
THOK!
THOK!
THOK!
THOK!
SLUMP!
LORD MIYAGI!
HE'S GULP! DEAD!
20.

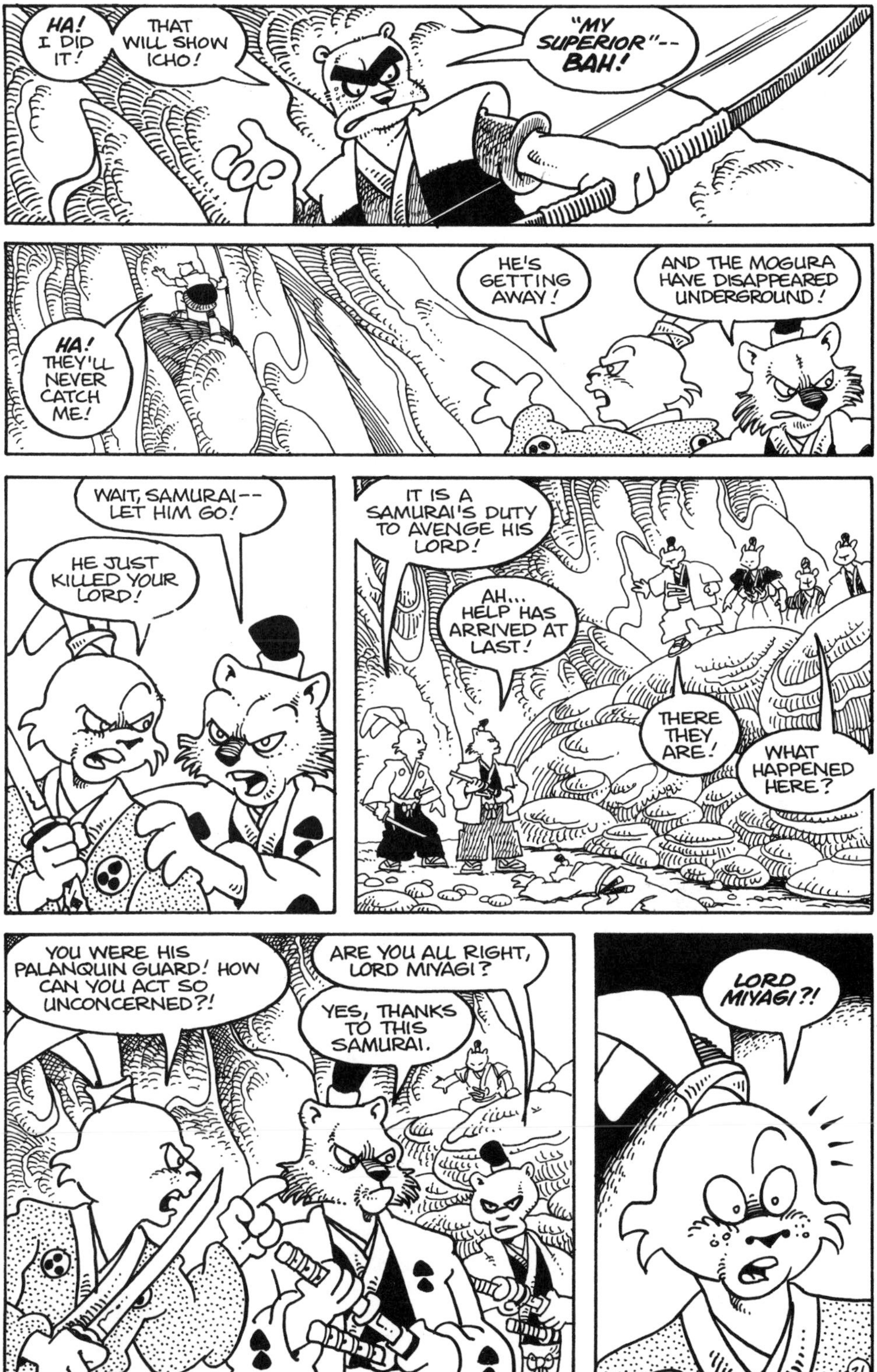
HA! I DID IT!
THAT WILL SHOW ICHO!
"MY SUPERIOR"-- BAH!
HA! THEY'LL NEVER CATCH ME!
HE'S GETTING AWAY!
AND THE MOGURA HAVE DISAPPEARED UNDERGROUND!
WAIT, SAMURAI-- LET HIM GO!
HE JUST KILLED YOUR LORD!
IT IS A SAMURAI'S DUTY TO AVENGE HIS LORD!
AH... HELP HAS ARRIVED AT LAST!
THERE THEY ARE!
WHAT HAPPENED HERE?
YOU WERE HIS PALANQUIN GUARD! HOW CAN YOU ACT SO UNCONCERNED?!
ARE YOU ALL RIGHT, LORD MIYAGI?
YES, THANKS TO THIS SAMURAI.
LORD MIYAGI?!
21.

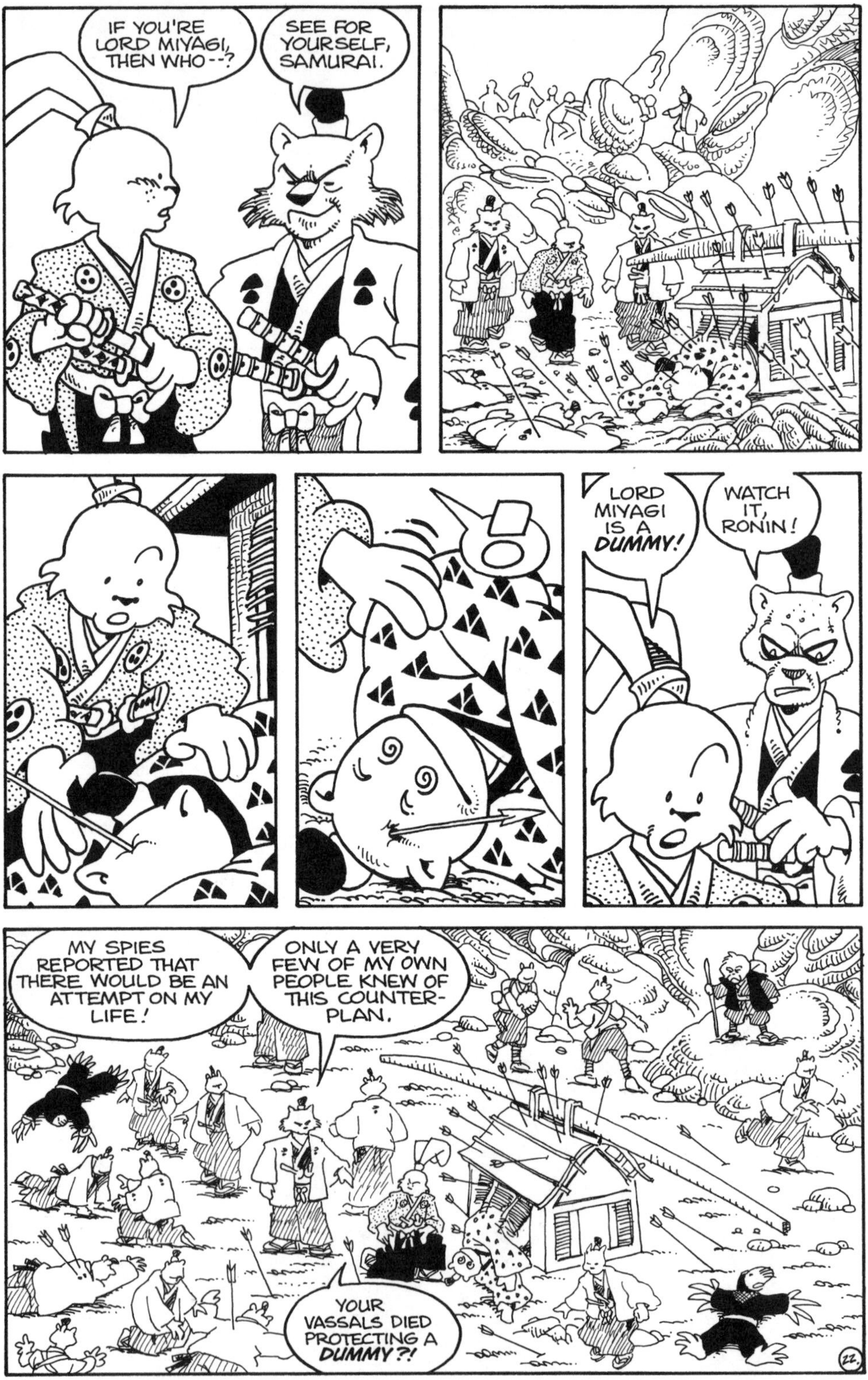
IF YOU'RE LORD MIYAGI, THEN WHO--?
SEE FOR YOURSELF, SAMURAI.
LORD MIYAGI IS A DUMMY!
WATCH IT, RONIN!
MY SPIES REPORTED THAT THERE WOULD BE AN ATTEMPT ON MY LIFE!
ONLY A VERY FEW OF MY OWN PEOPLE KNEW OF THIS COUNTER-PLAN.
YOUR VASSALS DIED PROTECTING A DUMMY?!
22.

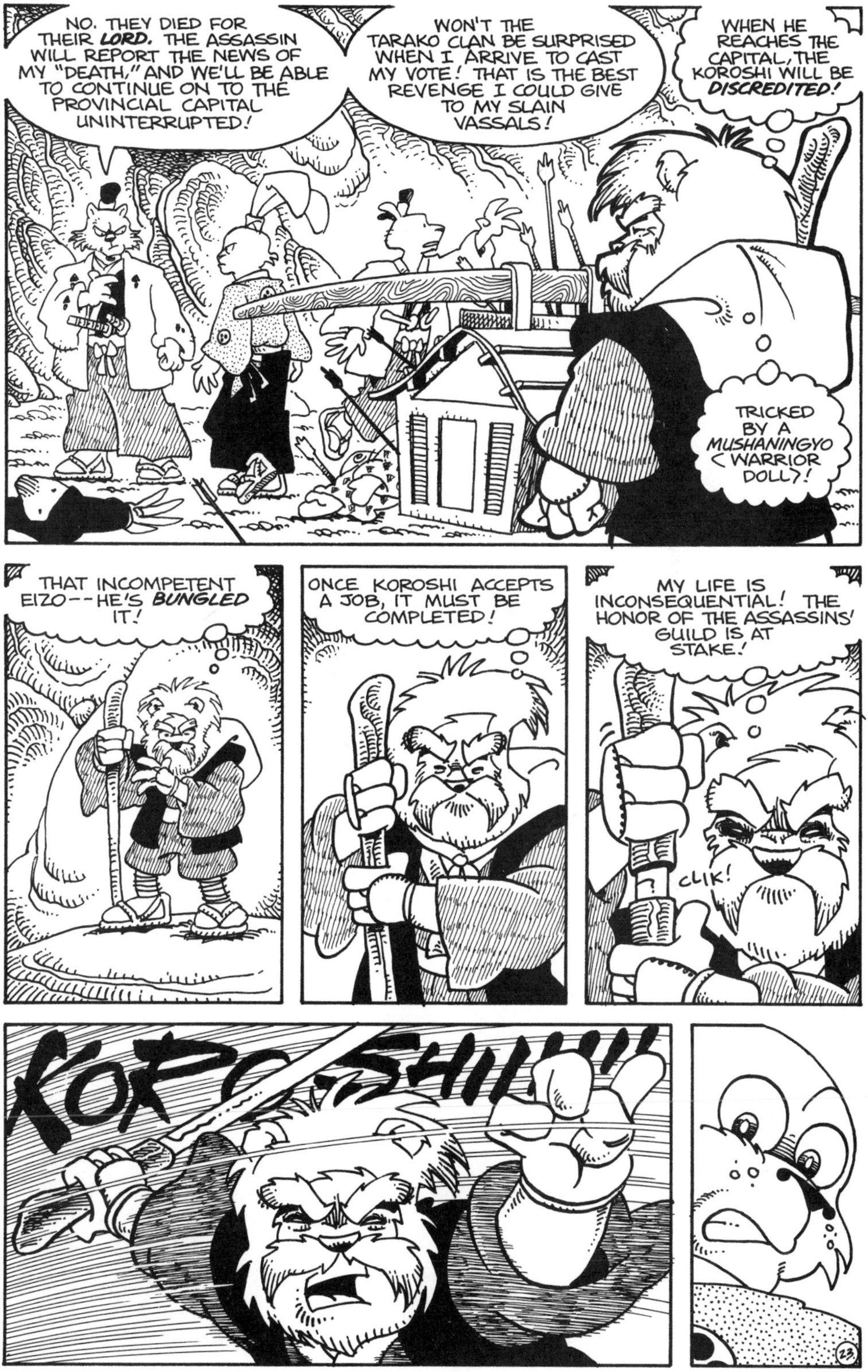

NO. THEY DIED FOR THEIR LORD. THE ASSASSIN WILL REPORT THE NEWS OF MY "DEATH," AND WE'LL BE ABLE TO CONTINUE ON TO THE PROVINCIAL CAPITAL UNINTERRUPTED!
WON'T THE TARAKO CLAN BE SURPRISED WHEN I ARRIVE TO CAST MY VOTE! THAT IS THE BEST REVENGE I COULD GIVE TO MY SLAIN VASSALS!
WHEN HE REACHES THE CAPITAL, THE KOROSHI WILL BE DISCREDITED!
TRICKED BY A MUSHANINGYO <WARRIOR DOLL>!
THAT INCOMPETENT EIZO--HE'S BUNGLED IT!
ONCE KOROSHI ACCEPTS A JOB, IT MUST BE COMPLETED!
MY LIFE IS INCONSEQUENTIAL! THE HONOR OF THE ASSASSINS' GUILD IS AT STAKE!
CLIK!
KORO-SHII!!!
23

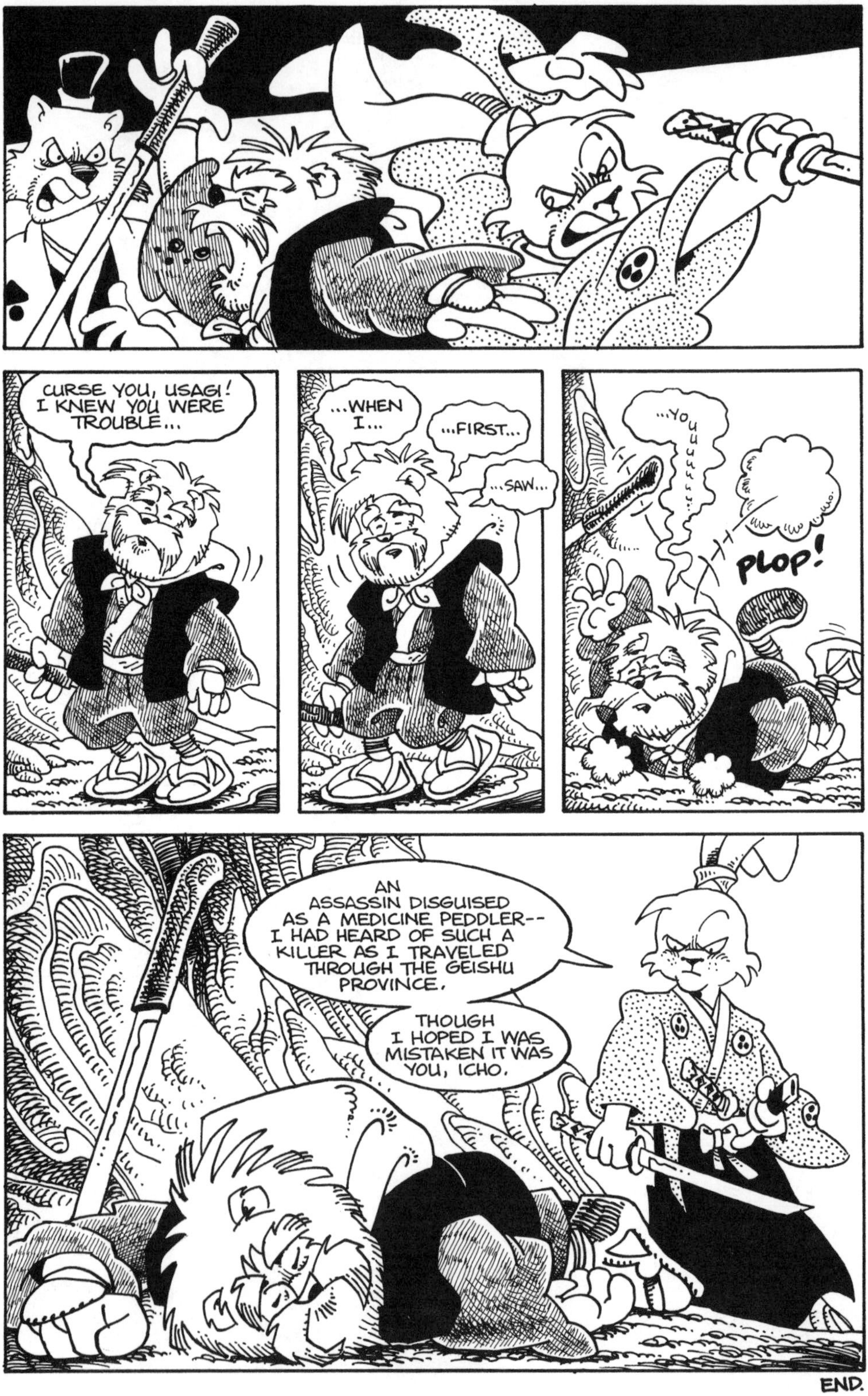
CURSE YOU, USAGI! I KNEW YOU WERE TROUBLE...
...WHEN I...
...FIRST...
...SAW...
...YOUUUUUUU...
PLOP!
AN ASSASSIN DISGUISED AS A MEDICINE PEDDLER-- I HAD HEARD OF SUCH A KILLER AS I TRAVELED THROUGH THE GEISHU PROVINCE.
THOUGH I HOPED I WAS MISTAKEN IT WAS YOU, ICHO.

END.

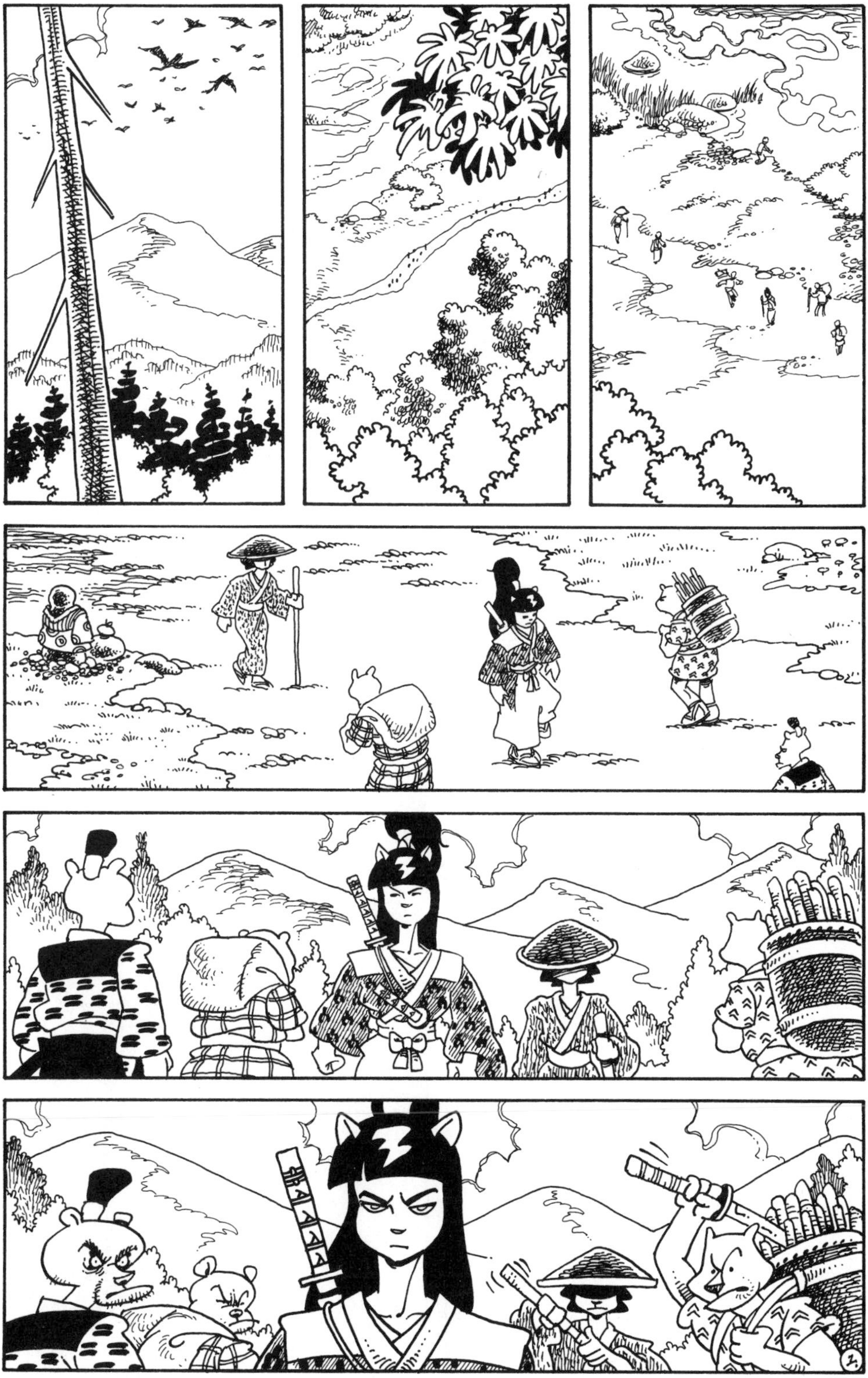

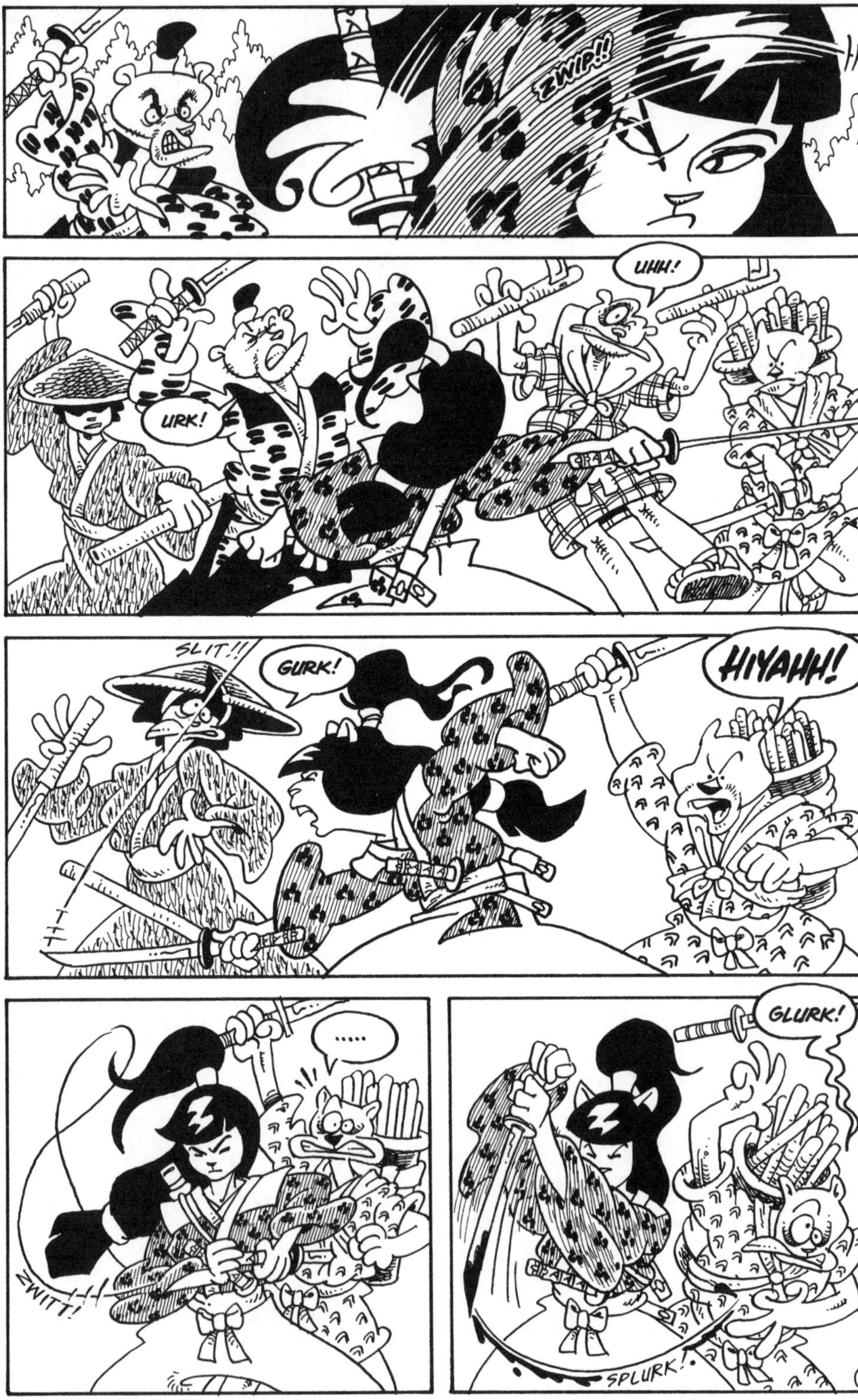
ZWIP!!
UHH!
URK!
SLIT!!
GURK!
HIYAHH!
......
ZWITT!
GLURK!
SPLURK!

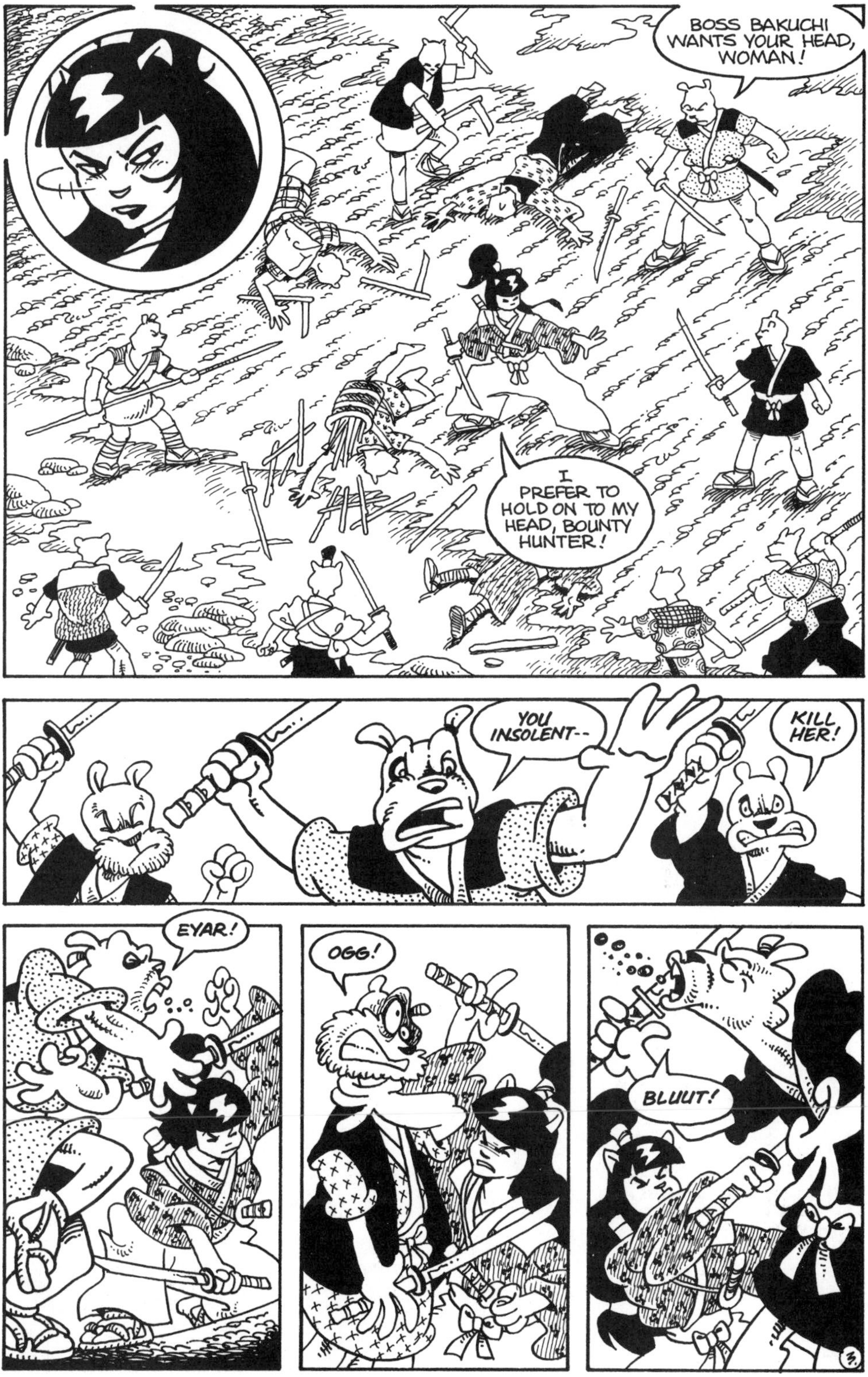
BOSS BAKUCHI WANTS YOUR HEAD, WOMAN!
I PREFER TO HOLD ON TO MY HEAD, BOUNTY HUNTER!
YOU INSOLENT--
KILL HER!
EYAR!
OGG!
BLUUT!

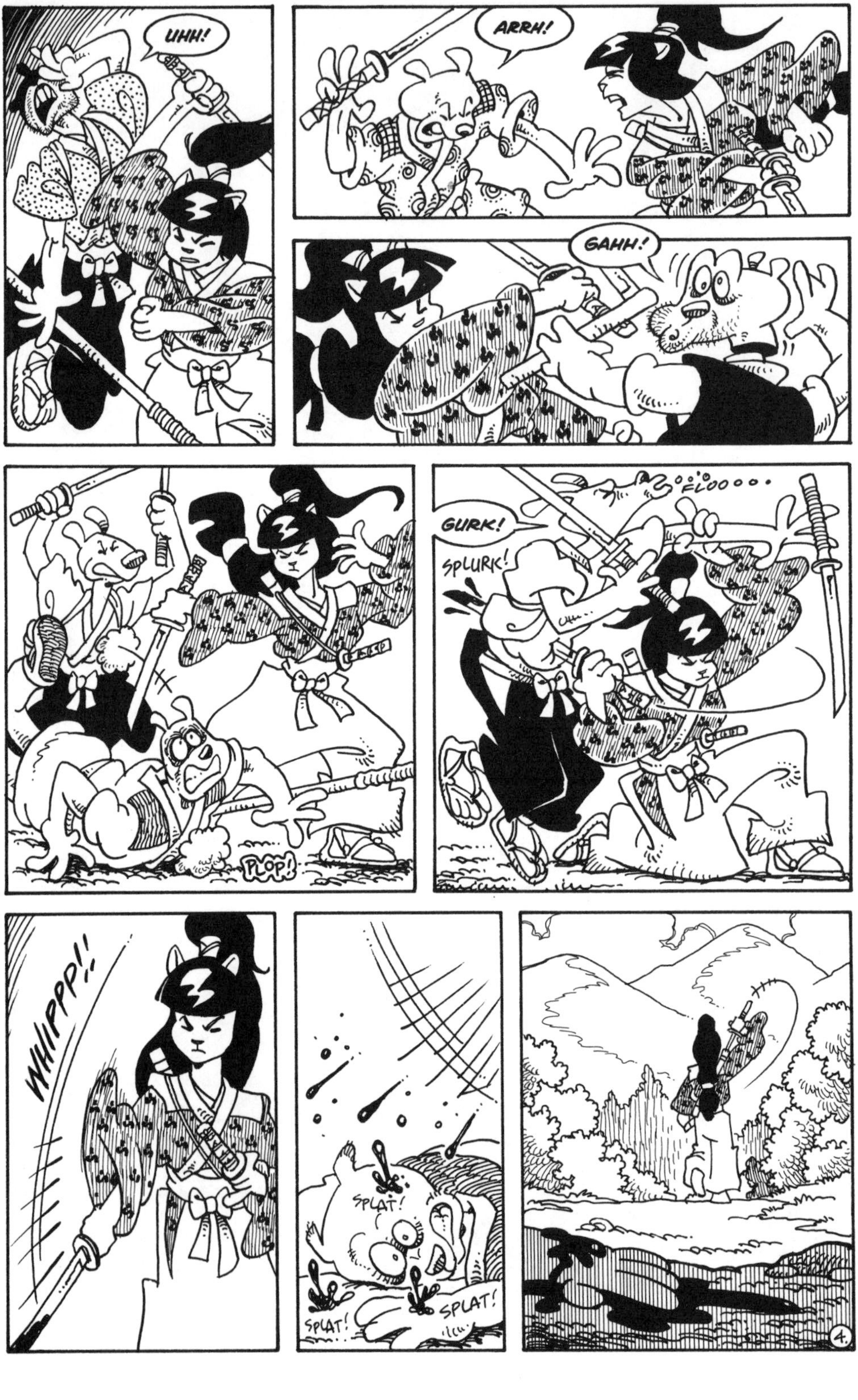
UHH!
ARRH!
GAHH!
PLOP!
GURK!
SPLURK!
FLOOOOO.
WHIPPP!!
SPLAT!
SPLAT!
SPLAT!
4.

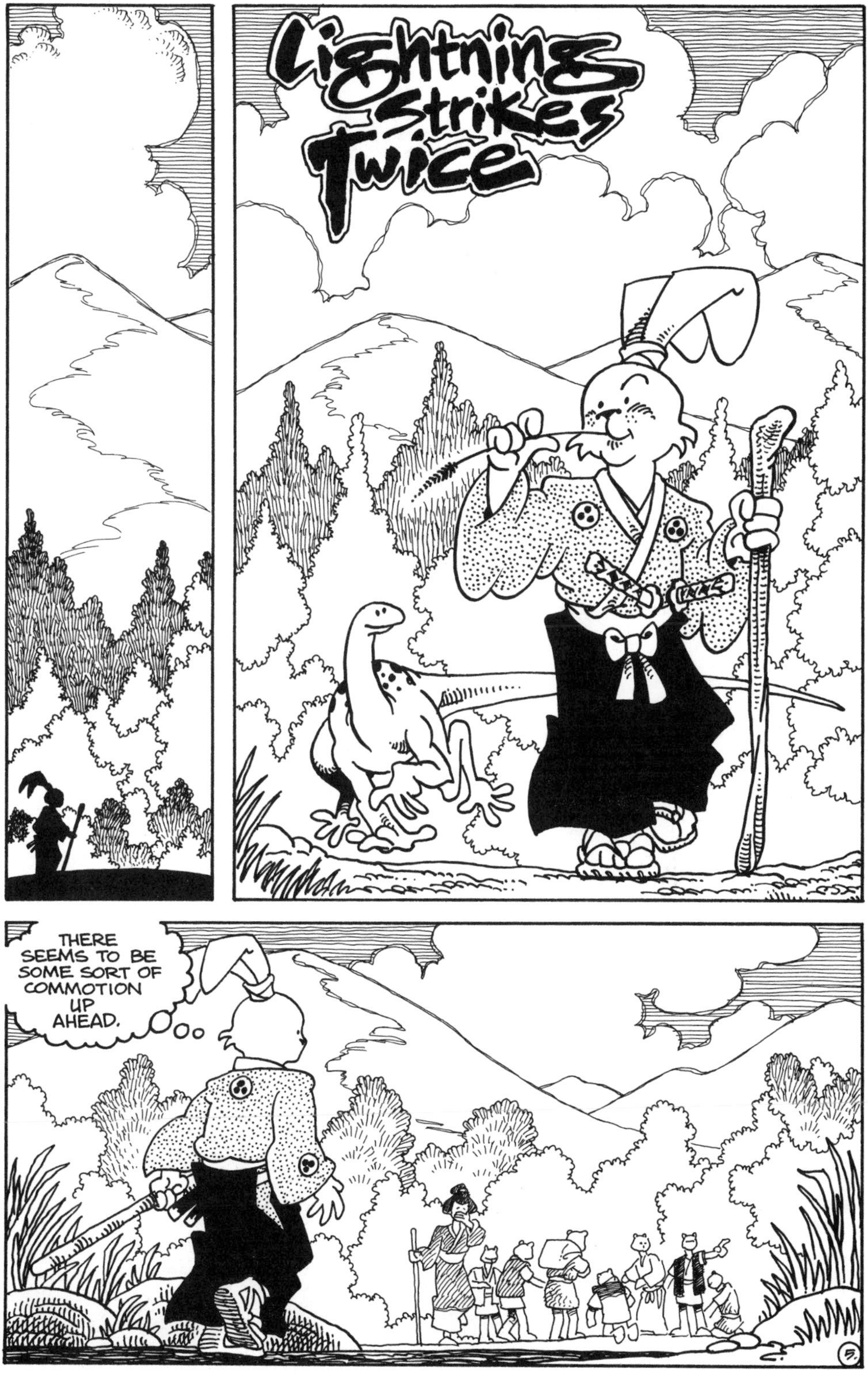
Lightning Strikes Twice
THERE SEEMS TO BE SOME SORT OF COMMOTION UP AHEAD.

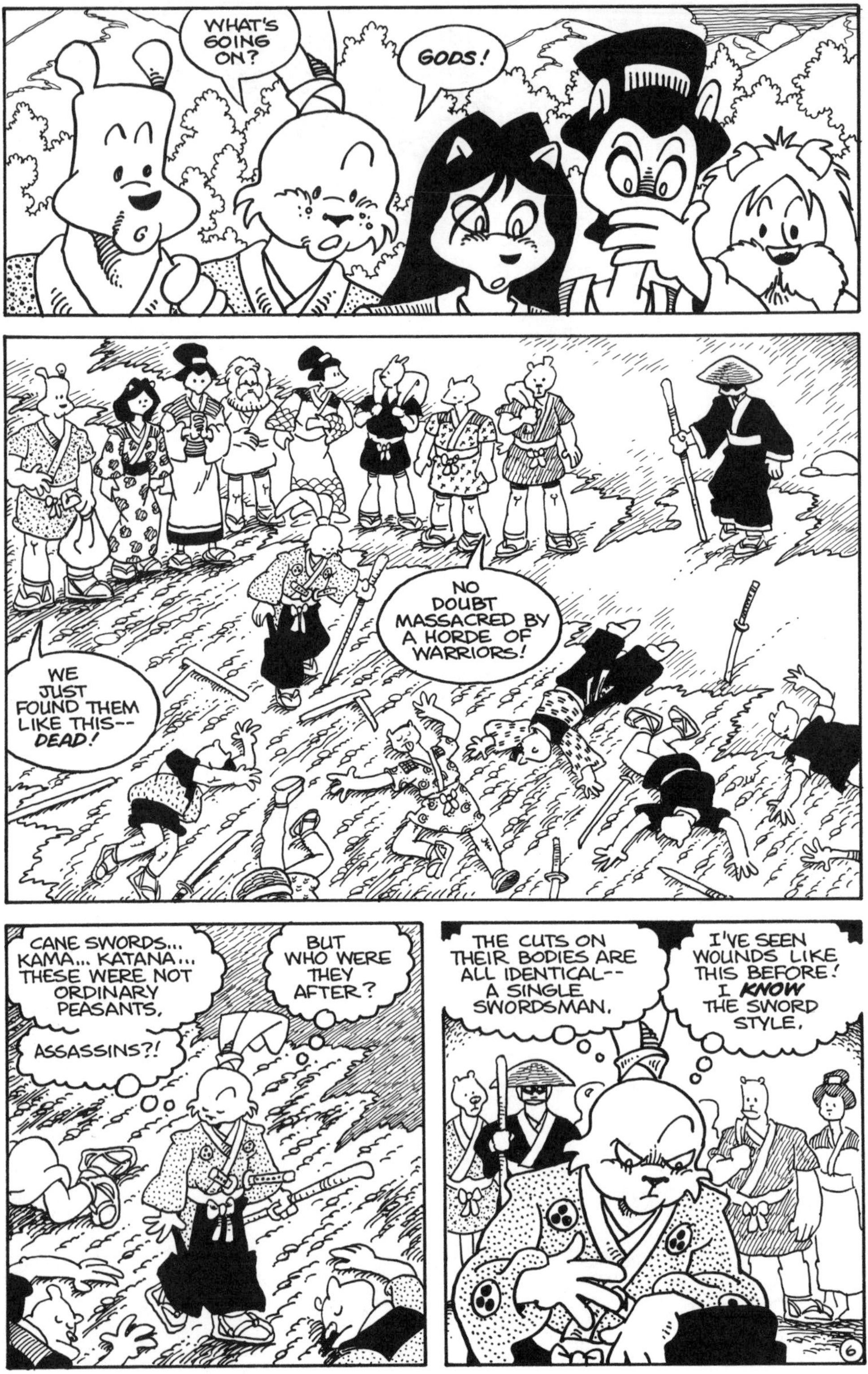
WHAT'S GOING ON?
GODS!
NO DOUBT MASSACRED BY A HORDE OF WARRIORS!
WE JUST FOUND THEM LIKE THIS-- *DEAD!*
CANE SWORDS... KAMA... KATANA... THESE WERE NOT ORDINARY PEASANTS.
BUT WHO WERE THEY AFTER?
ASSASSINS?!
THE CUTS ON THEIR BODIES ARE ALL IDENTICAL-- A SINGLE SWORDSMAN.
I'VE SEEN WOUNDS LIKE THIS BEFORE! I *KNOW* THE SWORD STYLE.
6

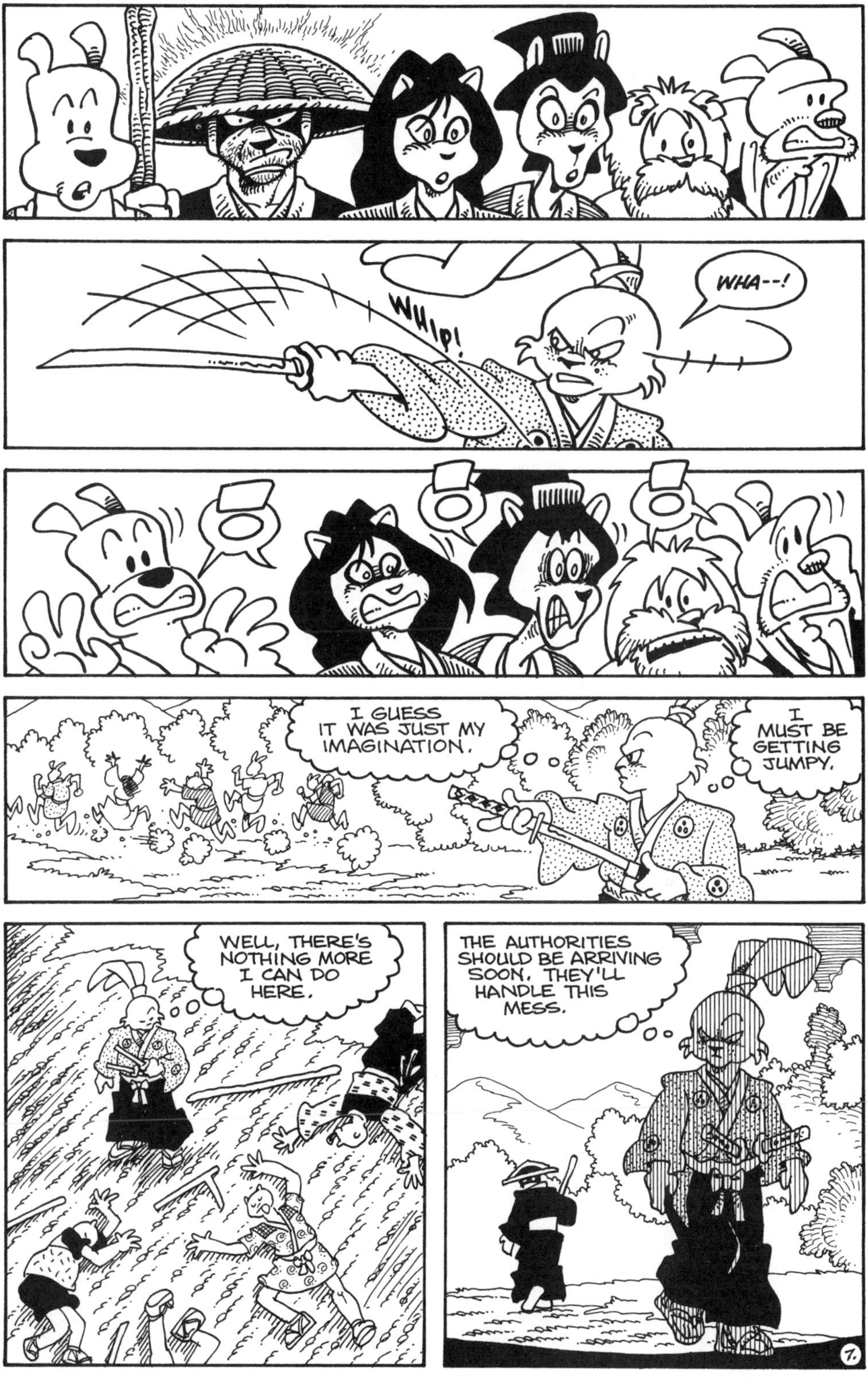
WHIP!
WHA--!
I GUESS IT WAS JUST MY IMAGINATION.
I MUST BE GETTING JUMPY.
WELL, THERE'S NOTHING MORE I CAN DO HERE.
THE AUTHORITIES SHOULD BE ARRIVING SOON. THEY'LL HANDLE THIS MESS.
7.

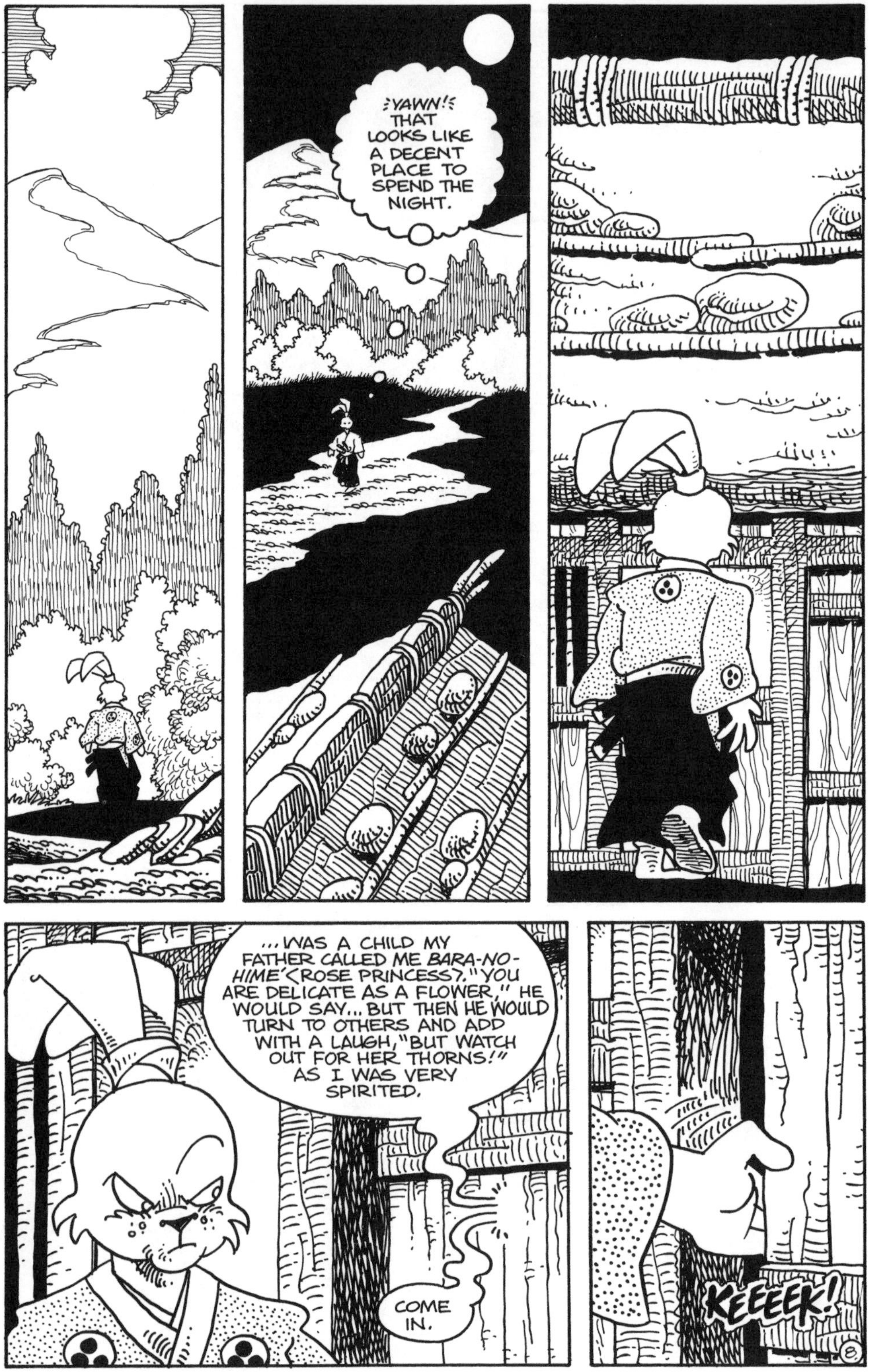
YAWN! THAT LOOKS LIKE A DECENT PLACE TO SPEND THE NIGHT.
...WAS A CHILD MY FATHER CALLED ME BARA-NO-HIME' <ROSE PRINCESS>. "YOU ARE DELICATE AS A FLOWER," HE WOULD SAY... BUT THEN HE WOULD TURN TO OTHERS AND ADD WITH A LAUGH, "BUT WATCH OUT FOR HER THORNS!" AS I WAS VERY SPIRITED.
COME IN.
KEEEEK!
8

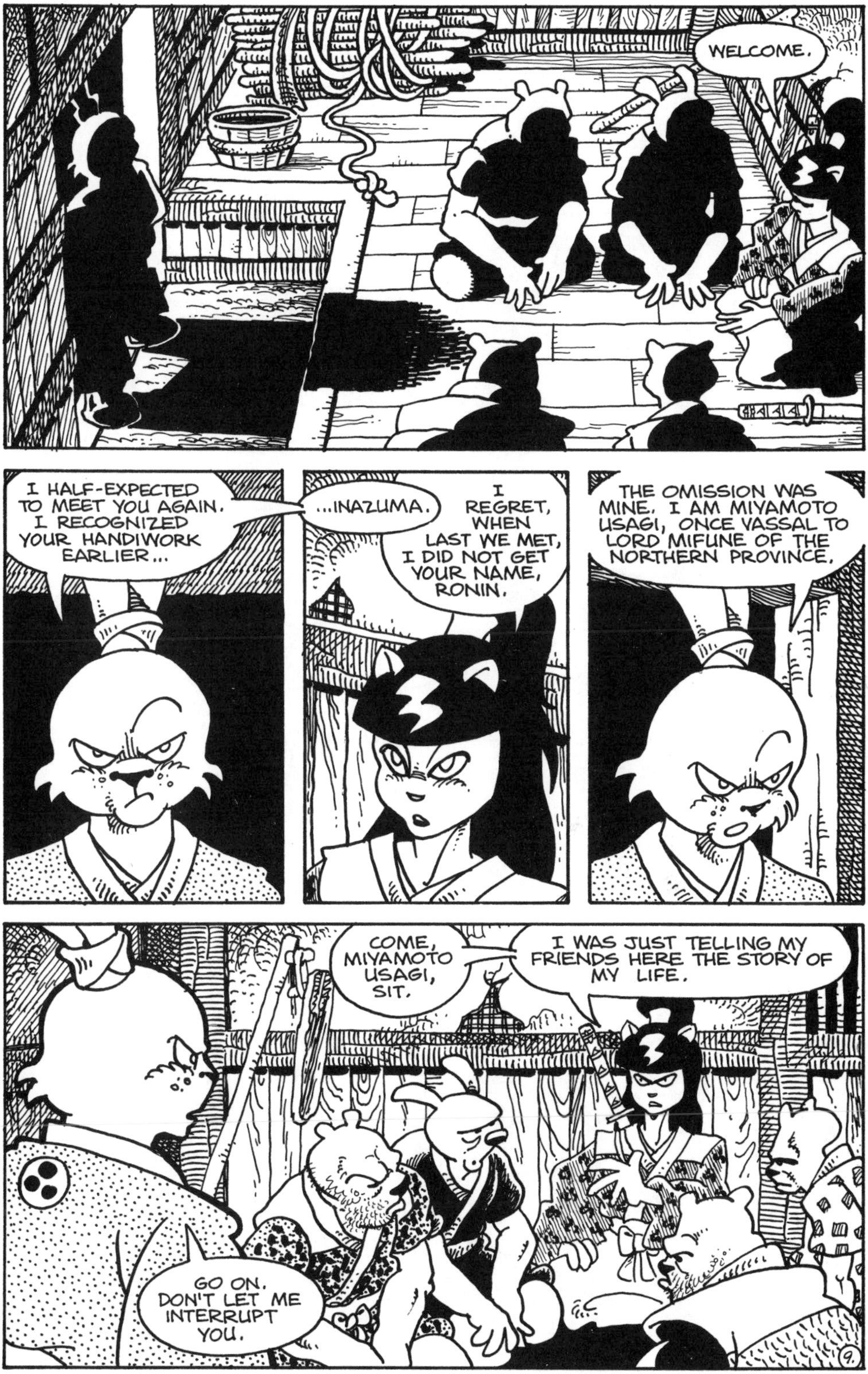
WELCOME.
I HALF-EXPECTED TO MEET YOU AGAIN. I RECOGNIZED YOUR HANDIWORK EARLIER...
...INAZUMA.
I REGRET, WHEN LAST WE MET, I DID NOT GET YOUR NAME, RONIN.
THE OMISSION WAS MINE. I AM MIYAMOTO USAGI, ONCE VASSAL TO LORD MIFUNE OF THE NORTHERN PROVINCE.
COME, MIYAMOTO USAGI, SIT.
I WAS JUST TELLING MY FRIENDS HERE THE STORY OF MY LIFE.
GO ON. DON'T LET ME INTERRUPT YOU.
9.

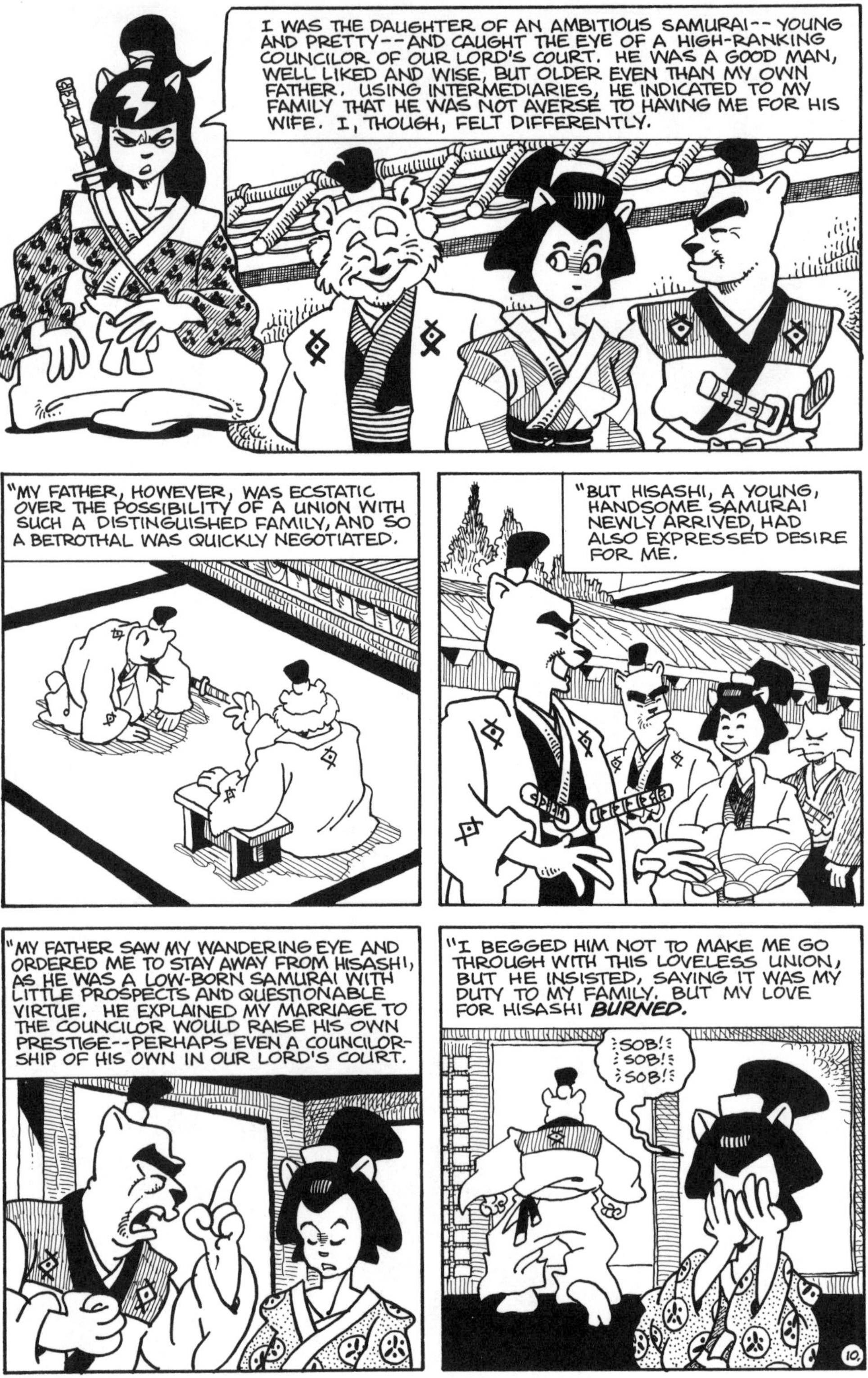
I WAS THE DAUGHTER OF AN AMBITIOUS SAMURAI-- YOUNG AND PRETTY--AND CAUGHT THE EYE OF A HIGH-RANKING COUNCILOR OF OUR LORD'S COURT. HE WAS A GOOD MAN, WELL LIKED AND WISE, BUT OLDER EVEN THAN MY OWN FATHER. USING INTERMEDIARIES, HE INDICATED TO MY FAMILY THAT HE WAS NOT AVERSE TO HAVING ME FOR HIS WIFE. I, THOUGH, FELT DIFFERENTLY.
"MY FATHER, HOWEVER, WAS ECSTATIC OVER THE POSSIBILITY OF A UNION WITH SUCH A DISTINGUISHED FAMILY, AND SO A BETROTHAL WAS QUICKLY NEGOTIATED.
"BUT HISASHI, A YOUNG, HANDSOME SAMURAI NEWLY ARRIVED, HAD ALSO EXPRESSED DESIRE FOR ME.
"MY FATHER SAW MY WANDERING EYE AND ORDERED ME TO STAY AWAY FROM HISASHI, AS HE WAS A LOW-BORN SAMURAI WITH LITTLE PROSPECTS AND QUESTIONABLE VIRTUE. HE EXPLAINED MY MARRIAGE TO THE COUNCILOR WOULD RAISE HIS OWN PRESTIGE--PERHAPS EVEN A COUNCILOR-SHIP OF HIS OWN IN OUR LORD'S COURT.
"I BEGGED HIM NOT TO MAKE ME GO THROUGH WITH THIS LOVELESS UNION, BUT HE INSISTED, SAYING IT WAS MY DUTY TO MY FAMILY. BUT MY LOVE FOR HISASHI ***BURNED.***
SOB! SOB! SOB!
10.

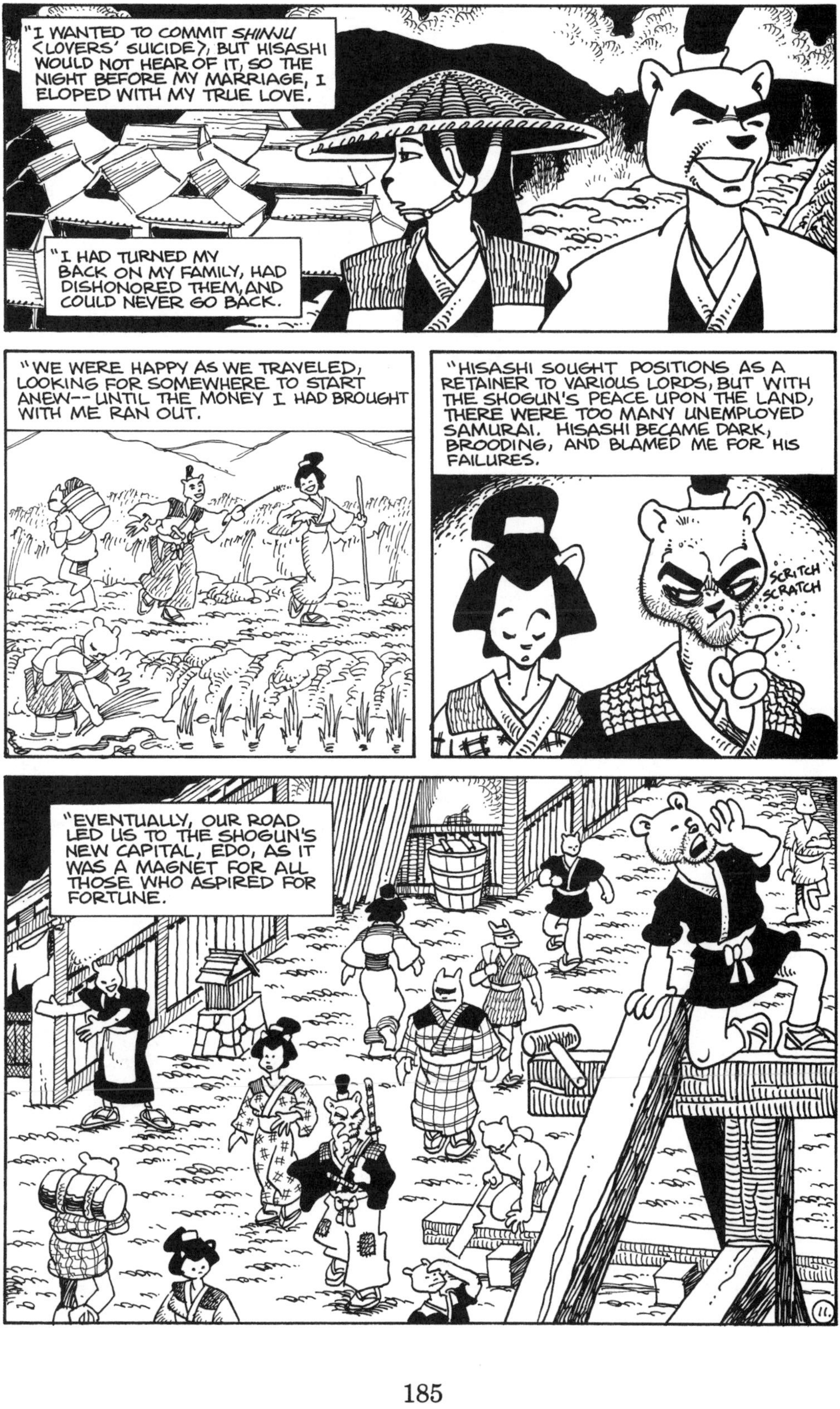
"I WANTED TO COMMIT SHINJU <LOVERS' SUICIDE>, BUT HISASHI WOULD NOT HEAR OF IT, SO THE NIGHT BEFORE MY MARRIAGE, I ELOPED WITH MY TRUE LOVE.
"I HAD TURNED MY BACK ON MY FAMILY, HAD DISHONORED THEM, AND COULD NEVER GO BACK.
"WE WERE HAPPY AS WE TRAVELED, LOOKING FOR SOMEWHERE TO START ANEW-- UNTIL THE MONEY I HAD BROUGHT WITH ME RAN OUT.
"HISASHI SOUGHT POSITIONS AS A RETAINER TO VARIOUS LORDS, BUT WITH THE SHOGUN'S PEACE UPON THE LAND, THERE WERE TOO MANY UNEMPLOYED SAMURAI. HISASHI BECAME DARK, BROODING, AND BLAMED ME FOR HIS FAILURES.
SCRITCH SCRATCH
"EVENTUALLY, OUR ROAD LED US TO THE SHOGUN'S NEW CAPITAL, EDO, AS IT WAS A MAGNET FOR ALL THOSE WHO ASPIRED FOR FORTUNE.
11.

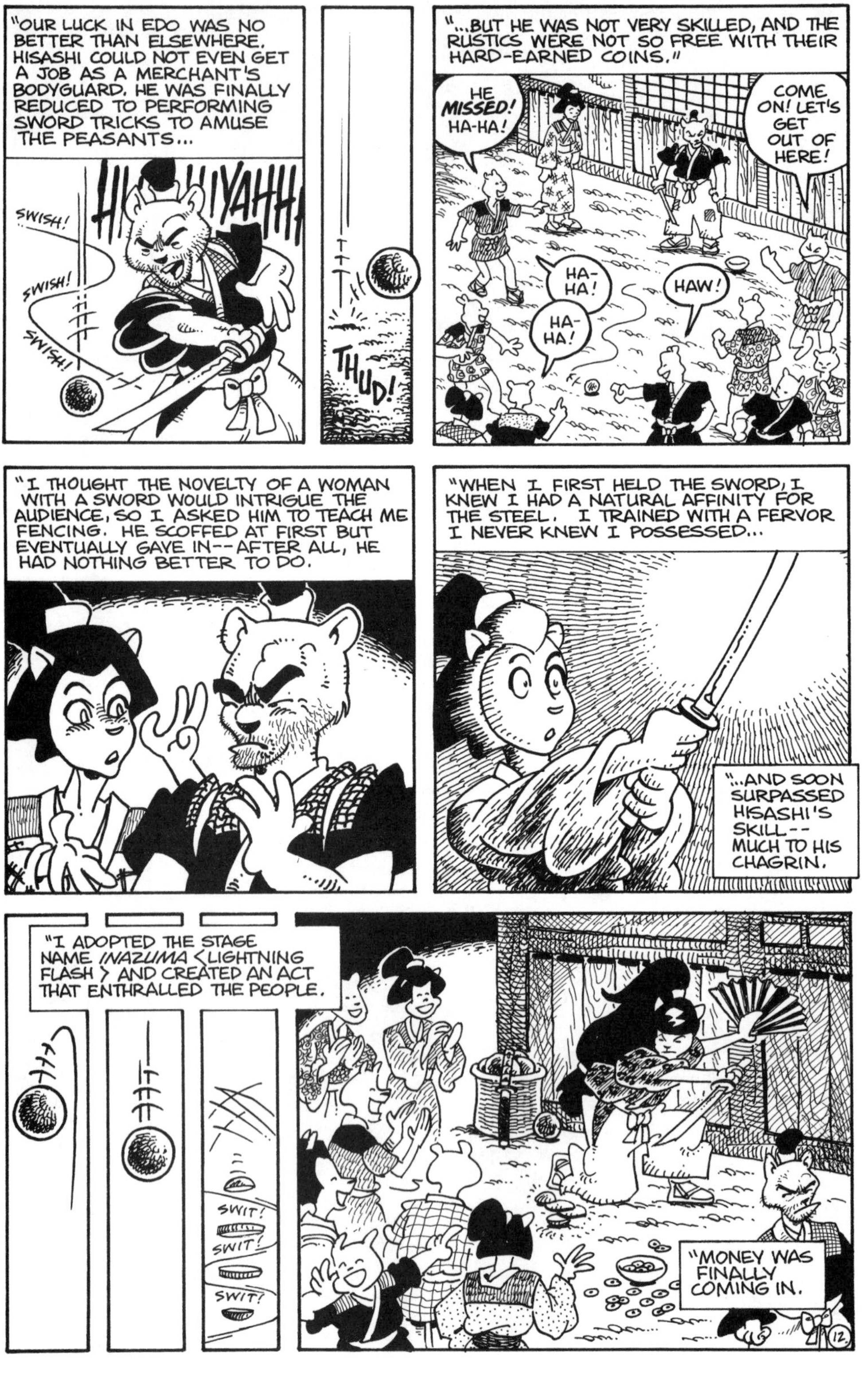

"OUR LUCK IN EDO WAS NO BETTER THAN ELSEWHERE. HISASHI COULD NOT EVEN GET A JOB AS A MERCHANT'S BODYGUARD. HE WAS FINALLY REDUCED TO PERFORMING SWORD TRICKS TO AMUSE THE PEASANTS...
HIIIIIIYAHHH
SWISH!
SWISH!
SWISH!
THUD!
"...BUT HE WAS NOT VERY SKILLED, AND THE RUSTICS WERE NOT SO FREE WITH THEIR HARD-EARNED COINS."
HE MISSED! HA-HA!
COME ON! LET'S GET OUT OF HERE!
HA-HA!
HA-HA!
HAW!
"I THOUGHT THE NOVELTY OF A WOMAN WITH A SWORD WOULD INTRIGUE THE AUDIENCE, SO I ASKED HIM TO TEACH ME FENCING. HE SCOFFED AT FIRST BUT EVENTUALLY GAVE IN--AFTER ALL, HE HAD NOTHING BETTER TO DO.
"WHEN I FIRST HELD THE SWORD, I KNEW I HAD A NATURAL AFFINITY FOR THE STEEL. I TRAINED WITH A FERVOR I NEVER KNEW I POSSESSED...
"...AND SOON SURPASSED HISASHI'S SKILL--MUCH TO HIS CHAGRIN.
"I ADOPTED THE STAGE NAME INAZUMA <LIGHTNING FLASH> AND CREATED AN ACT THAT ENTHRALLED THE PEOPLE.
SWIT!
SWIT!
SWIT!
"MONEY WAS FINALLY COMING IN.
12

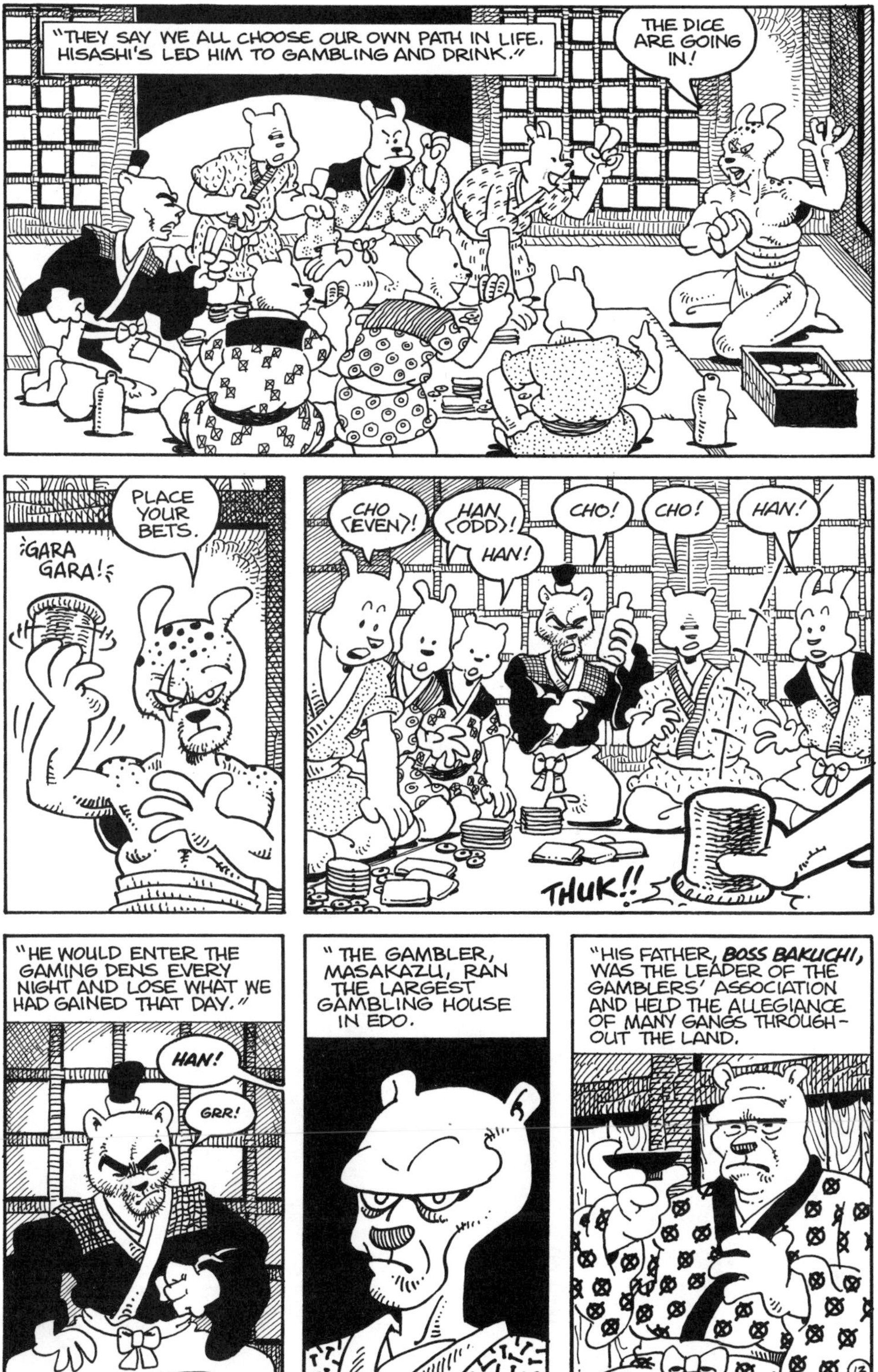
"THEY SAY WE ALL CHOOSE OUR OWN PATH IN LIFE. HISASHI'S LED HIM TO GAMBLING AND DRINK."
THE DICE ARE GOING IN!
PLACE YOUR BETS.
GARA GARA!
CHO (EVEN)!
HAN (ODD)!
HAN!
CHO!
CHO!
HAN!
THUK!!
"HE WOULD ENTER THE GAMING DENS EVERY NIGHT AND LOSE WHAT WE HAD GAINED THAT DAY."
HAN!
GRR!
"THE GAMBLER, MASAKAZU, RAN THE LARGEST GAMBLING HOUSE IN EDO.
"HIS FATHER, BOSS BAKUCHI, WAS THE LEADER OF THE GAMBLERS' ASSOCIATION AND HELD THE ALLEGIANCE OF MANY GANGS THROUGH-OUT THE LAND.
13

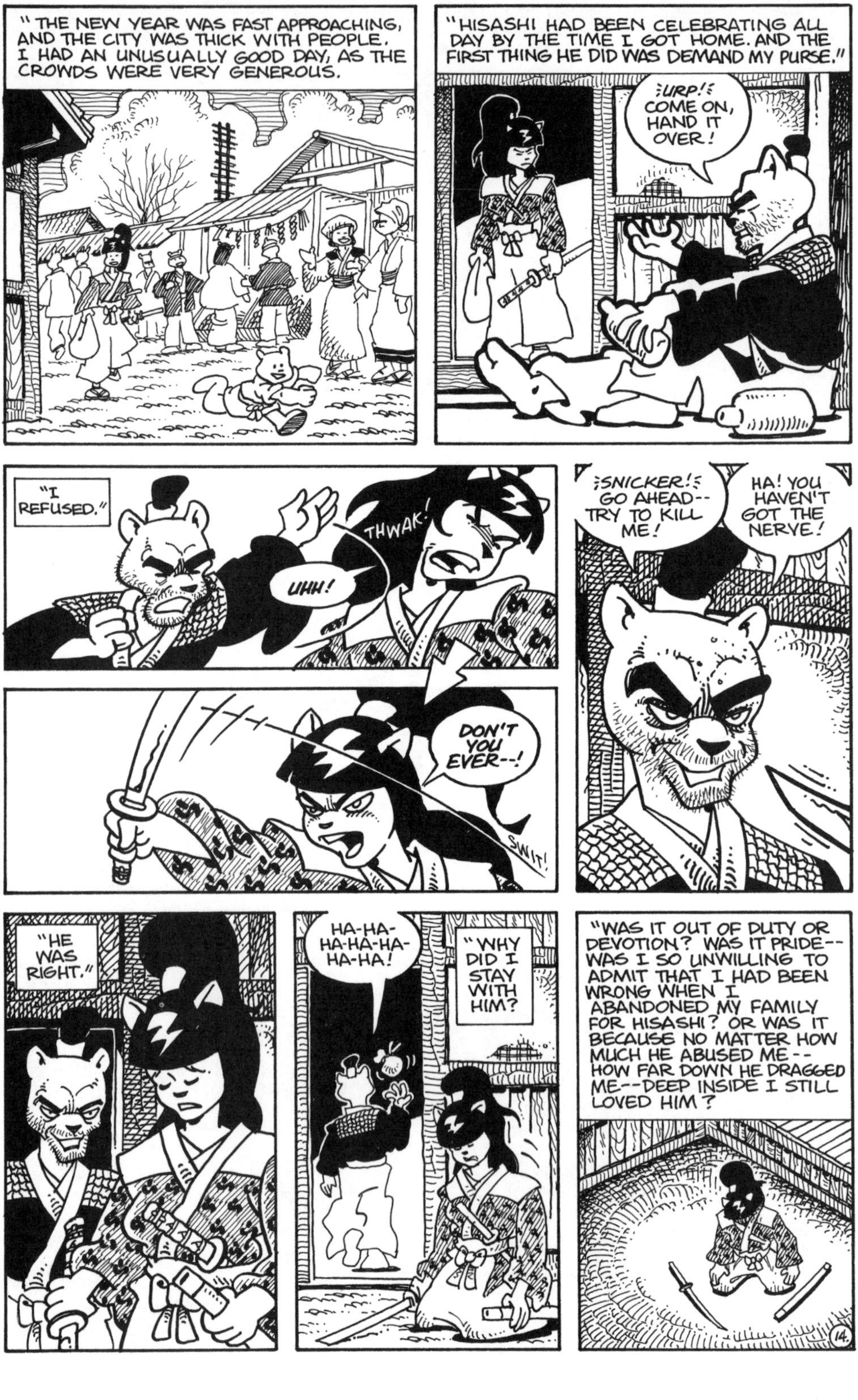
"THE NEW YEAR WAS FAST APPROACHING, AND THE CITY WAS THICK WITH PEOPLE. I HAD AN UNUSUALLY GOOD DAY, AS THE CROWDS WERE VERY GENEROUS.
"HISASHI HAD BEEN CELEBRATING ALL DAY BY THE TIME I GOT HOME. AND THE FIRST THING HE DID WAS DEMAND MY PURSE."
URP! COME ON, HAND IT OVER!
"I REFUSED."
THWAK!
UHH!
SNICKER! GO AHEAD-- TRY TO KILL ME!
HA! YOU HAVEN'T GOT THE NERVE!
DON'T YOU EVER--!
SWIT!
"HE WAS RIGHT."
HA-HA-HA-HA-HA-HA-HA!
"WHY DID I STAY WITH HIM?
"WAS IT OUT OF DUTY OR DEVOTION? WAS IT PRIDE-- WAS I SO UNWILLING TO ADMIT THAT I HAD BEEN WRONG WHEN I ABANDONED MY FAMILY FOR HISASHI? OR WAS IT BECAUSE NO MATTER HOW MUCH HE ABUSED ME-- HOW FAR DOWN HE DRAGGED ME--DEEP INSIDE I STILL LOVED HIM?
14.

"HE WENT TO MASAKAZU'S GAMBLING HOUSE AS USUAL..."

PLACE YOUR BETS!

CHO!

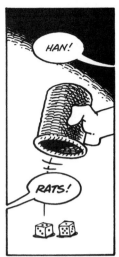

HAN!

RATS!

"...AND STAYED UNTIL HE WAS THE ONLY CUSTOMER LEFT."

YOU LOSE AGAIN!

YOU'RE CLEANED OUT, HISASHI!

NEXT TIME BRING MORE MONEY WITH YOU! HA-HA!

BAH!

THESE DICE HAVE BEEN AGAINST ME ALL NIGHT!

CRAK!

WHA--! THE DICE ARE WEIGHTED! THE GAME'S FIXED!

TAKE ME TO MASAKAZU! I'VE GOT SOME BUSINESS TO DISCUSS WITH HIM! HEH-HEH!

DO AS HE SAYS!

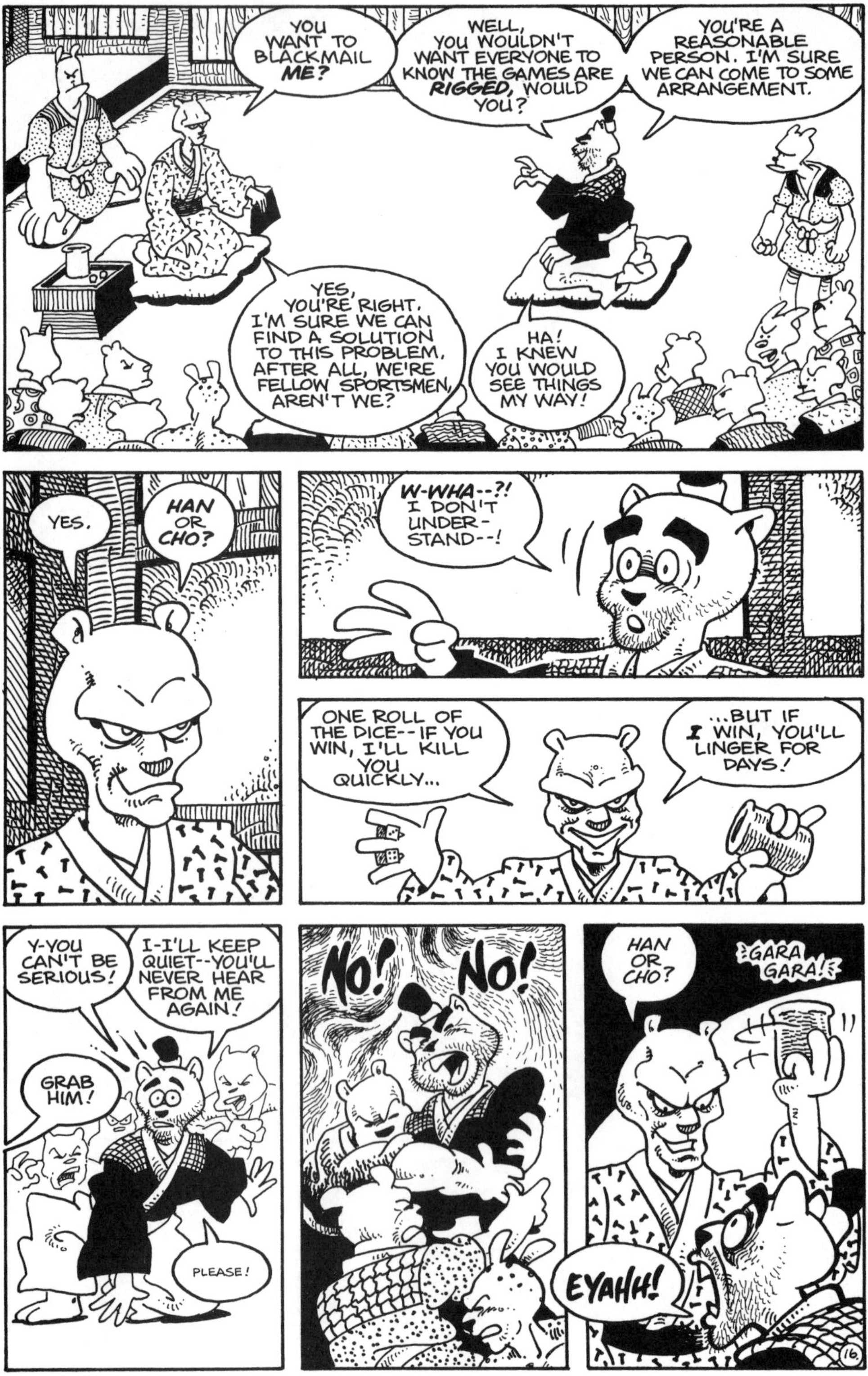
YOU WANT TO BLACKMAIL ME?
WELL, YOU WOULDN'T WANT EVERYONE TO KNOW THE GAMES ARE RIGGED, WOULD YOU?
YOU'RE A REASONABLE PERSON. I'M SURE WE CAN COME TO SOME ARRANGEMENT.
YES, YOU'RE RIGHT. I'M SURE WE CAN FIND A SOLUTION TO THIS PROBLEM. AFTER ALL, WE'RE FELLOW SPORTSMEN, AREN'T WE?
HA! I KNEW YOU WOULD SEE THINGS MY WAY!
YES.
HAN OR CHO?
W-WHA--?! I DON'T UNDER-STAND--!
ONE ROLL OF THE DICE--IF YOU WIN, I'LL KILL YOU QUICKLY...
...BUT IF I WIN, YOU'LL LINGER FOR DAYS!
Y-YOU CAN'T BE SERIOUS!
I-I'LL KEEP QUIET--YOU'LL NEVER HEAR FROM ME AGAIN!
GRAB HIM!
PLEASE!
NO! NO!
HAN OR CHO?
GARA GARA!
EYAHH!
16

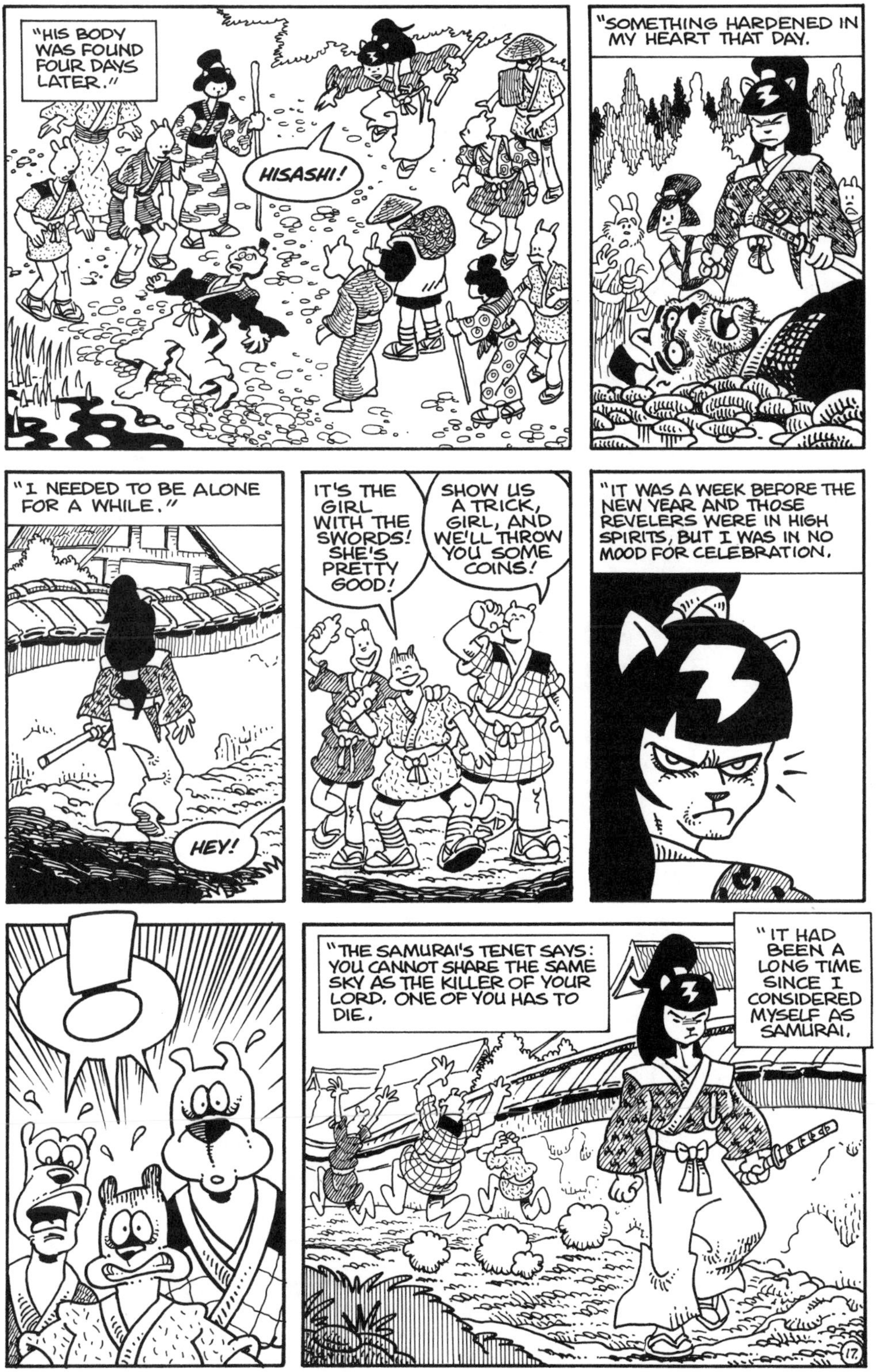
"HIS BODY WAS FOUND FOUR DAYS LATER."
HISASHI!
"SOMETHING HARDENED IN MY HEART THAT DAY.
"I NEEDED TO BE ALONE FOR A WHILE."
HEY!
IT'S THE GIRL WITH THE SWORDS! SHE'S PRETTY GOOD!
SHOW US A TRICK, GIRL, AND WE'LL THROW YOU SOME COINS!
"IT WAS A WEEK BEFORE THE NEW YEAR AND THOSE REVELERS WERE IN HIGH SPIRITS, BUT I WAS IN NO MOOD FOR CELEBRATION.
!
"THE SAMURAI'S TENET SAYS: YOU CANNOT SHARE THE SAME SKY AS THE KILLER OF YOUR LORD. ONE OF YOU HAS TO DIE.
"IT HAD BEEN A LONG TIME SINCE I CONSIDERED MYSELF AS SAMURAI.
17.

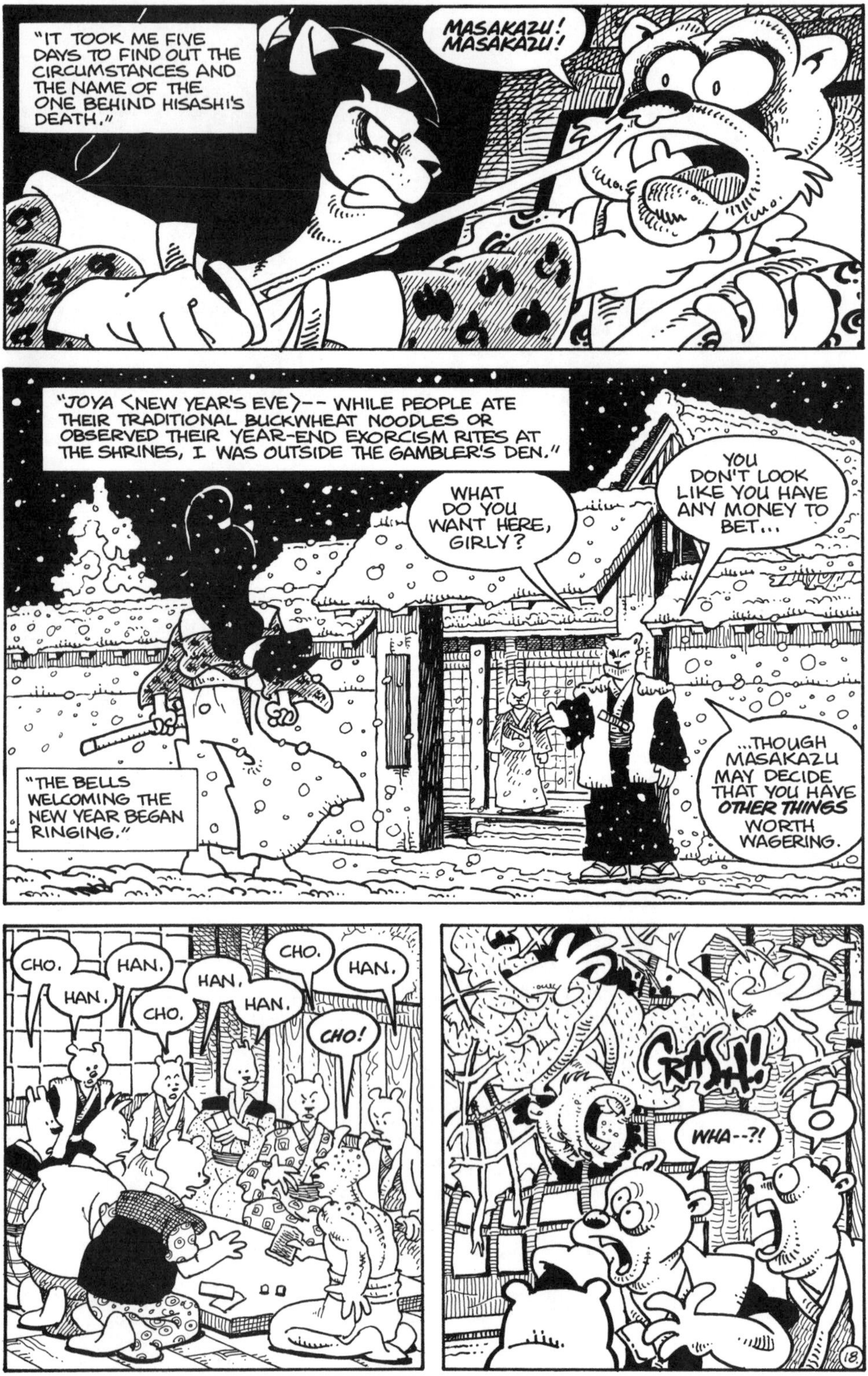
"IT TOOK ME FIVE DAYS TO FIND OUT THE CIRCUMSTANCES AND THE NAME OF THE ONE BEHIND HISASHI'S DEATH."
MASAKAZU! MASAKAZU!
"JOYA <NEW YEAR'S EVE>-- WHILE PEOPLE ATE THEIR TRADITIONAL BUCKWHEAT NOODLES OR OBSERVED THEIR YEAR-END EXORCISM RITES AT THE SHRINES, I WAS OUTSIDE THE GAMBLER'S DEN."
WHAT DO YOU WANT HERE, GIRLY?
YOU DON'T LOOK LIKE YOU HAVE ANY MONEY TO BET...
"THE BELLS WELCOMING THE NEW YEAR BEGAN RINGING."
...THOUGH MASAKAZU MAY DECIDE THAT YOU HAVE OTHER THINGS WORTH WAGERING.
CHO.
HAN.
HAN.
CHO.
HAN.
HAN.
CHO.
HAN.
CHO!
CRASH!
WHA--?!
!
18.

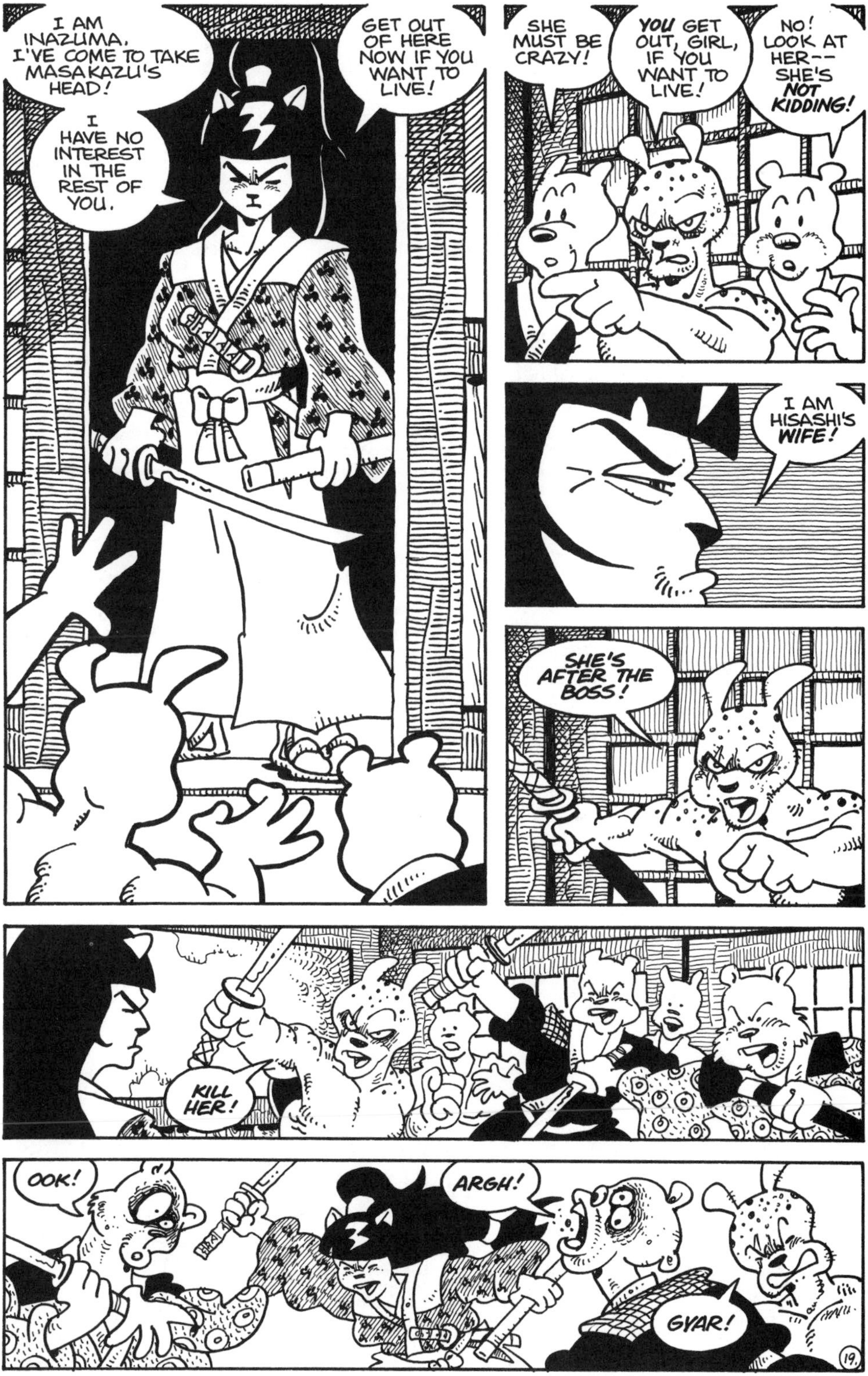
I AM INAZUMA. I'VE COME TO TAKE MASAKAZU'S HEAD!
I HAVE NO INTEREST IN THE REST OF YOU.
GET OUT OF HERE NOW IF YOU WANT TO LIVE!
SHE MUST BE CRAZY!
YOU GET OUT, GIRL, IF YOU WANT TO LIVE!
NO! LOOK AT HER-- SHE'S NOT KIDDING!
I AM HISASHI'S WIFE!
SHE'S AFTER THE BOSS!
KILL HER!
OOK!
ARGH!
GYAR!
19.

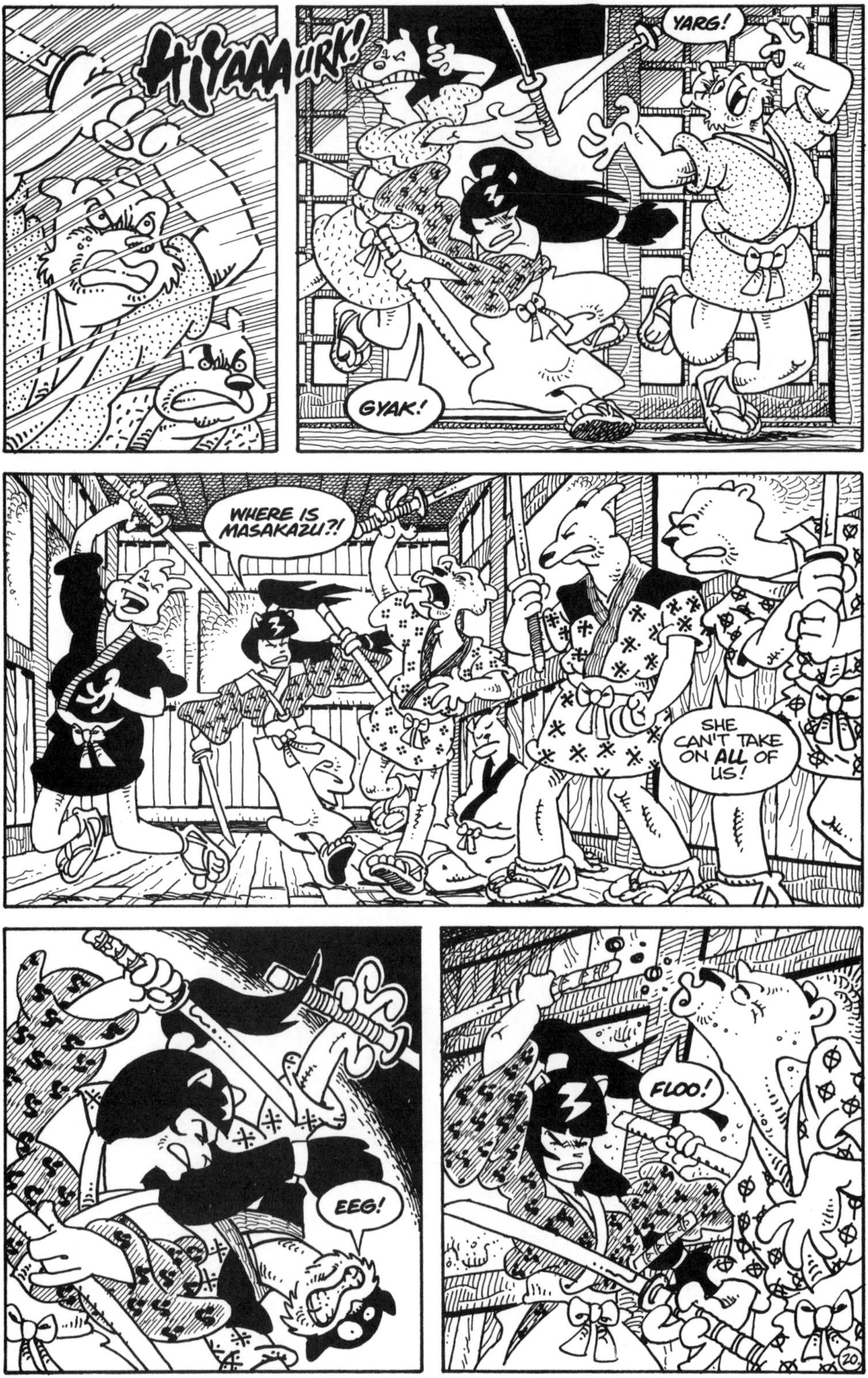
HIYAAAURK!
YARG!
GYAK!
WHERE IS MASAKAZU?!
SHE CAN'T TAKE ON ALL OF US!
EEG!
FLOO!
20

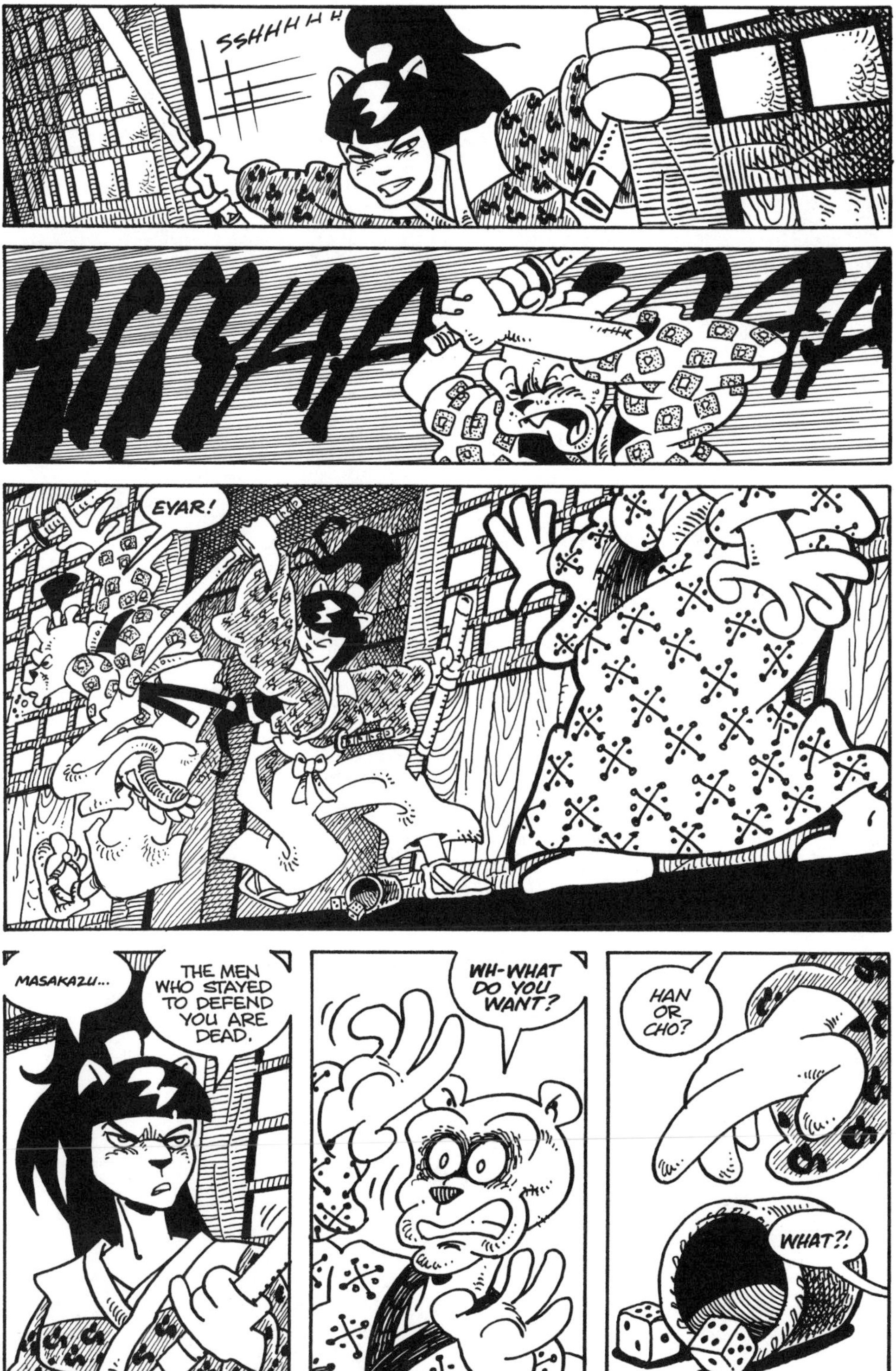
SSHHHHH!
EYAR!
MASAKAZU...
THE MEN WHO STAYED TO DEFEND YOU ARE DEAD.
WH-WHAT DO YOU WANT?
HAN OR CHO?
WHAT?!
21.

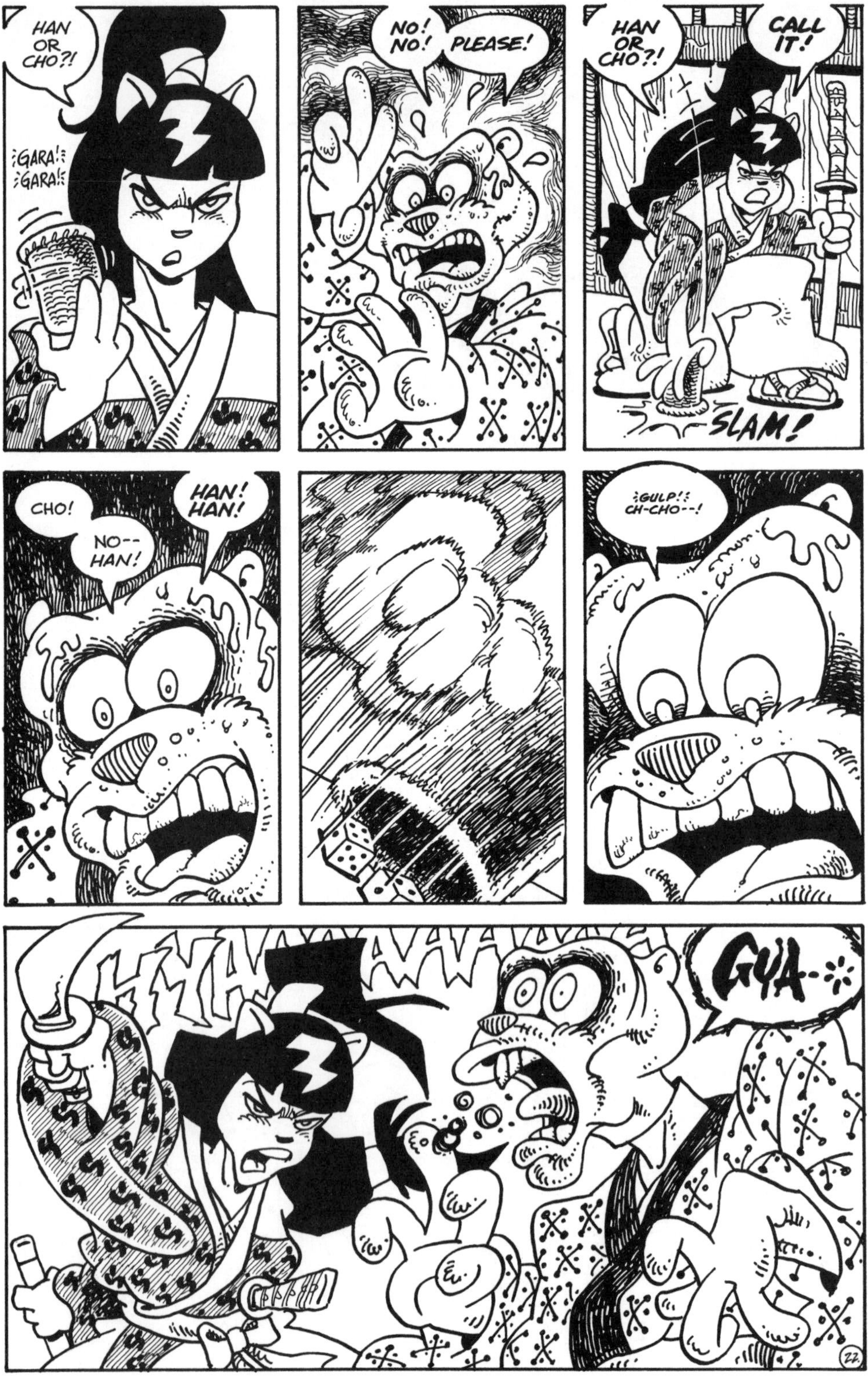
HAN OR CHO?!
GARA! GARA!
NO! NO!
PLEASE!
HAN OR CHO?!
CALL IT!
SLAM!
CHO!
NO-- HAN!
HAN! HAN!
GULP! CH-CHO--!
HYA
GYA--
22

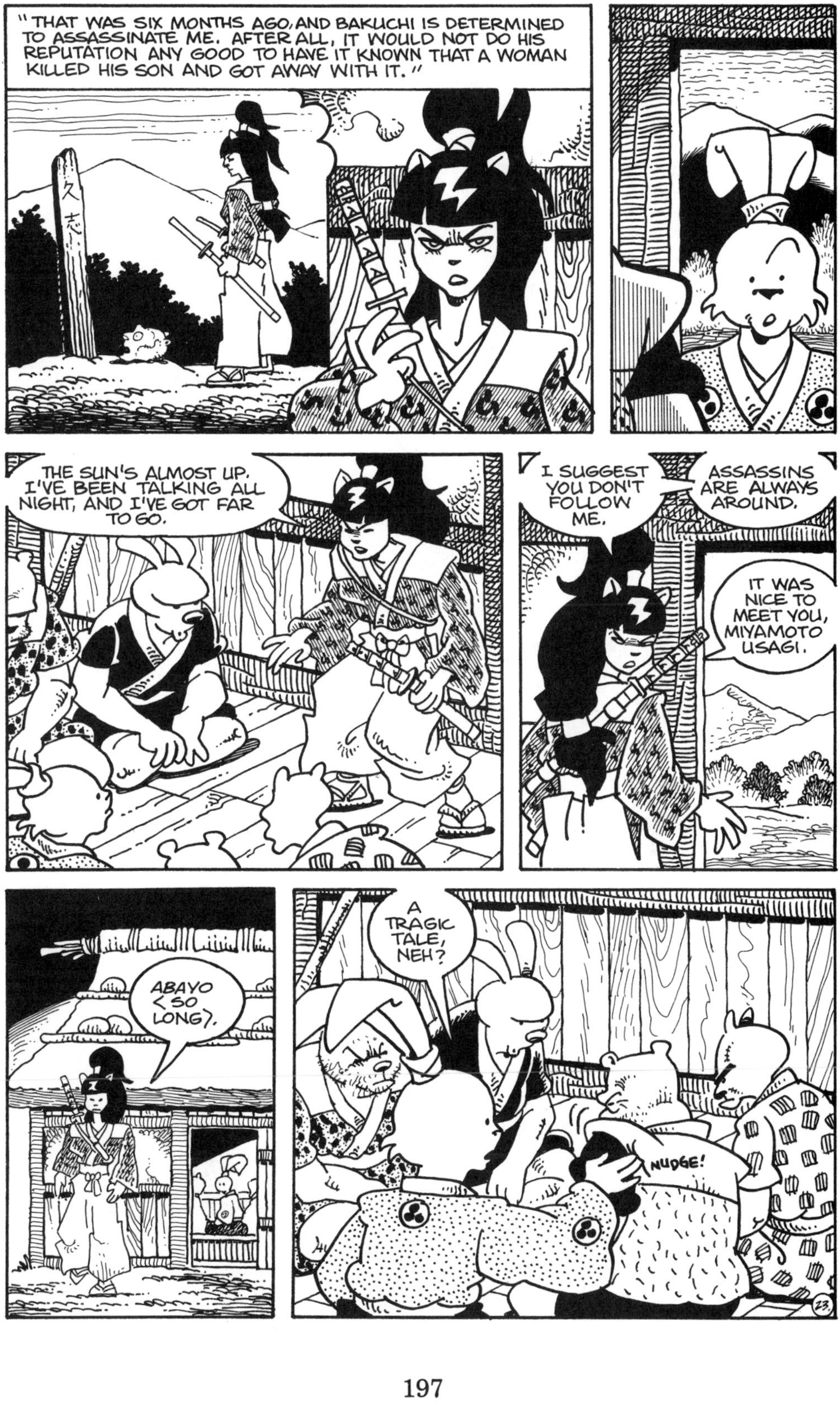
"THAT WAS SIX MONTHS AGO, AND BAKUCHI IS DETERMINED TO ASSASSINATE ME. AFTER ALL, IT WOULD NOT DO HIS REPUTATION ANY GOOD TO HAVE IT KNOWN THAT A WOMAN KILLED HIS SON AND GOT AWAY WITH IT."
久志
THE SUN'S ALMOST UP. I'VE BEEN TALKING ALL NIGHT, AND I'VE GOT FAR TO GO.
I SUGGEST YOU DON'T FOLLOW ME.
ASSASSINS ARE ALWAYS AROUND.
IT WAS NICE TO MEET YOU, MIYAMOTO USAGI.
ABAYO <SO LONG>.
A TRAGIC TALE, NEH?
NUDGE!
23.

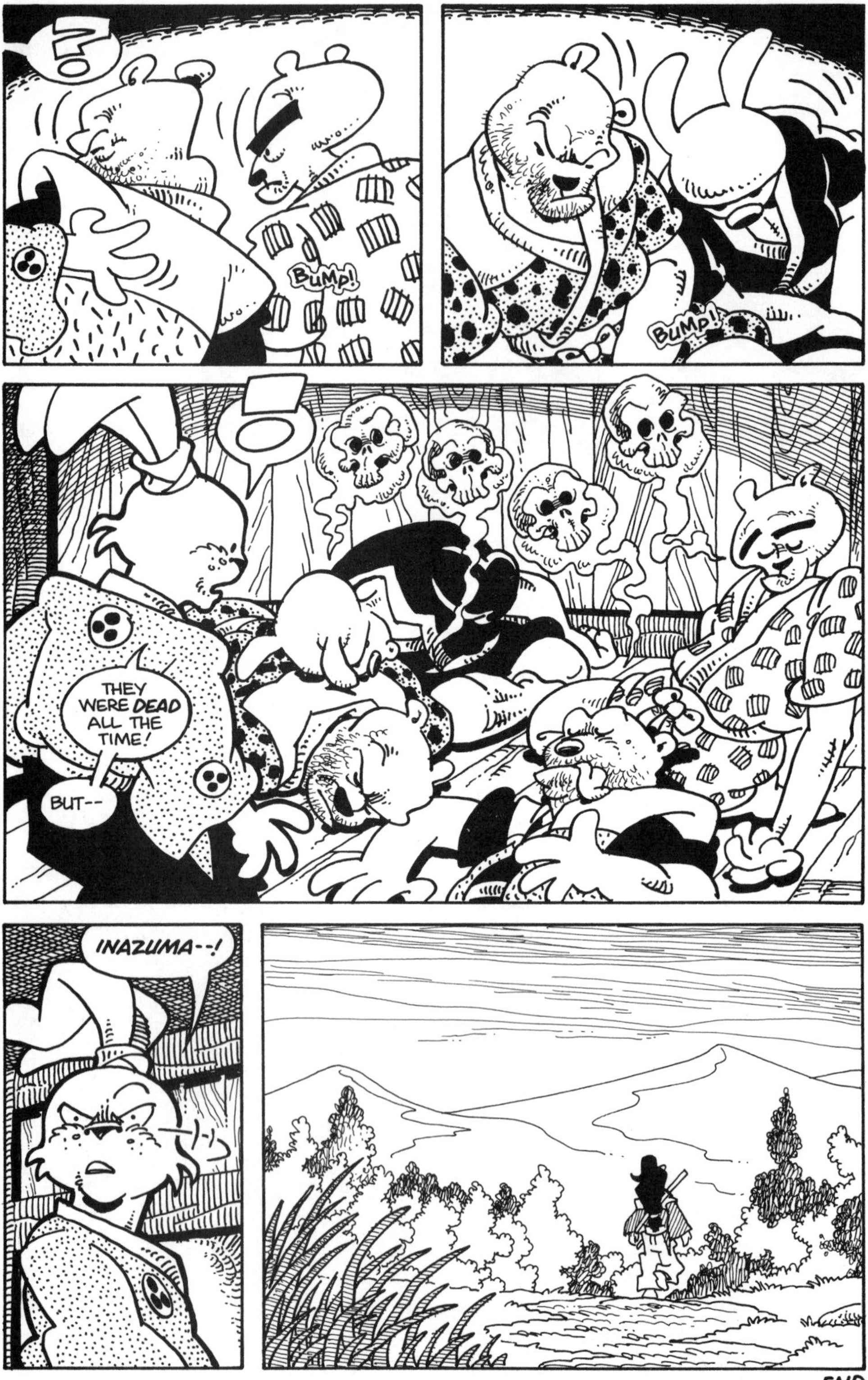
?
BUMP!
BUMP!
!
THEY WERE DEAD ALL THE TIME!
BUT--
INAZUMA--!
END.

Gallery

Stan Sakai's cover art from issue fifteen of Mirage's Usagi Yojimbo™ Volume Two *series and from issues four, five, and six of Dark Horse's* Usagi Yojimbo™ Volume Three *series.*

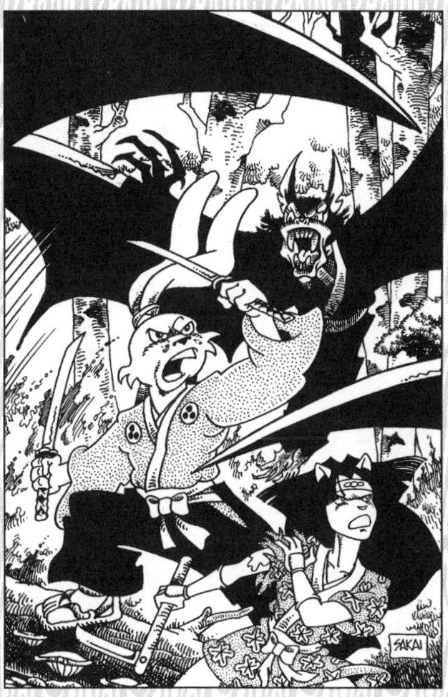
SAKAI

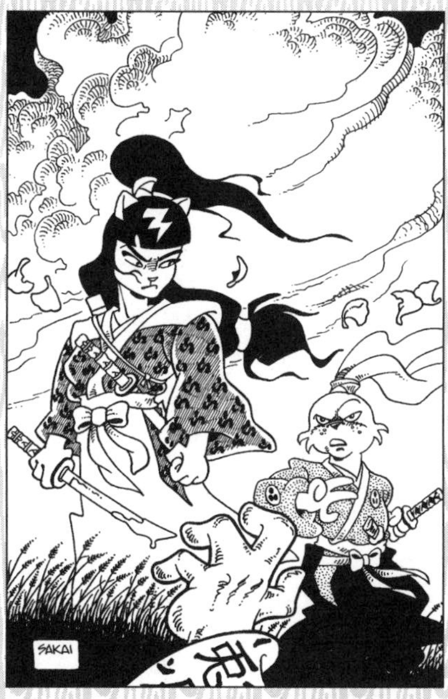
SAKAI

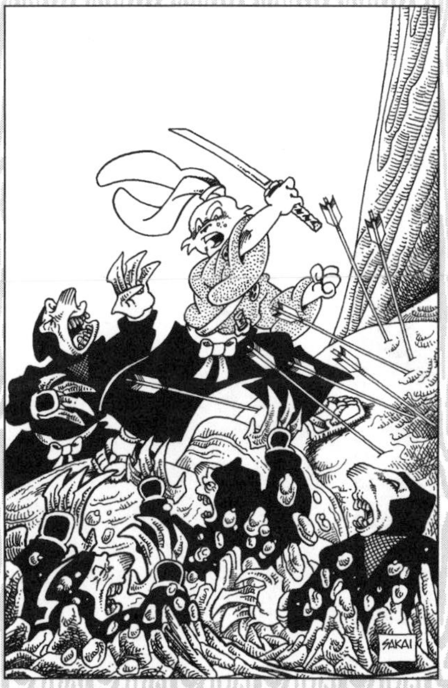
SAKAI

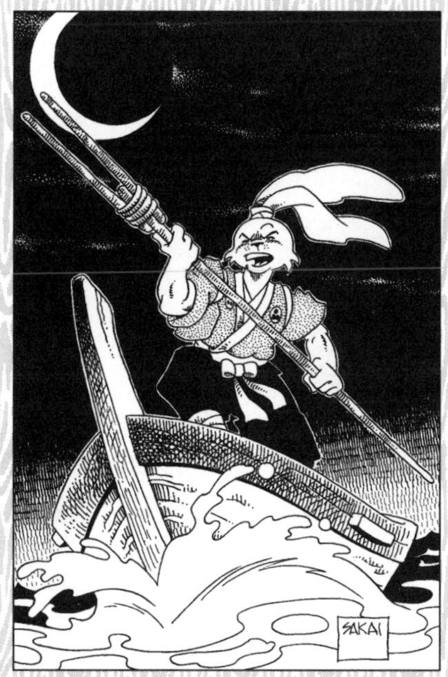
SAKAI

USAGI YOJIMBO

Trade-paperback and limited-hardcover
collections available from Dark Horse Comics

AVAILABLE AT YOUR LOCAL COMICS SHOP OR BOOKSTORE. To find a comics shop
in your area, call 1-888-266-4226. For more information or to order direct:
ON THE WEB: www.darkhorse.com E-MAIL: mailorder@darkhorse.com
PHONE: 1-800-862-0052 OR (503) 652-9701 Mon.-Sat. 9 a.m. to 5 p.m. Pacific Time

SHADES OF DEATH
200-page black-and-white paperback
ISBN: 1-56971-259-X $14.95
limited-edition hardcover
ISBN: 1-56971-279-4 $49.95

DAISHO
200-page black-and-white paperback
ISBN: 1-56971-292-1 $14.95
limited-edition hardcover
ISBN: 1-56971-293-X $49.95

THE BRINK OF LIFE AND DEATH
200-page black-and-white paperback
ISBN: 1-56971-297-2 $14.95
limited-edition hardcover
ISBN: 1-56971-298-0 $55.00

SEASONS
200-page black-and-white paperback
ISBN: 1-56971-375-8 $14.95
limited-edition hardcover
ISBN: 1-56971-376-6 $55.00

GRASSCUTTER
254-page black-and-white paperback
ISBN: 1-56971-413-4 $16.95
limited-edition hardcover
ISBN: 1-56971-414-2 $59.95

SPACE USAGI™
296-page black-and-white paperback
ISBN: 1-56971-290-5 $16.95
limited-edition hardcover
ISBN: 1-56971-291-3 $59.95